Two Much Trouble

Two Much Trouble

Lisa Jane Lordan

Two Much Trouble published in Great Britain in 2021 by:
ENIGMA PRESS
An imprint of PARTNERSHIP PUBLISHING

Written by Lisa Jane Lordan

This is a work of fiction. The characters, incidents and dialogues are products of the author's imagination and are not to be construed as real. Any resemblance to actual events or persons, living or dead, is entirely coincidental. The editors have ensure a true reflection of the author's tone and voice and it has remained present throughout.

A CIP catalogue record for this book is available from the British Library.

ISBN 978-18384243-3-6

Book Cover Design by: Partnership Publishing
Book Cover Images ©Shutterstock 84415306

Book typeset by:
PARTNERSHIP PUBLISHING
Barton upon Humber
North Lincolnshire
United Kingdom
DN18 5RG
www.partnershippublishing.com
Printed in England

Partnership Publishing is committed to a sustainable future for our business, our readers and our planet.

Book Two

IN THE

'Two Series'

One

"Evan, what are you doing here?" I ask with a shaky voice.

"Can we talk?" Evan replies nervously. He looks at me as I stare back at him.

"You've got some nerve turning up here I thought I made it clear I don't want to see you again."

"Please Kara just five minutes?" he pleads.

It has been a month since I last laid eyes on Evan Hamilton, the gorgeous hotel owner who came into my life when he walked into Walt's Coffee Shop one morning looking for directions. The man who swept me off my feet, the man I fell in love with, the man who broke my heart.

After meeting and spending nearly every day together, enjoying an intimate close relationship he led me to believe that we had something truly special but then I discovered it was all a sham when I read the hurtful text on his mobile phone 'The girl I was looking cosy with is no-one, she is just someone who works in a coffee shop

I picked up for a bit of fun. She is nothing to me, I've had my fun and I won't be going there again.'

Evan has tried numerous times to contact me since he left. At the time he said the text was not what he meant but how else can I take it when the words say it all.

When we first met we were only supposed to be a casual thing, but it turned into something so much more than that. Yes, he told me not to fall in love with him but how could I not when he is just so gorgeous and treated me so wonderfully.

Finding out that day when I read the text that it had all been an act, a complete lie I was devastated I didn't want to listen to what he had to say, I didn't want to hear him explain, to try and talk me around so every time he tried to contact me I repeatedly ignored him.

The day he left my whole world fell apart and it has been a hard miserable few weeks. Jodie my best friend and flat mate has been there for me every step of the way trying her best to help me through my heartache, listening to me pour my heart out, mopping up the tears I've shed repeatedly until I have no more tears left.

Some might say I am being overly dramatic for the time we have known each other but I knew from our very first encounter, the spark that brought us together like a magnet that he was the man I wanted to be with, the man I wanted to give me my happy ever after but unfortunately it just wasn't meant to be.

Now at the end of a busy week at Walt's Coffee Shop I am just getting ready to leave work for the weekend and he walks through the door. He is standing across the room looking at me with a serious face, the man who I constantly think about but tell myself not to because of the heartache he has caused.

'I wonder what he wants, forgiveness, more casual sex?'

We were so close and now he feels more like a stranger which I never thought possible. I stare back, my heart is pounding in my chest as I try to process everything.

"Are you okay Kara, do you want him to leave?" Sally my boss and friend asks looking concerned glaring at Evan displeased to see him.

"No, it's okay Sal I'm fine" I reassure her, but I am clearly not fine, not by a long shot.

'I suppose talking to him won't hurt will it seeing as he's come all this way to see me.'

"You've got five minutes; I'll meet you outside" I tell him.

"Thanks" Evan replies sheepishly and walks out the door.

Sally immediately locks the front door behind him, and I walk through to the back office to get my things.

"Are you sure you're alright, you look ever so pale, do you want to sit down for a minute?" Sally asks looking worried.

"I'm fine Sal it's just a shock seeing him that's all especially because I'm nothing to him, just someone he liked to use for sex. It's funny isn't it because he did say that's all we would ever be in the beginning, but he certainly didn't act that way."

I am still so hurt.

"I know love it's not like you imagined it we all saw the way he was with you, the flowers, the romantic weekend away, you don't act like that if it's just a casual thing. You don't have to talk to him if you don't want to, what do you think he wants? It's been a month hasn't it since you last heard from him?"

"Yes, it has. I don't know he probably wants to try and apologise then want more casual sex, he probably thinks he has given me enough time to cool down and that I'll be ready to just run back to him if he needs a sexual fix. The thing is Sal even after the way he has treated me seeing him just now I feel like I need to hear what he has got to say, you can't just turn your feelings off like that can you?"

"He doesn't look that good does he I hardly recognised him?"

"Yeah, I know what you mean, he looks like he's not been sleeping, he needs a good haircut and a shave, maybe he's been finding it hard like I have?"

"Yeah, maybe but then he caused all the upset so I don't feel sorry for him one bit, come on then you'd better go and hear what he has to say and Kara if you need me just ring me and I'll be there like a shot, Tim won't stand any nonsense from him either he thinks a lot of you he would soon send him packing."

"Thanks Sal maybe once I've heard what he's got to say I will be able to move on from it all."

"Okay love, don't be easy on him though because he doesn't deserve it using you the way he did."

"Don't worry I'm not going to welcome him back with open arms that's for sure."

I put my apron into the laundry box in the corner of the office ready for washing and get my bag. I then follow Sally to the front door shaking with nerves.

I feel sick.

Evan is stood outside leaning against the red brick wall of the coffee shop waiting for me.

'What is he going to say? What am I going to say? Why did he have to come back now just when I'm starting to feel slightly better about things?'

I take a deep breath and walk out the door.

"See you Monday Sal I'll text you later" I smile.

"Okay bye love don't forget if you need me" she replies with a serious face giving Evan a look that could turn him to stone before running off to meet Tim who is sat at the roadside in his car waiting for her.

"How are you?" Evan asks with a smile acting like nothing has happened between us.

I laugh nervously, "How do you think I am?" I cross my arms defensively and scowl at him.

"Well, that's why I'm asking."

"Look Evan just forget it." I walk off quickly towards home and he runs to catch up with me.

"Wait…wait I'm sorry, can we start again?" he says grabbing my arm to stop me.

I stop abruptly and shrug him off. "Just say what you came to say and then go."

"Let me take you for a drink it looks like you need one and then we can talk properly, I'm sure you don't want to stand here talking in the street, do you?"

I think for a moment and feel that an alcoholic drink is very much needed at this moment in time. "Okay." I huff.

"Where would you like to go, it's your choice?" Evan asks.

"We could go to that quiet pub you took me to on the way back from bowling if you like?"

"Okay great."

"I'm only having one drink though; I'll listen to what you have to say and then I'm leaving."

"Okay sure, the car is this way" he smiles.

I follow Evan to the car park across the road and look around for his Aston Martin. I can't see it parked anywhere and a car that flashy you would definitely notice. I'm surprised when he walks up to a metallic blue Audi R8.

"Where's your other car?" I ask.

"Oh, I had a little accident in it nothing major so it's having some work done I'm driving this for now."

"Oh, right you weren't hurt were you?" I reply shocked as he opens the passenger door for me to get in.

"No like I said nothing major" he smiles getting into the driver's side.

'I wonder if he crashed his car when he left my flat that day when I was upset after reading the text on his phone?'

It upsets me to think about that day even now and if anything serious would have happened to him I can't bear thinking about it. I shut down those thoughts and concentrate on the here and now. I can't let him know I still care about him; I mean I shouldn't care because of the way he treated me, but I do, and I think if I'm honest I think I always will.

The first thing I notice when Evan gets into the car is his aftershave, it has been replaced with a different scent and it's not the alluring smell that I love so much.

"You've changed your aftershave." I frown.

"Yes, I thought I would try a different one for a change my mother bought it for me do you like it?"

"Um if I'm honest I prefer your other one" I state folding my arms across my body and looking away from him out of the car window. If he thinks he is getting a compliment from me on smelling nice after the way he has treated me then he will be waiting a while.

Evan starts the car. "You'll have to direct me because I can't remember how to get to the pub" he smiles.

"Okay." I roll my eyes. He's not good at remembering how to get to places is he but then I suppose that is how we first met when he was lost and couldn't find his way.

After giving him directions, we soon arrive at the whitewashed pub which is a short drive away. I feel nervous as flashbacks of the last time we came here come to mind. I remember I had put a ban on having sex with him and after having a bottle of wine which had contributed to making me feel horny, I ended up breaking my own rule and having the most amazing sex back at the Kingsman Hotel.

'Stop it Kara now is not the time to think those thoughts.'

Evan opens the car door for me to get out and we walk side by side into the pub. I take a seat at the same booth we sat in last time. 'This feels strange.'

"What would you like to drink?" Evan asks.

"I'll have a glass of white wine please."

"Okay I'll be back in a minute."

While Evan is getting the drinks, I send Jodie a quick text to let her know that Evan has turned up wanting to talk and that I will fill her in on the details when I get home.

"Here you go" Evan says passing me a glass of wine and placing a glass of coke on the table for himself.

"I'm pleased to see you haven't bought the bottle like you did last time we were here."

Evan looks at me and smiles "Oh yes" and takes a seat next to me.

For a few minutes we sit in silence and I take a big gulp of wine to steady my nerves.

'This feels so awkward.'

"Have you had a good day at work?" he asks.

"Evan, I haven't come here to talk about my day at work" I snap.

"Why are you being so frosty?" he frowns.

I laugh. 'Oh my god seriously.'

"I haven't seen you for a month and that's all you can say, why do you think I'm being frosty?"

Evan doesn't say anything.

"Well let me enlighten you shall I maybe it's the fact that you used me all the time we were together, saying things to me to make me believe that I was more to you than just sex, that you actually cared about me. Yes, I know you said we were just having sex for fun, but you acted like it was so much more than that and reading that text you sent to god knows who saying I was no-one after the amazing times we have shared together... maybe that's why I'm frosty."

Evan looks serious. "I didn't use you."

"Really? Well, what would you call stringing me along the whole time making me think we had something special? You should never have treated me like I was more than a casual fling, buying me flowers, taking me on a romantic trip to Italy, that is not being casual Evan.

I guess it was all just some sick game to you wasn't it? Keep her sweet, spoil her so she will keep sleeping with you until you get bored. Unlike you I have feelings you can't treat people like that."

"Listen I'm sorry let me explain."

"Okay you can start off by explaining why you did that."

"I did want a casual thing and I thought we were both on the same page but spending time with you made me want more I'm sorry if I upset you."

"Why did you write that text saying I was no-one and meant nothing to you and who did you send it to anyway?" I scowl. I take another gulp of wine waiting and watching Evan carefully.

He takes a deep breath "I sent the text to Julia."

"Julia?" I frown shocked.

"Yes, I thought I still had feelings for her, she found out about you and well in a moment of madness I sent that text to her because I was confused."

"From what I remember the person who text you mentioned I was world class compared to Julia, that you were a friend and you owed them money so it couldn't have been her. Was it that guy you have fallen out with, your childhood friend?"

"Okay you're right I didn't send it to Julia and yes it was an old friend. I didn't want to tell you because I didn't want you to worry."

"Why should I worry? No more lies Evan just tell me the truth?"

"This friend I owe him a lot of money."

"Why do you owe him a lot of money?"

"It doesn't matter I'm not getting into that now."

"Are you going to pay him the money you owe him?"

"Not a fucking chance."

"But why not if you owe it to him?"

"Because if I pay him he wins and..."

"Oh, another game…" I roll my eyes.

"I'm not playing games Kara, this is very real believe me."

"Okay so the text why did you say that about me?"

"I was trying to protect you from him because he had seen us together and I didn't want you being involved so I said you were nothing to me."

"I see and am I nothing to you?"

"No, you are everything to me."

Seeing him again I am finding it hard to stay mad at him, I have missed him so much, but I need to keep my guard up because he could just be playing me. I need to be cautious. I take another sip of wine.

Evan notices me deep in thought. "Kara listen forget the text, forget about what's happened in the past and think about the here and now. It's you I love."

'What?' I almost spit my drink out onto the table in front of me. "Sorry, what did you just say?"

He smiles. "I said it's you I love."

"Now I'm even more confused." I shake my head in disbelief.

"Why?" Evan frowns.

"Because you have never said that to me before, all the times I've told you I love you and nothing and now you just turn up and say it to me casually."

"I thought I had told you."

"No, you haven't, you didn't." My heart is pounding in my chest, I don't know what to think.

"Well now you know can we please move on and forget about all this shit?" He strokes my face with the back of his hand and moves towards me for a kiss.

'I can't do this.'

"Evan stop," I place my hands on his firm chest and turn away from him. "move on to what having lots of sex for fun until you get bored of me again and find someone else. What did you think give her some time to cool down then turn up say you love me; we could pick up where we left off and all will be forgotten? After reading that text it really hurt me, what we had, the things you said to me, it's not that simple for me to just move on and forgive and forget. I can't do this right now I need to go." I stand up and grab my bag in readiness to leave.

"Wait," he says putting his hand on my arm making me flinch stopping me from going "I'm sorry please don't go, stay let me make it up to you."

I can see the desperation on his face, my head is saying walk away don't go there again but my heart is telling me to stay and give him a chance. I take a deep breath and sit down again. "Okay I'll stay a bit longer but just to be clear if you try and kiss me again I will get up and leave."

"Okay understood I'm sorry" Evan says looking relieved.

"There's something else I need to know" I say with a serious tone.

"What?"

"Do you still have feelings for Julia?"

"What, no I don't."

"I would rather know if you have any feelings for her at all, just tell me honestly Evan, do you?"

Evan laughs. "No, I don't I love you," he smiles looking me in the eye.

"You're sure because…"

"Yes, I'm sure I don't have feelings for Julia so does this mean we are friends again?"

I think for a moment then look at him and smile. "Okay sure we can be friends."

"Kara."

"Hmm..." I take a sip of my drink then put it down on the table and look at him.

"I know a lot has happened between us, but I want to be more than friends I want a relationship with you."

"But Evan Hamilton doesn't do relationships?"

"Please can I kiss you? I've missed you" he smiles asking me this time instead of forcing himself on me.

"No definitely not" I laugh.

'Cheeky sod he's got some nerve.'

Evan smiles and looks longingly at me "Please it will help you to remember what we have."

"What we had. No Evan, I can't I'm sorry." I pick up my glass and down the rest of the wine.

"Okay, I apologise, I'll behave" he grins.

'I've missed his gorgeous smile.'

"Listen let's just get one thing straight here, I may have made friends with you, but I am not jumping back into bed with you again not now or in the near future."

"We'll see" he smirks.

"Confident, aren't you?" I smile.

"How can you resist this face?" Evan puckers up his lips.

"Well, it's a different face from the one I'm used to."

"What do you mean?" Evan asks looking anxious and confused. Oh…he probably thinks I might have been seeing someone else.

"Well, you are normally clean shaven, and your hair could do with a cut."

"Oh, right yes, I haven't had a chance I've been busy."

"It's okay it's just I'm not used to seeing you looking so…"

"So…"

"Rough and ready, you're normally so well-kept."

"Well maybe I fancied a new look."

"New look, new aftershave, new car, you're like a different man."

"Don't you like it?" Evan says looking slightly hurt by my comment.

"Yes, I do. I'm sorry."

"I may look different Kara but I'm still the same in the bedroom" he winks.

"Let's not go there" I smile.

"Anyway, what are you doing tomorrow?" Evan asks changing the subject and taking a sip of his coke.

"I'm having a girly day out shopping with Jodie why?"

"I thought it would be nice to spend some time together getting reacquainted again, are you free tomorrow night?"

"I'm not sure." I hesitate, this is all happening so fast.

"Please I need to start making things better between us. Let me take you for a drink again."

"Okay" I sigh unsure as to whether I am doing the right thing. I really want to see Evan again but a part of me feels like I am being too forgiving and that I should make him wait a bit longer. I mean he shows up here says sorry and now we are friends again. I don't want to be some push over. I don't want him to think he can just click his fingers and I will come running back. I'm scared that if I let him in he will hurt me all over again and I don't think I can go through anymore heartache.

"I'll get us another drink?" Evan says finishing his coke.

"No, I'm fine thanks. I'd better go." I really need to talk to Jodie about things.

"Small steps eh, I understand, come on then I'll take you home."

I get up out of the booth feeling happy but confused as to how I am feeling. After telling myself these past few weeks that Evan is not worth it, it feels strange spending time with him again.

Placing his hand on the small of my back he leads me out of the pub and back to his car. As we get into the car thoughts of when we first met comes to mind. The sparks, the physical attraction between us was so strong. When our eyes met for the very first time, the first touch of his hand, the first time his lips met mine, just being with him caused me continuous excitement and happiness but looking at him now I feel different somehow. I know I love him but after all the emotional upset he has caused me I am concerned that I will never feel the way I did about him again? I can't help thinking how happy we were and now we are miles apart. Maybe spending some time together will help to find out if we do have something special worth fighting for or will it all end up just being 'Two Much Trouble'?

"You'll have to direct me to your place because I can't remember the way from here" Evan says snapping me out of my thoughts.

"You're not very good at remembering the way are you?" I laugh. "I suppose if you were though you wouldn't have needed my help that day when you got lost on your way back to the Kingsman Hotel, the first day we met" I smile.

"That's right and I do need you Kara more than anything" he replies giving me a knockout smile.

Arriving back at my flat Evan pulls up outside and cuts the engine of the car. "Here you go sweetheart I'll be in touch about tomorrow night."

"Okay." I grab hold of the door handle to get out of the car.

"Oh, before you go can you give me your mobile number again because I lost my phone and I had to get a new one, so I don't have your number anymore?" he asks.

"Oh, right okay give me your phone and I'll program it in for you."

"It's okay just read your number out and I'll do it" Evan replies.

"Okay then." I frown.

'I wonder why he's being cagey about giving me his phone. Maybe he has got something to hide like last time? I need to be cautious and think about this whole situation, can I really trust him?'

After swapping mobile numbers we say goodbye and I wave to him as he drives off down the road then I go inside for an interrogation from Jodie.

“I’m home” I shout as I walk through the front door of our two bedroomed flat.

“I’m in my bedroom Kar.” Jodie calls.

“Hi Jode” I smile sitting down on her bed.

“So, Evan showed up then I thought he might at some point.”

“Yeah, he wanted to apologise and explain things.”

“And did he explain things?”

“Yeah, he did but it was really awkward at first.”

“I bet it was, so what did he say then?”

I tell Jodie all about my evening and what Evan had to say also that he told me he loved me.

“Maybe having some time apart has made him realise how he really feels about you, so what now?”

“I said I would meet him for a drink tomorrow night to talk some more. You should have seen him Jode he looks so different to how I remembered him.”

“What do you mean he looks different?”

“Well, he doesn’t look that great for a start like he could do with a good night’s sleep and you know he always looked so clean-cut, well now he looks like he needs a good shave and a haircut.”

“Maybe he has been struggling without you and let his appearance slip.”

“Yes, that’s what I thought it did appear that way I mean god if he saw what I looked like when he first left me, he would definitely not be calling me beautiful like he used to.”

"Yeah, I know" she smirks.

"What do you mean yeah you know?" I laugh.

"I'm only joking" Jodie giggles.

"I'm not sure whether I should meet up with him tomorrow night or not Jode, am I forgiving him too easily after the way he treated me?"

"You need to see him Kar to work things out if that's what you want to do, it's good that you're talking?"

"Yeah, you're right, now he's explained about the text I feel like I do want to see him but I'm definitely not going to be jumping into bed with him because that's what I did the first time around and look where that got me. He's got a lot of making up to do first before we even get to that stage."

"Yes, I think that is wise, you need to make sure he is not stringing you along again. You have only just started to feel a bit better about things and you don't want to get hurt again, I hated seeing you so upset."

"Don't worry I've got my guard up now, he's not getting around me easily this time however hard he tries."

"So what time are you seeing him tomorrow then?"

"He said he would be in touch, oh and he also said he lost his phone, so he's got a new one, I had to give him my number again. When I asked him to give me his phone so I could program my number in he acted weird. All I could think is has he got something to hide like last time or do you think I'm being paranoid?"

"Maybe he smashed up his old phone in anger like you did yours? Also, he was probably nervous giving you it because of what happened last time when you read that text. He probably didn't want you to see something on his phone that is innocent like a business colleague and you would think it was something else. It doesn't hurt to be cautious though."

"Yeah, maybe anyway I'll just have to wait and see what happens I suppose."

"Yeah, just take each day as it comes and don't get stressed about it, what will be will be."

"Yeah, I guess, thanks Jode."

After having a late dinner Jodie and I are sat at the kitchen table having a cuppa when my mobile rings making us both jump.

"Shit." I nearly spill my tea. I put it down on the table and fumble in my bag for my phone, I look at the screen and see Sally is calling me.

I have a quick chat to Sally, she called to see if I'm alright after Evan's unexpected visit. I tell her what happened and after reassuring her that I am fine I tell her I will see her on Monday and end the call.

"That's nice of Sally to ring and see if you're alright" Jodie says sipping her tea.

"Yes, she's a good boss and friend" I smile.

"How's the baby making going?"

I smile. “Good Sally says she is having lots of practice, but nothing has happened yet.”

“I suppose it’s just when the time is right I suppose.”

“Yeah, she is enjoying the practising though I think poor Tim is worn out bless him.”

Jodie laughs “Poor Tim.”

Seeing Evan today despite being a total shock has been good. I have often wondered how he has been doing since the day he left and from the look of his appearance it looks like he has been struggling and had a rough few weeks just like I have.

I’m pleased he wants to make amends because I hate falling out with people but most of all I am pleased because it shows he does care, and I have really missed him.

Life can be so unpredictable at times yesterday I was focussing on getting through each day, a life without Evan in it and today he has come back into my life and we are talking again. Who would of thought? I know deep down that I must try again with him because what we had was amazing and maybe once he has made it up to me and I have gained his trust then maybe we can have that again.

Two

It's Saturday morning, I wake up and the first thought to enter my head is Evan paying me a visit yesterday. I sit up in bed and grab my phone off the bedside drawers and turn it on eager to see if he has text me.

After waiting a few minutes my phone beeps signalling a text has come through. Evan has text me; I open the message feeling nervous but also excited.

Good Morning it's a beautiful day outside. Seeing you yesterday, you have no idea how fast my heart beats when I see you, what time can we meet up later? Evan x

I can't help feeling impressed with his words. I wish all the bad stuff had just been a bad dream. I would give anything to go back to how it used to be between us. With a smile on my face, I send him a reply.

Good Morning, I can meet you about 7.00pm if that's any good? K x

I wait anxiously and after a few moments Evan sends another text.

7.00pm is perfect just like you. I'll see you later then. I'll pick you up. Evan x

Ok great, see you later K x

I get out of bed, put on my dressing gown, and go to the kitchen. Jodie is sat at the table eating some muesli for breakfast.

"Morning sleepyhead, I was just going to eat this and then wake you, are you ready for a fun day of shopping with your bestie?" she says popping another spoonful in her mouth.

"Yeah, I am, I can't wait, Evan's just text me." I smile.

"Oh, really what did he say?"

"Just that it was nice seeing me yesterday and that he's picking me up tonight about 7.00pm."

"I really hope you can work things out because you make such a great couple."

"Thanks, Jode I hope so too I've really missed him these past few weeks."

"Yeah, I know you have" Jodie smiles.

"Right, I'm off for a quick shower and to get ready."

"What about your breakfast you really should eat something Kara?" Jodie calls as I scurry off to the bathroom.

"I'm not that hungry I'll grab something later" I shout back.

After a quick shower I get dressed and go to find Jodie who is sat waiting for me in the kitchen. "I'm ready, are we walking into town or taking the car?" I ask feeling excited.

"Well, it depends how many clothes we are going to buy, and will we be able to carry all the bags back home?" Jodie laughs.

"Maybe we should take my car then" I grin.

"Good idea, I'll just go and get my bag, I'll lock up and meet you out front" Jodie says sounding excited.

"Okay great see you in a few minutes."

I grab my phone, my designer handbag that Sally bought me for my birthday and my car keys then go and wait in my Fiat 500 car for Jodie.

I love having my own car, I love having the independence of being able to drive to anywhere I want to go without having to walk or use public transport all the time. My mum always offered for me to borrow her car but it's not the same as having your own. Every time I see my car it reminds me of Evan because of the Italian stripes on the roof, it reminds me of the amazing weekend we spent together at Evan's villa in Lake Como, Italy. I wish I could turn the clock back and we were there now, we were so happy then.

"Right let's hit the shops, have you got your voucher for the beauty salon?" Jodie says getting into the passenger seat.

"Yes, it's in my bag, I'm so excited we are going to shop 'til we drop," I smile starting the engine and setting off towards town.

After parking the car, we leisurely make our way around town visiting every clothes shop in sight. The summer sales are on and after spending a few hours grabbing lots of bargains we decide we need a break and find somewhere to have lunch.

We choose a charming little bistro in the high street that has a few tables and chairs scattered outside under a sun canopy and take a seat at one of the tables, placing the shopping bags at our feet.

A waitress comes over to take our drinks order then we peruse the lunch menu.

"I'm going to have a steak & caramelised onion sandwich." Jodie says.

"Ooh that sounds nice I'm going to have the chicken Caesar sandwich."

"Okay and it's my treat" Jodie smiles.

"No Jodie I'm buying lunch today to say thank you for putting up with me these past few weeks, I've been a mess and you have been such a good friend to me, making me dinners and trying to cheer me up so I'm treating you, no arguments. I'm also treating you to have your nails done at the beauty salon as well."

"Aww thanks Kara, you really don't have to, you would have done the same for me, I was just looking after my best friend" she smiles.

"I know but I want to" I smile.

The waitress comes over with our drinks and then we order the food. We then sit and chat happily while we wait for the food to arrive. I check my phone; Evan has sent me another text.

I realised I was thinking about you and I began to wonder how long you had been on my mind then it occurred to me since I met you you've never left. Can't wait to see you tonight x

I read the text to Jodie with a smile.

"Oh my god, does he think saying cheesy romantic lines to you is the way to win you back?" she laughs.

"I don't know," I laugh "What do you think I should reply to that?"

"Just put something like 'it's going to take a lot more than cheesy lines for me to forgive you'."

"Yeah, okay I'll put that."

I type out the text and send it to Evan just as the waitress arrives with our food.

The lunch is delicious and after eating the sandwiches and having a refreshing cup of coffee to wash it all down I pay the lady and then we get ready to leave. I quickly check my phone to see if Evan has sent a reply but there is no message, maybe he didn't like what I put? Tough! I put my phone away.

"Right are you ready to go and get pampered?" I ask collecting the shopping bags at my feet.

"Yes, let's go" Jodie smiles and we head off to the beauty salon.

After having a manicure and a pedicure we go back to the car feeling happy and tired after enjoying a great girly day together and go home.

It's almost 7.00pm and Evan will be here soon, he is picking me up and taking me for a drink again so we can spend some more time together to work on our relationship.

After going through various outfits, I choose to wear a pair of black skinny jeans and a new cropped white t-shirt with the word 'Fashion' in black lettering that I bought in the sales today. I walk into the lounge and Jodie is sat on the sofa watching TV. "Does this look alright Jode?" I ask.

"Yes, you look lovely" she smiles.

"Thanks, oh god he should be here in a minute." I pace the carpeted floor of the lounge feeling sick with nerves. 'I can do this; I can do this.'

"Here have a mouthful of my wine it'll calm your nerves" Jodie says passing me her glass that she is holding.

"Thanks, but the way I'm feeling I need a bottle to settle my nerves not a glass" I reply taking the drink and having a big gulp.

The doorbell rings making me jump as I pass Jodie back her wine. "Shit he's here."

I take a deep breath and answer the door.

"Hi sweetheart, you look ravishing" he smiles looking me up and down with a lustful look on his face.

"Thanks, you look nice too" I smile looking at him dressed in a pair of blue jeans and a pale blue casual short sleeved shirt although he still hasn't shaved, and his hair is still too long for my liking.

"Are you ready to go?" he asks.

"Yes, I'll just grab my bag." I go into the kitchen, collect my phone and bag leaving Evan stood on the doorstep.

"Hello Evan" Jodie says walking into the hallway to greet him.

"Err hi" Evan replies looking anxious as soon as he sees her.

"How are you?" The atmosphere is slightly tense.

"I'm good thanks, you?"

"Yes, I'm okay, so you've come to make it up to Kara then?"

I stand there looking between them both feeling nervous and awkward because my best friend is making her feelings known loud and clear that she is not happy with him for upsetting me like he did.

"Yes, that's the plan" he smiles.

"Well make sure you treat her better this time" Jodie scowls.

"Of course, yes I will definitely."

Evan seems edgy and I kind of feel sorry for him, it must be hard coming back facing people knowing he is in bad books and with my best friend looking at him like he is the devil.

"Shall we go?" I ask wanting to escape the awkward atmosphere.

"Yes, let's go" Evan replies almost running away from the door.

I get into Evan's Audi R8 and I can feel my leg shaking because of how nervous I am, I take some deep breaths to try and calm myself. "Where are we going for a drink?" I ask.

"I thought we could have a drink at the hotel if that's okay with you?"

"Oh okay, are you staying at the Kingsman again?"

"Err no they were fully booked so I booked into a smaller hotel, it's not far from here, is that alright?"

"Yeah sure."

We arrive at the Swan Hotel which is quite different to the Kingsman. Evan parks the car and being the perfect gentleman opens the door for me to get out. I feel more relaxed now after the short car journey and placing a hand on the small of my back Evan leads me inside to the small reception area.

"Would you like to have a drink in my room so we can talk in private?" Evan asks looking me up and down then looking into my eyes.

'Does he think I haven't noticed him checking me out and looking like he wants more than just a drink. I don't think a drink in his room is a good idea, the further away we are from a bed the better.'

"No in the bar area is fine" I smile. I can't help noticing the disappointment on his face.

"Okay well there is a beer garden out the back, shall we sit out there it's a lovely evening?"

"Yes, that would be lovely" I smile.

Evan leads me through a door at the back of the pub to a quaint beer garden. The small garden is enclosed by wooden fencing and there are picnic tables evenly spaced throughout. Along the fencing there are fairy lights in the shape of small lanterns, and it adds to the ambience of the place.

"This is cute" I state sitting down at one of the tables.

"Just like you and the pretty fairy lights are twinkling just like your lovely blue eyes" he smiles.

"Evan you don't have to keep paying me all these compliments please just relax and be yourself."

"I like paying you compliments I'm only saying what's in my heart."

"Okay." I frown.

'God, I wish he would just relax so the old Evan will come back this new Evan is a bit much, he seems like he doesn't know what to say or do to make it up to me and his nerves are getting the better of him.'

"What can I get you to drink?" he smiles.

"I'll just have a glass of white wine, anything is fine."

"Okay I'll be back in a minute."

Evan walks off inside to the bar to get the drinks and while he is gone I look around at the other couples who are enjoying a drink on this warm summer evening, they all look so happy and in love and as Evan walks back towards me with the drinks I decide I need to try and put him at ease because he is clearly struggling with his nerves tonight. It makes me sad because he is usually such a confident man and now he is the complete opposite. It seems what happened between us has really affected him.

"There you go one glass of white wine" he says placing the wine in front of me.

"Thanks" I smile.

"You're very welcome." Evan takes a seat opposite me.

"So, what have you been up to since I last saw you?" I ask interested to know.

"Working mainly the hotels are really busy this time of year."

"Yes, I can imagine, we have been busy in the coffee shop, there are lots of tourists about at the moment. So how are the hotel renovations coming along at the Manor?"

"Really good thanks but I don't really want to talk about work."

"Okay… what do you want to talk about then?" I ask taking a sip of my drink.

"I'd like to talk about us."

"Evan there is no us, can we just work at being friends first, a lot has happened, and I can't think about anything else at the moment" I sigh.

"Yes, but I don't want to just be your friend Kara."

"Look we've only just started talking again, let's just be friends and see how it goes."

"Can we be friends with benefits?" he grins.

"No, we can't," I laugh. "Look I don't want to rush things because we did that before remember, so let's just take things slowly, no pressure, just friends." I take a big sip of wine. 'He is not making this easy for me.'

"Kara I've missed you and I know you have missed me too so why can't we just go back to enjoying each other again?"

"Because I want you to prove to me that I mean more to you than just sex. I want us to get to know each other properly with conversation this time rather than just our bodies."

"So, what's it going to take then?"

"What to have sex with me?" I frown.

"No to make it up to you so then we can have sex" he grins.

"Evan…" I sigh.

"Kara you are more than just sex to me I've told you that I love you."

"Then prove it to me, prove that you love me by making it up to me in other ways and by not having sex with me."

"Can I kiss you, is that allowed?"

"No sorry."

"Why, why can't I kiss you?"

"Why do you think, because when you kiss me it always leads to more."

"Well how about I promise to be the perfect gentleman and to just kiss you and that's all."

I laugh. "A perfect gentleman, you promised me that once before remember and then what happened, anyway can we change the subject please."

"But I like this subject" he grins.

"Evan please..." I sigh feeling frustrated.

"Okay I apologise, it's just hard you know."

"Evan." I laugh shaking my head.

'I bet it's hard because it was always hard when we were together before. I really don't want to be thinking about your manhood right now because I'm trying to be good. Oh, but the things he can do with his cock, the sex was amazing, and I haven't had an orgasm in weeks and Evan knows just how to...stop it Kara this is not helping.'

"No, I didn't mean it's hard as in my...," Evan laughs pointing to his crotch with his eyes "although it doesn't take much when I look at you. I actually meant it's hard being with you and not being able to touch you."

"It's okay I know what you meant" I blush giggling.

"Anyway, would you like another drink?" he smiles seeing that I have finished mine.

"Go on then" I smile pleased of an interlude from our topic of conversation because thinking about how amazing the sex is with Evan is making me aroused and feelings are beginning to surface again which I definitely need to put a stop to this time.

"Another wine?"

"Yes please."

While I am waiting for Evan to return with the drinks I send Jodie a quick text to let her know how things are going between us. I am just putting my phone away in my bag when Evan comes back.

"Thanks" I smile.

"Don't take this the wrong way but are you sure you don't fancy taking these up to my room so we can talk some more in private, I feel like people are listening to us sat in this small garden?" Evan says taking a seat and looking around him.

"No, I'm fine here thanks and people are having their own conversations so why would they be interested in ours."

"Yeah, I guess but it's a lovely room wouldn't you like to take a look?" he grins.

"Evan, I know what you are doing?" I smile.

"I'm not doing anything" he says shrugging his shoulders with a smirk on his face.

"How's Curtis?" I ask moving away from this subject.

"He's alright."

"What did he say about what happened between us?"

"Nothing much… why do you ask?"

"Oh, I just thought you might have talked to him about what went on and wondered what he'd said about it."

"Like I said nothing much."

"Oh okay." I take a sip of wine.

"Tell me what you missed about me?" Evan asks with a smile.

"No."

"Why not?"

"I don't want to because it will make you all big headed and besides, it should be you telling me because you're the one who is supposed to be making things up to me. So, what did you miss about me?"

"I missed seeing your gorgeous face, your beautiful eyes and I missed what we had together."

"Which was?"

"This, us, our relationship."

"It was weird not talking to you or seeing you after we had practically been seeing each other every day and night."

Evan looks lost in thought then looks at me. "Kara stay with me tonight let me help you to remember what we had?"

"Like I said what we had was just sex Evan."

"Don't say that, please let me touch you its killing me" he says grabbing hold of my hand on the table.

"Evan don't," I pull my hand away. "you need to stop pressuring me or I'm going home, I can't be with you like that it's too soon. I'm going to the toilet I'll be back in a minute." I get up from the table and walk off.

Evan

I sit waiting for her to return thinking about what she said when I receive a text message on my phone. Taking my phone out of my pocket I read the message and smile. I send a reply 'All is going well.' then put my phone back in my pocket and wait for her to return.

I look up and see Kara walking towards me. She really is beautiful I am so relieved to see she hasn't left, I think maybe I was coming on a bit strong, I'm so nervous and I don't want to scare her off, I need to tone it down a bit.

Evan watches me as I return from the toilet and walk back over to him. He looks serious when I sit down again.

"Kara I'm sorry for upsetting you I promise I'll stop pressuring you and I'll respect how you feel."

"It's okay you haven't upset me I just don't want to rush into anything this time."

"I know I understand. Will you let me take you out for dinner one night as friends?"

I think for a few moments, he looks nervous.

"Okay yes that will be nice."

"Great. I just need to check my diary because I've got a busy week planned then I'll let you know what night is best if that's okay."

"Okay I know you are a busy man" I smile.

"Yes, but I'm never too busy to see you. I will look forward to our friend's date."

"Yeah, me too" I smile.

We finish our drinks, and the night has been good, we have talked loads and things are beginning to feel less awkward between us. The glasses of wine I have drank tonight are starting to take effect and I'm feeling frisky as flashbacks of our nights of passion keep creeping into my mind. I really don't need those images right now when I'm feeling like I do. I tell Evan I'm ready to go home and we head back to the car.

We arrive back at my flat a short while later and Evan cuts the engine of the car and turns to look at me. I need to get out of this car and away from him because right now the way I'm feeling I could quite easily do something I would regret.

"Thanks for the lift" I smile trying not to give him eye contact in case he can read my mind which are thoughts of us performing some sort of sexual act. Seeing Evan has brought back all those feelings again, a desire that I have tried to block out of my mind every time I think about him and playing hard to get is not going to be easy.

"Can I have a goodbye kiss before you go, you know as friends?" he asks with a smile.

"No sorry I'd rather we didn't."

'Oh god don't ask me that, I'm struggling here as it is.'

"Just a kiss on the cheek, where's the harm in that, we're friends aren't we and friends say goodbye to each other with a kiss."

'Maybe one kiss won't hurt will it?'

"Okay a kiss on the cheek but that's all."

'I seriously need to get out of this car.'

Evan looks at me with his big brown eyes and taps his finger on his cheek for me to kiss it. I lean towards him and just as I am about to kiss him he turns his head, and we end up kissing on the mouth for a few seconds. 'Huh that felt weird?'

"Evan," I scowl. "you said just a peck."

"Oh yes," he grins "I'll look forward to the day when I can kiss you properly."

I shake my head feeling slightly annoyed that I fell for his trick but also feeling strange and confused because now I have kissed him the spark I felt every time we kissed before it's not there.

"Goodnight Evan." I go to get out of the car.

"Goodnight Kara. I'll call you about what night is best for going out to dinner."

"Okay." I get out and shut the car door then Evan drives off. As I watch him drive away my fingers go to my lips as I think about the awkward kiss we just shared.

'Why did it feel weird? Why didn't it feel like it did before when we kissed?'

I walk to the front door of the flat feeling deflated.

It's 9.30pm and Jodie is still up sat in the lounge with her boyfriend Matt watching television.

"Hi guys." I call taking my shoes off in the hall then walking into the lounge and flopping down onto the two-seater sofa.

"Hi Kar, how was your night?" Jodie asks.

"Hi Kara." Matt waves engrossed in a TV programme.

"Err…"

"It's okay Matt knows Evan is back."

"Oh right, it was alright I suppose."

"Just alright…" she frowns.

"Yes. no… it was good, we talked a lot and I told him clearly that we need to take things slowly and he seemed okay with that but I'm just not sure."

"What do you mean you're not sure, about what?"

"How I feel. I'm so confused just then when he dropped me home he wanted a goodbye kiss, I said no but he said a peck on the cheek wouldn't hurt so I thought okay why not what's the harm in that but then when I went to kiss him he turned his face and we ended up kissing on the lips and nothing."

"What do you mean nothing?"

"I didn't feel anything, no spark, no desire to carry on the kiss, nothing."

"Oh, that's not good." Jodie frowns.

"The thing is I know I love him Jode, I do I love him, I mean up to the point of the kiss I was thinking about when we used to have sex and how amazing it was but then when he kissed me just now, I felt nothing. Now I'm worried that my heart is not in it like it was before. Don't get me wrong I still fancy him and want to be with him but when he kissed me it felt different to how it was the last time something just doesn't feel right."

"Maybe it's because he hurt you plus you have been trying to get over him these past few weeks and I'm not surprised you're confused. Its early days Kar he only came back yesterday and I'm sure it's just that you've got your guard up because you're afraid of getting hurt again."

"I don't know, I'm so confused."

"Or maybe you thought you loved him but maybe it was just lust at the time" Matt says giving his take on things.

"Do you think? Before when he looked at me it did things to me, I felt this funny feeling of excitement but now it's like, it's like looking at you" I reply looking at Matt.

"Oh, thanks Kara." Matt laughs pretending to be offended by my comment.

"No, I mean like a friend, it's weird."

"I knew what you meant" Matt smiles.

"Don't stress about it, give it time and then you will know for sure, things are still raw, and you weren't expecting to see him again, so you are bound to feel that way" Jodie says sympathetically.

"Yeah, I guess, god why can't my love life be simple like yours? Anyway, I'm off to bed guys I've had enough for one day see you in the morning."

I change into my pyjamas, have a wash, and clean my teeth then get into bed. Hopefully after a good night's sleep things will be clearer tomorrow.

Three

It's 9.00am Sunday morning, after going to bed last night and sleeping on it I still feel strange about the kiss today. Evan is trying hard to make amends, but I am having doubts. Why do I feel like this? Why don't I feel like I did before? Why did I feel nothing when he kissed me last night? Maybe I should forget him and just move on, but I love him, or do I just think I love him? Evan hurt me so much when he said I was no-one and meant nothing to him and I think that is why I am feeling like this. Oh god I am so confused my mind is saying one thing, but my heart is saying another, aargh…

I sit up in bed and rub my eyes then turn on my mobile phone that's at the side of the bed. I open the gallery of photos and look for the ones of my time in Italy with Evan, we looked so happy together. He really is gorgeous with his dark chocolate brown hair and brown eyes, he was more clean-cut back then than he is now but it's not all about the looks it's the feeling, the trust and will we ever be that couple again?

My head is buzzing from all these thoughts and it's starting to give me a headache, so I get up and decide to go make a cup of tea. A cup of tea always makes you feel better.

I walk into the kitchen and Jodie is just putting the kettle on. 'Great timing.'

"Morning Jode." I smile taking a seat at the kitchen table.

"Morning Kar that was good timing" she smiles.

"Yeah, it was, where's Matt is he still in bed?"

"Yes, he's having a bit of a lie in, I think I wore him out last night" she giggles.

"Bless him."

"How are you today, feeling any better about last night and the kiss?" Jodie asks getting another mug out of the cupboard.

"No not really, I've been over and over it in my head and I'm still confused."

"You'll work it out" she smiles.

"Yeah, I guess."

"What are you doing today?" she asks.

"I'm going to see my mum and dad this morning then I thought I might go for a drive somewhere this afternoon, do you want to come?"

"I would but we are going to Matt's parents for Sunday lunch."

"Okay no worries just thought I would ask in case you didn't have plans."

"Thanks Kar, I bet its nice having your own car now and you can just take off somewhere whenever you want."

"I love it Jode I don't know how I managed before without one."

"Yeah," Jodie passes me a cup of tea. "I'll go and see if Matt's awake see you in a bit." Jodie takes two mugs of tea with her and leaves me sat at the kitchen table drinking my tea in my pyjamas. I look at the trees that are gently swaying in the breeze outside through the kitchen window and wonder where I should go for a drive in my car this afternoon after seeing my parents. 'Hmm...where shall I go? I know I could go and see how the renovations are coming along at Evan's new hotel? Then again I'm not sure whether that's a good idea? Maybe I should do something else? But I really want to have a nosy to see what it's looking like so yes that's what I'm going to do.'

After getting showered and dressed in a pair of denim shorts and a white tie front short sleeved shirt I knock on Jodie's bedroom door to say goodbye and go to visit my parents. My parents are always pleased to see me and to hear what I have been doing during the week and after having a good catch up over some lunch and a cuppa it's time to go. I say goodbye then get into my car to drive home.

Feeling happy I put on a pair of sunglasses then start the car engine. I wave goodbye to my parents and then turn up the stereo as 'Ain't Giving Up' by Craig David & Sigala plays on the radio. Hearing the song makes me smile, is this some sort of a sign to say don't give up on Evan? Thinking about Evan I remember my thought earlier about visiting the Manor to see how the renovations are coming along so I take a detour across town and head towards Danes Avenue where Evan's hotel is situated.

I pull off the main road onto the private lane that takes you to the Manor. I start to feel nervous because the last time I was here I was with Evan; we were so happy then. He gave me a tour of the place and thoughts of the games room springs to mind where we had mind blowing sex on the snooker table. We had such a great sex life, it was the best, I miss being intimate with him like we were before.

My stomach is churning with nerves the closer I get to the majestic building. "Oh god I hope he's not here" I mutter as the Manor comes into view. There are no vehicles parked out the front apart from a couple of diggers, I let out a sigh of relief as I pull up outside and get out of the car.

I look around and the place is like a building site. There are piles of bricks and building equipment dotted around the place, it's no way near ready for opening.

I wander around looking through the front windows then go around the back. The vast grounds that surround the property consist of mature shrubs and trees and acres of grass, I can see the renovations for the huge extension have begun and the footprint of the building is laid out before me. The foundations give you an idea of how large the building is going to be once completed and it's looking impressive already. 'Wow.'

I have a quick look through the windows at the back of the property and I can see work has started on the inside too. Once I've seen enough I walk down the side of the house back to the front and as I'm nearing the front I see a car driving down the private lane towards me. "Shit, who is that?"

'What shall I do? Oh god it's Evan he will think I'm stalking him; I need to hide.'

I'm panicking and seeing a nearby bush that is conveniently situated at the side of the path I quickly hide crouching down behind it. I hold my breath and listen and hear the car come to a stop at the front of the Manor then I hear a car door shut as someone gets out.

'Oh my god I am so stupid. What on earth am I doing hiding behind this bush hoping he won't see me when my car is parked out front, it's pretty bloody obvious I'm here.'

I casually get up feeling silly, luckily the person hasn't twigged (pardon the pun) that I was hiding behind a bush, so I casually walk to the front of the building. Not only do I feel silly, but I feel sick with nerves, I'm expecting to bump into Evan but when I walk around the corner it isn't Evan's car parked next to mine but his best friend Curtis' red Audi TT.

'Thank god.'

Curtis is looking at my car with a frown on his face obviously trying to work out whose car it is. He must sense me because he looks up and looks straight at me looking surprised.

"Hi Curtis" I smile walking sheepishly towards him.

"Hi Kara, this is a surprise, what are you doing here?" he smiles walking over to me and kissing me on both cheeks.

"You caught me, I was just having a nosy around to see how the hotel renovations are coming along, I'm sorry I shouldn't be here."

"Hey no it's fine, it's good to see you, it's looking great isn't it?" he smiles.

"Yes, it really is, it's come on leaps and bounds since I was here last."

I suddenly feel shy and don't know what else to say.

"So, how are you?" Curtis asks.

"I'm okay and you?"

"Yeah, I'm good, have you seen Evan at all?"

"Yes, he came to see me on Friday actually just as I was finishing work."

"Really and how did that go?"

"Okay but it felt a bit strange seeing him again after he used me like that."

"He wasn't using you Kara."

“That’s what he said but that’s how it felt after reading that text, I take it you know about the text?”

“Yes, I do, and you were never supposed to have seen it because it was not how it was meant.”

“How else was I supposed to take it when he says I’m no-one, just some girl he picked up to have fun with and he wouldn’t be going near me again.”

“I know I can understand why you were upset but trust me there is a lot more to it than you know.”

“What do you mean?”

“It’s not my place to say you need to talk to Evan.”

“Well, I have spoken to him about it and he says he just wants to forget it and move on. He mentioned about the guy he owes money to but not any more details than that really.”

“He’ll tell you when he’s ready I’m sure.”

“How has he been anyway since we parted ways?”

“Not good at all, he is really cut up about the whole situation.”

“It does seem that way, he looks so different from the last time I saw him.”

“In what way different?” Curtis asks looking confused as to what I mean by that.

“Well, he looks like he hasn’t slept for days and he could definitely do with a haircut and a shave, he looks so rough and ready compared to his usual clean-cut look.”

"Hmm... I know he's been really down he hated that he hurt you."

"He did hurt me."

I think about the past few weeks and how I have been feeling, and I start to feel emotional. I don't want to cry in front of Curtis, so I take a few deep breaths to stop myself. "Anyway, he said he is going to make it up to me, so we'll just see what happens I suppose. We've been out for a drink a couple of times so that's some progress I guess."

"Really that's good when did you go out for a drink, he didn't mention it?" Curtis asks sounding curious.

"We went out for one Friday night after work and then last night, we had one at the Swan Hotel where he's staying."

"Oh right, yeah."

"Sorry I don't mean to go on at you about Evan."

'Poor Curtis he's obviously come to the Manor for a reason and here I am going on about Evan and I'm keeping him.'

"Hey no it's fine anytime you want to talk I'm a good listener" he smiles.

"Thanks Curtis anyway I'd best go and leave you to do whatever you came here to do."

"Yes, I left some paperwork here by accident the other day and I need it, it's been good to see you Kara."

"Yes, you too" I smile.

"Don't give up on him Kara, Evan is a good bloke."

I think of the song that was playing in the car on my way here saying the same thing 'Ain't Giving Up' and now Curtis has said not to give up on him either, another sign, I feel like something is trying to tell me something, maybe we do have a future after all?

"Thanks Curtis I wish we could go back to how it was before the text you know when things were good, and we were happy enjoying each other's company."

"I know just give it time and I'm sure things will work out for you both, Evan is not good at expressing how he feels because he doesn't, he can't, there are things you don't know about him in his past."

"Yes, but if he won't tell me how am I supposed to know?"

"You're right but you are the best thing that has ever happened to him, he just needs to sort his life out. Trust him Kara."

'That's what he said before he left.'

"Look I'll be seeing him tomorrow and I'll tell him I've seen you."

"Probably best not tell him I was snooping around his new hotel I don't want him to think I'm stalking him or something."

"Okay I won't mention where I saw you, it's our little secret," he winks. "he's also coming here on Friday we have a slight problem that he needs to look at."

"Nothing serious I hope."

"No, he just needs to look at something before a decision can be made on what to do about it so he is having to come over, he can't make it until Friday though because he's got a busy week this week."

I remember Evan saying he has a busy week this week, he is supposed to be letting me know what night is best to go out for a meal. I almost tell Curtis about our meal plans but stop myself because I have already taken up enough of his time talking non-stop about Evan.

"Okay well I'll get off then and thanks Curtis." He kisses me on both cheeks to say goodbye and I walk off towards my car.

"Hey Kara" Curtis calls catching up with me. "Take my mobile number and if you ever need to talk or anything just call me okay and that's not a chat up line, I genuinely want you two to sort things out so if I can help in any way I'm here okay."

"Okay thanks." I programme Curtis' number into my phone and give him my number. "I've got Evan's new number as well he told me about losing his phone and my number."

"Oh, when did he lose that?"

"I'm not sure, why?"

"I just wondered that's all, I mean it Kara if you need to talk just give me a call. I hope you can work things out, he's been really miserable without you, you know."

"Thanks Curtis, me too, bye."

"Bye Kara."

Curtis

Once Kara has driven away and is out of sight I take my phone out of my jeans pocket and dial Evan's number.

"Hi, mate it's me… yeah I'm fine I've just seen Kara… no she's fine mate… she told me you've been to see her… I know… yeah of course I'll call on my way back from the Manor… see you soon."

Four

"Good Morning Sal" I smile walking into Walt's Coffee Shop Monday morning ready to start work.

"Morning love, did you have a good weekend after your unexpected visit from Evan on Friday?"

"Yes, it was good thanks. I had the best day on Saturday shopping with Jodie. We found lots of bargains on the sale rails and then we went to the beauty salon where I spent my birthday voucher that Jodie bought me, we got our nails done, do you like them?" I ask showing Sally.

"Oh wow, they look lovely. Did Stacey do them?"

"Thanks, yeah she did, she's good isn't she."

"Yeah, I always ask for her when I go to get my nails done there."

"Did you and Tim have a good weekend?" I ask prepping the coffee machine for the day.

"Yes, we did thanks, anyway I'm dying to know how are things with Evan? Have you seen him anymore since Friday?"

"We're okay I guess; he took me out for a drink again on Saturday night and it was nice, but we are a long way off to how things were before."

"Well, he did hurt you Kara so it's going to take some time before you are that way again."

"Yes, I know, he's taking me out for dinner one night this week. I wasn't sure whether to go at first when he asked me but then I thought the more I see him the more it will make things clearer as to what is going on between us, it will either make us or break us I suppose."

"If you want to give him another chance then you need him to show you how sorry he is and taking you out for dinner is a good start. He has a lot of making up to do."

"Yes definitely, I'm still not 100% sure how I feel to be honest though Sal."

"Just take each day as it comes, that's all you can do."

"Yeah, you're right, I will do."

The day passes quickly and no sooner had we opened we were flooded with customers and now we are heading out the door on our way home after a hard day's work.

"God my feet are killing me."

"Yes, I know what you mean I can't wait to get home and have a nice long soak in the bath." Sally says locking the coffee shop door.

"Yeah, me too."

“See you tomorrow.” Sally calls walking off to meet her husband Tim who is parked across the road waiting for her.

“Bye Sal, see you tomorrow.”

As I walk home wearily in the sunshine all I can think about is Evan. ‘I wonder what he is doing. I wonder if he is thinking about me. I wonder when he’s going to text me about which night is best to go for dinner?’

Feeling brave I decide to send him a text.

Hi, just walking home after a busy day at work, how was your day? K x

A few minutes later my phone signals a message and I open it with a smile.

Hi sweetheart I've had a busy day too. Sorry I haven't had a chance to let you know which night to go out for dinner, how about Friday night? Evan x

I read his text and although I’m feeling confused about things he always manages to make me smile. I had a feeling he might suggest going out Friday considering Curtis told me he is going to be at the Manor that day sorting out a problem. I send him a reply.

Dinner on Friday night will be lovely. I will look forward to it. K x

So, will I but I was hoping I could see you before then if you are free, what are you doing tomorrow night? Evan x

'Hmm…what do I do on a Tuesday night, oh yes, nothing!'

I have looked at my schedule Mr H and it appears I am free tomorrow night what do you have in mind? K x

What I have in mind is not what you will be willing to do (winking emoji) so how about we go for another drink and talk some more? Evan x

'Oh god don't put things like that because now you've got me thinking about sex and I'm finding this hard as it is because I remember how good you are in bed. Just talking that's all because I need to sort out how I feel first before I go down that road. Remember he needs to prove that I mean more to him than just sex but god I've missed how he makes me feel and the orgasms, oh jeez.'

Hmm… Jodie is out tomorrow night so rather than keep going to some pub maybe he could come to mine and we can talk some more in private. I text him back.

How about you come around to mine, Jodie is out for the evening so we will have some privacy to talk? K x

After pressing send I suddenly regret inviting him to my flat because now he is going to think that I have an ulterior motive especially after his last text. "Shit."

My phone beeps almost instantly, I nervously open the message.

Perfect I would love to come to yours, I'll bring us a bottle of wine, what time? Evan x

'Oh god what have I done?'

About 7.00pm, can you remember the way? (Laughing emoji) and just to clarify talking is all we will be doing, do not get any ideas Mr H. K x

How can I not remember the way to my girl, and I don't know what ideas you are talking about (winking emoji), see you tomorrow Evan x

Ok see you then. K x

'Oh god I've done it now.'

I put my phone back in my bag and arrive home.

"Hi Kara" Jodie calls from the kitchen. I kick my shoes off in the hallway then walk into the kitchen and slump down onto a chair.

"Hi Jode."

"Have you had a good day?"

"Yes thanks, it went so quick, we've been ever so busy."

"That's good, what do you fancy for dinner tonight?" Jodie asks looking in the fridge.

"Err…how about something easy, scrambled egg on toast?"

"Yeah okay, would you like it now?"

"No, I'll have mine later thanks, you have yours Jode, I'm going to go and have a bath."

"Okay, how are things with Evan? Have you heard from him today?"

"Yes, we've just been texting on my way home actually."

"Oh right and...?"

"Um…I don't know if I've done the right thing, but I've invited him here tomorrow night while you are out at your work's meal."

"Oh okay." Jodie says sounding surprised.

"Why did you say it like that? You think I'm rushing things don't you? I knew I should have waited and just gone out with him on Friday."

"Whoa stop, I don't think you're rushing things, relax."

"Sorry I just don't know what to do for the best Jode, I hate feeling like this my head is all over the place."

"Hey, it's fine don't worry."

"Yes, but I do worry, I worry if people think I'm an idiot for giving him the time of day, I worry if I'm being too easy on him or too hard on him, I worry what if I let him in and he hurts me again."

"Babe listen, the road to love is never a smooth ride, there are always bumps along the way and there is no right and wrong answer you just have to go with your heart. Yes, it is scary, and you don't know if he is telling you the truth, but you have to trust your instincts and sometimes just go with how you feel. If it ends badly again then at least you will have given it a go otherwise you will always wonder and don't worry what people think it's your life and you live it how you want to live it. Like I always tell you I will support you whatever so stop with the worrying and relax or I will…I will…"

"You will what?" I smirk.

"I'll give you lines and a detention" she laughs.

"Sorry miss, yes miss." I laugh.

"That's better. I love hearing you laugh because you haven't done much of that lately."

"I know I've been a right miserable cow haven't I?"

"Well…" Jodie smirks.

"I'm sorry I just don't know what to think or how I feel anymore and it's stressing me out."

"Then don't think and don't feel, just go with the flow and everything will work itself out."

"Yeah, you're right."

Five

Tuesday at work is pretty much the same as the day before, busy with customers all day wanting a nice cup of coffee in Walt's Coffee Shop.

I arrive home just after 5pm and I am greeted by Jodie as I walk through the door wearing a lovely floral summery tea dress.

"Hi Jode, you look nice are you just heading out?"

"Yes, I'm going to the Italian with my work colleagues remember, I'm looking forward to having a catch up."

"Oh yes it will be nice, it's not that long until you go back to school is it?"

"No, I'm so ready to go back now."

"Oh, I don't know I would love to have the summer holidays off work. I'd go on holiday to somewhere hot, lie on a beach and read a good book and just relax…hmm I can picture it now."

"How is the holiday fund going, have you saved up much?" Jodie asks with a quizzical look on her face.

"Err…no not much because I raided it to buy those clothes we bought the other day" I laugh.

"Kara the whole point of saving is to save otherwise if you keep dipping into it you won't be going anywhere on holiday."

"Yes, I know, I know, I'll start again next payday," I smile. Jodie grins and rolls her eyes. "anyway, shouldn't you be going?"

"Oh god yes I'm going to be late," she says grabbing her handbag off the back of the chair "see you later."

"See you later, enjoy your meal."

I look at the time mindful that Evan will be arriving at 7.00pm so I have a quick dinner and shower then get dressed into some white cropped jeans and a black t-shirt thinking the trouser option is a good idea because it's not easily accessible if Evan tries anything.

I'm sat at the kitchen table lost in thought when I'm startled by a loud knock at the front door. I look out of the kitchen window and see Evan's blue Audi parked out front. "Shit he's here." I feel nervous suddenly as I go to answer the door.

'Come on Kara you need to be strong.'

"Hi" he says grinning at me stood on the doorstep with a bottle of Prosecco in one hand and a bunch of flowers in the other that look like they are from the local garage.

"Hi, come in" I smile.

"Thanks, these are for you" he smiles looking really pleased with himself.

"Thank you I'll just put them in some water" I smile accepting the flowers thinking they are quite different to the last bouquet of pink roses he bought me but it's thoughtful of him, I'm impressed that he is making an effort.

I walk into the kitchen as Evan shuts the front door and I look for a vase under the sink.

"You look nice" Evan says, and I turn to look at him and see he is staring at my bum while I am bent over looking in the cupboard.

"Err… thanks, so do you" I smile standing up and noticing he is wearing a pair of black jeans and a white t-shirt. He's also shaved. His hair is still long but this new look is kind of growing on me.

After putting the flowers in some water and arranging them in the vase I put them on the windowsill. They look nice. "Would you like a drink?" I ask.

"Yes, here let's have a glass of this." Evan hands me the bottle of Prosecco he brought, and I get two wine glasses out of the kitchen cupboard and pour us both a glass.

"Shall we sit in the lounge, it's more comfortable in there?" As soon as the words come out of my mouth I regret saying them because now he is going to think I'm suggesting getting more comfortable with him and that's not what I meant.

"Yeah sure" he smiles with a glint in his eye liking the sound of that.

We sit down on the three-seater sofa and after a few minutes of sipping wine and not speaking to each other, I feel awkward. I don't know what to say which is odd because we were never stuck for conversation before and we were normally so relaxed in each other's company. This feels like an awkward first date.

"So how was your day?" Evan asks choosing general conversation as an opener.

"It was very busy and you?"

"Yes, very busy" he replies. More awkward silence.

After a few moments I feel like I need to address it.

"This is weird isn't it?"

"What's weird?"

"This, us, it was never this awkward before."

"Then maybe we should just kiss and get over the awkwardness between us."

"Evan, I said don't get any ideas because it's not happening."

"But you kissed me the other night" he smiles.

"Well, that was because you tricked me" I frown.

"Okay but you can't blame a man for trying can you?" he grins.

"Maybe we should talk some more about everything that's happened because it still seems to be causing friction between us?"

"Do we have to?" Evan sighs.

"I just thought it might help, I can't move forward with you until I feel like we've moved on from what happened and I'm struggling to at the moment."

"What more do you need to know I thought we discussed everything?"

“Why do you owe your friend money?”

“For fuck’s sake,” he mutters under his breath “I just do okay and I don’t wish to discuss it with you, it’s personal between me and him.”

I sigh. ‘Why can’t he answer me? What is he hiding? Something doesn’t feel right.’ “Well, if you won’t talk about that then let’s talk about Julia.”

“What about Julia I told you she’s history so what do you want to talk about her for?”

“Does she still ring you?”

“No.”

“Evan, don’t lie to me ever since we’ve been seeing each other she has been constantly ringing you.”

“Okay occasionally yes but that doesn’t mean anything.”

“Have you seen her?”

“No.”

“Does she still want to get back with you?”

“No.”

“Is that all you can say ‘No’?”

“Yes” he smirks.

“Evan this isn’t funny I’m serious if we are to carry on seeing each other then I need to know the truth and for you to be honest about what’s happening with her.”

“Nothing is happening with her and nothing will be okay.”

“Why do I not believe you?”

"I don't know, and it really pisses me off that you keep asking me about her and I keep telling you she is nothing to me and you don't believe me."

"What like you said I was nothing to you Evan."

"No... you know that's not true."

"Do I? You say you love me, but something just doesn't feel right."

"Don't say that." He looks anxious.

I feel tearful my emotions are getting the better of me, so much for being strong.

Evan moves closer to me and places his hand over mine that is resting on my leg. "Please don't torture yourself about what happened in the past, please can we just move on from all that and concentrate on now, on us, I want you Kara, only you."

I wipe a stray tear falling down my cheek with my other hand. "Okay I'll try but I'm still not sleeping with you" I smile.

"Okay but don't make me wait too long because I'm desperate to have you, I can imagine what it's going to be like and I'm excited thinking about it."

"Have you forgotten already what it's like to be with me?"

"No but I would love for you to remind me" he grins.

"Evan" I warn. 'He is so cheeky.'

"Sorry just saying" he smiles, and I shift slightly so he removes his hand from my leg.

I need to change the subject. "So where are you taking me out for dinner on Friday?"

"I'm not sure any ideas?"

"There's a new restaurant that opened up recently, Jodie and Sally have been and say it's really good we could go there if you like?"

"Yeah, sounds good, would you mind booking it though because you know where it is, and I don't know this area very well?"

"Yeah sure, what time would you like me to book it for? You're going to the Manor on Friday aren't you?"

'Did I just say that out loud? I'm not supposed to know he is at the Manor on Friday. Now I have dropped myself in it because the only reason I know was because I was snooping around his new hotel and saw Curtis and he told me. Now I am going to have to confess why I know, great nice one Kara.'

"Going to the Manor?" he frowns.

"Yes," 'I may as well just tell him.' "I went to the Manor the other day to see how the hotel renovations are coming along and I bumped into Curtis while I was there, he mentioned you were going to the Manor on Friday."

"Oh right, you've been snooping have you and what else did Curtis have to say?" he scowls.

'He doesn't look happy.'

"Nothing much" I smirk. I recall when I had asked Evan what Curtis had said about what had happened between us he had said the same thing 'nothing much' so I throw his comment back at him.

"What are you smirking at? Yes, I am going to the Manor on Friday and I don't want you going there anymore. I also don't want you talking to Curtis about us either" he says with a serious tone.

"Okay I'm sorry," 'Jeez what's eating him?' "I was only talking to Curtis for a little while and we didn't really say much."

'I'm not telling him I was quizzing Curtis about him and about the guy he owes money to because that will make him even more grumpy.'

"Okay fine, I just don't want people interfering in our relationship that's all."

"Okay understood" I sigh.

"Anyway, we were saying dinner on Friday night if you could book the table for about 8.00pm that will give me enough time to go home get showered and changed before I come and pick you up."

"Okay," I almost offer for him to come back here for a shower and to change but it's a bit soon to be doing things like that especially how things are between us. "I'll book it for 8.00pm then."

"Great" he smiles.

"Would you like another drink?" I ask.

"I would love a cup of coffee."

"Okay I'll go and put the kettle on."

I hope things improve between us because as far as the night is going it's not going great.

Evan follows me into the kitchen and sits down at the table. I wait for the kettle to boil, filling two mugs one white with one sugar and one white with no sugar. "When will you be getting your other car back?" I ask looking out the kitchen window at Evan's Audi referring to his Aston Martin.

"I'm not sure why?"

"Oh, I was just wondering I thought you might be getting it back soon that's all."

"They can't find the fault so who knows when I will get it back."

I pass a cup of coffee to Evan "Thanks" and then I join him sat at the kitchen table. Evan looks at me seriously. "I know it's a bit strange between us now, but I've really missed you Kara and if you can just let your guard down then I'm sure things will be better between us. I can tell you are holding back."

I take in his features I love so much especially his chocolate brown eyes that are looking at me intensely. I've really missed him too and in a moment of weakness and not thinking I blurt out "I've really missed you too, I miss what we had, I miss feeling so incredibly happy that I don't know what to do with myself, I just wish we could go back in time, but we can't, and I'm scared that if I let you in you will hurt me again."

Evan takes a hold of my hand that is resting on the table. "You need to let me make it up to you, I'm trying here but if you won't let me in then we're not going to be able to move on from everything."

I don't say anything, and I don't remove Evan's hand on mine either, he strokes the back of it with his thumb. I just look at him and smile then look down to our joined hands.

"Kara look at me."

I lift my head to find his eyes. "You really are gorgeous, please let me love you, let me touch you, kiss you, I miss being with you" he smiles making me blush and moving towards me.

I almost drop my guard and kiss him, but I stop myself suddenly feeling panicked that things are moving too quickly again, I'm not ready. "Evan." I back away and remove my hand from under his and pick up my coffee mug with two hands as a distraction, Evan is watching my every move.

"I'm sorry I can't I just need more time." I take a sip of my drink.

"Not too much time I hope" he sighs.

'I feel awkward. I hate this. Why can't I just move on, what is stopping me? Why can't I let Evan be close to me again?'

Evan senses I am struggling and decides to move away from this line of conversation. "So where is Jane tonight?" he asks taking a sip of his coffee.

"Jane?"

"Your flatmate."

"Don't you mean Jodie?"

"Yes, that's who I said didn't I?"

"No, you said Jane."

"Did I?" Evan laughs "I meant Jodie sorry I've been interviewing a lady today at work and she is called Jane, I must have got the names mixed up."

"Oh, is she going to be working at the Manor?"

"No one of my other hotels I had a staff member leave and so I needed to replace them."

"Oh, right, well Jodie," I grin "is having a meal with her work colleagues, in fact she should be back soon" I say looking at my watch.

"Oh, that's nice," he says finishing his coffee "well I'd better be going anyway so thanks for a lovely evening."

"Yes, I suppose it is getting late, thanks for coming over."

"It's been good to see you again" he smiles getting up from the table.

"You too, I'll see you out."

I follow Evan to the front door, and he turns to look at me. "I'll see you Friday then gorgeous."

"Yes, I'll see you Friday" I feel slightly awkward with the awkward goodbye.

As I look at him and he looks at me I can feel a glimmer of hope that maybe things are going to be okay between us. I drift off into a trance thinking private thoughts of how we used to be and how it could possibly be in the future, but I'm soon brought back to the here and now when Evan grabs hold of me and kisses me. Holding the back of my head I can feel his tongue swipe across my lips as he tries to coax my mouth open. He seems desperate as he kisses me hard, rough, and forceful.

"Evan stop," I mumble trying to break free as he holds me tight.

"Remember how good we are, let me kiss you" he says briefly before finding my lips again. I manage to move my head away from him "Evan get off me." I'm just about to knee him where it hurts when he steps back breathless realising what he's doing and hearing the anger in my voice that I'm clearly not impressed.

"What the hell do you think you're doing?" I shout glaring at him wiping my mouth with the back of my hand.

"I'm sorry I shouldn't have done that it's just that I'm finding this really difficult, I can't help it if I want to kiss the woman I love." Evan runs his hands through his hair looking stressed.

"Jeez why did you have to do that, why did you have to ruin it, I told you it was too soon, I'm not there yet Evan, I need more time, I need to be able to trust you and what you're saying before we're intimate again" I scowl.

"I'm sorry Kara, I thought you wanted to, you were looking at me and…please forgive me?" he says moving towards me as I back away from him.

"No, I didn't, I think it's time you went." I open the front door.

"Don't be mad at me please, I'm sorry."

"Evan it's fine just go and I'll see you on Friday okay."

"Okay I'll text you" he smiles and then walks through the front door and leaves.

I shut the door behind him and let out a long breath that I didn't realise I had been holding and lean on the back of the door. "Shit." I feel strange and overcome with a mixture of emotions. His kiss, the feel of his lips, the spark, there's no denying it because it just isn't there anymore, the hurt has made my love for him fade away, I feel nothing.

Tears roll down my cheeks as the reality of it all becomes too much, the man I claim to love is now just a man, a man who no longer has my heart, a man who I thought was going to be my happy ever after but now I realise is never going to be. I stand against the back of the door wiping my tears with the backs of my hands thinking about what just happened, I feel numb.

After a few moments, my thoughts are interrupted when the door is being shoved into my back and I hear a voice saying, "Bloody hell what the hell is wrong with this door?"

"Jodie" I whisper turning around just as Jodie prepares to give the door another shove and I open the door and she comes bursting through it into the hallway almost falling into a heap on the floor.

"What the hell?" she says stumbling to a stop and seeing me looking at her trying not to laugh.

"Are you okay Jode?" I smirk my tears of sadness now turning to tears of laughter.

"I'm fine thank you," she says adjusting her dress "what the hell just happened and what's wrong with the front door?" she frowns.

"Nothing's wrong I was just leaning against it when you tried to open it" I giggle.

"Something funny?" she smirks. "Where's Evan?"

I can feel the tears coming again. "He's just gone."

"Are you alright Kar?" she asks noticing my tears.

"Evan just tried to kiss me and in that moment I realised that everything I felt for him before, its gone Jode, the spark, the excitement has all gone." I burst into tears and sob covering my face with my hands.

"Oh Kara, come here," Jodie says hugging me "are you sure?"

"Yes, I'm sure, when he kissed me before it felt like the whole world stood still, there could have been an earthquake and I wouldn't have noticed because I was totally consumed and lost in the love I felt for him, it was earth shattering Jode but now I don't feel any of that, how can that be, how can it all just go?"

“He’s obviously not the man for you Kara, maybe it was just lust before and you thought you loved him, come on let’s get out of this hallway and I’ll make us a cup of hot chocolate and you can fill me in on your evening okay.”

“Okay.” I wipe the tears from my eyes, I’m so pleased to see my best friend home she always gives good advice and makes me feel better.

After Jodie has made us both a cup of hot chocolate we sit in the lounge and I tell her all about my evening with Evan up to the point of the kiss.

“I knew it was going to be an awkward goodbye. I was thinking about how it used to be between us and before I knew what was happening he was holding me tightly and kissing me hard and it just felt so wrong.”

“What are you going to do?” Jodie asks concerned.

“I don’t know, I’ve said I will go for dinner with him on Friday night now.” I stress.

“If I were you I wouldn’t do anything drastic I would still go for the meal and then if you still feel the same on Friday tell him then. You might just be rushing things and being too hard on yourself about it all and of course it will feel different to how it was before because the situation is different.”

“Okay I’ll go for the meal and if my feelings haven’t changed then I’ll tell him afterwards. God it will be like the last supper,” I laugh feeling less tearful now. “thanks

for always being there for me Jode and giving me advice."
"Hey that's what good friends are for aren't they?" she smiles.

Six

Friday soon comes around and as I arrive at work on this lovely sunny morning I am just walking through the door when I hear my phone go off in my bag.

"Morning Sal" Sally is stood at the counter, I walk over to her.

"Morning Kara, how are you feeling today?"

"Yeah, I'm alright a bit nervous about tonight."

I've told Sally all about the situation with Evan, the kiss the other night and how I'm feeling, Sally thinks if this is how I feel then it's better to tell Evan now than to leave it any longer so we both know where we stand.

"Yeah, I can imagine you're feeling nervous, do you know what you are going to do yet?"

"I still don't know to be honest I suppose seeing him later will clarify whether I want to keep on seeing him or not."

"Yes, as soon as you see him and spend some more time with him I'm sure you will know then."

"What shall I say though if I don't want to carry on with things, I mean I know we are only friends at the moment, but he's made it clear he wants to pick up where we left off and he's not going to like it when I tell him I don't want to and that my feelings have changed?"

"Just be honest with him Kara that's all you can be, and he will just have to accept it. You can't force it if you're not feeling it anymore."

"I know I keep thinking am I rushing things, should I give him a bit longer but then I remember what it felt like when he kissed me, and it should have made me feel like it did before."

"Yes, admittedly in the beginning of a relationship you should feel like that especially because the relationship is new, I mean I could understand it if you were an old married couple. So, I guess after tonight you might be on the lookout for a new man again?"

"Maybe but to be honest I think I'm going to stay single for a while and concentrate on saving for a holiday somewhere, going to Italy really gave me a taster of what there is to discover beyond our hometown."

"Sounds like a good plan" Sally smiles.

"Anyway, I'll just put my bag away and grab my apron then I'll get started on the coffee machine."

"Okay love."

I hang up my bag on the coat hook and remember I received a text earlier; I retrieve my phone from my bag and see that Evan has sent me a message.

Hi gorgeous, sorry I haven't text since I saw you the other night but I've been busy at the hotel and I've been getting home late. I'm really looking forward to our meal tonight I'll pick you up at 7.30pm. Evan x

Reading his message, I feel bad because I'm not looking forward to the meal one bit. Thinking he must be on his way over to the Manor by now I send him a reply keeping it short and sweet.

Hi it's okay, see you later, Kara x

I put my phone back in my bag and put on my apron putting all thoughts of Evan and tonight's meal to one side and go to start work.

As soon as 5 o'clock comes around I'm starting to feel sick with nerves, my stomach is full of nervous butterflies because in a few hours I will be seeing Evan and possibly ending it with him and I'm still unsure as to what to do or say.

'Do I still have feelings for him? If I decide to end things how am I going to tell him and how is he going to react? Is our relationship really over?'

"Are you okay Kara?" Sally asks seeing my anxious worried face as we walk out of Walt's Coffee Shop ready to leave work.

"Not really" I sigh.

"Do you really think it could be over between you two?"

"How I'm feeling at the moment yes I think it is Sal."

"I know it's not nice finishing with someone especially if they don't take it well, but you need to do the right thing Kara."

"I know oh god I hope he doesn't cause a scene. I think I will have to get through the meal first and then tell him when he drops me home."

"Yes, I think that's a good idea. Text me tomorrow and tell me how it went, I'll be thinking about you."

"I will do."

"Bye love."

Sally runs off to meet Tim and I wave at them as they drive past and take a leisurely walk back home in the lovely evening sunshine.

I arrive home and as I walk through the front door I find Jodie and Matt canoodling in the hallway.

"Hi guys, get a room" I laugh and they both stop what they are doing and look at me.

"Hi Kar" they both say in unison laughing.

"Good idea come on Jode" Matt grins dragging Jodie towards her bedroom.

"Matt get off you idiot, you'll have to wait now," she giggles as Matt pulls a disappointed face. "I want to talk to Kara." Matt leaves us to it and goes to watch some TV in the lounge and Jodie follows me into the kitchen.

"How are you feeling about tonight?" she asks.

"To be honest I'm dreading it and I feel sick."

"Do you think you are going to end it tonight then?"

"I think so oh I don't know…aargh what's wrong with me? I'm going to go and have a shower hopefully it will destress me."

"Alright babe, try not to stress, it will all work out, see you in a bit."

I pick up my bag off the back of the kitchen chair that I slung there earlier and go to my room. I throw my bag on the floor and flop onto my bed.

'Aargh why does my love life always have to be so complicated, why I can't just have a normal relationship like everyone else?'

After laying on the bed thinking for a few moments I get up and get in the shower. The hot water cascading over my head starts to relax me and I think of how I can word it to Evan, the breakup speech.

'Hmm… what shall I say? I'm sorry I don't want to be with you anymore my feelings have changed, I'm sorry but things aren't working out, I'm sorry but you shouldn't have come back, I'm sorry it's not you it's me …oh god what the hell do I say? Whatever I say it's going to be awkward and shit. Think Kara think.'

After agonising for a while, I get out of the shower and go back to my bedroom. I put on my watch and see it's 6.30pm, Evan will be arriving in an hour. I blow dry my hair then look in my wardrobe for something to wear. I decide on a new blue knee length dress that's fitted on the top and flares out at the waist that I bought on the girly day out with Jodie. 'Yes, that will do.' I put it on. I look in my jewellery box to get some accessories to go with it and the first thing I see is the bracelet that Evan bought me for my birthday. I pick it up and read the words on the back of the heart 'With Me Always.' I sigh as tears spring in my eyes and put it straight back into the box. I can't possibly wear that when I'm thinking of ending things, so I choose a simple silver bracelet, silver earrings and a silver necklace that match perfectly and put them on. I still feel sick with nerves and taking one last look in the wardrobe mirror I go the shoe rack in the hallway and put on some white strappy shoes. Once ready I go into the kitchen to find Jodie washing up and Matt is drying.

"Wow you look nice" Jodie smiles.

"Thanks, I don't feel very nice though."

"Are you still feeling stressed? Did your shower not do the trick?"

"No not really, I still feel sick I don't know how I'm going to eat a meal, have we got any wine in the fridge, I feel like I need a large glass of it?"

"Yes, there's half a bottle left."

I open the fridge, take out the bottle of wine then pour myself a glass and sit down at the kitchen table.

"What time is he picking you up?" Matt asks.

"About 7.30pm."

"Oh, he won't be long then."

"Oh god don't remind me."

"You'll be fine Kara, don't worry," Jodie says taking off the pink rubber gloves and joining me. Matt sits down too.

"If you are feeling like this why don't you just cancel and tell him when he arrives?" Matt says trying to help.

"I could but it's all arranged now, I've booked a table and I'd feel guilty cancelling this late."

"Yeah, I guess" Matt says as there is a loud knock at the door.

"Shit he's here." I get up and look out of the kitchen window and see Evan's Audi parked out the front.

I straighten my dress and grab my clutch bag and phone. "Wish me luck guys, see you later."

"Yeah, good luck, see you later" they both reply.

I open the door and the first thing I notice is that Evan has had his hair cut, it's still longer than he had it before when we first met but it looks much better. 'Oh god he's made an effort and now I feel even worse.'

"Hi" I smile.

"Hi gorgeous wow you look hot" he says looking me up and down. He's still wearing the different aftershave but at least he has had a shave and with the new haircut he looks smart wearing a pair of black jeans and a light blue shirt.

"Thanks, you look nice too." I close the front door behind me and walk down the path following Evan to his car. Being the perfect gentleman, he opens the car door for me. I feel terrible knowing that I might end things with him tonight because he is being so nice.

I fasten my seatbelt and Evan gets into the driver's side and looks at me. "I won't be able to take my eyes of you all night, you really are gorgeous" he smiles starting the car.

'I can't deal with this, the more he pays me compliments the more guilty I feel because I've realised that it doesn't matter how much time I spend with Evan my heart just isn't in it anymore. I don't feel right which means I have to tell him...tonight.'

We arrive at the restaurant and we are shown to a table for two by the window. The waiter takes our drinks order, Evan orders a coke because he is driving, and I opt for a large glass of white wine. The wine I drank at home earlier has certainly helped with my nerves but to get through the rest of this evening, I need some more Dutch courage.

"What are you having then?" I ask looking at the menu.

"I'm going to have the steak. What are you going to have?"

"I'm going to have the lasagne and salad."

'I couldn't possibly eat a steak right now with how I'm feeling, my stomach is doing somersaults from nerves and chewing on a piece of steak would probably take me all night. The sooner this meal is over with the better.'

The waiter arrives with our drinks then makes a note of our food order then leaves us alone again.

"What are your plans for the weekend?" Evan asks.

"Oh, I'm really busy this weekend, I'm going to see my parents and then I've got washing and cleaning and I said I would do something with Jodie."

"Oh, that's a shame I was hoping we could do something" he says looking disappointed.

"Sorry but I wasn't expecting to see you was I, so I already have plans."

"No, it's fine, how about Monday night, we could do something then?"

"Err maybe… sorry will you excuse me, but I need to go to the ladies, I'll be back in a minute."

"Okay gorgeous" he smiles.

I get up from the table feeling Evan's eyes on me the whole time as I walk through the restaurant towards the toilets. I walk through the toilet's door feeling relieved to see that no-one else is in here. I pace the floor thinking for a moment then I get my phone out and call Jodie.

"Hey it's me" I whisper.

"Hi where are you and why are you whispering?" Jodie asks sounding surprised to hear from me.

"I'm at the restaurant in the ladies toilets and I don't know why I'm whispering." I laugh nervously. "I can't do this Jode."

"What do you mean?"

"I can't do this with Evan I've made my decision I don't want to be with him."

"Okay so that's good seeing him has made things clearer for you."

"Yes, it has, I think I knew deep down that I felt this way but seeing him tonight my heart's just not in it anymore so I'm going to tell him."

"Good I'm pleased that you now know how you feel so it's just a matter of telling him."

"Yes, but it's not going to be easy, he is being really nice to me and he keeps paying me all these compliments, I feel so bad. He has even made an effort with his appearance and had a haircut. He's just asked me what my plans are for the weekend."

"Oh, so what did you say?"

"I said I was busy and was doing something with you to try and put him off but then he suggested we do something Monday night."

"Oh god, so what excuse did you give him then?"

"I didn't I said I needed the toilet and came to phone you. I mean what do I say, oh sorry I can't because after this meal is over I don't want to see you anymore."

'I'm so stressed right now.'

"Calm down, you sound in a right state take a few deep breaths and get yourself together, you can do this Kara."

"I am in a state I'm fucking shaking, I hate this, I'm not a horrible person Jode and I don't want to hurt anyone, it's so hard breaking up with someone, not that we are actually dating because we're not, but you know what I mean."

"Kara listen just get through the meal then when he brings you home tell him and then you don't have to see him again. Yes, he will be disappointed and hurt but you can't carry on if it's just one sided, it's not fair to you or him."

"I know, oh god I'd better get back or he'll think I'm having a number two or something."

Jodie laughs. "Go on, good luck and I'll see you later."

"Thanks Jode, bye."

"Bye babe."

I end the call and check myself in the mirror above the sinks then take a deep breath to calm myself down before I return to the restaurant back to Evan.

"Are you okay?" Evan asks as I approach the table.

"Yeah, sorry there was a queue" I lie and take my seat at the table again just as the waiter arrives with our food.

The food is delicious just like Jodie and Sally said it would be but feeling anxious and the somersaults that are happening in my tummy its affecting my appetite and I pick through my meal and Evan notices.

"What's wrong? Don't you like the food?"

"Yes, it's lovely I'm just not as hungry as I thought I was, is your meal nice?"

"Yes, it's great and don't worry I'll help you out if you can't eat it all" he grins.

"Okay thanks" I smile.

After pushing the food around my plate and preferring the liquid food instead I'm feeling rather tipsy after all the wine I've drank tonight.

"Are you finished?" Evan asks referring to my food.

"Yes thanks."

"Swap plates and I'll finish yours" he smiles.

"Okay thanks." 'I hate wasting food.'

After clearing everything on the plates Evan asks, "Would you like a dessert?"

"No, I'm fine thanks but you can have one though."

"No, I'm good I feel stuffed now after eating two meals," he smiles "I'll get the bill then. I thought we could go back to yours and have coffee if that's okay with you?"

"Oh, okay yeah sure." I smile.

'Damn it, that wasn't part of the plan. I was just going to get him to drop me home then tell him that this, whatever this is between us is over and now I've agreed to invite him in for coffee, aargh what was I thinking?'

"Great I don't have to rush off either" he grins.

'Oh god...don't say that.'

Evan beckons the waiter over and after having a disagreement that I can't pay for my meal he pays the bill and then we leave.

Arriving back at the flat Evan parks the car and I look at him, his big brown eyes staring at me. I'm about to make an excuse and say I'm tired so he doesn't come in for coffee and then give him the breakup speech when he leans in quickly and tries to kiss me. I turn my head to dodge the kiss and he plants a kiss on my cheek instead.

"Evan what are you doing, don't?" I warn then get out of the car. 'Jeez why does he keep doing that?'

I'm so annoyed that he thinks he can just keep trying to kiss me when I've already told him it's too soon. In fact, I don't want him kissing me at all especially since I've decided I don't feel that way about him anymore which reminds me I need to tell him, and I need to tell him now.

"Evan I'm sorry…"

"No Kara I'm sorry I shouldn't have kissed you it's just you are so gorgeous I can't help myself."

"No, you shouldn't" I snap walking off up the path towards the front door to get away from him. I turn around and I'm just about to tell him when I see the look on his face, he looks so sorry that he's upset me, and I chicken out. I unlock the front door and walk inside, and Evan follows me. "I'm home" I shout walking into the hallway.

"How did it go did you tell him?" Jodie calls from the lounge and walking into the hallway.

"Told me what?" Evan replies stood behind me.

"Err… just that Matt's here and he hoped that you didn't feel awkward seeing him again, you know because he told you to leave when you were here last." I ramble.

"Oh right" Evan replies looking uncomfortable.

Matt hearing the conversation joins us in the hallway. I look at Jodie and secretly shake my head at her signalling to her that I haven't said anything to Evan yet. Matt looks at Evan who is looking anxious.

"Hi mate, how are you?" Matt says holding out his hand to shake Evan's to say no hard feelings.

"Err I'm good thanks you?"

"Yeah, I'm great."

The atmosphere is awkward.

"Would you like a hot drink you two I was just going to make us a coffee?" I ask looking at Jodie and Matt.

"No, we're fine thanks we've just had one" Jodie replies.

"Okay Evan is just having a drink before he goes home so…"

"Okay we'll leave you guys to it" Jodie says looking at me with a knowing look then grabbing hold of Matt's hand and dragging him back into the lounge.

I walk into the kitchen and put the kettle on, and Evan takes a seat at the table. I get two mugs out of the cupboard and can feel Evan watching my every move. I just want to run away, my heart is beating fast in my chest, I hate this, I hate ending things with someone, but it must be done.

After the kettle has boiled, I make the coffees and then join Evan sat at the table. I take a deep breath. "Evan, we need to talk."

"Okay" he frowns looking at me with a serious face. I am just about to say the words when the doorbell rings. "I'll get it" I shout wanting to avoid the awkward break up speech because I am still not clear in my mind as to what I am going to say.

"Okay" Jodie shouts carrying on watching television.

I look at my watch, it's just past 9.30pm. 'I wonder whose calling at this time of night?'

"Excuse me I'll be back in a minute" I say looking at Evan before walking out of the kitchen to the front door.

I open the door and see a man stood on the doorstep dressed in black jeans and a white t-shirt and he looks extremely nervous running his fingers through his dark brown hair staring at me. "Hi Kara." I stare at the man for a few moments then stumble backwards grabbing hold of the door for support. The man's face, those eyes, his voice "Oh my god…" I whisper.

"Jesus Kara, are you okay?" he says, "you've gone as white as a sheet." I stand frozen on the spot, my pale face looking back at the man on my doorstep. "Kara." Everything is hazy and muffled; I think I'm in shock. "Kara baby are you okay?"

I feel like I can't breathe.

"Oh my god…what the hell is going on?" I shout.

Jodie hears me shout and comes rushing into the hallway closely followed by Matt to find out what is going on. Jodie looks at the man stood outside and the look on her face of total shock and disbelief matches my own. "What the hell?" she says looking at him then looking at me. "What the fuck?" Matt says shocked at what he is seeing too because the man stood on the doorstep is a mirror image of the man sat in my kitchen drinking a cup of coffee.

"Evan" I whisper.

The man in the kitchen comes into the hallway to see what all the commotion is about. "Are you okay darling?" he asks then notices the man stood on the doorstep outside and laughs.

"What the fuck is going on here?" I yell backing away from the pair of them to stand next to Jodie and Matt.

"Oh, this is just great," the man laughs who was sat in my kitchen moments ago. "Hello dear brother."

"Evan," I look between them both "you have a twin brother I thought you said were an only child?" I'm surprised, shocked and angry that he lied to me.

"Yes, I'm a twin and I'm sorry I didn't tell you" Evan says with a serious face looking at me then looking at his brother. "Sebastian what the hell are you doing here, I swear to god if you have laid one finger on her?" he says glaring and pointing a finger at him. "You need to step outside…NOW" Evan shouts making everyone jump pacing up and down on the doorstep, his face and body language showing so much anger.

Sebastian laughs. "Well, I would but Kara has just made me a nice cup of coffee and I don't want it to get cold, so I'll pass if you don't mind. Oh, and I've laid more than a finger on her alright when I was fucking her last night in my hotel room, she really is world class dear brother."

Evan lunges at Sebastian grabbing him around the throat then pushes him up against the hall wall "You fucking bastard, I'm going to fucking kill you" he says before punching him in the stomach. We all jump backwards to get out of the way and the twin brothers start laying into each other. Fists are flying and Matt tries to intervene to break them up but ends up getting punched himself.

"Evan no he's lying we didn't," I shout. "Stop, please...STOP" I scream.

Evan looks murderous, I have never seen him look so angry, he drags his brother outside by his shirt and they both start throwing punch after punch.

"Matt please you need to stop them" I cry standing at the door with Jodie watching them fight.

The twin brothers ferociously attack each other their faces are becoming bloody from the heated punches they are giving and receiving, there shirts are torn, and I'm scared someone is going to end up seriously hurt.

"Matt please" I shout sounding desperate.

"Shit" Matt quickly puts on some shoes then barges past us running through the doorway like a bull charging at its target separating the two men. He grabs hold of one of them in a headlock but with all the commotion going on and the twins being identical it's difficult to tell which one is the real Evan and who he has a hold of. It's only when Evan shouts "Matt get the fuck off me I'm going to fucking kill him" that Matt knows it's Evan. Matt lets go of him and Sebastian runs off down the path, jumps into his car and wheel spins away with Evan running after him down the street.

"Stay the fuck away from her or I swear I'll fucking kill you" he shouts looking weary from the fight putting his hands on his knees and slumping over.

"Hey man are you okay?" Matt says walking over to him and patting him on the back. Evan stands up to face him.

"No, I'm not…FUUUCCCKK" he shouts letting out his anger and frustration and flexing his hand which is hurting from the punches he has been giving.

"Well, that was a total shock" Matt laughs trying to make light of the situation.

"You're telling me, Jesus…what the hell is going on here?"

"I was going to ask you the same question" Matt replies.

"Thanks for helping I'm sorry you got caught up in our fight mate."

"Hey, no worries mate I'll survive" Matt says rubbing his jaw which is stinging after being punched by one of the brothers.

"He is not fucking doing this to me anymore…" Evan pants also rubbing his jaw as the after-effects of the fight start to kick in. "I need to speak to Kara I need to explain" he says sounding desperate noticing my confused tear-stained face stood looking at him from the doorway. I turn and walk back inside the flat.

"Come on mate let's go inside, we'll give you some space" Matt says rubbing him on the back then walking over to Jodie telling her they are going out for a bit. Matt grabs his car keys out of the kitchen and then leaves with Jodie. As the front door closes Evan walks into the kitchen.

"Kara I…" I hold my hand up to shush him from speaking.

"Before you say anymore, I need a stiff drink, take a seat at the table and I'll get something to clean you up with" I say looking at his bloodied face then opening a cupboard to get the first aid kit out and a bottle of vodka putting them on the kitchen worktop.

"Kara please I need to explain…"

"Evan I just need a moment; I need to process what has just happened." I look at him. "Would you like one?" I ask pouring a glass of vodka and downing it in one go feeling the burn on the back of my throat.

"No thanks I'm driving. Look I know you've had a shock but if you'll just come and sit down, I need to talk to you, I need to explain everything."

"Yes, you do" I snap filling my glass again and carrying it in my shaky hand to sit down at the table opposite Evan.

Evan takes a deep breath and lets out a big sigh. "You've met my brother then" he says looking awkward after telling me he is an only child when we first met.

"Yes, you could say that." I glare at him.

Evan's facial expression changes and he looks at me with hurt in his eyes "Before I explain everything, I need to know did you sleep with him Kara?"

I look at him, his eyes close and I can see the hurt written all over his face as he waits for my answer.

"No Evan I didn't" I reply firmly.

"Please just be honest with me, I need to know" he sighs.

"I swear, he was lying, I never slept with him. Evan look at me…look at me" I urge.

Evan opens his eyes and looks at me, my eyes are brimming with tears. "I'm telling the truth, nothing happened between us, he wanted something to happen, but it didn't feel right."

"I don't know what I would have done if he had touched you, just the thought of it I'm so sorry…" he says looking distressed.

"Hey, he didn't, we didn't okay…honestly."

"Okay I believe you I'm so sorry," He is genuinely upset. "I'm sorry I told you I was an only child, I'm sorry

I didn't tell you about Sebastian and for hurting you for everything."

"I wish you had told me because then things would have been quite different. So, explain, tell me now."

I down my second glass of vodka I think I might need it hearing what Evan has to say. I don't give him any eye contact while I wait for his explanation.

"Okay so the reason I didn't tell you about Sebastian is because I was trying to protect you. Somehow Sebastian found out about us, maybe he had seen us together and seen how happy we were. Anyway, he's trying to hurt me Kara, Sebastian thinks I owe him money and he is trying to hurt me any way he can so I will pay him. He is the one who sent me the text. When I received it from him saying you were world class compared to Julia, I knew then you were going to be a target, so I sent him a reply to try and warn him off you. I told him that you were no one, just a bit of fun and didn't mean anything to me because I knew it was only a matter of time before he tried to hurt me through you. The text you read which you were not supposed to have seen was my way of warning him off you. I wish you had given me the chance to explain it to you back then, but you just kept ignoring my texts and calls and..."

"I'm sorry, I was really hurt, I thought you didn't care about me, I thought when I read that text that you meant it, that I was nothing to you and..."

"Kara you mean the fucking world to me."

I look at him and he looks at me intensely. I feel a single tear fall down my cheek. I quickly swipe it away with my hand.

"I'm sorry you thought I didn't care. I honestly thought keeping things from you I was protecting you and keeping you out of his little game. I thought if I made out you were nothing to me he would leave you alone, but how wrong was I?" Evan looks angry again.

We are both silent for a few moments while we think about what just happened and what has been said.

"Did he kiss you?" Evan asks obviously still seething that Sebastian has been close to me.

"Yes" I whisper.

"Fuck." Evan thumps the table making me jump forgetting his hand is hurting. "Bastard."

"Evan it wasn't a proper kiss."

"He still kissed you Kara, do you know how that makes me feel?"

"Yes, well you should have just been honest with me in the first place then it wouldn't have happened would it" I snap.

"I know and I'm fucking regretting it now I can tell you."

"Yes, your brother kissed me, but it didn't feel right, the spark wasn't there, it wasn't there with him and now I know why because it wasn't even you."

"Can you feel the spark now… with me?" he asks with hope in his voice looking at me.

"Evan" I look away from him.

"Shit I've ruined everything haven't I, Sebastian has won…again." He gets up from the table.

"Evan, no wait where are you going?" I panic. I get up from the table, grab hold of his arm and he looks at me. "you haven't ruined everything; Sebastian hasn't won because the spark that drew us together yes it's still there it's always there with YOU" I smile.

"I'm so sorry baby" he says looking at me regretfully moving towards me, but I stop him.

"Come on let's get you cleaned up." I smile.

Evan sits down again; he has a cut above his left eye. While I clean his face, he watches me looking tormented.

"I'm sorry if you thought I only wanted you for sex."

"I'm sorry for ignoring your calls and texts when you wanted to explain things."

"It's okay I forgive you" Evan smiles.

I smirk. "Well, I forgive you too but don't ever keep things from me again even if you are trying to protect me, you should have told me."

"I know…okay" he smiles breathing out a sigh of relief and then wincing from the pain in his face as I clean his eye.

"Are you alright?" I ask concerned.

"I am now" he grins.

"Evan why didn't you tell me you were a twin? Why did you tell me when we first met that you were an only child? I mean you could have said you had a brother, but you don't get on with him, why did you act like he doesn't exist?"

"I didn't tell you because for a long time now I have thought of myself as an only child he is not someone I wish to call my brother. Yes, we are identical twins and look the same, but we couldn't be any more different, I have morals Kara, he doesn't. He doesn't care about anything or anyone all he is interested in is the money he thinks is owed to him and he will do whatever it takes to get it."

"Why don't you just pay him then so you will be rid of him?"

"Because after everything he has done to me he doesn't deserve a single penny and that's my way of making him suffer."

"I'm so glad I'm an only child."

"Yes, and it's not just the money he is the one who seduced Julia and she had the affair with."

"Oh my god, I can't believe this, so when you told me about Julia having an affair with some guy it was your twin brother you were talking about?"

"Yes, I'm afraid so."

"Why didn't you just tell me this before?"

"I didn't tell you because we were only supposed to be a casual thing and..."

I look serious for a moment and Evan notices.

"Kara what started out as a casual thing turned into something so much more than that, the more time I spent with you things changed. I loved being with you, you made me forget all about the shit going on with Sebastian. You were such a breath of fresh air when you came into my life and yes as far as I was concerned at the beginning all I wanted was a bit of fun but after meeting you and our first night together I couldn't get you out of my head, I still can't. As soon as I got that text from Sebastian and knowing he would try to hurt me through you I knew I had to do the right thing and let you go because I didn't want you caught up in his games but after all I've said and done to try and keep you out of it he got to you anyway."

"I can't tell you how much that hurt me when I told you that I loved you and you told me you didn't feel the same."

"I know and I'm sorry for hurting you the way I did but I honestly did do what I thought was best."

"So, you do care about me then?"

"Yes Kara I do, from the first moment I met you I felt like I had won the lottery but I'm not good at dealing with my feelings after the whole Julia thing. It was the hardest thing I have ever had to do to push you away like that" he says looking up at me with his captivating brown eyes which make me melt every time.

We stare at each other for a few moments not saying anything.

“Am I fixed now?” he smiles.

“Yes, all done.” I smile putting the cleaning cloth down on the table.

“I don’t think I’m quite fixed yet” he smiles.

“Oh, what’s left for there to fix?” I ask.

“Just us.” he smiles. “I promise I’m going fix things Kara, I’m going to make it up to you if you’ll let me?”

I smile cupping his face in my hand looking into his gorgeous brown eyes.

“I’ve missed you so much” he says staring at me like he wants to kiss me but unsure how I will react.

“I’ve missed you too” I smile.

He gently pulls me onto his lap and brushes my hair out of my face. We look at each other tenderly for a few moments and then our mouths slowly find each other. The slow, gentle, tender loving kiss reminding us how we feel about each other and that as long as we have each other then everything will be okay.

“I’ve missed having you in my arms and kissing you” Evan says holding my face in his hands carrying on the kiss not wanting to stop.

“Evan” I moan softly.

He breaks the kiss and looks into my teary eyes. “Kara the worst decision I ever made was walking away, I should have stayed, I should have made you listen, I should have told you how I really feel.”

"Evan it's okay" I look into his eyes as tears appear there too. "So… how do you feel about me?" I ask longing to hear the words for so long.

"I am completely and utterly in love with you Kara Davis" he smiles finally able to say the words out loud.

"I'm completely and utterly in love with you too Evan Hamilton."

Tears roll down both our cheeks as we hug, kiss, and reunite with each other, our love so strong that nothing or no one is going to come between us again.

"You made up then?" Jodie smiles walking into the kitchen followed by Matt after giving us some time alone seeing me sat on Evan's lap kissing him. We quickly wipe our eyes.

"Hi guys thanks for giving us some space. Yes, Evan has explained everything and we're fine." I say with a big grin on my face.

"I'm sorry for hurting Kara the way I did but it wasn't intentional and I'm sure Kara will fill you in on all the details later" Evan says sounding guilty.

"Hey, no hard feelings," Jodie says, and Matt agrees. "It's good to see Kara smiling again, she has been so miserable without you."

"Yeah, and I've been miserable too" Evan smiles looking at me adoringly.

"So, does this mean you are officially together now?" Matt asks.

"Matt" Jodie says giving him a shove.

"Err..." I look at Evan not knowing what to say.

Evan smiles. "Kara, spending time apart made me realise just how much I want to be with you. I need to stop dwelling on the past and think about the future, our future so if you'll have me, I would love for you to be my girlfriend?" he grins.

"Really the man who doesn't do relationships?" I reply pretending to be shocked.

"Yes really, the man who doesn't do relationships would like to be in a relationship with you if you'll have me, I love you Kara so what do you say will you be my girlfriend?"

"Oh god...yes...yes...yes...I do I will err yes please." I smile kissing him all over his face.

"Ouch steady I've just had my face punched numerous times remember" he laughs loving my reaction.

"Oh god sorry," I laugh "I'm just so happy."

"Aww that's brilliant." Jodie says with tears in her eyes.

"Aww Jode come here." I get up off Evan's lap and give my best friend a hug.

"Sorry you just make such a gorgeous couple and I'm so pleased you have worked things out."

"Me too" I smile looking at Evan who is smiling at us both.

Matt walks over to Evan and shakes his hand "Shall we have a drink to celebrate?" he suggests.

"I think we should maybe leave them too it because they probably want to celebrate on their own." Jodie says taking hold of Matt's hand.

"Oh right, yes okay." Matt winks at me making me blush.

"Oh, just before we leave you two to get reacquainted what are you going to do about your brother?" Jodie asks Evan.

"Don't worry if he tries anything again he will be dealt with."

"Okay come on then Matt let's go to my room for a bit" Jodie says dragging him by his hand.

"Well, there's an offer I can't refuse" Matt grins smacking her on the bum and following her out of the kitchen.

I look at Evan "Do you want to go to my room for a bit?"

"Okay but I can only stay for a little while because it's getting late and I have an early meeting at Hamilton Tower in the morning."

"Okay," I smile "would you like a cup of tea or coffee?"

"A coffee would be great thanks."

I discard the remnants of Sebastian's coffee cup in the sink and after putting the kettle on I notice the flowers he bought me the other day in the window when he came to see me. I pick up the vase, open the bin and deposit the flowers inside. "Good riddance to bad rubbish" I scowl. I look at Evan and he is looking at me with a confused look on his face. "The flowers they were from Sebastian."

"Oh, I see, cheapskate" he sneers referring to the small bunch of flowers that are different to the large bunches of flowers he normally buys for me.

I make us both a coffee and then I carry the mugs to my room and Evan follows. He sits on the bed with his legs outstretched and leans on the headboard. I sit next to him. It feels a little awkward at first, it feels like we are a couple of teenagers feeling nervous of one another and I've just invited him to my room for the first time.

"So how have you been?" Evan asks as I pass him a mug and he takes a sip of his coffee.

"Honestly, a mess, how about you?"

"Same!"

"When I saw Curtis the other day he told me you hadn't been great."

"Yes, he said he'd seen you."

"Oh," I suddenly feel embarrassed remembering that I was snooping around Evan's hotel at the time. "I guess he told you where I saw him then?"

"Yes, he did happen to mention it" Evan smiles.

I blush. "I went for a drive and somehow ended up at the Manor. I told him not to mention it to you because I didn't want you thinking I was stalking you or something. I was just interested to see how the renovations are coming along."

Evan smiles. "So, what did you think, the Manor's looking good isn't it?"

"Well, I only had a quick look around but from what I could see that you have done so far it looks really impressive."

"Yes, it is. I'm really pleased with how everything is going."

I start to laugh. "When Curtis came, I had been around the back having a look and I was just walking down the side of the building on my way to the front when I heard a car. I thought it was you, so I hid behind a bush."

"You did what?" Evan laughs.

"I know it was stupid considering my car was parked out front, but I felt really awkward because things were strange between us but luckily it turned out to be Curtis."

"After you left Curtis phoned me to say he had seen you, he told me what you had said, and things didn't add up and that's when I realised Sebastian had been near you and was pretending to be me. I didn't want to phone or text to warn you about my brother because we were not on great terms and you didn't even know about him. I wanted to explain to you in person. I just wish I had got here sooner; I could have stopped you from being with him, who knows what might have happened if I hadn't turned up tonight?" Evan's face turns serious and angry.

"I wouldn't have been with him."

"You say that but how do you know?"

"Because like I said there was no spark, I was going to tell him just before you turned up actually, I was making him a coffee and then I was going to say I didn't want to see him anymore and things were over."

Evan looks at me. "Really?"

"Yes, honestly" I smile trying to reassure him.

"It would have killed me if he had touched you, if you had slept with him, it's bad enough that he kissed you" Evan says looking angry and tormented.

"He tried to kiss me numerous times and every time I turned away apart from the time when he forced me and that's when I knew."

"He forced you, Jesus Kara."

"No, it was nothing like that, he just grabbed hold of me and tried to kiss me goodnight, it was unexpected. I'm kind of pleased now that he did though because that's when it confirmed to me that I didn't feel anything for him."

"I can't think about him kissing you, it makes my blood boil." Evan looks agitated like he wants to punch something.

"I promise you it wasn't a proper full-on kiss." I take his cup out of his hand and place it on the bedside drawers alongside mine then straddle his legs and sit on his lap.

"It wasn't a kiss like this" I smile cupping his face and leaning into him placing my mouth over his as I kiss him slowly and passionately.

Evan pulls me closer and we hold each other kissing and making up for lost time.

Breaking the kiss Evan looks at me seriously "You are the best thing that has ever happened to me Kara and I genuinely mean that. I see a future with you and I'm so thankful to have met you and to be here with you now."

Tears spring in my eyes. "I see a future with you too and I've never felt this way about anyone either, I love you Evan."

"I'm so glad to hear that, I love you too" he smiles pulling me to him again for another deep and meaningful kiss. "Lay with me, let me hold you" he says moving me off his lap.

We lay cuddling each other on my bed feeling contented to be back where we both belong, with each other.

"So how did Sebastian find you?" Evan asks stroking my arm while we talk.

"He turned up at the coffee shop last Friday after work and said he wanted to talk."

"I wonder how he knows where you work?"

"I don't know but I was shocked to see him and obviously thought he was you, so I agreed to go for a drink with him."

"The sly git and then you saw him today as well?"

"I actually went for drink with him on Saturday night too and he came to see me here on Tuesday night as well."

"Oh my god I can't believe this."

"If I had known he wasn't you I would never have met up with him."

"It's okay it's my fault, you didn't know and if I had of known you had been seeing him regularly I would have put a stop to it straight away, but I only found out when Curtis told me and then I had to go to Spain at short notice, so work kept me away and..."

"I know it's okay, you didn't know what he was up to."

"Yes, but I should have realised he would do something like this especially after the whole Julia thing."

"Please don't blame yourself." I look at his tormented face.

"So, what happened when you saw him?"

"When he first showed up he took me to that pub we called at on the way back from bowling."

"Oh yes I remember the whitewashed pub."

"Yeah, that's the one, anyway we just had a drink and he asked me why I was being frosty with him, so I told him about the text and basically gave him all the information he needed. He then kept up the pretence after I had told him everything. He kept apologising saying he wanted to forget and move on."

"Did he try and kiss you that night?"

"Yes, in the pub but I told him if he tried it again I was leaving so he got the hint I wasn't happy and didn't try again."

"Okay and Saturday night."

"We arranged to go for another drink, and he suggested going for one at the hotel where he was staying. I thought he meant at the Kingsman, but he came up with a story that they were fully booked, and he was staying at the Swan Hotel, so we went for a drink in the garden there at the back. He kept saying he wanted to go back to how things were and that we should be together, he was trying to convince me to go to his room so we could talk in private, but I kept refusing. Thinking about it now he was trying to get me to sleep with him, he kept saying things like it would make me remember how good we are together."

"Jesus Kara, I'm fucking fuming."

"Do you still want me to carry on telling you if it's upsetting you?" I ask seeing Evan's fists clenched, anger and frustration written all over his face.

"Yes of course I'm sorry he just makes me so angry carry on I need to know."

"So, he dropped me home and tried to kiss me again, in fact he had been trying it on all night. I kept refusing but he kept on at me and he said a peck on the cheek wouldn't hurt so I went to kiss him, and he turned his head, so I ended up kissing him on the lips and that's when I felt strange."

"Strange?"

"Yes, the spark that I feel when we kiss wasn't there with Sebastian. Anyway, after that night I was having doubts about how I was feeling but I agreed to see him on the Tuesday night and stupidly I invited him here for a drink. That's when he bought me those flowers. Jodie was going out with her workmates so I thought it would give us an opportunity to talk some more in private. It was really awkward I didn't feel relaxed with him at all like I do with you, but I didn't know why, I just knew something didn't feel right."

"So, what did you talk about?"

"I was asking him about the hotel which he was cagey about and had he seen Julia that sort of thing. Anyway, as soon as I mentioned Jodie would be coming back he said it was time to leave. He even called Jodie Jane by mistake when he asked me where she was. I should have been suspicious then, but he just said he had been interviewing someone called Jane and got the names mixed up, so I never thought anymore of it. How stupid was I?"

"He's clever babe."

"Yeah, he is, he knows what he's doing that's for sure. Anyway, when it was time for him to leave that's when he tried to kiss me forcefully. I think he'd had enough of me saying no to his advances, so he basically grabbed hold of me and held me, so I had no choice."

"I want to kill him."

"Don't say that, he's not worth it and I don't want you doing anything stupid because you will go to jail and then where will we be."

"I know don't worry I won't do anything stupid and then you saw him tonight as well is that it?"

"Yes, he took me out for a meal and like I said I was going to tell him that it was over between us. When you showed up and he told you that we had slept together I was so scared that you would believe him."

"I thought you might have done thinking it was me."

"Well, I didn't and now you know for sure I wouldn't have slept with him because I wasn't into him at all."

"My brother is such a liar, a cheat and a manipulator this is what he does. I can assure you he is not doing this to us anymore."

"Why does your brother think you owe him money?"

"It's a long story. Growing up my father and I were close, and Sebastian was closer to mother. Sebastian hated the relationship I had with my father and was always jealous that I got on with him so well. Seb would often clash with my father they used to argue a lot. Anyway, from the age of 18 we both received a monthly allowance and when we turned 21 we both received a good sum of money each, I think it was from some trust fund my parents had set up for us when we were born. Not long after receiving the money Seb got mixed up with some wrong people he was partying a lot and to keep in with his friends he used to splash the cash. Small things to start with you know, buying them rounds of drinks, putting fuel in their cars. Anyway, as time went on he started splashing out on bigger things like fancy holidays for all his friends and my father warned him numerous times he was heading for trouble, but he wouldn't listen. Seb took his friends to Vegas to the Casinos and they drank, seduced women, and lost a huge amount of money, well Seb's money. Anyway, when Seb returned he was broke and because my parents were well off he expected my father to give him some more money and my father refused. They had a huge argument and my father basically told him that he was stopping his allowance until he changed his ways and his lavish lifestyle. After that things were not good between them and because Seb was close to Mother she used to give him money on the quiet behind my father's back. My father found out and he was so angry, I have never seen him so angry he had a huge row with my Mother and Seb, then Seb left. My Mother pleaded with my father to go after him, but he wouldn't. Seb went to live with a friend and the months that followed my parents were arguing all the time as my Mother kept supporting him. My Mother felt my father had wronged Seb, but my father felt he had given him enough chances to change. I remember my father getting chest pains one day from the stress of it all. Seb always said I was the golden child and that I was the favourite and over time it ate away at him and he began to hate me as well as my father. When my father had a heart attack and died Seb soon came sniffing around to see how much money he had been left in his will and this is where it all started. My father left 50% of his millions to my Mother, I got 40% and Sebastian got 10%."

"Oh wow so that's why he thinks you owe him because you got most of his inheritance when your father died?"

"Yes, it's not good is it?"

"What a mess."

"I didn't agree with my father's decision, so I was going to pay Seb his rightful share but after father died Seb was drinking heavily and I didn't want to contribute to that, so I decided to postpone paying him. Anyway, Seb started blaming me saying I influenced our father and has been making my life hell so I would give in and pay. At one time I did consider handing it over but the way he has treated me over the years, the things he has said and done has stopped me from giving it to him."

"So, what sort of things has he been doing then?"

"Setting up fake accounts in my name, he's vandalised my car which I have proof of because he was caught on CCTV at my house, lots of things and worst of all he used my long-term girlfriend Julia to get to me by having an affair with her and making her pregnant. It's funny because I actually feel sorry for him. He is angry and hurt because he never made peace with our father before he died, it must be hard knowing he will never get that chance and he has to live with that for the rest of his life."

"Can't your Mother do something? What does she think about it all?"

"She has tried to pay him some money out of her share, but he is adamant it must come from me. She thinks I should just pay him and make it up with him and then everything will be alright again. She forgets the way he is treating me and how he is constantly trying to ruin my life."

"What did she say about the affair with Julia?"

"She said if Julia was meant to be the one she wouldn't have gone off with him and things happen for a reason."

"I can't believe you have a twin; you look the same, but you are so different."

"I know like I said I have morals he doesn't."

"So, what are you going to do about him you can't keep living like this, he has already come between us once and I'm scared he will again?"

"I'm not sure but enough is enough, I assure you Kara he will not come between us again. Now that I have found you and you have given me hope for the future, I will not lose you. I am going to stop this once and for all."

Seven

Sebastian

I pull up at the side of the road inspecting my bloody cut lip in the rear-view mirror. "Fuck!"

I pull at my blue shirt and see the blood splats all over it. 'Well, that's ruined a perfectly good shirt, I liked this shirt.'

I hit the steering wheel in frustration.

'Evan turning up wasn't part of the plan and now he's fucking ruined things.'

"Shit." I pull my phone out from my jeans pocket and look through my contacts and dial a number.

"Hey gorgeous it's me."

"Hi how did it go?"

"It was going great until Evan turned up and found me with Kara."

"Oh god Sebastian what did you do?" she laughs.

"Well after I'd told him I had slept with her he wasn't best pleased, and we got into a fight" I laugh.

"Oh baby are you okay?"

"Yes, I'm fine I managed to get away with just a cut lip, but my shirt is fucked. You should have seen Evan's face it was a picture when he found me with Kara and from the look on her face seeing double it was priceless, I'm guessing he hadn't even told her about me."

"Really I bet she was shocked then."

"Yep, you could say that, so we are going to have to think of a Plan B."

I put the key in the door of my one bedroom first floor flat, open the door and kick it shut behind me. I throw my car keys onto a nearby table and walk down the short hallway towards my bedroom. Leaning against the doorframe of the bedroom rubbing her leg up and down in a teasing way my woman greets me wearing a red lace teddy suit with stockings and suspenders. "Welcome home" she says staring at me with a sultry look on her face.

"I hope you are ready for me Liv because I'm fucking pissed off and feeling horny, so you are going to get fucked hard" I state stalking over to her.

She smiles and backs away from me and crawls backwards onto the bed. "What are you waiting for?" she says licking her lips.

I take hold of my blood-stained shirt from the fight with Evan, rip it open and throw it onto the floor. "I can't believe my fucking brother ruined our plan, so we are going to have to think of something else to get him to pay me my money now."

I take off my trousers and boxers and throw them to one side on the floor. My cock is as hard as stone as I stand looking at her laid on the black silk sheets on my bed dressed in red sexy lingerie waiting for me to have my wicked way with her.

"Sebastian…"

"Don't say another fucking word and come here." I point my finger at her and beckon for her to come to where I'm stood at the foot of the bed. Liv crawls over to me and my cock twitches in excitement.

"Give me your greedy mouth, I want you to suck my cock you dirty bitch."

She looks up at me and smiles then opens her mouth and I fill it with my cock. "Aargh fuck."

I look down at her taking every inch of me, she sucks me so good. I hold on to her head as I hit the back of her throat every time moaning loudly while she gives me just what I need. "Aargh fuck Liv."

My fucking brother infuriates me so much, I'm so wound up and Liv giving me good head is going to make me forget for a while. "Aargh you like sucking my cock don't you?" I grin watching my cock slide in and out of her greedy mouth.

"Hmm…Sebastian" she moans giving me pleasure turning us both on more and more.

"You like me fucking your dirty mouth don't you Liv?" I thrust in and out as she moans around my cock, sucking and licking and taking me deep. I don't want to blow in her mouth not tonight, I need to fuck so I pull out of her mouth. "Take off your underwear now, I want you naked." I watch her intensely as she quickly strips from the red lacy underwear. "Sebastian…"

"Shut up and hurry the fuck up." She smiles, she loves it when I order her around in the bedroom, she loves it when I talk dirty to her.

Once she is naked, she lays down on the bed and waits for my next instruction. I walk over to a set of drawers at the side of the room and pull out a set of black velvet handcuffs. "Lay back and hold onto the bed frame." Liv looks so turned on, her cheeks are flushed and she's excited. She does as she is told, and I walk over to her and fasten the handcuffs to her wrists then attach them to the metal bed frame while she watches my every move. I climb onto the bed and spread her legs wide open. "Look at you all wet and greedy for my cock, your soaked." I look into her eyes.

"Sebastian, I love it when you're like this" she pants.

I stroke my cock in front of her. "You love it when I tell you what to do don't you?"

"Yes" she breathes.

"That's because I know what you need, you need to be fucked like a whore."

"Sebastian please" she moans begging me, looking at me, wanting me desperately to take her. I smile and just stare at her continuing to stroke my cock up and down.

"Fuck me you bastard, please" she pleads sounding desperate.

"All in good time Liv, all in good time" I smile. I climb onto the bed and wipe the precum off my cock over her lips and she licks the tip tasting me. "How much do you want my cock Liv?"

"So fucking much."

"Beg me" I whisper teasing her some more. She is so turned on she is getting frustrated as she pulls on the handcuffs that are restraining her. "Sebastian, I swear to god if you don't fuck me now" she shouts.

I laugh and make my way down her gorgeous body giving her eye contact as I lower my head and lick straight up her core causing her to buck upwards off the bed "OHHH...."

"Hmm you taste so good Liv." I lick around and around her clit and sink two fingers inside her.

"OHHH Sebastian... I want you, FUCK ME..." she begs.

"I say when and don't you forget that."

Liv writhes around on the bed as my fingers work her up more and more. "Hold still."

She stops moving and I carry on fingering and licking her getting her to the point where she is almost ready to come and then I stop.

"Fuck why are you stopping, I was ready to come." If looks could kill I would be dead.

I smirk. "I thought you wanted me to fuck you."

"I do, you are such a fucking tease Sebastian."

"You love it Liv." I smile and position my cock at her entrance but only enter her a little way getting her more and more frustrated.

"Hmm... you're so wet." I grab hold of her hips and she lifts her body slightly pushing down on the bed with her feet to try and get me to enter her fully, but I hold back.

"Sebastian" she moans waiting for me and looking at me with pleading eyes.

My eyes roam up and down her naked body. "Say please."

"Please, fuck me please." On hearing the words, I ram my cock into her hard making her scream my name loudly. "SEBASTIAN.... OHHHHH...." I hold still for a few moments. "Again." I pant.

"YESSSS.... AGAIN...." she screams, and I thrust into her hard again making us both moan long and loud.

"I need to hear you" I say ramming into her again.

"FUCK ME" she screams.

"Hold on baby." Liv holds onto the bed frame as best she can and I take her forcefully, fucking her hard repeatedly, the bed is creaking, and the headboard is banging against the wall.

When we fuck it's fierce, passionate, and intense and I can't get enough of her. "Aargh fuck Liv you feel so good…" I can't help the loud moans that escape from my mouth as I give it to her hard repeatedly, building us both up to our release.

"Oh god Sebastian you're feel amazing."

"You know it baby."

I fuck her with everything I have, and I know she's getting close because her breathing changes and this encourages me on even more desperate to reach the finish line.

"YES…YES…OHHHHH YEESSSSS…" she screams "I'm coming…. OHHHHHHH…" she orgasms, her insides grab my cock which tips me over the edge, and I come too. My cock is deep inside her as I fill her with my come. My body is sweaty and I'm breathless as I slump over her body.

"Sebastian…" she grins her eyes are glazed, and her cheeks are flushed as she smiles at me.

"That's just what I needed after the evening I've had" I smile pulling out of her and undoing the restraints. "Come here Liv." I lean against the headboard and hold my arms out to her.

"How's the lip, it looks swollen?" she asks climbing onto my lap and cuddling me.

"I'll survive" I reply holding her.

"So, what happened then?" she asks as we get our breath back, the street lights shining through the window of my London apartment.

"My brother turned up unannounced that's what fucking happened and then when told him I had slept with his little tart he saw red and we ended up fighting in the street."

"Oh god," she laughs. "I'm pleased you didn't end up sleeping with her, I know we discussed it and decided that you might have to keep up with the pretence, but I didn't really like the idea. I want to be the only person you put your cock in."

"Are you jealous Liv?" I grin.

"Fuck off Seb."

"Well, it didn't even get to that because she was playing hard to get the frigid bitch."

"So, we need a plan B then" she smiles.

"Yes, got any ideas?"

"I might have" she smiles.

Eight

"I'd better go" Evan says looking at his watch "It's 10.30pm."

"Are you sure you can't stay?" I sigh "I've not seen you for weeks and I don't want you to go."

"I can't baby I've got meetings tomorrow all day at Hamilton Tower, so I need to get home."

"But it's a Saturday you normally have weekends off."

"I know but it's been one of those weeks and because I've been away in Spain, I've got some things I need to attend to, so I've had to organise a meeting for tomorrow to catch up. How about when I'm finished I'll come and see you then?"

"Please I'd love that, and I'll cook us something if you like for when you get here."

"Okay thanks that sounds great."

Evan gives me a kiss then gets up off the bed ready to leave.

"I'll see you out then." I gather up the empty mugs and carry them to the kitchen and Evan follows. "Can I have your mobile number again because I changed yours to

Sebastian's number thinking it was you and you had a new number?" I ask.

"Of course, keep hold of Sebastian's number just in case he tries to contact you again, so you know it's him."

"Okay will do."

I programme Evan's number into my mobile phone and then show Evan to the front door.

"Lock the door as soon as I've gone."

"I will, don't worry I'm sure your brother won't be coming back anytime soon."

"Yes, but you don't know that Kara. I don't trust him so lock the door okay."

"Okay."

I can't help the big smile on my face because the real Evan is back in my life where he belongs and I'm looking forward to spending time with him again. Evan takes me in his arms for a cuddle, he kisses my neck and sniffs my hair taking in the scent of my apple shampoo that he loves so much, it's like he can't believe I'm back in his life too.

"I don't want to go" he says taking my face in his hands and kissing me slowly and passionately.

"Then don't, stay because I don't want you to go either" I whisper continuing the kiss.

"I can't," he sighs "I'll let you know what time you can expect me tomorrow."

"Okay."

"If you see or hear anymore from Sebastian stay away from him and let me know okay" he stresses.

"Okay I will, don't worry."

"I love you Kara" he says looking into my eyes and planting soft kisses on my mouth and all over my face.

"I love you too."

With a big sigh Evan opens the front door. "Bye babe, see you tomorrow."

"Bye." I watch him walk down the path to his car standing in the doorway waving at him.

Evan waves then gets into his car and drives away. I shut the door and lock it and as I turn around to walk back to my room Jodie's bedroom door opens slightly and my messy haired friend peers through a gap in the door looking at me with a big smile on her face.

"Hi, everything okay?"

"Everything is perfect, Evan's just gone, is Matt in there with you?"

"Yes, he's staying tonight."

"I thought he was."

"Why do you say that?"

"Well, the only time you have wild hair like that is when Matt stays for a sleepover."

Jodie laughs. "He likes to be a bit rough sometimes."

"None of my business" I laugh screwing up my face.

"I'm so pleased you have made it up with the real Evan, what a load of drama on a Friday night hey."

"I know I felt like I was in an episode of EastEnders earlier. I feel so relieved and better about everything now."

"Pleased to hear it and you'll be able to sleep better tonight."

"Yeah, I will. Goodnight Jode, see you in the morning."

"Goodnight Kar."

I go to the kitchen and get a glass of water to quench my thirst before I go to bed, and I'm stood drinking it in the kitchen when I hear a noise outside and then I hear footstep up and down the path.

'Shit…Sebastian's come back.'

My heart is thumping fast in my chest.

'What shall I do? What shall I do? I'll get Jodie and Matt, yes that's what I'll do. But what happens if it's just me being paranoid because of the night I've had, no I'll leave them alone. I can handle Sebastian. I am brave, I am the do not mess with me type of woman…Who am I kidding no I'm not I'm shitting myself, whoever you are please go away.'

I put my glass down quietly on the sink and turn the kitchen light off. I then bob down behind the kitchen unit to hide. It might just be my imagination running away with me but I'm not going to be able to sleep if Sebastian is lurking outside. I need to be brave and check. I pull the blind up slightly and peer through the gap and take a quick look to see if I can see anything, there is definitely someone out there because I can see a dark figure walking up and down the path. Luckily, they didn't see me.

'Oh god, what does he want? Just go away will you.'

I jump down behind the kitchen unit again and then open a draw to grab the rolling pin to use as a weapon in case I need it.

'There is no way you are coming in my house again Sebastian.'

I pull the blind up slightly again and peer through the gap and see that the dark figure has gone.

'Maybe it wasn't Sebastian, maybe it was a drunk on his way home and he had walked up the wrong path?'

I stand up and put the rolling pin on the kitchen worktop and walk quietly into the hallway, I don't need to put the light on to see because I can see enough from the street lights shining outside. I grab hold of the front door handle to check the door is locked and as I grab hold of it there is a light knock on the door making me jump.

"Shit..." I run into the kitchen grab the rolling pin again and then stand behind the door.

"Who's there?" I whisper but no one answers. I call louder this time but still no one answers. My heart is hammering in my chest and the adrenaline is pumping. Feeling brave because I'm armed with a rolling pin, I put the safety chain on the door and unlock the door. I open it slightly to see if I can see anyone and then I call out again. "Who's there?"

"It's me!" a voice whispers and then Evan's face appears in the gap of the door.

"Shit… Evan what are you doing you scared the hell out of me I thought Sebastian had come back?" I quickly put the rolling pin down on the kitchen table, take the safety chain off and then open the door to him.

"I'm sorry baby I didn't mean to scare you. Can I come in?"

"Yes sorry." I let him in and then shut the door.

"What are you doing here I thought you were going home?"

"I was but I was driving down the road to go home and I just couldn't leave," he is staring intensely into my eyes. "I've been pacing outside your house for the last five minutes wondering whether I should come to the door or not."

"Why?"

"Because after what I put you through, the hurt I caused, it's been a month of not having you in my life and…" He pauses. "I need you…"

I smile.

"I need you too." I move towards him and pin him up against the back of the door placing my lips on his. I kiss him slowly to start with and then the intensity of the kiss becomes more needy, the longing on both sides has us both feeling breathless.

"Kara," Evan pulls away from me and places his forehead on mine. "I don't want you to think I just came back here to have sex with you because I didn't, I just need you, I want to hold you, be near you…"

"Shush," I put my finger over his mouth to stop him talking. "Evan I've missed you so much, I want you to make love to me?" I say smiling at him.

"Are you sure, we can wait I…?"

"Please I want you to."

"Okay then I'd love to, more than anything" he smiles.

I lock the front door and grab hold of his hand and lead him to my bedroom. Shutting my bedroom door behind us I take him in my arms and kiss him slowly and softly while fumbling with his belt on his trousers trying to undress him. Evan helps me and we both get undressed quickly then carry on with the slow, passionate kiss. I can feel his erection pressed up against my stomach, my body pressed against his. My hands are in his hair and his hands are on my naked bum pulling me to him while he grinds his cock into my front.

"God I've missed you so much" he whispers.

"I've missed you too" I pull him over to the bed and we fall happily onto it kissing each other and caressing each other's naked bodies. I run soft finger tips up and down his back while Evan cups my breast with his warm hand.

"I've been dreaming of this moment for so long hoping to be with you again" he says looking at me.

“I’m so pleased you came back to me, I hated being apart.” He strokes my face with the back of his hand looking lovingly into my eyes and then he kisses me slowly delving his soft wet tongue into my mouth which I accept gladly.

“I’ve missed your kisses and this gorgeous body” he says continuing the kiss, our tongues entwined tasting each other while he cups my breast in his hand and rolls my nipple with his thumb and finger as I enjoy the feel of his hands on me again.

“Hmm…” I sigh.

I can never get enough of this man, this man who I love with all my heart and I never want to be apart from again.

Evan lowers his mouth onto my neck and trails soft kisses from my shoulder up to my ear and then down again. I move my head to one side giving him better access. I want him to go lower and to take my nipple in his mouth like he always used to, he turns me on so much this way, and it’s been too long since he did that to me.

As if he can read my mind he kisses the soft plump mounds of my breasts before sliding his soft wet tongue over my erect nipples, I arch my back “OHHH god I love that.” He circles his tongue around and around “Hmm I know you do baby and I love doing it, your breasts are so perfect” he says before sucking and flicking my nipples with his tongue giving me sensations of pleasure that go straight to my core.

"Evan, I want you" I plead my breathing escalating as he moves from one nipple to the other giving each one his undivided attention. "Oh god you're so good" I moan enjoying his expert strokes that turn me on every time.

After getting his fill he moves down my body trailing his tongue further and further "I need to taste you" he whispers finding my most sensitive part and nestling his face in between my legs. "Evan…" I pant as he circles my clit slowly with his wet tongue making me cry out "OHHH god…" I grab hold of the duvet as he hits the spot with his tongue giving me goosebumps, my insides are pulsating and twitching, I am so wet from excitement.

"You taste fucking amazing" he says licking and sucking making me cry out some more "OHHHH…. Evan…. you turn me on so much." His tongue explores every part of me around and around, in and out of my opening and Evan seems to be relishing in the sounds I'm making showing my enjoyment because with every moan he tastes and devours me more and more like I'm his favourite treat that he can't get enough.

"Evan oh god, stop or I'm going to come, I want to come when you are inside me…" I pant.

Evan desperate to be inside me too stops and climbs up my body. It feels like a lifetime ago since we made love. I open my legs wide making room for him.

"My girlfriend is so beautiful, I'm so lucky" he whispers making me smile hearing the word girlfriend. He kisses me passionately nestling his body in between my legs and enters me slowly. The sensation of his hard cock entering me makes us both let out a loud satisfied moan. I've missed this feeling when our bodies connect to become one, it's just the best feeling in the world.

"Wow, you feel amazing" he says thrusting his cock in and out me slowly, filling me deeply, feeling every part of me, my insides clenching and grabbing hold of him drawing him in.

"Evan…" I moan holding onto his muscly back while he plunges deep into me repeatedly.

"I know baby, I know."

Evan starts off slow to begin with and then after a while he picks up the pace as I hold onto him, his firm bum cheeks are in my hands as he pushes his cock in and out of me giving us both so much pleasure with every stroke. The love we feel for one another is so strong and the most special feeling as we make love reconnecting in my double bed.

"Evan I can't hold back any longer, it's too good I'm getting close" I pant as he carries on thrust after thrust driving towards the end goal.

"I'm with you baby" he pants feeling the same and close to his own release.

"Oh yes that's so good, oh god…" the pressure building more and more.

"Feel it baby…it feels so fucking good."

"Yes… so good…" I cry.

"Me and you babe always…"

"Always," I pant. "OHHHHHH…….."

I let out a long moan as I orgasm, and the incredible feeling takes over my body.

"FUCCKKK…" Evan cries and after a few more thrusts he comes too as the out of this world feeling fills both of our brains and we moan repeatedly as our orgasms gives us such a rush of overwhelming pleasure.

"Wow." Tears are running down my face.

"I've dreamt of making love to you, holding you, kissing you." Evan says breathless with tears in his eyes knowing just how I'm feeling as he kisses me softly. My tears fall quickly, and I can't help but sob.

"Hey, shush don't cry baby I'm here" he says holding me in his arms.

"I'm sorry I'm just so pleased you came back to me, I thought I'd imagined it all, the things you said to me and what we had together and then you left and…"

"Shush…it's okay baby I know, I'm sorry, please don't cry."

Evan pulls out of me and then lays down at the side of me and takes me in his arms again, his brown eyes searching mine. "You were with me always Kara, I never really left," He is looking at me with so much love and affection. "I'm so sorry for hurting you."

"Evan you love me and that's all I ever hoped for. I can't believe someone like you wants someone like me."

"Hey, don't say that, why wouldn't I?" he says leaning in and giving me a meaningful kiss.

"Well, you could have the pick of any girls, you are gorgeous, you have a fit body, you're rich, I just can't believe I'm the lucky girl who gets to have you."

Evan lays back and puts his arm around me and I snuggle into his side for a cuddle. "I don't care about other girls you are the only girl I want; you have shown me how love can be, and you have given me hope for the future. I have met girls in my past and all they are interested in is status, the money, the fancy car, and I have never once wanted more from any of them until you. When I met Julia, she was a nice girl, but she soon became focussed on money over time, the nice things I could buy her, where she wanted me to take her on holiday, my mother has always been like that too because my father spoilt her, and I never knew women could be any different until I met you. You have never wanted anything from me but ME."

"Thank you." I look at him and smile.

"You don't have to thank me; I should be thanking you for being with me and loving me. Or are you thanking me for the mind-blowing orgasm I've just given you that you are accustomed to?" he grins digging his fingers in my side tickling me making me laugh.

"Hey, don't start with the tickling and I'm thanking you for both," I grin. "So, when did you know that you had fallen in love with me?"

"I think I knew you were special from meeting you that very first day in the coffee shop, I developed feelings for you quite quickly and the more time I spent with you I realised I was falling in love with you."

"So why did you think I was special?"

"I knew you were special because I've never felt like this before with a woman, I remember feeling strange it was like being struck by lightning, the strong connection we had right from the start, when you looked at me, when I touched your hand when you dropped the change all over the counter, the spark it was unbelievable but also fucking scary."

"I know what you mean, I felt the same the first time I saw you. I have never been dumbstruck before when meeting a man and it was like you had cast a spell on me that day, I could hardly speak and I felt turned on by the way you looked, your voice everything and when you touched my hand when you passed me the change that I dropped it was like I could physically feel the sparks between us."

"Getting to know you, every moment we shared together just confirmed how I felt about you. After Julia, the idea of loving someone again was a no go for me, I felt so betrayed when she had the affair but meeting you, you have shown me how love can be with the right person and that it is worth taking a risk."

My tears start to fall again.

"Hey, I don't mean to upset you" he says noticing my tears and holding me closer.

"Sorry it's just no-one has ever made me feel special like you do."

"But you are special, you are beautiful, kind, funny, fantastic in bed, great at giving directions, good at riding my motorbikes and especially giving me pleasure on the bonnet of my Ferrari" he grins making me feel better.

I look at him, wipe away my tears and smile. "Okay you can shut up now I can't take all these compliments." I blush.

"And there is that cute blush which is one of the other things I love about you."

"Alright no more." I laugh lunging at him and kissing him.

After having a heart to heart we lay in each other's arms for a while feeling contented and happy.

Evan stretches feeling sleepy and looks at his watch to see what the time is. "I really need to get going baby it's 1.00am."

"Hmm..." I reply sleepily snuggling into his side some more.

"Babe I need to get going." He nudges me gently and sits up in bed stretches and yawns.

"Why don't you stay and go from here in the morning, I can set the alarm?" I mumble.

"I can't another time babe, I haven't got any stuff with me and it will be a rush in the morning otherwise plus I could do with some sleep and if I stay here I don't think I will get any especially with you laid next to me naked and with not seeing you for a month, I can already feel my cock getting excited again." Evan smiles.

"I don't mind not sleeping" I grin sitting up and smiling at him with a pleading look on my face.

"Don't look at me like that, I need to go." Evan smirks getting up and finding his clothes.

An unwelcome thought suddenly pops into my head as I watch him get dressed. "You didn't sleep with anyone else did you while we were apart?" I ask.

I feel anxious while I wait for his answer because knowing that Evan has such a high sex drive and we have just had unprotected sex I couldn't bear it if he says that he has.

"No, no way, I didn't, I couldn't. Please don't tell me you did?" he asks sounding worried and looking at me with a serious face.

"Thank god and no I didn't I couldn't either."

"Thank fuck for that," he smiles relieved "so we both have plenty of catching up to do then" he winks pulling on his boxer shorts then his jeans.

"Yes definitely" I grin.

After Evan has finished getting dressed I show him to the door.

"I'll see you tomorrow babe" he smiles giving me a lingering kiss.

"Yeah, I can't wait."

Today Evan came back to me, I am now officially his girlfriend and he loves me, things just couldn't be any more perfect. I just hope things stay that way especially now I know his brother Sebastian is playing games and he is definitely up to something.

Nine

It's Saturday morning and after yesterday's events I awake this morning with a big smile on my face feeling rested and contented.

I sit up in bed and reach for my mobile phone and turn it on desperate to see if Evan has text me. A text comes through instantly and feeling excited I open the messages and scowl when I see it's a text from Sebastian.

I was really looking forward to getting to know you more Kara, but my dear brother has ruined our plans. I can assure you despite what my brother has told you about me I am definitely the better twin and if you are still interested in meeting up I would love to take you out again sometime. Sebastian x

'Oh my god the nerve of that guy, he makes me so angry.' I send him a reply.

Evan and I are together and nothing is going to break us apart so you are wasting your time trying to come between us. Evan has told me all about you and what you did to him with Julia and I can assure you that your charms will not work on me so you may as well just give up now. Goodbye Sebastian.

I press send then decide to send Evan a message to let him know that his brother has been in contact. Just as I'm typing the text my phone starts ringing in my hand. "Shit." I almost drop it as it rings and vibrates in my hand. I look at the screen anxiously expecting it to be Sebastian, but my concern soon turns to happiness when I see Evan's name on the screen.

"Hello boyfriend" I answer with a smile.

"Good morning my beautiful girlfriend, how did you sleep?"

"Really good how about you?"

"Same after having amazing sex with my girlfriend and then driving home I was knackered I didn't want to get up this morning when my alarm went off."

"Hmm the sex was good wasn't it I woke up this morning with a big smile on my face."

"Me too and a huge erection thinking about last night in fact every time I think of you and your incredible body it sends a signal to my dick."

I laugh. "Well sorry to put a damper on things but I need to tell you something I've just had a text from your brother."

"Unbelievable what did he have to say?"

"He said he's still interested in meeting up with me and that he's the better twin."

"That's a fucking joke ignore him Kara I don't want you getting involved in his mind games."

"Too late I already text him back sorry."

"Kara please babe you need to ignore him."

"I couldn't help it he wound me up."

"So, what did you say?"

"I told him that we are together, and nothing is going to break us up. I said his charm is not going to work on me like it did Julia and he may as well give up now."

"Okay babe but promise me you will ignore him if he contacts you again."

"I will I'm sorry he just made me mad that's all."

"I know thanks for telling me and obviously if he does contact you again you need to tell me. I don't want you dealing with him I will sort my brother out you just concentrate on us alright."

"Okay are you still coming later?"

"Oh, I'll be coming alright and so will you."

"Evan," I giggle "I meant are you coming to see me after work."

Evan laughs. "I knew what you meant just try and stop me that's why I'm ringing I should be with you about 6.00pm if that's alright?"

"Yes, that's great and can you stay over?"

"I was planning to if that's okay?"

"Of course, it's okay and don't forget I'm cooking."

"I haven't forgotten I'm looking forward to it, what are you making for me?"

"It's a surprise. I'll see if Jodie can make herself scarce so we can have the place to ourselves, I've done that for her plenty of times before."

"Sounds perfect, I'm sorry babe but I've got to go to my meeting now, but I'll see you later, I can't wait."

"Me too, see you later love you."

"Love you, bye."

"Bye."

I end the call and jump out of bed desperate for a wee. 'Hmm what shall I wear tonight, that's easy something sexy and what the hell am I going to cook?'

Deep in thought about what I can make and needing the toilet I put on my dressing gown and hurry to the bathroom. I open the door and walk in and squeal as I am faced with a sight I would have preferred not to have seen. "Matt…" I shout.

"Sorry mate I forgot to lock the door" he grins laughing at the look of horror on my face seeing him having a wee.

"Oh my god…urgh." I back out of the bathroom and close the door behind me and wait cross legged in the hallway for him to finish. "Hurry up Matt I need a wee, I'm desperate" I shout.

A few minutes later he opens the door and walks out with a big grin on his face. "I know it's big isn't it, it makes Jodie squeal too."

"Really Matt, I don't wish to discuss the size of your penis thank you very much." I roll my eyes and Matt is proper belly laughing.

"What's so funny?" Jodie asks walking out of her bedroom in her pyjamas to see what all the commotion is about.

"Your boyfriend here was having a wee and forgot to lock the bathroom door I've just walked in on him and seen his manhood and he clearly thinks it is funny." I pull a face of disgust.

"Matt you need to be more careful and remember to lock the door," Jodie says telling him off like one of her schoolchildren. "I'm sorry Kara you shouldn't have seen that."

"Yes, I'm sorry Kara." Matt laughs and Jodie hits him on the arm to tell him off for laughing.

"It's okay, just remember to lock the door next time maggot" I laugh waggling my little finger at him.

"I don't think so Kara, I think you mean more like Mr Python" Matt shouts laughing and following Jodie walking to the kitchen.

"Maggot" I call.

"Python" Matt calls catching up with Jodie and lifting her up from behind making her squeal "I'm sorry babe" he says and starts kissing her making her giggle. "You're terrible" she laughs.

I shake my head laughing and making sure to lock the door I quickly use the toilet then get dressed in a black mini skirt with a white t-shirt with the slogan 'Choose Love' in small black letters on the front. I apply minimal make up then go to the kitchen to have some breakfast.

I have a chat with Jodie about what I can cook for Evan tonight and Jodie suggests homemade lasagne with salad. Being the good friend that she is she even offers to help me make it this afternoon, which I'm pleased of because she is a much better cook than me.

I also mention about having the place to ourselves tonight and she happily agrees to go out with Matt somewhere.

After having breakfast and talking to Jodie I go to the supermarket to buy the ingredients for the lasagne. While I'm in town I also pay a visit to my favourite lingerie shop to buy something sexy to wear for my dinner date with Evan tonight.

I'm driving home in the sunshine in my Fiat 500 car when 'Give Me Your Love, Sigala featuring John Newman' starts playing on the radio making me smile and think of Evan. I turn up the volume and drive home feeling great singing along to the tune looking forward to seeing Evan again at the end of the day.

Feeling refreshed from a shower I put on the new black lace teddy that I bought from town this morning which Jodie kindly washed for me so I could wear it tonight, a red mini skirt and a fitted black t-shirt showing some cleavage, my blonde hair is flowing around my shoulders and I feel sexy. I apply some strawberry flavoured lip gloss to my lips and after having one last check in the bathroom mirror I go to check the lasagne that is cooking nicely in the oven.

Evan text earlier to say he was running late but he is on his way now. It's 6.15pm on a sunny Saturday evening and just as I am finishing prepping the salad on two plates I look out of the window and see Evan pull up outside in his Aston Martin. I'm feeling slightly nervous if I'm honest, I feel like I did when we first met, I've got butterflies in my tummy as I go to the front door to greet him.

I open the door and my gorgeous boyfriend presents me with a big bouquet of pink roses with white gypsophila that he had hidden behind his back.

"Wow thank you" I smile accepting them from him.

"Hi beautiful you look stunning as always sorry I'm a bit late" he says giving me a lingering kiss on the lips.

"I think you are forgiven" I smile "The flowers are beautiful, thank you."

"Beautiful flowers for my beautiful girlfriend" he smiles making me blush. "Aww am I making you blush" he smiles.

"You always make me blush when you say sweet things to me. Come in."

"Thanks, have you been eating strawberries?" Evan asks walking through the front door as I close it behind him and placing his overnight bag on the floor in the hallway.

"No," I frown and then I realise. "Oh, it's my lip gloss, it's strawberry flavoured." I smile.

"Hmm I wouldn't mind another taste you know how much I love strawberries" he grins taking me in his arms and kissing me again more passionately this time.

'Hmm me too especially when you are eating them off my body.' I break away breathless remembering him doing it. 'Jeez I'm getting turned on, shall we just go to bed now?'

"Hmm it was good wasn't it."

"Yeah."

"Something smells good what are we having?" Evan asks following me into the kitchen.

"Thanks, its homemade lasagne I hope you're hungry because I've made plenty?" I smile placing the flowers on the windowsill that are already in water.

"I'm very hungry" he smiles eyeing me up and down, his eyes drawn to my cleavage. I blush because I know he is not just talking about the food. I can feel myself becoming aroused because I know what is coming later and we have got some serious making up for lost time.

'Calm down Kara, stop thinking about sex and concentrate on the meal first, you've got all night.'

"It's nearly ready would you like a glass of wine or a beer?" I ask.

"A glass of wine would be great thanks" he smiles.

"I've got a bottle chilling in the fridge." I open the fridge door and take out a bottle of Prosecco.

“Here let me do the honours” he says taking the bottle from my hands and I get two wine glasses and put them on the kitchen table in front of him. Evan pours the chilled liquid into the glasses and passes one to me then picks up the other. “Cheers babe, to us.”

“To us” I smile.

“You’ll make the perfect wife one day cooking for me being all domesticated,” Evan grins making me almost choke on my mouthful of wine. “Relax your face,” he laughs. “I’m just teasing.”

I love the comment that Evan just made even if he was just joking, I know we have only just made things official, but I hope that one day we will end up saying I do and that we will live happily ever after just like I’ve always wanted in life. I love him so much; he makes me so happy.

My mind wanders and all I can think of is Evan, a family home and a couple of kids running around. Evan is chasing them around the house, and they are running away laughing while he tries to catch them. I picture a little boy who is the spitting image of his father with dark brown hair and chocolate brown eyes and a little girl who is blonde like me. They are squealing ‘Daddy no Daddy, you can’t catch us.’

“Hey, I was only joking, I didn’t mean to upset you” Evan says seeing me lost in my own thoughts looking serious bringing me back to the here and now.

"Oh no you haven't upset me sorry I was just… never mind, please sit down and I'll check to see if the lasagne is ready" I put on the oven gloves and open the oven door, hmm it smells good, it's ready.

Evan takes a seat at the kitchen table and watches me enjoying the view of me bent over with my bum in the air while I get the lasagne out of the oven. I dish up two plates then join him at the table.

"I hope you like it" I smile feeling proud that I've made it even if Jodie did help me a little bit.

"I'm sure I will it looks delicious thank you" he smiles picking up the knife and fork and tucking in. "Hmm this is great."

"So how did your meetings go today?" I ask finishing my mouthful.

"Very well thanks, what have you been up to today apart from cooking this gorgeous meal?"

"Well, I went to town this morning to buy the ingredients to make the lasagne and then once I had made it I've been trying to make myself beautiful for you."

"You don't need to try; you always look beautiful."

"Thanks" I blush.

"Have you heard any more from Sebastian since this morning?"

"No have you?"

"No nothing."

"Have you thought about what you are going to do about him?"

"I'm always thinking of ways and the only solution is to pay him the money which is not what I want to do."

"Yes but isn't it worth paying him off and then he will leave you, us alone."

"You don't know my brother Kara; I don't think it's just about the money anymore I think he wants to see me suffer because he feels that he suffered because our father always favoured me and he is very bitter about it especially after what my father did with his will."

"Sounds like he's got serious issues and needs professional help."

"I believe he does; I've approached him in the past after father died about getting some professional help, but he didn't react to well when I suggested it. Anyway, enough about him I don't want to talk about him anymore and let him spoil our evening."

"Okay I agree so… I have a little surprise for you later" I smile.

"Oh, I'm intrigued, what is it?" Evan asks his eyes lighting up wondering what it could be.

"You'll just have to wait and see" I grin clearing the plates away having finished our meals.

"Well, I will look forward to it, whatever it is. Thank you, the meal was delicious. Now come here so I can thank you properly" Evan gestures for me to sit on his lap.

I sit on his knee and he takes me in his arms and kisses me softly plunging his tongue into my mouth sending tingles straight to my core.

'Oh god when he kisses me like that it just does something to me, hmm…'

I can feel Evan's erection becoming harder beneath me and it appears our kiss does something to him too as we enjoy the passionate embrace.

"Would you like some dessert?" I ask breathless becoming more aroused by the second as he trails sweet kisses from my neck up to my ear.

"Yes please, can I have you for dessert?" he whispers in his sexy voice looking at me with so much love in his eyes then kissing me softly all over my face.

I could quite easily take him to bed right now because I want him desperately, but I had planned to spend the evening doing normal stuff like talking or watching a film before we jump into bed together. I'm beginning to think it's a stupid idea now because he turns me on so easily and I just want to have sex, but I want our relationship to be more than just sex, so I need to slow things down a bit.

"I want you too," I whisper "but let's not rush we've got all night. Would you like some ice cream instead?"

Evan smiles. "I'm alright, I'm quite full thanks."

"Okay do you fancy snuggling on the sofa and watching a film?"

"I would love to. I just need to use the toilet, so you pick a film and I'll be back in a minute."

"Okay." I smile getting up off his lap.

Evan goes to use the loo while I take the rest of the wine and our glasses into the lounge to look for a film. I dim the lights in the room giving it a romantic feel and then go to choose a DVD from the cabinet.

As I'm bending over looking for a DVD Evan comes up behind me and grabs me by the hips.

"Oh hello" I smile.

"You look good bent over like this" he says rubbing himself against me.

"Hmm....do you fancy watching an action movie or a romance film?"

'He's not making this easy for me, I'm trying to be good here but all I want to do is to take him in my bedroom and have my wicked way with him. Stay strong Kara you can do this, oh god, deep breaths, deep breaths.'

"I would love some action" Evan replies, and I know he's grinning as he continues to rub his cock against my backside, I can feel him getting hard.

"Evan" I giggle.

"Sorry I don't mind you choose" he says getting more turned on by the minute.

"Oh god… Evan" I laugh feeling his cock as hard as stone as he continues to rub against my backside.

"What baby?" he laughs cheekily.

"I'm trying to be good and you are not making it easy for me."

"Why are you trying to be good I like it when you are naughty?" he says turning me on grinding his cock against me slowly and firmly.

'Oh god his cock feels so good. I need to move away from him before I give in.'

I stand up and he lets go of my hips and I look at him and smile. "I'm trying to be good because our relationship before was mainly sex, sex and more sex."

"But I love having sex, sex and more sex with you, you won't hear me complaining" he smiles giving me that 'I want to fuck you look.'

"Yes, and I love having sex with you too, a lot, but I want us to be like other couples and have quality time as well as having great sex all the time." I stop him from coming any closer by placing my hands on his chest because if he starts kissing me again, I know I will be putty in his hands.

He smiles. "Okay babe I'm sorry I'll try and behave but it's not easy when you look so sexy and I haven't had you that much recently."

"I know" I smile.

Evan takes a seat on the three-seater sofa and I carry on looking for a film. "Hmm...what's this?" I pull out a DVD from the shelf that has a plain black cover on it, I don't recognise it. "I haven't seen this before."

"What's it called?" Evan asks.

"I don't know it's just in a blank box I think it's probably one of Matts, he borrows them off his mate from work all the time, Matt brings them around here to watch with Jodie, let's have a look."

I load the DVD into the machine and then take a seat next to Evan and press play on the remote. We snuggle in each other's arms ready to watch the film.

The titles come on then the film starts with a businessman in his late 30s dressed in an expensive suit being driven in a limousine by his driver to a posh hotel, the man is obviously rich. After dropping him off at a swanky club, he walks in and up to the bar ordering himself a glass of whisky. There are lots of men and women chatting and drinking socially and some of the men are sat at tables playing poker while the women stand over them watching.

"It looks like a James Bond type film; I love James Bond films" I say excitedly.

"Hmm maybe..." Evan smiles.

The businessman sips his whiskey then a dark-haired lady who looks to be in her forties appears dressed elegantly in a plain red dress which has a split up one leg and gives him a kiss on both cheeks. "Mr White" she says, and the gentleman says, "Hello Petra" and then he walks with the lady as she escorts the man up a grand staircase and down a corridor to a private room. "Please take a seat Mr White I will tell Gloria you are here." "Thank you." Mr White replies taking off his suit jacket and hanging it on the back of a chair before sitting down. The woman then walks off leaving him alone in the room.

"I wonder who Gloria is?" I say looking at Evan.

"I don't know" Evan replies.

"I reckon she's someone like M in the James Bond films who is the Head of the Secret Intelligence Service."

"Maybe" Evan smiles pulling me closer to him and kissing me on the side of the head as we carry on watching the film.

After a few moments, another woman walks into the room who is blonde and looks to be in her early thirties wearing a business suit, she sits down in a chair opposite the man at a large oak desk. "Mr White how are you, its lovely to see you?" she smiles.

"Hello Gloria, I'm good thank you and it's always a pleasure seeing you."

"Why thank you Mr White and what can I do for you today?"

"I would like my usual please."

The woman smiles "Of course I will just be a moment." The woman walks out of the room again.

"I wonder what he means by that?" I look at Evan and he's smiling. We continue to watch the film to see what is going to happen next.

The same woman reappears but now she is wearing a black and white sexy maid's outfit, her boobs are pushed up and almost popping out the top of her dress. She is also wearing some black stockings and suspenders and she's holding a feather duster in her hand.

Evan laughs "I don't think this is a James Bond type film."

"Oh my god..." My eyes widen as the woman walks over to the man and tells him to remove all his clothes then to sit down on the chair that is placed in the centre of the room. The woman then walks around the room in red high heels pretending to clean things but not touching anything and sweeping the feather duster lightly through her fingers smiling at him.

The man is now naked, and the woman is tickling his erection with her feather duster as he moans and holds tightly onto the sides of the chair. The woman bends down shoving her cleavage in his face reminding the man that he isn't allowed to touch her and that if he is good, she will reward him greatly. She tickles him some more teasing him for a while before moving down his body to perform oral sex while he moans loudly as she takes him in and out of her mouth.

"Are you sure you didn't know what sort of film this was? Is this the surprise you were talking about earlier?" Evan laughs looking at my shocked face.

I blush. "I promise you I didn't know, and this is not my surprise although this is definitely a surprise to me, Matt must have brought it around for him and Jodie to watch, the dirty buggers." I laugh. "Err…do you want to carry on watching this?" I ask looking at Evan.

"I don't need to watch these films to be turned on I have everything I need right here." Evan leans towards me for a kiss making me breathless and cupping my breast through my top.

"Okay" I moan turned on from what I have just been watching on screen but also by my gorgeous boyfriend.

I climb onto Evan's lap pushing my skirt up slightly so I can straddle him and kiss him passionately.

"Forget what I said earlier about we've got all night I can't wait any longer." I breathe.

Our kiss becomes urgent, our tongues duel together in our mouths and we both moan feeling turned on.

Evan slips both his hands under my skirt and feels something lacy covering my bum. He stops kissing me.

"Hmm… what's this?" he asks trying to have a look at what I'm wearing underneath.

"Wait," I smile grabbing his hands to stop him from pulling up my skirt any further. "I think it's time for your surprise now." He smiles as I get up off his lap and walk over to the TV and turn it off. I then turn to face him. "Go and wait for me on my bed naked and I'll be there in a minute."

"Jesus Kara with pleasure" he replies grinning looking excited and quickly getting up off the sofa and moving swiftly to my bedroom already beginning to undress as he walks.

I lock the door of the flat and turn off the lights then go into the bathroom and get undressed just leaving on my sexy new lingerie. I fluff up my hair in the mirror and once ready I open the door slowly and call to Evan to close his eyes. I then walk out the bathroom and lean against the doorframe of my bedroom in a seductive manner and slide my leg up and down it. "Open your eyes" I say in a sexy voice.

The bedside lamp is turned on and Evan immediately opens his eyes and is taken aback at his girlfriend giving him a provocative sidelong glance dressed in a black lace teddy suit which is see through and barely covering my assets.

"Oh my fucking god" he says getting up off the bed quickly and coming over to me, his erection as hard as stone with pre-ejaculate glistening on the tip.

"You like Mr H?" I smile giving him a twirl so he can take in every inch of me.

"I fucking love" he says placing his hands on my body and feeling my curves, the lace beneath his fingers. "Jesus Kara I'm so hard feel me" he says taking my hand and placing it on his cock.

"Hmm..." I stroke his cock a few times while he kisses me fiercely moaning into my mouth and I can tell he's feeling wild with desire.

Moving his hands onto my impressive sized breasts he rubs my nipples with his thumbs through the delicate material making me moan. "Oh god Evan…" He slowly massages my breasts and then trails his hands down the lacy material down my back and then cups my bum cheeks in both hands while pressing his erection into my front gyrating his hips making me breathless and needy for him.

"Evan, I want you" I moan.

"And I want you, your body looks incredible dressed in lace" he breathes kissing my neck and then licking my ear giving me tingles all over my body. I move my hair out of the way, so he has better access. "Evan…" I moan becoming more and more turned on. I'm still stood in the doorway of my bedroom when Evan lowers to his knees and pulls the lace material of my teddy suit to one side "Jesus Kara you're soaked" he says finding my sensitive spot and circling it with his tongue as I hold onto the door frame for support while he makes me go weak at the knees.

"Oh god, wait…" I protest, his tongue having the desired effect and I can feel the pressure building for an explosive orgasm.

"You love that don't you baby" he says grabbing hold of my hips and pulling me onto his greedy mouth.

"Oh shit, Evan wait…"

Evan is giving me so much pleasure and the more he sucks and licks my clit the more I moan in appreciation because I'm getting close to my release, but I don't want to come yet because I have plans.

"Evan stop…wait...stop."

He stops and looks at me concerned. "What's wrong?"

"I've got plans." I smile.

"Plans?" he grins "I'm intrigued, what plans?"

He gets up with a cheeky smile on his face and looks at me.

"As much as I would love to have come just then I want to do something for you first."

"Okay" he smiles as I take his hand and lead him towards the bed.

"Just lay down on the bed and think of me and I'll be back in a minute, I just need to get something" I smile cheekily.

"I love this dominant side to you Kara" he grins making himself comfortable while he waits for my next move.

"I'm just going to the kitchen; close your eyes and I'll be back in a minute."

Evan does as he's told, and I leave the room briefly then return moments later with a small tub of creamy custard which I place on the bedside table.

"Hmm what's that I can hear?" Evan asks with a grin hearing me putting it down.

"You'll soon find out. Don't open your eyes just feel what I'm going to do okay…"

"Okay" he smirks, his cock twitching with excitement.

I start off by kissing him slowly slipping my tongue into his mouth and Evan returns the kiss moaning softly. "Hmm…" I then trail light kisses around his face leaning over him and then pulling down the straps on the lace teddy I'm wearing to expose my breasts I take hold of one of my breasts in my hand and guide it to his mouth. He teases my nipple with his tongue licking and sucking the sweet nub and the feeling is incredible. His hand strokes up and down my back a few times before moving to my bum where he performs light circles with his fingers.

"I love your tits" Evan says as I swap breasts and he gives my other nipple the same treatment making me moan in appreciation as he gives me just what I need with his expert mouth and tongue. After enjoying the sensation for a few moments, I move away from him. "Hey, I was enjoying that" he complains.

"So was I but I think you are going to enjoy what I'm going to do to you a whole lot more and don't forget keep your eyes closed" I warn whispering into his ear before moving to the bedside table to pick up the pot of cold creamy custard.

"Okay baby I'll keep them closed...jeez I'm so turned on right now" he pants.

I look at him laid on my bed with his eyes closed and can't help smiling, he is so gorgeous and I'm so lucky because he's mine, my boyfriend who I love and can't get enough of.

I lean over him and blow cold air onto his hard and imposing cock making him flinch and his cock twitch. The anticipation of what I'm going to do to him is turning him on to the extreme.

I scoop some of the cold custard onto my finger. "This might feel a bit cold okay." I warn.

"Okay baby" The rise and fall of his chest as his breathing escalates tells me he is excited for what's to come.

"Are you ready?" I ask kneeling at the side of him on the bed.

"Yes...I'm more than ready."

"Don't open your eyes," I warn. "remember just feel."

"Okay" he smiles.

With my fingers covered in yellow custard I smear it into my palms and then place my hands on his hard length making him flinch and moan as I rub up and down coating him.

"Fuck that's cold, what is it? Aargh god that feels good?" he moans thrusting his hips forward as I move my hands up and down his shaft. I smile because the look on his face of pure enjoyment with his eyes closed makes me so happy, I love pleasing him. I lean down and place my mouth onto his awaiting erection "Aargh… fuck..." I lick and suck the custard from his cock while he enjoys the thrilling feeling.

"Hmm…you taste delicious…" I clean him of all the custard teasing and tasting him with my tongue.

"Aargh fucking hell woman…" I take him deep in my mouth then slowly moving up and down from root to tip pleasuring him while cupping his balls at the same time.

"Oh baby that's so fucking good..." he pants while I give him the best blow job of his life.

"Baby stop or I'm going to come..." He grabs hold of the back of my head like he's losing control.

"Don't come I want you to come inside me."

"Jesus Kara you need to stop baby, seriously I'm almost there."

I can feel his cock swelling in my mouth getting ready for his release, so I stop what I'm doing and climb up his body with a smile on my face. "You can open your eyes now." He opens his eyes and gives me the biggest smile before I kiss him slowly delving my tongue into his mouth.

"Hmm...you taste of...custard" he laughs.

I giggle. "Hmm... I love custard and even more so when it's smeared all over your cock," I whisper looking at him.

"Hmm...and I love custard too especially when you are sucking it off my cock, I very nearly came in your mouth just then" he whispers.

"I know I could feel you getting close, I want you to make love to me now."

"I'd love to," he says as I lay down on the bed on my back at the side of him and Evan climbs on top of me. "How do I take this lace thing off you?" he asks unsure as to where to start."

"I'll do it." I smile quickly removing it and throwing it on the floor then laying back down again and Evan is on me straight away. He sucks one of my nipples into his mouth and teases it with his tongue.

'Oh god I love it when he does that.'

With each flick of his tongue the tingles I'm feeling between my legs become stronger and stronger.

"Evan please I want you…" I'm desperate now I need to feel him inside me. Evan positions his cock at my entrance and enters me swiftly making me cry out and call out his name. "EVAN…" He gyrates his hips moving his hard length around and around, in and out, in and out.

"OH… Evan…. Oh god…yes…." I cling to him as he plunges his cock slowly deep inside my body hitting the spot every time. The feel of his cock rubbing against my insides as he enters me repeatedly feels so good and I'm not going to be long before I finish. I can feel every gorgeous inch of him, and it feels amazing.

"I love you Kara" he moans.

"I love you too, OHHHH…." After a few more deep thrusts penetrating me I'm there and a powerful orgasm takes over my body. I pulsate around him moaning repeatedly enjoying the incredible feeling. Evan comes too.

"Wow that didn't take us long, are you okay baby?" he grins holding me as I lay beneath him breathless.

"Wow, yes I'm good, are you?" I smile.

"I'm good," he smiles "every time is just so incredible, you make me come so easily" he says rolling off me and pulling me to him for a cuddle.

"I know what you mean." I smile.

As we lay holding each other getting our breath back we hear a phone ringing and it's coming from Evan's jeans pocket.

"Perfect timing as always" he sighs getting up off the bed to look for his phone in his jeans that are on the floor.

Evan

Without taking any notice of who is calling I answer the call.

"Hello."

"Evan hi it's Julia, are you okay you sound out of breath?"

"Julia," I sigh. "yes, I'm fine I've just been err doing a workout in the gym." 'Great what does she want?' I look at Kara feeling uncomfortable and her annoyed face is looking back at me. "Sorry" I mouth to her; she doesn't look happy.

"I'm sorry to bother you Ev I know it's late it's just…" Julia burst into tears.

"What's the matter, why are you crying?" I ask stood looking at Kara who rolls her eyes and shakes her head.

"I'm sorry I didn't know who else to ring and I know you'd understand."

"Understand what, what's happened?"

"Sebastian... he came to see me earlier, he was really angry, I didn't know what to do, he kept banging on the door and to shut him up I answered it to tell him to go away and he..."

"He what? What did he do?" I listen feeling awkward having a conversation with my ex when my girlfriend is sat on the bed looking annoyed.

"He was really drunk, and he kept ranting about you, that you'd had some fight, he forced his way into my flat and kept saying that you still owe him his money and that he would get it if it was the last thing he ever did. He then brought up about me losing his kid and said I would have been a useless mother, so it was a blessing I lost it. He called me a whore for sleeping with two brothers at the same time and that we have both ruined his life and then he glared at me with crazy eyes and then just left."

"I'm sorry that my brother said those things to you."

"It's not your fault Evan" she cries.

"Did he hurt you physically?" I ask running my hands through my hair feeling angry and stressed.

"No not physically but I guess he's right I am a whore I should never had slept with him and continued to sleep with you, what sort of a person am I?" Julia sobs.

"Julia, don't."

"I couldn't help having a miscarriage, it's not my fault I lost the baby, the doctors say it's common and there was nothing I could have done but then I suppose that was my comeuppance for having the affair wasn't it."

"I'm sorry and if that's what the doctors said then you mustn't blame yourself."

"Yes, but if I hadn't slept with Sebastian everything would be different, I hate him Evan all he cares about is the god damn money and himself, he continues to try and hurt people when really he is the one hurting over your father, he was never the same after your father died."

"I know look the best thing you can do if he calls again is don't answer the door to him."

"Okay but I'm scared Evan, he was so angry I'm worried he might hurt me."

"My brother is many things Julia, but he is no woman beater."

"I'm not so sure you didn't see how he was acting towards me."

"If you're feeling scared why don't you go and stay with Jackie tonight."

"No, it's okay I think I'm just shaken that's all I'll be fine in a minute. Thanks Evan I'm so sorry to have bothered you."

"It's okay look I've got to go."

"Of course, I'm sorry I just wanted to let you know that Sebastian had been and what he had said."

"Thanks, I appreciate it anyway lock the door and if he comes around again call the police."

"Okay I will, thanks Evan."

"Goodbye Julia."

Evan cuts the call and looks at my scowling face. "What did she want? let me guess what she always wants…YOU." I huff.

"She sounded really upset babe, Sebastian has been to see her, he was ranting about what happened yesterday, she said he was really angry, and he'd been drinking."

"Oh right."

"She said he forced his way into her flat, ranting about our fight and the money, he was also saying some really hurtful things about Julia losing their baby. She said she was scared and didn't know who else to call."

"I'm sorry that your brother has done that, and it mustn't have been very nice for her but is she always going to be calling you Evan when she has a problem because if Sebastian is going to keep interfering in our life then that means Julia is too?"

"No, I've told you I will sort it, but I can't just ignore her when she rings me."

"Yes, you can," 'Oh my god seriously?' "How would you like it if my ex kept ringing me all the time?"

'I already know the answer to this he would be fuming.'

"You know how I would feel" he frowns.

"Exactly so..."

"Okay I'll speak to her, tell her to stop calling me."

"You'd do that?"

"Yes, I'd do anything for you, I don't want you upset and if it means not talking to Julia anymore then I won't."

Evan puts his phone on the bedside drawers then sits on the edge of the bed. I take one look at him then push him backwards and dive on top of him kissing him all over grinning from ear to ear.

"Alright alright," Evan laughs. "Calm down woman."

"Thank you" I smile.

Evan grabs hold of me and flips me onto my back "Your welcome. Now I think it's time for round two don't you think?"

"Why that sounds just perfect" I giggle, and we make love again forgetting about Julia and the phone call.

Ten

It's 8 o'clock Sunday morning and I'm rummaging in the fridge looking for something to make for breakfast. I'm going to surprise Evan with breakfast in bed. I find some bacon and some fresh bread and decide to make bacon sandwiches.

While I'm cooking the bacon, the smell must have wafted down the hallway to my bedroom and woken Evan up, I sense him as I look over my shoulder and see him stood in the doorway watching me.

"Good morning" I smile, and he walks over to me wearing just his boxers puts his arms around my waist and nuzzles his face into my neck.

"Good morning beautiful, something smells good."

"Hmm I was going to surprise you with breakfast in bed."

"Oh, sorry do you want me to go back to bed?"

"Yes, and I'll bring it to you when it's ready? I wouldn't want Jodie coming home early and finding my boyfriend half naked in our kitchen."

"Oh yes I forgot about Jodie, okay."

As I watch the bacon sizzling in the frying pan I can't help the big smile on my face. I've never cooked breakfast for a special man in my life before and it's a lovely feeling.

After plating up the bacon sandwiches I carry them to my room to find Evan sat up in bed waiting for me.

"Here you go." I pass him a plate and climb into bed at the side of him.

"Thanks baby these look and smell delicious" he says taking a bite.

"Damn I forgot to make the tea." I go to move but Evan stops me. "Hey, you eat your breakfast, I'll make the tea in a minute, you cooked that lovely meal last night and a bacon sandwich this morning the least I can do is make us a cuppa."

"Okay thanks" I smile tucking into my sandwich.

"So, what do you fancy doing today?" Evan asks.

"I'm not sure what do you fancy doing?"

"Well, we could just stay in bed all day?"

"Hmm sounds good but we spend a lot of time in bed already" I smirk.

"Yes, and what's wrong with that? My favourite pastime is being in bed with you."

"I know" I giggle.

"Well, you have a think what you would like to do, and I'll go and make us that cuppa." Evan gets up, puts his jeans on and then goes to make the drinks.

While Evan is making the tea, I try to think of something we can do today, and I suddenly have a great idea. Evan walks back into the bedroom carrying two mugs of tea. "I know what we can do" I say smiling at him.

"Okay what?"

"Let's go to the beach."

"The beach?"

"Yes, it looks like it's going to be a nice day so let's go to the beach. We can take a picnic and just chill out in the sun, what do you think?"

"Okay why not, sounds good, the beach it is then."

After having a shower, I change into some summer clothes deciding to wear a yellow sun dress with a white bikini underneath. Evan gets dressed in some blue jeans and a white t-shirt because he hasn't brought any shorts with him in his overnight bag, he wasn't expecting to go to the beach. We are just in the kitchen making a picnic to take with us when we hear the front door open, Jodie is home.

"Hello, is it safe to come in?" Jodie shouts walking through the front door.

"Hi Jode, yeah we're in here" I call.

Jodie walks into the kitchen and sees us making some sandwiches.

"It's a bit early for lunch isn't it?" Jodie smiles.

"We're making a picnic we're going to the beach for the day" I reply sounding excited.

"Sounds great, it's going to be a lovely day for it, hi Evan."

"Hi Jodie, how are you?" Evan smiles.

"I'm good thanks, I've just left Matt he's doing some washing then he's coming over later to take me out for lunch. So, did you two have fun last night then?" Jodie smirks walking over to the kettle, filling it with water and switching it on.

"Yes, we had a great night thanks, we had a lovely meal the lasagne was scrumptious and then afterwards we watched a DVD."

"Oh, that sounds nice, what film did you watch?"

"Well, it's funny you should ask that, I found a DVD on the shelf, it's one that Matt borrowed from his mate at work, we decided we would see what it was like."

"Oh yeah his mate at work lends him them all the time, we've watched some great films courtesy of his friend, which one did you watch then?"

"Well, we didn't watch all of it, but it started off with this rich guy going to a club and then being seduced by a woman in a maid's outfit." I grin.

Jodie looks shocked, her face turns bright red from embarrassment "Oh" she laughs.

"You dirty buggers" I laugh looking at Jodie as her face becomes more and more red.

"Well, what can I say there's not much on TV nowadays I mean you pay your TV licence and what do you get eh?" Jodie laughs. "Wait until I see Matt later, he shouldn't have left that on the shelf. Anyway, changing the subject do you guys want a cuppa?" she asks getting a mug out of the cupboard.

"No thanks we need to get going."

"Okay" Jodie smiles making herself one.

After finishing preparing the food for the picnic and putting it into a cool bag we say our goodbyes and then head out the door. It's a perfect sunny day to go to the beach and I feel on top of the world as Evan drives us in his Aston Martin with feel good tunes playing on the radio. I am loving life right now; we are back together again, and everything is perfect.

"What a gorgeous day" Evan says placing a hand on my leg and smiling at me.

"Hmm it was a good idea of mine wasn't it going to the beach."

"Yes, I can't remember the last time I went to the beach, not in this country anyway."

"I love going to the beach, I have lots of fond memories going to the seaside as a child with my mum and dad."

"We never really went to the beach much, my father was always too busy working, we mostly hung around the hotel pool, my mother is a sun worshipper, and she would lay on the sun lounger all day reading a book while my brother and I played in the pool."

"Have you never made a sandcastle then?"

"No, I can't say that I have."

"Really not when you were little?"

"Nope not even when I was little."

"Oh, I wish we'd bought a bucket and spade now, making sandcastles is fun."

"Oh, that's a shame" Evan says sarcastically laughing and putting his hand back on the steering wheel.

"Hey, it's fun I'll just have to bury you in the sand instead then."

"What? Bury me in the sand."

"Don't say you've never been buried in the sand either?"

"Hmm…nope can't say I have."

"Oh Evan..."

"I think I would rather be buried in you than in the sand if that's okay" he grins.

"Oh okay." I laugh.

Arriving at the secluded beach Evan parks the car. We collect the picnic that we made, a blanket from Evan's car boot and then we walk hand in hand down to the sandy beach. We have chosen this beach because it is quiet and secluded so we can relax and enjoy our time together without crowds of people surrounding us.

Finding a nice spot, we lay out the blanket and lay down next to each other staring at the blue sunny sky above us and listen to some seagulls flying over ahead and the gentle waves lapping on the shore. “Hmm what a lovely sound” I sigh.

“Hmm…” Evan agrees stretching putting his hands behind his head.

“Will you put some sun cream on me?” I ask taking off my yellow sun dress to reveal my white bikini underneath and getting the sun lotion out of my bag.

“Wow you look hot in a bikini” Evan says his eyes nearly popping out of his head.

“Thanks,” I blush. “Um sun cream” I laugh passing it to him snapping him out of a trance as he stares at my body.

“Oh yeah sorry” he grins taking the bottle and squeezing a small amount into his hand. I lie down on my back. “I don’t think I’m going to be able to do this without getting a hard on” he laughs rubbing some onto my smooth silky legs.

“I do seem to have an effect on you don’t I.” I giggle.

‘I love that I affect him like this.’

“Always I seem to have a permanent stiffy these days.”

“Hmm, I’m not complaining because I know what your stiffy can do” I smile making him laugh as he rubs some lotion onto my stomach and then my arms and shoulders.

“It’s a good job we’re not at a nudist beach,” he laughs “I wouldn’t survive seeing you walking around naked I’d be poking everyone’s eyes out.”

I proper laugh at the thought because he is definitely well-endowed in that area. "Yes, I think you would, plus there would be lots of other naked people walking around too."

"Oh yeah and I definitely wouldn't like that, men ogling you, your naked body is for my eyes only" he says looking serious.

Knowing how jealous Evan is I move away from this line of conversation because I want us to have a fun, chilled day. "Aren't you hot in your t-shirt?"

"Yeah, I am so do you want to return the favour and put some sun cream on me" he smiles taking off his t-shirt showing his toned abs.

'Oh my god every time I see his perfect body it gives me tingles, he is so hot, I am one lucky girl.'

"Hmm I'd love to." I lick my lips; I am going to enjoy rubbing cream all over his muscly body. Evan lays down on the blanket and I sit up and straddle him. Squeezing some lotion into my hands I start at the top and rub some into his shoulders and on his chest.

"Hmm it's a gorgeous view" Evan says looking up at me, I look over my shoulder at the sand and sea in the distance. "Yes, it is gorgeous isn't it."

"I wasn't talking about that view" Evan grins cupping my breasts over my bikini top as I lean over him applying the cream.

"Oh," I laugh "behave."

"Sorry I can't resist" he smiles. I can feel him becoming hard beneath me which is not helping because rubbing lotion onto his gorgeous body is affecting me too and I could quite easily succumb to a sexual need that is increasing more and more every minute.

'No Kara, put those thoughts out of your head you are on a public beach so you will just have to wait, it's not like you haven't had him enough times already but oh god he's just so good and too tempting.'

After we are both lathered in sun cream we lay down on the blanket again next to each other and soak up the sun's rays.

"This is nice being here with you and relaxing" I sigh.

"Yeah, it is, I need to do this more often."

"Yes, especially when you have such a busy working life it does you good to just chill out and forget about work for a while."

"I know for the past few years I've been working so hard to make my hotel business a success I haven't really taken much time off to do fun stuff. Julia always used to have a go at me when we were together for not spending enough time with her because I was constantly working but spending time with her didn't really have the same appeal as it does with you. I remember she had booked to take me away for my birthday and she had to cancel it because I couldn't go due to work commitments, she was really annoyed about it. It's funny though because since meeting you all I want to do is spend time with you I hate it when we are apart, you've changed me."

"I love spending time with you too," I smile leaning over and giving him a kiss. "Oh my god I've just realised something."

"What?" Evan frowns.

"I've known you all this time and just talking now I don't even know when your birthday is?"

Evan laughs "Yeah when we first met you asked me my age but never my birthday."

"Sorry is that bad I was so nervous, and you were distracting me with your good looks I wasn't thinking straight?"

"Don't be daft, it's the 24th of March."

"Oh, thank god I haven't missed it because I would have felt awful because you spoilt me so much on my birthday."

"No don't worry you haven't missed it and you deserve to be spoiled."

"I loved my birthday presents," I smile admiring the bracelet on my wrist. "Did you have big birthday parties when you were little being twins, double the celebration and all that I bet you were quite close to your brother when you were little weren't you?"

"Yes, we were close when we were young, but we didn't really have big parties because we used to travel around a lot, and we didn't have big friendship groups either. We tended to get taken out for the day to somewhere of our choice."

"Oh, I bet that was nice though."

"Yes, it was. It was only as we got older and my brother got in with the wrong people that we started to drift and then obviously my father dying and his will."

"Yeah, do you miss being close to your brother?"

"Yes, I guess I do miss him being my twin, it's a shame because I never wanted any of this, if only my father had not been so stubborn and made up with him then maybe now things would be different."

"Yeah, I sometimes wish I had a sibling but then I suppose I have the next best thing, my best friend Jodie, she's always been like a sister to me."

"Yes, she's a lovely girl, I really like her, and Matt is nice too do you think they will end up getting married one day?"

"Definitely," I think for a moment wondering whether I should ask what's in my head and then I decide to just come straight out with it. "Would you like to get married one day?"

"Why it's not a leap year is it, are you asking me?" Evan grins.

"No, it isn't… I wasn't asking… I…" I blush.

'Why didn't I keep my big mouth shut, now I feel awkward.'

"Relax I'm only winding you up." Evan laughs and I playfully hit him on the side of his leg.

"I was just wondering because of the whole Julia thing has that put you off marriage now?" Evan's face turns serious. "Err… I've never really thought about marriage since Julia and I've never been in a relationship since to warrant thinking about it. I suppose maybe I would get married one day; do you want to get married one day?"

"Yes, I would love to" I smile looking at him then looking away feeling my cheeks become red as I blush more and more. Even though I feel awkward asking these types of questions seeing as we have only just got back together, I feel that this is a good a time as any to ask because I need to know what his thoughts are and what he wants out of life. I ask him another question that I would love to know the answer to. "So…what about kids? I know you said once before that you didn't think having kids would be a good idea, do you still feel that way?"

"I'll be honest the idea of having kids scares the hell out of me."

"Really I think you would make a great dad one day?"

"Do you want kids?" Evan asks with a serious face.

"Yes, one day I would love to have at least two kids but if you don't want kids and we are still together then we might have a problem."

"Look I'm not saying I don't want kids and yes I did say before that having kids wouldn't be a good idea but now I've met you and I want to be with you I suppose I would need to rethink that one wouldn't I if you want them?"

"Yes, but you can't just have kids because I want them you've got to want them too or our relationship won't work because wanting different things can break a relationship."

"Kara listen when we discussed the kids thing before it was when I was closed off from having any sort of a relationship but since meeting you it appears my whole perception has changed on a lot of things, you have completely changed my outlook on relationships, about being in love, about the future so I guess in time maybe I could see myself becoming a father."

"I just think it's important to say how we feel now about these sorts of things than further down the line into our relationship, we need to be on the same page."

"You're right and I'm pleased we have had this discussion" Evan says looking serious.

"I haven't upset you have I talking about marriage and kids?" The look on Evan's face tells me I have because he is now deep in thought.

"What no not at all it's just feels strange to me that's all, come here" he says pulling me to him.

"I'm sorry I don't know why we are having this deep conversation it's not like it's going to happen for a good few years anyway, I guess I just wanted to know what your thoughts are on the subject" I smile trying to make light of the conversation.

"As long as you keep taking your pill it won't happen for a few years," he smiles "and it's good that we have had this discussion so don't apologise, everything is cool okay."

"Okay. Oh my god speaking of the pill I forgot to take it the last few days" I say looking at Evan with a worried look on my face.

"Oh Kara you didn't, seriously."

"Gotcha!" I laugh.

"Kara Davis you little tease" he says pulling me on top of him and digging his fingers into my sides to tickle me.

"Aargh no stop no I'm sorry" I giggle wriggling and laughing trying to break free.

He stops and manoeuvres me off him and soon has me on my back on the blanket pinning me down by straddling me. "Kara" he says looking at me intensely.

"Yes Evan" I smile looking into his chocolate brown eyes I love so much.

"I love you" He moves towards me and kisses me slowly and softly delving his tongue into my mouth.

"Hmm…" I moan putting my arms around his neck and caressing the back of his head, my hands in his brown hair massaging it with my fingers. "I love you too. Anyway, don't worry I want to do some travelling first before I settle down and have kids."

"Okay where shall we go?" he smiles making my eyes light up.

"What do you want to go on holiday?" I smile.

"Yes, why not? I loved our time in Italy so let's go somewhere. I'll speak to Curtis to see if he can manage things this end, I'll only be able to manage a weekend at the moment though."

"Oh my god really?"

"Really" he laughs.

"Oh god where can we go, where do you want to go?"

"Well, I've been to quite a lot of places already so it's up to you, think about it, do some research and let me know" he grins.

"Okay I will, obviously it won't be too far, eek we're going away." I kiss him again.

Evan climbs off me, lays at the side of me and leans on one arm looking at me. I turn to look at him as I lay on my side. "When we got back from Italy, I loved it so much I decided to start saving for a holiday. Jodie bought me a suitcase money box for my birthday and so I thought I would put some of my wages in it each month."

"Oh right, have you saved much then?"

"Err no not exactly I've already spent what I'd saved buying some clothes in the sale the other day, but I will start saving again this month, I might have to pay you back."

Evan laughs. "Listen you don't need to save your money or pay me back because wherever you decide to go, I will be paying."

"But…"

"No buts Kara I have worked hard, and my hotel business is thriving so if I can't treat my girlfriend to a nice holiday then what can I do."

"I also kind of agreed with Jodie that we would go somewhere together."

"Well, if you want Jodie to come too then let's make it a foursome and she can bring Matt."

"What you'd do that, you'd go on holiday with Jodie and Matt?" I smile.

"Yeah, I really like them, and I think we'd have a laugh and I'd treat them too."

"Oh my god Evan but I'm sure they would want to pay for themselves."

"I know but I will insist I can afford it trust me."

"I can't believe this wait until I tell Jodie she is going to be so excited." I squeal making Evan laugh.

"You are so cute; do you know that?" Evan says leaning over and giving me a kiss then looking at his watch to see what the time is. "Anyway, I'm starving so let's eat and then we can go for a dip in the sea?"

"Okay."

After having a nice lunch and relaxing on the picnic blanket for a while underneath the warm rays of the sun Evan gets up "Right fancy a dip?" he asks.

"No, I'm quite happy laid here thanks you go."

"Come on it'll be nice" Evan says looking down on me trying to persuade me.

"Evan I'm comfortable here you go."

"Kara Davis you can't go to the beach and not have a dip in the sea come on" he says holding out his hand for me to take. I begrudgingly take hold of his hand and he pulls me up to a standing position then before I know what's happening he has picked me up and thrown me over his shoulder making me squeal.

"Evan no put me down" I scream laughing.

"I will in a minute when you're in the sea" he laughs striding towards the water.

"No Evan please no it'll be cold" I protest.

"More than likely but you'll find out in a minute won't you" he laughs.

"No please Evan no."

As we reach the sea he wades in a little way and then gently lowers me down the front of his body. My feet hit the cold water first as I'm lowered down into the water until I'm stood in front of him up to my knees.

"Aargh god its bloody freezing."

"Yes, I can see it's making you cold" he grins looking down at my chest my nipples poking through the material of my white bikini.

"Well, we'd better do something to warm us up then" I smile seductively unwrapping myself from his arms. I walk back a few paces and splash him with the cold water before running off slowly trudging through the sea.

"Oh, you want to play that game do you?" he says kicking the water and it splashes all over my back.

"Nooooo…. aargh…" The cold water is giving me goose bumps. I turn around and scoop up some water in my hands and splash him again.

"Water fight" Evan shouts and we splash each other repeatedly forgetting about the coldness of the water and enjoy having fun in the sea.

After happily splashing each other for a while we stop and look at each other and we are soaked.

"Oh dear, we're all wet" Evan says brushing his hair back from his face and stalking towards me.

"Oh dear, so we are" I grin. The water from my hair is dripping down my face and I brush it back with my hands as I look at Evan, he looks divine.

"I like you wet" he smiles taking me in his arms and kissing me passionately massaging my breast with his hand over my wet bikini top while he holds me with his other.

"Hmm I know…." I moan into his mouth feeling the bulge in his jeans which is hard and solid just like the masculine body wrapped around me.

I am so turned on and Evan is too at the sight of my wet body and my erect nipples from the cold water. "I think we need to go" I say before I pull him to me again for more kisses. "Kara" he says picking me up and kissing me passionately as I cling to his body.

"Hmm…"

"We really need to go" he urges looking turned on manoeuvring me so he can carry me in his strong arms to carry me back to the beach where we have left our things.

We arrive back at the picnic blanket and Evan looks around the secluded beach before laying me down and lowering himself on top of me.

"Oh, I thought we were going" I smile when he takes me in his arms and kisses me again.

"I've changed my mind now we are coming" he grins pulling down the front of my bikini top and sucking my cold wet nipple and warming it with his tongue and mouth.

"Oh god Evan I soon will be if you keep doing that…OHHH…"

"Jesus you turn me on so much when you moan like that, I need you Kara, I need to be inside you" he says.

"Evan what if someone sees us?"

"Relax there's no one around I've already checked."

'Of course he has.'

"Okay hurry then because I need you too."

Evan tries to take off his jeans which is a hard task seeing as they are stuck to his legs from being so wet. He rolls onto his back to try and take them off, but they are really stuck. "Shit" he curses trying to slide them down his legs to free his cock making me laugh. I watch him desperately trying to get rid of his jeans and I can't help giggling.

"Do you need some help?" I ask laughing.

Evan laughs. "Jesus this is a fucking task in itself. Fuck it." He stands up to make the job easier and prises them down his legs before kicking them off onto the golden sand. "Right where were we" he laughs looking around again before lowering himself down onto the picnic blanket. He pulls down the front of his boxers letting his erection spring free and then climbs on top of me. I move my bikini bottoms to one side, and he thrusts into me quickly making me cry out "OHHHH…." We both moan as he fills my insides completely "Oh Jesus you feel good, you're so wet" he pants "Are you ready baby this is not going to take long."

"Yes, I'm ready and I don't think I'm going to be long either." He starts to move in and out of me and it feels amazing.

"Oh, fuck yes…" Evan pounds into me on the secluded sandy beach, the sounds of the water lapping against the shore in the distance as I hold onto his back. "Evan oh god." He gives us both just what we need and with each thrust the feelings intensify as we enjoy the most incredible sex on the beach but not in the drink form but in the form of two people with a strong physical connection who can't get enough of each other.

"Evan shit…" I pant as Evan drives into my wetness sending tingles to my core as he rubs against my sensitive spot. "Oh god I'm close."

"Me too baby, shit" he moans getting ready for the amazing feeling that is soon to take over our minds and bodies.

After a few more thrusts, in and out I cry out "I'm coming" and then I orgasm letting out a long satisfying moan as ripples of pleasure spread throughout my body to my brain. Triggering Evan's release, he comes too and lets out a long moan, his cock jerking inside of me as he fills me with his come. "Oh my god," I laugh suddenly conscious that we are on a public beach. "I hope no-one heard us."

"Relax its fine there's only us and a few seagulls" he smiles as one swoops over our heads and drops down to pick something up off the sand before flying off again.

Evan pulls out of me and pulls up the front of his boxers. He then sits on the picnic blanket at the side of me and hands me a clean tissue to clean myself with. I make myself presentable and then we lay on the blanket cuddling each other.

"I can't believe we just had sex on the beach" I laugh.

"I know, thank you" he smiles.

"No thank you" I grin.

"Right, I'll get dressed and then shall we head off?" he says standing up putting on his t-shirt and retrieving his jeans that are all covered in sand.

"Yeah okay." I sit up and look at the state of his jeans. 'He is never going to get them back on.' I watch him shaking all the sand off and trying to straighten them out and I can't help giggling.

"If I knew we were coming to the beach today I would have packed some shorts to wear" he laughs trying to get one leg in.

"Sorry, it would have been better for you" I smirk.

"You could say that…Oh shit." He loses his balance as he gets one leg stuck in the wet jeans and falls over into a heap on the sand causing me to let out a proper belly laugh. 'Oh my god.' I am in hysterics.

"Something funny?" he says standing up laughing attempting to put the jeans on again.

"No nothing at all" I snort laughing with tears in my eyes.

"It's alright for you wearing a dress" he laughs watching me put my dress back on easily and getting frustrated because he can't put his jeans on because they are so wet.

"Oh, fuck it I'll leave them off" he says throwing them down on the floor laughing.

"You can't travel back in just your boxers," I laugh "what if we get stopped or something. Maybe you could wrap the picnic blanket around your waist and wear it like a sarong skirt." I suggest giggling.

"A sarong what?" he says looking puzzled. "What the fuck's one of them?"

"Come here," I stand up move my bag and shake the sand off the blanket. I then wrap it around his waist and tie it securely around his waist sniggering "There you go, like that."

"Oh, and I suppose a lot of men wear these do they?" he laughs feeling stupid.

"Only men that can't put their jeans on after getting them wet and having sex with their girlfriend at the beach" I grin.

"Well, I guess this will have to do, I just hope we don't see anyone or get stopped like you said because that would be extremely embarrassing" he laughs.

'He could have just worn his boxers on the way home, he obviously hasn't twigged I was joking about the sarong skirt but I'm not going to tell him that because this is far more entertaining.'

"Come on let's go" I giggle collecting our stuff.

Once ready we make our way back to the car and I can't help giggling as I walk behind him watching his bum swaying as he walks in the blanket skirt.

"It's alright you can laugh" Evan smiles.

"I'm sorry I'm just not used to seeing you wear a skirt."

"Yes, and why is that, because I don't wear them do I."

Tears are rolling down my face as we get into the car, I have not laughed this much in a long time. "I'm sorry baby but there is one benefit to wearing a skirt though" I say looking at him.

"Oh, and what's that?" he asks raising an eyebrow at me.

"Easy access." I slide my hand under the blanket skirt and give his cock a rub making him smile.

"Oh yes maybe I could get used to this skirt thing."

"Oh god, don't" I laugh pulling my hand away.

"Joking this is the first and last time you will ever see me wearing a skirt" he laughs.

"Oh good, now take me home."

Arriving back at my flat it's late afternoon and I get out of the car first to make sure the coast is clear before Evan gets out. After finding Jodie has gone out I give the signal of a thumbs up to Evan and he quickly gets out of the car and runs up the path in his blanket skirt and inside so not to be seen by any of my neighbours.

Shutting the door behind him he rips off the blanket skirt throws it onto the floor and stalks over to where I'm stood in the hallway looking at him with a smile on my face. Pushing me up against the wall he kisses me fiercely as I cling to his neck. "So, you think it's funny dressing your man in a skirt do you hey?" Evan says gyrating his hips against me.

"Maybe" I smile feeling his erection growing in his boxers.

He starts to tickle me, and I wriggle in his arms. "I'm sorry I shouldn't have laughed, aargh…" He continues to tickle me.

"So, are you going to make it up to me?" he smiles stopping and kissing my neck and licking his way up to my ear.

"Hmm… what did you have in mind?" He kisses his way to my mouth and then kisses me slowly pushing his tongue inside to find mine.

"Hmm… well how about…" We are so engrossed in each other we don't hear the door open and Jodie walks in finding us in a compromising position.

"Oh god sorry" she squeals turning away from us.

"Shit." Evan quickly runs off to my bedroom wearing just a t-shirt and his boxers feeling embarrassed and awkward shutting the bedroom door behind him leaving Jodie and I sniggering in the hallway.

"Sorry about that" I giggle.

"Well, I wasn't expecting to see that when I walked through the door," she grins "he's got a lovely bum hasn't he" she whispers smiling.

"He's got a lovely everything" I smile grinning at her then walking off to my bedroom to find Evan.

I peer around the door seeing Evan routing around in his overnight bag. "Hi."

"Well, that was awkward" he laughs blushing slightly.

"Are you blushing Mr H?" I walk over to him.

"No" he smiles taking me in his arms.

"Don't worry that was nothing I walked in on Matt the other day having a wee, he forgot to lock the bathroom door and that was really awkward I can tell you."

"Yes, I can imagine" he frowns.

"Jodie thinks you have a nice bum by the way."

"Oh, does she, it's not as nice as yours though" he says grabbing hold of my bum giving my cheeks a squeeze while kissing me.

"Anyway, do you want to have a shower?" I ask.

"Yes, that would be great I don't fancy travelling home as I am." He lets go of me and finds some clean clothes to change into.

"I've got a skirt if you want to borrow one seeing as yours is covered in sand" I smirk.

"Very funny" he laughs shaking his head.

After having a shower and washing away all the suntan lotion, sand, and sea water we get changed into some clean clothes and Evan packs his overnight bag leaving it in the hallway ready to collect when he leaves.

Jodie is in the kitchen making a drink, so we join her for one sat at the kitchen table and tell her about our day at the beach. We also mention to Jodie about going on holiday together and she loves the idea and says she will mention it to Matt later when she sees him and that she knows he will definitely be up for it.

"Right, I'd best make tracks" Evan says finishing his coffee and standing up looking at his watch.

"Okay babe I'll see you out." I yawn. All the fresh sea air and the sexual activities we have been enjoying over the weekend has made me tired, I think I'll have an early night to recharge.

Evan says goodbye to Jodie then I show him to the door.

"I'll call you when I can get over next okay."

"Okay."

He takes me in his arms and gives me a slow goodbye kiss then picks up his bag and the sandy blanket. "Bye baby, see you soon, love you" he smiles.

"Bye love you" I smile.

Another week is due to begin, it's Monday tomorrow, since meeting Evan my life has certainly been an adventure, I wonder what will happen next?

Eleven

"Morning Sal." I walk through the door of Walt's Coffee Shop on Monday morning with a big smile on my face.

"Morning love, I take it the meal went well and you have sorted things out with Evan, or have you ended things and you're happy because you feel like a weight has been lifted?" she smiles.

"Oh god I've got so much to tell you Sal, let me just sort the coffee machine out and then I'll tell you what's been happening."

"Ooh I'm intrigued."

I prepare the coffee machine and other things in readiness for opening for the day then fill Sally in on Evan being a twin and the man that turned up last Friday at the coffee shop was his twin brother Sebastian pretending to be him, the fight and getting back together with the love of my life. To say Sally is shocked is an understatement.

"When Evan's brother turned up here, he seemed arrogant, dark somehow compared to Evan. They really are identical aren't they I'm not surprised you thought it was Evan because I did too?"

"Yes, I know I'm so glad I found out sooner rather than later though because I could have been intimate with him and oh god just the thoughts of it makes me feel sick."

"I know it doesn't bear thinking about does it."

"Evan asked me to be his girlfriend Sal and he told me he loves me."

Sally squeals with excitement "Oh really that's brilliant, I'm so happy for you," she says giving me a hug "I'll look forward to my invite to the wedding."

I laugh. "Don't get too excited Sal it's early days but I'm feeling more positive about everything this time around."

"Good, you just need to get rid of the brother and then you can have your happy ending."

"Yes, I hope so."

"It's going to happen Kara…I just know it is."

Lunchtime soon comes around and after Sally has taken her half hour lunch break I decide to eat my lunch in the office and to send Evan a text.

Hi gorgeous, hope you are having a good day. I can't stop thinking about you, when are we seeing each other again? I can't wait K xxx

Taking a bite of my sandwich I smile when a text comes through instantly.

Hi my sexy girlfriend, I can't stop thinking about you either and I'm struggling to work with a hard on when images of you laid wet on the beach with my cock deep inside you keeps coming to mind. I've got a busy week here and I will be finishing late most days, but I'll see what I can do because I can't wait to see you either, we've got a lot of making up for the time we've lost haven't we. E xxx

I recollect the same image and it makes me want to see Evan even more. I send another text.

Yes, I know what you mean. I'm just sat eating my lunch in the office what are you doing? K xxx

I wait for a reply and I don't have to wait long before a text comes through.

I'm wading through some reports, very boring but important. I'll call you later beautiful, enjoy your lunch, love you. E xxx

Ok, speak to you later, love you K xxx

I love the fact we can tell each other how we feel about each other now, yes it's early days but I love him, and he loves me and it's a great feeling.

After finishing work, I arrive home, kick off my shoes in the hallway then say a quick hello to Jodie who is in the kitchen cooking tea.

"It smells lovely Jode, how long?"

"About 10 minutes, you can go and get freshened up if you like."

"Thanks Jode, won't be long."

I return minutes later feeling fed up.

"Are you alright Kar you look cheesed off since I saw you earlier, has something happened?"

"No nothing's happened I'm fine I've just got my period that's all."

"Well, you don't look very happy about it, was you wanting to get pregnant or something?"

I laugh. "God no nothing like that it's just that I've only just got back with Evan and now we can't have sex because I've got my period."

"Evan will understand."

"I know he will but..."

My mobile starts ringing, Evan is calling me.

"Speak of the devil, I'll just take this, be back in a minute."

I take my phone with me into my bedroom for some privacy.

"Hi babe,"

"Hello beautiful, have you had a good day?"

"Yes thanks, have you?"

"Not bad, what are you up to?"

"I'm going to have some dinner in a minute, Jodie is just cooking it."

"Oh, I won't keep you long then, are you alright you sound fed up?"

"I'm okay I got my period today so I'm afraid we won't be able to have sex for a few days, sorry."

"Hey, you don't have to apologise I would be more bothered if you didn't get your period."

"Well, I have so you don't have to worry" I snap.

I burst into tears.

"Hey baby what's wrong? I'm sorry I didn't mean to upset you I just know we are both not ready for kids."

"No, it's fine I'm sorry I'm just being silly, it's just that we've only just got back together and now we can't have sex and you have such a high sex drive and…"

Evan interrupts me. "Baby I'm not just with you for the sex, yes the sex part is amazing but it's you I love not how many times we have sex."

"It's just that in the beginning it was such a big part of our relationship and..."

"Yes, and now we have so much more than that."

I wipe my eyes with the back of my hand.

"I'm being silly, aren't I?"

"Yes, you are, so stop thinking silly things and go and get your dinner and I'll speak to you soon."

"Okay, I love you."

"Love you too, bye."

I end the call and go into the kitchen to see Jodie is ready to dish up.

"Hey, are you okay you look like you've been crying?" Jodie asks carrying two plates of food and placing them on the kitchen table.

"Yes, I'm fine. I told Evan I got my period, and he was fine about it.

"I told you he would understand."

"I know it's just I want everything to be perfect between us, I can't lose him again Jode."

"You are not going to lose him because you got your period Kara and can't have sex. Evan loves you; you only have to see the way he looks at you to see a man totally in love."

"I love him so much Jode."

"I know you do now tuck in or the food will be getting cold" Jodie smiles sitting down at the table.

"Thanks Jode."

"Have you heard anything from Evan's brother?"

"No nothing but Evan reckons we will definitely hear from him again."

"Why can't he just leave you both alone?"

"I know life would be so much simpler if he did, did I tell you it was Sebastian that had the affair with Julia?"

"Oh my god really that man is evil, poor Evan it's bad enough his girlfriend having an affair but when it's with your own brother that's terrible."

"I know Evan said Sebastian has always been jealous of him, I think that's why he went after Julia and he thought he could do the same with me."

"Families eh, has Evan heard any more from Julia?"

"She rang him the other night saying Sebastian had paid her a visit and she was scared what he might do, she said she didn't know who else to call."

"You need to be careful of her Kar you don't want her getting in the way of you two now you've just got him back."

"I know she has already made hints in the past that she wants him back and she is always contacting him but if she thinks she is getting him she has got a fight on her hands."

"Yes, and I'll fight her with you."

"Thanks Jode you really are the best."

"I know" she grins.

Twelve

It's Tuesday and after a lovely walk in the sunshine I arrive at work and walk over to where Sally is stood at the counter.

"Morning Sal, how are you today?"

"I'm feeling a bit off today actually."

"Oh no you do look a bit pale are you okay to be at work?"

"Yes, I'm fine I just keep feeling a bit nauseous there's probably a bug going about or something."

"Are you sure you're not pregnant Sal?"

"No, I don't think so, I mean we are trying for a baby as you know but we haven't been trying that long and it doesn't always happen straight away does it."

"Yes, but sometimes it does Sal, oh god you need to do a test, have you got one?"

"At home I have."

"Go and get one or I'll go to the chemist at lunch for you."

"Kara calm down I really don't think I am I'm sure it's just a tummy bug." Sally laughs.

"I think you are" I say excitedly clapping my hands in excitement.

"Oh you've got me thinking now, do you really think I could be?"

"Well, there is only one way to find out, go and get a pregnancy test it won't take you long and I'll hold the fort."

"What do you think I should do it now, aren't you supposed to do it first thing in the morning."

"No, you can do it any time of the day if the pregnancy hormone is strong enough it will pick it up so get your bag and go get one unless you want to do the test with Tim?"

"Nah because I don't want to get his hopes up if the test is negative. If you're sure you will be alright on your own for a while."

"Don't be silly I'll be fine; I'm dying to know if I'm going to be an auntie."

"Okay I'll pop to the chemist then because it will be quicker than going home."

"Okay and hurry up not because I won't be alright but because I want to know."

"Alright, alright." she laughs going into the office to get her bag.

Sally returns a while later and walks through the door smiling looking excited. I smile at her as she walks past and into the back office. A few moments later she reappears.

"Have you done it?" I ask.

Sally laughs "I'm not that quick Kara and I'm not doing it now I'll wait until we have a quiet spell."

The lunchtime rush comes to an end and finally there are no customers wanting to be served so we can have a break for a while.

"Go on then Sal go and do it now."

"Okay I won't be long" Sally shrieks running off into the back to use the toilet.

Five minutes later Sally beckons me over to the office. Standing in the doorway so I can keep an eye on the shop the first thing I see is Sally's teary face with her head in her hands.

"Oh Sal don't worry it's fine there will be plenty of other times. I'm sorry for encouraging you are you okay?"

"Yes I'm…" She holds up the pregnancy stick and shows me the word saying pregnant on the tiny screen.

"Oh my god, you're pregnant." I dance around clapping and jumping up and down on the spot.

"Shush, people will hear you" she laughs with tears rolling down her face. "I can't believe it I can't wait to tell Tim he's going to be a father."

"Its brilliant news you will make a wonderful mother Sal."

"Thanks Kara." she smiles, and I run over and give her a quick hug.

"Tim's banana must have super sperm or something" I laugh.

Sally laughs. "Well, it must have because I never expected to fall this quickly."

"So now you know why you are feeling nauseous. How are you going to tell Tim?"

"I guess I'll just tell him tonight when we get home."

"I've got an idea how you can tell him" I grin.

"Have you what?" Sally smiles.

"Well why don't you take a cake box home with you put the test inside and tell him you bought him a cake home for dessert and then when he opens it he will see the test and voila you're pregnant."

"That's a brilliant idea yes I'll do that thanks Auntie Kara" she says hugging me.

"Oh god don't you'll make me cry," I wipe my eyes feeling tears appearing and go and get her a cake box. "Here you go."

"Thanks love I'll tell you how Tim takes the news tomorrow."

"You'd better."

Arriving home after an eventful day, I kick off my shoes and walk into the kitchen placing my bag on the back of a chair. A few minutes later the front door opens, and Jodie walks in laden with shopping bags. Jodie has been to the supermarket getting supplies. I get up to help her carry them into the kitchen then after helping to put it all away I put the kettle on.

"So, I've got some news" I say with a big grin on my face carrying two mugs of hot tea to the table.

"What have you done now?" Jodie smiles raising her eyebrows with an intrigued look on her face.

"No, it's not me, it's Sally she's pregnant."

"Really aww that's brilliant news, I bet she's thrilled."

"Yes, she is, she's telling Tim tonight."

"Aww that's lovely."

"Yeah, it is, oh did you speak to Matt about going on holiday?"

"Yes, and he said let me know the time and the place and he will be there for sure."

"Great, did you tell him Evan is treating you."

"Yes, and he said he's not paying for us."

"He won't let you pay you know, I guess when you own as many hotels as he does, he must have a bit of money in the bank."

"Yes, you've fallen lucky there Kara."

"I wouldn't care if he didn't have any money Jode I just love him for who he is."

"I know you do but it always nice to have money."

"Don't know never had any" I laugh.

The doorbell rings and I open the door hoping it's an unexpected visit from Evan but it's not, a man is stood on the doorstep holding a big bunch of yellow roses.

"Delivery for Miss Davis" the man smiles.

"Oh yes that's me thanks." I accept the flowers from him then shut the door.

I walk into the kitchen and Jodie looks at me and smiles. "Wow I wish Matt bought me flowers like that, I take it they are from Evan" she says looking envious as I admire the huge bouquet.

"Well, I hope so, I read the card 'With Me Always' yep they are definitely from him." His words make me smile.

I take the flowers that are already in water and put them in the lounge because there is no space left in the kitchen. I then walk back into the kitchen to see Jodie staring into thin air looking all dreamy. "What are you thinking about?"

"Just that it's nice to see my friend happy and smiling again after the rough few weeks you've had." Jodie smiles.

"Yeah, I'm so happy Jode."

"You deserve to be," she smiles "right we ought to think about something for dinner."

"Let's go to the pub and have dinner out, my treat" I suggest.

"Really?"

"Yes, why not, I feel like taking my best friend out to say thank you for always being there for me."

"Okay," she grins. "give me 10 minutes."

After getting ready we lock the door of the flat and set off walking to the pub which I pass on my way to work that serves great food.

Walking through the doors of the traditional pub with beams and wooden tables dotted about the place we order two glasses of wine at the bar and choose to sit at a table by the window. The pub is not overly busy for a Tuesday night and as we sit and drink our wine we peruse the menu to decide what to eat. I'm trying to decide what to have when I suddenly remember I haven't thanked Evan for the flowers, so I send him a quick text.

Hi my gorgeous boyfriend thanks for the beautiful flowers, they are a lovely surprise. I'm currently sat in a pub with Jodie we decided to have dinner out for a change. Will call you later when I get home K xx

After pressing send I look at the menu again and choose to order steak and chips, Jodie opts for the same, I go to the bar and place the order. While we are waiting for the food to arrive Evan sends me a reply.

Hi beautiful you are very welcome, I thought they might cheer you up after being upset last night. It must be the night for it because I am just heading out the door to meet Curtis for a few beers. Don't get too drunk and I'll speak to you later then E xx

Evan's text makes me smile.

"Evan's gone out tonight too he's meeting Curtis for a few beers."

"Oh, I like Curtis, he's lovely."

"Yes, he is."

"So, I've been meaning to ask you Kar have you thought any more about your job and what career you want to do?"

"Not really I think I'll still be working in Walt's Coffee Shop in another 10 years' time."

"No, you won't you'll be helping Evan run his empire of hotels."

"Ooh there's a thought maybe I could ask Evan for a job at his new hotel."

"Yes, you ought to have a word with him."

"Hmm...maybe I will."

The food arrives and we sit and eat our meals chatting about everything from work to where we can go on holiday with Evan and Matt.

"I'd love to go on a cruise" Jodie says, "I've always fancied holidaying on one of those big ships you know like Jane McDonald advertises on the telly, err what's her show called again?"

"Cruising with Jane McDonald."

"Yeah, that's it." Jodie laughs "I guess I should have known that."

"We are not going on a cruise Jodie."

"I know but I can dream can't I."

"Why don't we go to Paris, it could be so romantic?"

"Yeah, that's a good idea, it's not too far and we could visit all the tourist spots I've always fancied going to see the Eiffel Tower."

"So, have I shall I suggest it to Evan then?"

"Yes, do it" she smiles.

"It will only be a weekend thing though."

"Oh, that's great, I've got school anyway, I'm so excited I can't wait" Jodie says grinning and finishing off her glass of wine.

"Oh my god..." 'It can't be.'

"What?"

"Is that? Oh god it is." I recognise someone in the corner of the pub and quickly hide behind my hand trying not to be noticed making Jodie laugh.

"Who is it?" Jodie asks looking around.

"Over there in the corner," I whisper, "It's Greg from the newsagents and it looks like he's on a date."

"Really where?" Jodie says straining her neck to try and spot him. "Oh yes I see him, so he is."

"Have you seen who he's with?"

"Oh god is that Windy Wendy from school?" Jodie laughs.

"The one and only."

"Oh god I've not seen her in years, she hasn't changed at all has she, can you remember she was always farting in class and sometimes it was really loud, and everyone knew it was her, but she always denied it."

"Yes, I used to have to sit next to her sometimes and it was hard I can tell you; I wonder what her parents used to feed her?" I giggle.

"I don't know but they seem quite into each other don't they."

"Yes, it seems so."

"Shall we go over and say hello?" Jodie suggests laughing.

"No definitely not."

"I don't think he will be bothering you anymore," Jodie smiles "Look."

"Ugh are they going to kiss, oh no, of all the places and they had to be in this pub, are you ready to go Jode?"

"Yeah, come on" Jodie laughs. "Who would have thought eh... Windy Wendy and Greg."

"I know" I giggle.

After a chilly walk back, we are pleased to arrive home. I put the kettle on for a hot drink to warm us up deciding a nice mug of hot chocolate will do just the job.

"I'm just going to give Evan a call while the kettle's boiling, I'll make the drinks when I come back Jode."

"Okay" Jodie smiles filling two mugs with hot chocolate powder in readiness.

I go to my bedroom for some privacy and call his number, he picks up instantly.

"Hi sexy did you have a nice meal?" 'He sounds happy.'

"Yes, it was lovely, where are you it sounds noisy?"

"I'm in a pub in Chelsea it's really busy I can hardly hear you hang on."

I can hear Evan moving to a quieter spot away from all the noise. "Can you hear me now?" he asks.

"Yes, that's better."

"Sorry about that" Evan says sounding slightly tipsy.

"Sounds like you're having a good night, are we feeling a bit tipsy Mr H?"

"Yes, how can you tell?" he laughs.

I can picture him grinning down the phone at the other end of the line.

"Where's Curtis?"

"Oh, he's stood at the bar chatting up some woman."

"Oh really, as long as her mate doesn't think she has a chance with you" I say feeling jealous that girls will be looking at him and trying it on because why wouldn't they because he is so gorgeous.

"I'm taken so they can try all they like but they won't succeed because I'm in love with this hot girl I met in a coffee shop, she's the sweetest, kindest, sexiest woman I've ever met and she's amazing in bed."

"She sounds really nice."

"Oh, she's more than nice I wish my girlfriend were here now because there are so many things that I want to do to her. Did I mention she's got fantastic tits and she's great in bed?"

"Evan," I giggle "I hope no-one can hear you."

"I don't care if they can I want the world to know."

"What that I've got fantastic tits and I'm good in bed" I laugh.

"No, that I have a girlfriend who I love very much. Oh, here's big lad coming over with the girl now."

"Okay I'd better let you go then."

"No Kara, don't ever let me go."

"Don't worry I'm not now I've got you back."

"Hey big lad Kara's on the phone, here say hello." Evan passes Curtis the phone. 'God he really is tipsy.'

"Hi Kara, how are you?" Curtis says sounding merry.

"I'm good thanks it sounds like you are having a good night."

"Yes, we are, I think Evan's had a few to many."

I laugh. "Yes, I think he has by the sounds of him."

"I'll pass you back, see you soon."

"Bye Curtis." I hear Curtis pass the phone back to Evan and then he is back on the phone.

"Hi baby I'm really sorry but I've got to go now because we are moving on apparently, I'll call you tomorrow beautiful."

"Okay babe, I love you."

"Love you too, miss you, bye..." Evan sends kisses down the phone making me laugh. I've never heard Evan drunk before; he is quite entertaining.

Walking back to the kitchen I make two mugs of hot chocolate then carry them into the lounge. Jodie is sat on the sofa talking to Matt on the phone.

"I've got to go now my hot chocolate is here, I'll see you tomorrow. Love you" Jodie says.

"Bye Matt, love you" I call joking around in the background and hear him shout love you back down the phone making us laugh. Jodie ends the call. "Is Evan alright?"

"Yes, he's in a bar in Chelsea, he sounded drunk."

"Is he and on a work night too."

"I know, Curtis was chatting up some woman, I just hope this woman's friend doesn't come on to Evan, especially him being drunk I don't want anyone trying to steal him away from me."

"Don't worry, Evan won't be doing anything to jeopardise your relationship this time, so stop panicking."

I wish I could stop this jealous feeling that keeps creeping into my mind, but I worry that being with Evan and feeling this happy is just all too good to be true. I know I must trust him but it's everyone else I don't trust and especially with Julia sniffing around it doesn't make me feel any better.

Thirteen

After a good night's sleep, I wake up feeling concerned as to whether Evan made it home last night so the first thing I do is to turn my phone on hoping there is a message from him but there's nothing, so I decide to send him a quick text before my shower.

Hi my gorgeous boyfriend, just checking you are okay and not too hung over this morning, what time did you get home last night? K xx

Leaving my phone on the bedside table I gather up my clothes to wear for work and after waiting for a reply and nothing comes instantly I go and take a shower.

Feeling refreshed dressed in a pair of black three-quarter cropped jeans and a tie front red spot top I check my phone to see if Evan has sent a reply but still nothing. 'That's strange?'

Feeling confused about what to do next because I don't want to come across as an overprotective, jealous girlfriend I go to find Jodie to ask her advice.

“Morning Jode.” I walk into the kitchen to find Jodie eating a bowl of cereal.

“Morning Kar, sleep well.”

“Not bad, did you?” I get some cereal then join Jodie sat at the table to eat it.

“I slept great thanks, have you heard from Evan since last night?”

“No and I’m worried, it’s not like him. I’ve just sent him a text, but he hasn’t replied.”

“I’m sure everything is fine Kara, sometimes Matt doesn’t always contact me straight away when he has been for a night out with his mates, maybe Evan overslept, or his phone has run out of charge.”

“Yeah maybe.”

Eating my breakfast all I can think is the worst, I had a bad feeling when I woke up this morning and something doesn’t feel right.

I finish getting ready for work and I am just making a sandwich for my lunch when a text notification sounds on my phone. ‘Oh god I hope it’s him.’

Feeling excited that Evan has finally sent me a text I open the inbox but it’s not from Evan it’s from Sebastian. There is a text with an attachment.

Seems like Evan isn’t the good twin after all, oh dear, I’m sure he was only catching up with Julia for old time’s sake and it doesn’t mean anything but then again I never kiss my friends like that.

'Oh my god, no, what have you done?'

I feel sick as I open the attachment accompanying the text and tears fill my eyes as I stare at a photo of Evan kissing some woman, her arms are draped around his neck and it's definitely him because I recognise the shirt he is wearing.

'Oh my god' Tears roll down my cheeks "No." I cry out and Jodie hears my sobs and comes running from her bedroom into the kitchen.

"Hey what's the matter?" Jodie asks.

"Don't worry you said, look." I pass my phone to Jodie to show her the photo and a look of horror appears on her face."

"Shit Kara, what the hell."

"I know." I sit down at the kitchen table and put my head in my hands and cry.

"I can't believe it" Jodie says sounding angry pacing the floor looking mad.

"Why me Jode, why do I always get shit on by men, I may as well have a sign on my head saying 'Mug'?"

"I don't know what to say Kar I never thought he would do that especially after being so sorry for hurting you before."

"Neither did I what am I going to do?" I sob.

"You need to have it out with him."

"I don't want to talk to him Jode."

A text sounds on my phone and we both look at each other. I open my phone and this time it is a message from Evan.

Morning gorgeous, sorry about last night being a bit drunk on the phone, I'm heading over to the Manor today. I've got a busy day planned so will call and see you after work if that's ok? E xx

I debate what to put then type a reply.

Okay I need to talk to you anyway. K

Evan replies instantly.

Is everything alright? E x

'No, everything is not alright.'

Fine, I'll see you later. K

I dry my eyes and finish making my lunch. "Are you going to be alright?" Jodie asks concerned.
"Yeah, I'll be fine."

Arriving at work I walk through the door of the coffee shop to see Sally stood at the counter grinning from ear to ear. Seeing Sally so excited about her baby news makes me so happy. Yes I've got problems with Evan but for now Sally is all I care about and I will deal with the problem of Evan and that woman later.

"Morning Sal" I smile putting on my happy face.

"Morning love."

"So how did Tim take the baby news I can't wait to hear all about it?" I grin.

"Oh, Kara it was so emotional. Put your bag away and then I'll tell you."

I go into the office and return moments later then Sally tells me how surprised Tim was after dinner when he saw the pregnancy test inside the cake box.

"I think it took him a few seconds to realise what he was actually looking at. He then looked at my teary face and said, 'You're pregnant' and then I sobbed, and he held me and cried too."

"Oh god Sally." I wipe the tears from my eyes.

"I know." We give each other a hug.

"So, what happens now?" I ask.

"I've got to ring my doctors to make an appointment to see a midwife."

"Aww you're going to have a little bubba and I can't wait. I can't tell you how happy I am for you both."

After putting on a brave face earlier my emotions get the better of me and I can't help bursting into tears.

"You daft thing come here" Sally says hugging me and rubbing my back.

"Sorry I'm so happy for you but I'm also emotional because something has happened."

"What?" Sally asks letting go of me and passing me a napkin to wipe my eyes with.

"I'll show you," I get my phone out of my pocket and Sally looks at me confused. "Evan's brother sent this to me this morning, Evan went out last night and well look." I show Sally the photo.

"Oh, are you sure it's him and not what's his name the twin brother?"

"It's him Sal."

"Oh god and who's Julia?"

"She's Evan's ex-girlfriend."

"Oh yes I don't know what to say?"

"Evan text me this morning acting like nothing's happened he's coming to mine later after work so I'm going to confront him about it then."

"There's always something isn't there, why can't life be straightforward. I hope it's just a misunderstanding."

"I hope so too. Just when I was feeling happy about everything this happens."

"I know it's not fair Kara you do seem to have your fair share of dramas don't you when it comes to men."

"Tell me about it."

After a hard day at work, I arrive home get freshened up and then have a quick chat with Jodie over a glass of wine, a bit of Dutch courage is just what I need before I confront Evan about the photo.

We are sat in the kitchen and my stomach is filled with nervous butterflies. Jodie is waiting for Matt to pick her up because they are going to his mum and dad's for dinner which I'm glad about because it means I have the place to myself and it will give us some privacy when I have the chat with Evan.

Matt arrives and Jodie wishes me luck then leaves. Two glasses of wine later Evan pulls up outside and I watch him through the window walking up the path to the front door. My heart skips a beat as it always does when I see him, his gorgeous features, his fine physique, and those chocolate brown eyes of his that glance my way catching me looking at him through the window.

He gives me one of his knockout smiles, but I don't smile back, and he frowns. I feel sick with nerves because I know as soon as I open the front door and we have discussed the photo then it could be over for us all over again.

I open the door and he smiles instantly taking me into his arms for a kiss. "Hi beautiful god I've missed you" he says pulling me to him, but I turn my head and push him away.

"Hey what's wrong, why are you being like that?"

I laugh sarcastically. "You really don't know?" I give him a dirty look. Evan shuts the front door and follows me into the kitchen. I lean against the worktop and Evan sits down at the table looking at me confused.

"What's going on? Why are you treating me like I've done something wrong?"

"Have you done something wrong?" I scowl.

"What do you mean?"

"Have you got anything to tell me about last night?" I ask folding my arms defensively.

"Last night?" Evan replies trying to think. "I went out with Curtis for a few drinks as you know and then went home why?"

"Did you see Julia by any chance?"

"Oh Julia, yes I did briefly how do you know about that?"

"Well, your dear brother decided to inform me this morning with a text and a photo of the two of you kissing."

"Kissing? What? I didn't kiss her well not the way you think I did and how the hell did Sebastian know?"

"I don't know but he had the pleasure of telling me. Here look." I show him the photo and the text message on my phone.

"Kara listen, I know this looks dodgy, but it really isn't what it looks like."

"You were kissing her Evan how else can it look?" I swallow the lump in my throat as tears spring in my eyes.

"No baby we didn't I promise you, please don't get upset let me explain" Evan gets up from the table and walks over to me.

"No stay where you are," I hold my hands up to stop him in his tracks and he frowns and sits down again.

"Okay explain to me why I get a photo of my boyfriend kissing his ex-girlfriend" I snap.

"Look obviously Sebastian is playing his games again, he must have been in the pub at the same time and saw me with Julia. She was out with her friend Jackie and she was drunk, we spoke briefly. She told me she missed me and wanted me back and I told her I was with you and I was not interested, I also told her to stop bothering me and phoning me. I thought about what you said, and I know I thought she would be useful finding out what Sebastian is up to but then I thought I don't care what's he's up to it's you I care about and if speaking to her is upsetting you then I will put a stop to it."

"So why does it look like you were snogging her face off then?"

"Like I said she was drunk stumbling about and then the next thing I know her arms were around my neck and she was holding me trying to kiss me. Sebastian must have taken a photo of us."

"It doesn't look like you were trying to fight her off."

"Look it all happened so quickly and I did fight her off I can assure you, just ask Curtis, in fact I'll ring him now he'll tell you."

Evan takes out his mobile from his pocket and calls Curtis, when he answers he explains the situation to him about the text and the photo then hands the phone to me.

After Curtis has confirmed Evan's version of events I pass the phone back to Evan and he ends the call.

Evan gets up from the table and comes over to me. "Baby I promise you nothing happened, you have to believe me I wouldn't do that to you, can't you see it's Sebastian trying to come between us again." He looks into my teary eyes with a pleading look.

"I just saw the photo and…"

"I know" he says cupping my face with his hand as I look at him.

Evan pulls me into his arms and before I can say anymore he brings his lips to mine and kisses me, I bring my arms up around his neck and hold him closer.

"I'm sorry for jumping to conclusions I should have trusted you."

"It's alright but I would never do that to you or anyone for that matter, I've told you before how important fidelity is to me and how it felt when Julia had the affair so please know that it will never happen."

"I'm sorry."

"Hey, it's fine and thank you for being so understanding if it had been the other way around I would have reacted a lot worse than you I can tell you" he says with a serious look.

"I can't believe I thought…"

"Forget about it" Evan says cuddling me and reassuring me that everything is okay.

"Have you eaten?" I ask trying to lighten the mood.

"No, I haven't, I came straight here from the Manor."

"Do you fancy a takeaway because I've not eaten either, I wasn't hungry earlier."

"I fancy you and a takeaway" he grins.

I smile. "What do you like Chinese, Indian, Mexican?" I ask opening a kitchen drawer and pulling out a handful of menus.

"I don't mind I'll eat anything."

"I fancy Chinese if that's okay."

"Yes babe, that'll be great."

After perusing the Chinese menu, we decide to go for a set meal for two so I ring through the order and I'm told it will be delivered in 30 minutes.

"Would you like a beer while we're waiting?" I ask.

"I'll just have a soft drink please because I'll be driving home later."

"Oh, are you not staying tonight?"

"No sorry not tonight babe."

"Oh okay, would you like coke, lemonade, water…?"

"A coke would be great thanks."

I pour Evan a coke and a glass of wine for myself because I'm in need of another glass after the stressful conversation we have just had. All this stress recently is seriously turning me into an alcoholic. We sit in the lounge on the sofa to wait for the Chinese.

“So how was your day?” I ask sitting next to him looking into chocolate brown eyes full of desire.

“It was busy but good” he says bringing his hand up to my face and caressing it with soft strokes of his fingers.

“What did you...?”

“Shush” he says putting a finger over my mouth to stop me from talking and moving towards me for a kiss.

Evan kisses me and his hand caresses my breast over my t-shirt. “Evan…”

‘Why did I have to have my period right now?’

“Kara, I know you’ve got your period,” he says continuing what he is doing.

I enjoy the feel of his hands on me, a small moan escapes from my lips and my nipples harden from his touch. Evan moves me so I’m lying back on the sofa and manoeuvring his body over the top of mine I can feel the hard bulge in his trousers as he rubs it against me rubbing me up and down in just the right spot.

“Hmm I love kissing you, your lips are so soft” he says sucking my bottom lip gently before kissing me some more. I know Evan can’t do anything to me, but I can do something to him.

I fumble with the belt and zip on his trousers and pull his trousers down at the front enough so I can slide my hand into the waistband and inside his boxers to feel his erection hard and weeping with excitement. Evan moans as I rub his length up and down, “Hmm…” we are both getting lost in the moment as desire takes over us.

Wriggling out from beneath him I push him back onto the sofa and then lower my mouth eagerly onto his cock sucking and tasting him as he holds my head in his hands.

"Oh fuck, you're so good at that… I love it when you do that with your tongue" he moans as I circle the tip around and around before taking him deep into my mouth hitting the back of my throat.

I lick along his shaft and around the tip again before taking him fully into my mouth giving him pleasure.

"Aargh Jesus Kara you turn me on so much" he pants.

I devour him like he is a delicious treat as I guide my mouth expertly up and down his erection while cupping his balls. I stroke and lick and suck driving Evan to the brink of no return.

"Kara fuck baby… oh Jesus I'm so close…oh fuck…" he moans.

Bang…Bang…Bang.

I let him fall from my mouth and sit up startled. "Shit what was that?" We look at each other.

Evan laughs "That my love will be the Chinese."

"Oh yes," I giggle getting up off the sofa looking at Evan's erection pointing proudly towards the ceiling. I smile at him "Are you going to answer the door then?" I giggle.

"I don't think that's a good idea, do you babe?" he laughs grabbing hold of his cock. "He doesn't want to see my big chopstick."

Bang…Bang…Bang…

There is another loud knock, and it makes me jump. I quickly grab my purse from the kitchen and answer the door. I pay the man some money and take the food off him before he heads off down the path for his next delivery.

"Yum… it smells good" I call shutting the front door peering into the lounge to see Evan tucking himself away. I walk into the kitchen, put the Chinese bag of food on the table and Evan joins me.

"Well, that was close" he laughs cuddling me from behind while I stand at the table taking the silver dishes out of the bag and placing them on the table.

"Yes, he was earlier than expected I didn't get to finish what I started." I turn to look at him and smile.

"You nearly did a few minutes more and I would of have finished" he grins.

"Don't worry I'll make it up to you." I smile.

Evan lets go of me and I grab two plates from the cupboard and some knives and forks. I've tried using chopsticks numerous times before, but I can't seem to get the hang of it.

Evan opens the lids on the foil dishes while I fetch the drinks from the lounge, I top up our glasses and then we sit down at the table to eat.

"So how did you get on at the Manor today?" I ask before putting a forkful of chicken chow mein into my mouth.

"Really good it's coming on nicely, the extension is well under way and some of the existing rooms have been painted ready for the furniture to go in."

"Will you be interviewing soon for any staff?"

"Yes, Curtis is just going through the draft job descriptions at the moment and then we will be advertising around Christmas why?"

"Oh, I was just thinking if there would be any jobs I could do, I don't really want to work at Walt's Coffee Shop forever. Sally has always said to me when she has a baby she will leave because she wants to be a stay-at-home mum and it won't be the same without her so I wondered if there are any jobs I could do?"

"Hmm, I'm sure there is something you can do, you do have a lot of good skills, especially oral" he smiles. "What about being my personal assistant and I can fuck you over my desk everyday" he grins.

"Evan I'm being serious" I smile.

"So am I" he laughs.

I shake my head and roll my eyes smiling at him as I place another forkful of Chinese into my mouth.

"Okay let me have a think and I'll get back to you."

"Okay thanks I really appreciate it. Have you finished; do you want anymore?" I ask seeing his empty plate.

"Yes, I'm finished thanks, and I insist on paying for it."

"No, you are always treating me, so I want to treat you for a change."

"Well, if you fancy treating me you can finish what you started earlier" he says cheekily grinning at me.

I match his grin "I think I can manage that."

Fourteen

It's a cloudy Thursday morning and I wake up with a smile on my face feeling relieved that my relationship with Evan is back on track after Sebastian tried to sabotage it, yet again.

I get out of bed and take a quick shower before getting ready for work. I'm not seeing Evan until tomorrow tonight now because he has stuff to do so I have a free evening.

I arrive at work ready for another day of serving coffee and making sandwiches. Now that there is a chance I can work at Evan's new hotel working in a coffee shop is becoming more and more unappealing, and when it's time for Sally to leave and have the baby I want to have something in place, so I don't have to continue working here.

"Morning Sal." I walk into the office and Sally is sat at the desk doing some paperwork.

"Morning love, how's things I'm guessing you sorted everything out because you look happier today?" Sally knows I was having a chat with Evan last night about the text and photo.

"I'm pleased to say all is good, apparently Evan saw Julia drunk in some bar and she came onto him. He reckons Sebastian must have been in the pub at the same time and taken a photo of them and sent it to me to cause trouble. I feel bad now because Curtis backed up his story and I jumped to conclusions before I had even heard his side of the story."

"Don't worry I would have been the same, oh god excuse me." Sally gets up holding her hand over her mouth and runs towards the toilets.

"Are you okay Sal?" I call after her.

A few moments later Sally appears looking pale and sickly "No not really morning sickness, it's getting worse" she says rubbing circles on her tummy.

"Oh Sal, can I do anything?"

"Oh god I'm going to be sick again" she says rushing off to the toilets again.

I suddenly remember my mum telling me she used to eat lots of ginger biscuits when she was pregnant because it's good for morning sickness.

"Here have one of these apparently they do wonders for morning sickness" I smile handing the biscuits to Sally as she walks back in the office and slumps down in the office chair.

"Thanks Kara I'll try anything."

When 5 o'clock comes around we are both eager to shut up shop, Sally is ready for home so she can go to bed and rest and I'm excited about an evening of research for my future job whatever that maybe.

After having dinner with Jodie, I lock myself away in my room borrowing Jodie's laptop so I can find out some information on courses and possible hotel jobs that I could do.

After looking for a while my thoughts turn to holidays. I realise that I haven't mentioned to Evan about going to Paris, so I grab my phone and send him a text.

Hi babe hope you have had a good day. I've been thinking about our little holiday and I had a chat to Jodie and Matt and they are both up for it and thought we could go to Paris, what do you think?" K xxx

After a few minutes of waiting my phone beeps.

Hi gorgeous Paris sounds great; we just need to sort out when and I will book something. I keep thinking about the treat you gave me last night before I left, and I keep getting a hard on (laughing emoji). Have you finished your period yet, I need to have you ASAP? Evan xx

Mr H I'm pleased you enjoyed it, yes when I see you tomorrow night you can have me then and you had better be ready because I want you desperately too. K xxx

Oh god I'm hard now thinking about what I'm going to do to you. Wear some sexy underwear in fact don't wear any underwear E xx

Okay what time are you coming to mine, I will be ready? K xx

I've just had an idea, pack a bag, I'll pick you up and you come to mine for the weekend, you can see where I live and I'll take you out somewhere nice then bring you back on Sunday, how does that sound? Also you will be able to make as much noise as you like when I have you over and over again. E xxx

I read his text feeling excited because I haven't been to Evan's house before, I'm interested to see where he lives and what his house is like. Also, the fact that we will be able to have sex again and we can make as much noise as we like because we will be on our own sounds great. When Evan makes love to me or fucks me hard trying to keep quiet is a task in itself, he is just so good. A weekend of having lots of amazing sex with my amazing boyfriend, I can't bloody wait.

Sounds perfect, I would love to come, I'm feeling horny now just thinking about it, what time are you picking me up? K xx

Oh, you will be coming alright. About 6.00pm, you are not going to be able to walk by the time I've had my way with you this weekend. See you tomorrow, love you E xx

I can't wait, see you tomorrow, love you K xxx

At last, it's Friday and Evan will be arriving soon to pick me up and take me to his house for the weekend. I'm so excited, I can't wait to see him.

After soaking in a bath full of bubbles for a while I get out and put on a dress deciding not to wear any underwear remembering Evan's request in his text.

I'm sat at the table chatting to Jodie while I'm waiting for Evan to arrive.

"Have you told your mum and dad about Evan yet?" Jodie asks.

"Err no I haven't she doesn't even know he exists."

"Why not I would have thought you couldn't wait to tell them now you're in love and have a boyfriend."

"I know I need to tell them, oh god I haven't even told them I won't be popping to see them this weekend. I'm surprised my mum hasn't called me to find out what time I will be going. I'd better let her know."

"Tell her now" Jodie says excitedly.

I smile and call my mum and dad's phone number. After a few rings, my mum answers.

"Hi Mum it's me" I say happily.

"Hi love, how are you?"

"I'm good thanks Mum, I wasn't sure if you would be at one of your clubs tonight."

"No not tonight I couldn't be bothered."

"Oh, are you alright Mum?"

"Yes, I'm fine love, just didn't fancy shaking my booty tonight doing Zumba, I've been doing some gardening this week and so I think I deserve a night off."

"Oh right" I laugh imagining my mum doing a high energy aerobics routine.

"What time are you coming to see us tomorrow?"

"Well actually that's why I'm ringing, I can't come this weekend."

"Oh, why not, are you doing something with Jodie?"

"No not exactly."

"Oh, what are you doing then?" my mum asks sounding intrigued.

"Um I'm going to London for the weekend."

"Really who are you going there with, is it that girl Jess you went to stay with for the weekend?"

I hate that I lied to my mum when I went to Italy making her believe I was with an old school friend.

"No, it's not her it's another friend."

"Which friend?"

"You don't know them."

"Why does it sound like you are being cagey, is this so-called friend a boy by any chance?" she laughs.

"Err…yes, it is."

"Really," my mum squeals down the phone. "Who is it I need to know all the details?"

"Mum…" I laugh.

"So, what's he called then and how did you meet him?"

"His name is Evan, and he came into the coffee shop one day."

"Oh, is he local then?"

"No, he actually lives in London."

"Oh, I see, so you are going to London to see him."

"Yes."

"How long have you known him?"

"A little while."

"So..."

"So what?"

"So, is he your boyfriend Kara?" my mum asks excitedly.

"Yes, he is, but it's only been official since Monday."

"Oh, how exciting, so when are we going to meet this young man of yours?"

"I'm not sure it's early days Mum." I'm not sure how Evan would feel about meeting the parents so soon into our relationship.

"You're not embarrassed of us are you?"

"No Mum don't ever think that it's just..."

"Then what's the problem?" my mum says sounding disappointed.

"Nothing I'll ask him and arrange something okay."

"Great, why don't you both come around next Sunday, and I'll cook a roast."

"You don't have to do that just a coffee and cake would be fine."

"Nonsense you'll both come for dinner and then we can get to know him properly, oh how exciting it's ages since you had a boyfriend?"

"Okay great, look I've got to go but I'll ring you in the week to confirm okay."

"Okay love, ooh I can't wait until next Sunday now, hmm…what shall I cook he's not a vegetarian is he?"

"No Mum he isn't a vegetarian and anything will be fine."

"Oh good, chicken or beef or shall I do my speciality fish pie?"

"I'll speak to you soon then Mum" I laugh hearing my mum getting carried away with excitement.

"Oh yes sorry I'll speak to you soon love and Kara make sure you're careful if you know what I mean."

'Oh god how embarrassing.'

"Yes Mum, bye Mum."

"Bye love."

I end the call and laugh. "Well, that went well mum has invited us both for Sunday lunch next weekend."

"Great, you can't keep him a secret forever Kara."

"I know you're right oh and mum told me to be careful if we you know."

Jodie laughs. "Bless her I bet she's so excited to meet your boyfriend."

I sigh. "Yes, I think she is, but I'm scared to ask Evan if he wants to meet my parents, the man who didn't do relationships, I'm scared he will freak out."

"I'm sure he'll be fine, but you won't know unless you ask him."

"So, you think I should ask him and not make an excuse to my mum like he can't make it?"

"Ask him, and here he is now" Jodie says hearing a car pull up outside and I stand up and join her looking out the kitchen window.

We watch him get out of the car and walk up the path to the front door. I am such a lucky girl to have such a gorgeous, charismatic boyfriend, how on earth did I get this lucky? I rush to open the door and greet him with a lovely smile "Hi."

"Hi yourself," he grins "are you ready to go, have you got everything you need for the weekend?"

"I have now you're here," I smile. "I'll just get my stuff."

"Hey, let me get that" Evan says picking up my weekender case from the hallway floor while I grab my phone and bag.

"Have a good weekend both of you" Jodie says walking into the hallway to say goodbye.

"Thanks, we will" we smile.

We walk out the door towards Evan's car.

"Have you eaten?" Evan asks putting my case in the boot.

"No, I didn't have time."

"Great well I haven't either so I thought we could stop off somewhere on the way before I take you home and ravish you" he says with a cheeky smile as we both get into the car.

"Okay" I smile.

"Are you wearing any underwear?" he grins rubbing his hand up and down my leg.

"No because my boyfriend told me not to."

Evan sucks in a breath then a big smile appears on his face.

Arriving in London Evan parks the car in a small car park at the back of an Italian restaurant. He gets out and opens the car door for me making me smile.

'He is such a gentleman.'

I take hold of his hand feeling excited and hungry.

"This looks a nice place."

Evan leads me to the front of the small restaurant and opens the door for me to walk inside.

"It is, I've been here a few times, the food is great" he smiles.

'I wonder who he's been here with?'

A waiter shows us to a table for two by the window and asks us what we would like to drink.

"I'll just have a coke please" I smile, and Evan orders the same.

"So, are you excited about staying at mine for the weekend?"

"Yes, I'm looking forward to seeing where you live. Will your housekeeper be there?" I ask remembering

Evan has a housekeeper who does his washing, cleaning, and shopping.

"No, she's never there at weekends it's just us so you'll be fine walking around my house naked." he grins making me blush. "What would you like to eat?" he asks while we peruse the menu.

"Hmm…I'm going to have a Ham and pineapple pizza please."

"Sounds good, I'm going to have the Meat Feast."

"I'm so hungry" I smile looking at Evan who is staring at me.

"Hmm so am I, I could eat you right now especially knowing you are not wearing any underwear" Evan says licking his lips and looking at me suggestively.

I blush.

The waiter returns with our drinks and takes our food order and it's not long before it arrives. The food is delicious just like Evan said it would be and we chat happily eating and drinking only having eyes for one another.

We are in the middle of a conversation when a lady walks over to our table making us both look up. "Evan hi" she smiles.

"Julia… hello" Evan answers surprised looking awkward looking between us both.

'So, you're the ex who was trying to kiss my boyfriend because you want him back. I am not impressed.'

"I couldn't not come over and say hello. I'm just having some dinner with Jackie, she's over there." Evan looks over to where she is pointing and Jackie waves.

Evan nods at her looking uncomfortable.

"Anyway, aren't you going to introduce me to your friend?" Julia says with a smile.

"Julia this is Kara, Kara this is Julia."

Julia holds out her hand to shake mine.

"Hi" I say shaking her hand wanting to wipe the smug grin off her face.

Julia retracts her hand. "It's lovely to meet you, I'm Evan's girlfriend, sorry ex-girlfriend," she laughs. "How silly of me."

"Yes, how silly of you because I'm Evan's girlfriend now and you might want to remember that when you are trying to kiss him whilst drunk in some bar" I scowl.

"Oh, I take it you are talking about the other night," she smiles "well he wasn't fighting me off sweetheart."

"Julia don't lie" Evan warns.

"Well, you weren't" Julia grins.

"I've explained to Kara what happened so if that's all you came over for to cause trouble you can leave."

"Relax I'm only joking, stop being so serious Evan, you used to be so much more fun when you were with me."

'What a bitch, what on earth did he see in her?'

I give her a filthy look and just as I'm about to say something back Evan steps in. "That's enough Julia, I think it's time you went."

"Well actually I was wondering if we could have a quick word in private."

"I'm sorry but anything you have got to say you can say in front of Kara."

"Oh, it's okay Ev, I'll catch you another time then" she says placing her hand on his shoulder and rubbing her hand up and down. "I'll leave you two to enjoy the rest of your night." She gives Evan a sweet smile then glares at me before walking away.

As she walks off Evan looks at me apologetically. "I'm so sorry babe."

"So, she's the ex-girlfriend, charming isn't she" I say sarcastically.

"I'm sorry you had to endure that, of all the places in London and she had to choose to eat in this restaurant."

"God the nerve of that woman, I was this close to…"

"I know babe, don't let her upset you she just wanted to cause trouble between us, I don't think she enjoyed me telling her the other night that what we have is beyond anything I ever had with her and that I'm not interested."

"It seems like it fell on deaf ears though because I get the impression that she is going to keep trying to win you back until she succeeds."

"She will never succeed Kara just remember it's you I love and want to be with."

He places his hand over mine and holds my hand across the table trying to make me feel better.

"Have you been here with Julia before then?"

"Yes, I have, but a very long time ago, if I knew she would be here I would have chosen somewhere else trust me."

"It's okay you didn't know." I look down at my plate, I've lost my appetite now, I can't eat the last two pieces of pizza on my plate because Julia is here and I feel like she's watching us, I just want to leave.

"Are you okay?" Evan asks concerned.

"Yes, I'm fine." I try to sound unaffected, but I am clearly not fine. Evan's ex-girlfriend, the one he was going to ask to marry him and the one who tried to kiss him the other night is in this restaurant and I don't want to be here anymore, I feel uncomfortable.

"Have you finished your meal?" Evan asks.

"Yes, I'm full thanks."

"Are you ready to go?"

"Yes, but I just need to go to the toilet before we do."

"Okay babe you go, and I'll wait here and settle the bill then we can go back to mine and have some alone time."

"Sounds perfect" I smile getting up from the table.

After using the toilet I'm just washing my hands when Julia walks into the restroom.

'Oh my god, really, I can't get away from this woman.'

I look at her in the reflection of the mirror while I finish washing my hands in the sink.

"Hello again" Julia smiles walking over to me.

I give her a half smile and place my hands under the drier hoping Julia will go into one of the toilets and I won't have to speak to her, but she doesn't.

"I'm sorry if I made you feel uncomfortable before you know meeting the ex and Evan kissing me the other night."

"Evan didn't kiss you the other night."

"Okay well whatever, so you two are an item then, how long have you been together?"

"Yes, we are and a while not that it's any of your business" I exclaim.

"Oh, but it is my business when someone is standing in my way of what I want."

"I'm sorry." I turn to look at her.

"You heard me."

"Well Evan is not interested and frankly why would he be when you had an affair with his brother."

"Oh, he told you about that did he, well yes I made a mistake, but I can assure you Evan still loves me, he was going to ask me to marry him you know and when you have strong feelings for someone like that they don't just go away sweetheart."

"You're wrong, what you did, what you both did to him, he will never forgive you and you are deluded if you think you can win him back."

"We'll see, anyway I just wanted to warn you not to get too comfortable because you will only end up getting hurt when he comes running back to me."

"Goodbye Julia." I have heard enough of her shit and not wanting to hear anymore I walk out of the toilets feeling angry.

"Are you ready to go babe?" Evan smiles as I walk towards him.

"Yes, I'm more than ready" I smile as he gets up, takes hold of my hand and we walk out of the restaurant. As we get outside Evan stops and looks at me. "Are you alright, you seem agitated?"

"No, I'm not alright I've just had an encounter with your ex in the ladies toilets, she had some interesting things to say to me."

"What did she say this time?" Evan asks looking angry.

"Just that I shouldn't get too comfortable because she wants you back and that I will end up getting hurt when you go running back to her."

Evan laughs "That's a joke, I'm sorry she accosted you in the toilets I will be having words with Julia because I'm not having her upset you with the bullshit that comes out of her mouth. In fact, I'll go and speak to her now." Evan lets go of my hand and starts walking off back towards the restaurant.

"Evan wait," I catch up with him "please don't, let's just forget about her and enjoy our weekend" I smile cosying up to him. Evan smiles and puts his arm around me. "Okay." He gives me a kiss then we walk back to the car.

Arriving at Evan's three storey house I walk through the classic black front door of the London Terrace and I'm immediately drawn to the high ceilings and modern interior; pictures and prints adorn the walls.

Evan leaves my case on the parquet floored hallway and directs me towards the kitchen situated on the ground floor. "Would you like a drink?" he asks.

"I'd love one please, wow your home is gorgeous Evan I love your kitchen." I admire the high glossed white units with an island centre of the room.

"Thanks, I'll show you the rest later, glass of white wine I've got a bottle chilling in the fridge."

"Lovely, thank you." I look around and admire Evan's home, I can see a dining room leading off the kitchen with French doors leading to a private garden terrace.

"Here you go" he says passing me a glass of the cold liquid, I take a sip and it tastes divine.

"Have you lived here long?"

"About three years now." Evan smiles looking at me leaning against the island. "Would you like to sit and relax in the lounge for a while?"

"Lead the way Mr H" I smile.

I follow Evan to the first floor into a stylish lounge overlooking the front with its high ceilings, wooden parquet floor, large black leather sofas and ornate fireplace. There is a separate study area located off the lounge at the back of the house.

"Wow this is nice, I'm impressed" I smile taking a seat on one of the black leather sofas.

"Thanks, I'll put some music on" Evan says walking over to a music system. "What do you like to listen to?"

"Err I don't mind really; I love all types of music."

"Hmm…do you like Ed Sheeran?"

"I do" I laugh.

"Oh, why did you laugh, what's wrong with Ed?" Evan asks with a questioning look.

"Sorry it's just Sally has a thing for Ed Sheeran, she loves men with ginger hair, her husband Tim has bright ginger hair it just does something to her if you know what I mean."

"Oh, I see" Evan laughs.

He puts on a compilation of Ed Sheeran songs and then sits down next to me putting his arm around my shoulder.

"It's so good to have you here and be alone with you" he grins.

"I know, it's good to be here." I nestle into the crook of his arm while I drink my wine.

"I'm sorry about earlier bumping into Julia, honestly if I'd have known she was going to be there..."

"Hey, it's fine, I've forgotten about her now."

"So, what do you fancy doing tomorrow?" Evan asks.

"I don't mind?"

"Well...I thought we could do a tour around the city visiting the London Eye, Buckingham Palace how does that sound?"

"Oh, I'd love that, I haven't really done much sightseeing in London since I was little when my parents took me."

"Great, it's going to be a nice day tomorrow, so we'll make a day of it."

"Will we have to get up early?"

"Not particularly why?"

"Just that I was rather looking forward to a lie in with my boyfriend."

"Hmm I like the sound of that" Evan leans towards me for a kiss and just as our mouths touch Evan's mobile phone rings.

"Timing eh, I'll just see who it is in case it's important."

Evan looks at his phone and chooses to ignore it.

"Who is it?" I ask.

"No-one important, right, where were we?" he says taking my glass out of my hand and putting it onto a coffee table next to his.

He then sits down and takes me in his arms again sealing his mouth over mine. I will never get bored of kissing Evan, the feel of his soft lips, his tongue that dances with mine, the way he caresses my face in his hands when he kisses me, he really is the perfect man, my perfect man.

The kiss is slow to begin with but soon becomes more urgent we want each other desperately and with Evan knowing I'm not wearing any underwear his hands start to wander up my dress.

"Hmm…" a soft moan escapes from my lips as I am gently lowered down onto my back on the couch and just as Evan is about to lay down next to me the house phone rings interrupting us.

"Fuck what is it with these phones?" Evan says annoyed getting up to go and answer it.

Evan

'This better be urgent because if it's a bloody scam call, I won't be happy.'

"Hello" I answer sternly.

"Evan hi it's Julia sorry to bother you I tried your mobile and it went straight to answer phone so I thought I would see if you were at home."

"Julia" I sigh.

'For fuck's sake why can't she just leave me alone, didn't she get the memo, we were over a long time ago, I don't want to talk to you.'

"I was just ringing to apologise about earlier I hope it wasn't awkward introducing me to your friend."

"You mean my girlfriend?"

"Yes her, is everything okay you sound annoyed with me?"

"You could say that."

"Well, I apologise if I said the wrong thing, it was a shock seeing you with another woman I mean since we broke up I've never really seen you with anyone."

"Well, that's because you destroyed all my faith in women when you had an affair with my brother, well that is until I met Kara."

"I'm sorry Evan, how many times can I keep saying it I thought we had moved on from that now we are on speaking terms again."

"Yes, we are on speaking terms, but it will always be there Julia, what you did, what you both did. Anyway, I don't want to go over all that again, what do you want?"

"Did you enjoy your meal; I love that Italian restaurant it's one of my favourite places to eat after you took me there?"

"Yes, well that was a long time ago now..."

"Listen I hope sorry what was your friend's name again."

"Girlfriend and it's Kara."

I look at Kara because I know she knows who I'm speaking to and I know she won't be happy. Yes, I'm right she isn't happy she is scowling at me from the sofa.

'Well, this is awkward.... again.'

"I hope Kara didn't feel awkward I mean it must have been strange for her meeting the ex, the woman you were going to marry."

"Well actually I wanted to speak to you about that because I understand you said some interesting things to her in the ladies toilets and you were being quite bitchy."

"Really?" Julia says sounding shocked "You know me Evan I'm not a bitch."

"Well, whatever you said I don't want you upsetting Kara and I would appreciate it if you could stop phoning me all the time, I've moved on Julia and so should you."

"Is she there?"

"That's none of your business, I've got to go."

"She is there, well I'm sorry but just because your little tight assed girlfriend wants me to stop calling you, I'm not going to stop having a relationship with you because of her."

"Julia, we don't have a relationship anymore and don't ever speak of Kara in that way again do you hear me."

"I meant a relationship as friends; we've known each other a long time Evan and I know I have treated you badly in the past but I'm sorry. I'm trying to build bridges with you, and I want to show you how sorry I am. I'm not going to have your new girlfriend dictate if you can talk to me or not. We used to get on really well and I miss having you in my life."

"Look I've really got to go."

"Jackie bumped into Sebastian again the other night and he told her he was going to pay me another visit."

"Why?"

"I don't know, I'm scared Evan, when he's been drinking he can be quite volatile."

"Like I told you if he comes to see you again don't open the door and if you see him hanging around just call the police."

"Yes, but it's not that easy he can be so persistent when he wants and what are the police going to do, they are not interested Evan."

"Look I don't know what else to say to you." I look at Kara and she has a face of thunder.

'Thanks Julia, for ruining my night.'

"Okay well it's obviously not a good time so I'll let you go, it was nice seeing you and talking to you, I'll see you around sometime then."

"Goodbye Julia."

"Goodbye Evan."

Evan puts the phone down and walks over to me sat on the sofa, sits down, and looks at me.

"I'm sorry about that, what a great start to the weekend this is turning out to be isn't it?"

'You could say that.'

"She just keeps popping up doesn't she, first the restaurant, then she's constantly ringing you." I huff folding my arms defensively.

"I'm sorry if I knew it was her phoning I wouldn't have answered it." Evan runs his hands through his hair looking stressed.

"So, what did she want?"

"She wanted to apologise for the way she was acting in the restaurant earlier for making you feel awkward."

"Any excuse to phone you more like."

"She said she wasn't being bitchy when she spoke to you in the toilets."

"Oh my god seriously."

"Well, I don't know because I wasn't there but knowing Julia she isn't really a bitchy person."

"So, you're going to take her side, you don't believe me."

"I'm not taking anyone's side and yes of course I believe you I was merely saying she's not really a bitchy person that's all." He stands up and starts pacing the floor.

"Evan she was being a total bitch, she is obviously acting one way towards me and telling you a different version, I'm meant to be your girlfriend you should have my back not hers." 'I am so angry right now.'

"Hey," Evan says walking over to me and sitting down next to me again taking hold of my hand. "I do have your back I was just saying the Julia I know is not a bitchy person but then what do I know, I didn't even know she was having an affair with my brother for months, so it appears I don't really know her at all does it."

"She was warning me off you, she wants you back."

"And like I told you before I'm not interested."

He looks so sincere and I feel bad for getting annoyed at him.

"I'm sorry it's just she always seems to come between us Evan, we never argue but then she pops up and that's all we end up doing, I hate it, I don't want us to argue, I just wish she would leave us alone."

"So do I believe me, can we just forget about Julia and get back to enjoying our evening, I don't want her ruining our weekend."

"Okay" I sigh.

Evan takes me in his arms and the look on his face, those chocolate brown eyes staring into mine make me melt every time.

"Now where were we before we were rudely interrupted?"

He soon has me forgetting when his mouth touches mine, when he kisses me slowly and seductively.

'Hmm... Julia who?'

He puts his hand on my leg, but I stop him from going any further as I remember something else from the call.

"Wait one last thing. What did Julia say about Sebastian, I heard you say something about calling the police?"

"Oh, apparently Seb told Julia's friend that he will be paying her a visit again and she's scared."

"Oh, so she wants you to protect her does she?"

"No but if my brother is treating her or any woman badly I can't just sit back and let it happen he needs to be dealt with."

"Yes, I know, but..."

"Look can we please stop talking about them now because I can sense this is going to turn into another heated discussion and I just want to have a nice weekend with my girlfriend."

"Okay, okay I'm sorry."

I stroke the side of Evan's face as he looks at me.

"Now if you don't mind I would really like to take my girlfriend to bed and make love to her because knowing she is not wearing any underwear is turning me on big time."

"Where's your bedroom?" I smile standing up and holding my hand out for him to take.

"This way" he replies but instead of holding my hand he picks me up in his strong muscly arms making me giggle and carries me up the stairs to his master suite on the second floor.

I hold onto him tightly as Evan walks with me into the huge master bedroom with a king size bed centre of the room and he places me gently on the bed.

My heart is racing as I lay back and Evan climbs on top of me. He kisses me making me breathless from the passionate kiss, desire spreading throughout my body.

Moving down my body he lifts my dress seeing me naked from the waist down. "Gorgeous" he says as he lowers his face to between my legs.

I open my legs wide for him and he trails his wet tongue along the length of my folds stopping on my clit and circling it gently.

"Oh god..." I cry out arching my back from the sensation.

"Hmm... I've missed this" Evan says swirling his tongue around and around causing me to moan and cry out some more.

"Evan, I want you" I plead.

"You've got me, always" he smiles looking up at me before giving me more pleasure with his mouth.

"OHHHH...." I sit up slightly on my elbows and see the back of his head moving up and down as he gives me more tongue action turning me on to the extreme.

"Evan... oh god, watching you doing that to me is turning me on so much, oh...that's so good you're going to make me come." The intensity of the feelings in my groin are getting stronger and stronger as I lay back down on the bed.

"Hmm... you taste so good" he says pushing his tongue into my opening and circling it around before finding my clit again teasing and sucking it making me cry out.

"Evan…OOHHHH…. please I need you inside me."

The pressure is building and building, and I don't know how much more I can take before the inevitable happens.

"I want you to come, I want to feel you pulsate around my tongue while I lick you, I want to hear your cries when you orgasm."

"Oh shit…."

"That's it baby you're nearly there aren't you?"

"Ohhh god yes…yes…."

Evan gives me the ultimate pleasure licking, sucking, and sliding his wet tongue around and around repeatedly until I am ready to explode.

"OHHHHH YES…I'm coming, I'm coming." Evan continues with his tongue on my clit until I can't stand it anymore. I orgasm, the feeling is so intense, and Evan moves his tongue away and watches me have the most incredible orgasm. I moan loudly from the sensations it's giving me; it feels amazing. I can feel my heart thumping fast in my chest and the once the incredible feeling ends my eyes are glazed as I come down from such a rush.

Evan climbs up my body and kisses me, his erection pressing into my front as we enjoy a slow, lingering sensual kiss.

"I love you" Evan whispers smiling at me.

"I love you too." I wrap my arms around his neck and pull him closer to me as our lips find each other again.

Helping each other to undress we are soon naked and ready for more. Evan climbs on top of me and looks at me "Oh baby I have been looking forward to this all day." He kisses me softly and I feel his erection pushing against my front.

"I feel the same, all I can think about is you and how you make me feel." continuing our passionate kiss.

"I want to make love to you, nice and slowly," he says positioning his hard length at my entrance. "are you ready?"

"I'm all yours" I smile because I am, my heart, body and soul belongs to Evan now and for always.

He pushes his cock inside me we both draw breath because the strong physical connection we have is out of this world and every time he makes love to me it feels like the first time, magical, exhilarating and earth shattering as my body draws him in.

"You always feel so good," he moans slowly easing in and out of me.

I moan too still feeling sensitive from the orgasm I've just enjoyed.

Holding onto his muscly back I can't help thinking how far we have come, ever since Evan came back to me, he is more open with his feelings now instead of masking how he really feels. We are totally consumed by the love we have for each other and it's a love like no other and if things continue like this I truly believe that I will get my happy ending after all and my happy ending is Evan Hamilton.

"Oh Jesus, this is too good." Evan pants his urges becoming stronger as his slow pace now takes on a different form and he begins to fuck me with more force, the power of his drives driving us both insane.

"Yes baby, that's so good, give it to me." I claw at his back trying to hang on, his flesh becoming marked from my fingernails as I dig them into his back.

"Fuck…" The more I dig my nails in the wilder and more dominant he becomes.

"Yes, like that, oh god that's so good."

In and out, harder, faster, deeper and we are desperate to reach the end goal.

"Oh, shit Kara, are you nearly there?"

"Yes baby..." I pant.

Repeatedly he claims my body and with every stroke he brings us closer to our release.

"Fucking hell…, aargh fuck…"

"I'm coming" I cry.

"I'm with you baby, come for me."

A few more thrusts and "YEESSSSSS…... OHHHH……." I orgasm and Evan follows too.

"FUUUCCCKK….", his seed spills into me as he stills, his cock twitching inside of me. We are breathless and elated as our powerful orgasms takes us to a place of mind-blowing ecstasy.

"Wow," Evan laughs "Are you okay babe?" he grins looking at my satisfied face then rolling off me hot and breathless.

"I'm good" I grin.

"Yes, you are" he smiles as I nestle into him. He puts his arm around me and kisses the top of my head. I can hear his heart pounding as I lay my head on his chest.

"Every time we make love it feels like the first time, it's amazing, you're amazing." I smile.

I turn to look at his gorgeous face.

"I never knew it could be this way until I met you."

"I love that you're my girlfriend" he smiles.

"Me too and I love that you're my boyfriend." I smile laying my head on his chest again cuddling while we get our breaths back.

Speaking of Evan being my boyfriend I suddenly remember my phone call with my mother.

"Evan." I look at him with a serious face.

"Yes baby." Evan frowns obviously wondering what I'm going to say next and why I'm looking so serious.

"I need to tell you something and ask you something."

"Okay is everything alright, why do you look so serious?"

"Everything is fine it's just… I… I spoke to my mum to let her know that I wouldn't be able to see her and dad this weekend and she started quizzing me about what I was doing, where I was going and who with."

"Okay" he grins.

"Yeah, so I don't want you to freak out because I know we have only just made our relationship official, but she was probing me asking me lots of questions and I kind of mentioned you."

"Okay" Evan says still smiling at me.

"Why are you smiling at me like that?" I sit up to look at him properly.

"Because you're cute, go on."

"So, I kind of mentioned you and she really wants to meet you. She has invited us for Sunday lunch next weekend. I understand if it's too soon and I don't want to scare you off by introducing you to my parents so if you want to say no that's cool. I'll just come up with an excuse or something..."

"Kara." Evan says interrupting me.

"Yes, sorry was I rambling?"

"You were," he laughs. I blush. "I would love to meet your family. I'm in this for the long term so please tell your mum I would love to come for dinner."

"Really?" I can't help the big smile that appears on my face.

"Yes really."

"Oh, thank you" I squeal launching myself at him kissing him making him laugh.

"Will it be sausage and mash?" he asks.

"What, oh like I had when I went for dinner that time, no I think my mum wants to cook you her speciality roast."

"Oh, I'm honoured" he grins.

"I apologise now, I haven't really taken a boy home to meet my parents since my ex whom I dated when I was 18 so my mum is rather excited about meeting you and getting to know all about you."

Evan laughs. "Well, I feel even more honoured and like I told you once before I would like to shake your mum and dad's hand for creating such a beautiful person who I am totally in love with," Evan rolls me onto my back and lays on top of me. "and who I can't get enough of, fancy another orgasm?" he smiles making me giggle.

'Oh my god yes please.'

"Bring it on" and without hesitation Evan takes me again.

Fifteen

"Good morning sleepyhead" Evan smiles carrying a tray with two mugs of tea and some toast into the bedroom.

"Good morning" I yawn stretching and sitting up leaning against the headboard giving Evan an eyeful of my breasts.

"Hmm what a beautiful view" he says grinning at me as I realise what he is referring to blushing and covering myself with the bed sheet. "You look so cute when you blush" he says putting the tray down on the bedside drawers and sitting on the bed at the side of me and giving me a kiss.

"What time is it?" I ask yawning again.

"It's 9.30am."

"Is it really, I slept like a log, what time did you wake up I didn't hear you get up?"

"I got up at 7.00am you were fast asleep, and I didn't want to disturb you."

"Oh, you could have woken me up."

"No, it's fine, after all the sex we had last night I'm not surprised you were tired. I'd had enough sleep, so I got up and I've been checking my emails and doing a bit of work."

"It was a good night wasn't it" I smile.

"The best, I've made you breakfast in bed." Evan says obviously pleased with himself from the look on his face looking at the breakfast tray.

'A girl could get used to this.'

"Thanks, that's so sweet of you."

"Well, you deserve to be spoilt and I like looking after you" Evan smiles blushing slightly.

"Are you blushing Mr H?"

"No, I don't blush."

"I think you are" I giggle looking at him with my head cocked to one side.

"Oh, you think so do you eh?" Evan laughs climbing onto the bed and straddling my legs.

"Well, it looked like a blush to me."

"Well, I can assure you that I do not blush" he says digging his fingers into my side tickling me.

"Aargh no, stop no you didn't blush, aargh..." I squeal as Evan carries on tickling me making me laugh. "Evan please stop seriously I need you to stop." I look serious at him.

Evan stops and climbs off me looking concerned "Sorry babe did I hurt you?" he asks worried he was being too rough.

'Well, that worked in getting him off me.'

Before he knows what's happening I push him down onto the bed and straddle him then start tickling him to get him back.

"You little tease I thought I'd hurt you" he laughs, my attempts at trying to tickle him clearly not having any effect on him whatsoever like it does me.

Evan smiles looking at my naked breasts that are dangling in front of him as I lean over him trying to get a reaction.

"Nice breasts" he smirks looking at them then to my face.

"Oh" I giggle.

"Carry on I was enjoying looking at my fun bags jiggling in front of my face."

"Fun bags?" I laugh.

"Yes, my fun bags" he says placing his hands on them and massaging them.

"Well, I've never heard them called that before."

"Really well now you are wide awake I'd like to have some fun with my fun bags if you don't mind."

"Knock yourself out" I smile removing his hands from my breasts and pushing them into his face.

"You could quite easily knock me out with these beauties" Evan laughs nuzzling his face into them.

"Hmm…" Evan takes one of my nipples into his mouth and nibbles it gently.

"You can play with my fun bags anytime" I moan as he moves from one nipple to the other sucking and teasing me with his tongue.

After a few moments he lets go.

'What no I was enjoying that.'

"Okay that's all you're getting for now because breakfast is getting cold" he grins knowing I'm turned on and seeing the disappointment on my face.

"Evan that is so unfair you've got me all hot and bothered now and I want you" I huff as he gently pushes me off him and stands up to look at me with his gorgeous brown eyes.

"And I want you as you can see," he says referring to his erection that is clear to see "and as much as I would love to have you we need to have our breakfast and get showered because I really want to take you out today around London, I'm looking forward to it" he smiles.

"So am I" I smile.

Evan passes me a plate of toast and a cup of tea. He takes a bite of his toast and chews it for a while then takes a sip of tea to wash it down with. "Yuck that's disgusting."

"It's fine it's just a bit cold that's all."

"Leave it, let's get ready and then we'll have breakfast out somewhere."

"Okay sounds good."

After getting showered and dressed we catch a tube into the heart of London and find a nice little bistro to enjoy a Full English cooked breakfast before heading off to the London Eye, the first tourist spot on our list of things to do.

"Wow, it's massive!" I exclaim looking at the London Eye in all its glory.

"Why thank you it is pretty impressive isn't it" Evan smiles looking down at his crotch smirking. I hit him playfully on the arm "I wasn't referring to your dick, although I agree it is pretty impressive" I smile. "The London Eye it's huge."

"Come on beautiful we're getting on it" Evan says grabbing hold of my hand and leading me to an area for priority boarding.

"Really, I've always wanted to do this" I say excitedly following him.

Unbeknown to me Evan has secretly booked Cupid's Capsule, a private capsule for two guests which includes a bottle of Champagne and a luxury box of Champagne Truffles with a 30-minute rotation included, the ideal way to view London.

"Oh, wow Evan, this is simply breath-taking." I snuggle into his side as we take in the impressive London skyline.

"I thought you'd enjoy it, it's a first for me too" Evan replies enjoying it just as much as I am.

"Something else we have in common then." I smile.

"Yes, I've never really done the tourist thing in London much because I've always been busy working or doing other things but since meeting you I want to spend more time doing things to enjoy together."

"I like the sound of that" I smile.

After 30 minutes of sightseeing from a bird's eye view, we leave the London Eye feeling elated and head off to the next attraction we want to visit Big Ben and the Houses of Parliament en route to Buckingham Palace.

"I'm having a great time," I say giving Evan a kiss as a thank you as we walk hand in hand in the sunshine close to Big Ben "Thanks for taking me out today."

"You're welcome and I'm having a great time too."

"So how big is Big Ben then?"

"No idea but it's a lot bigger than Big Evan."

"Big Evan?" I frown looking confused.

"Yes, Big Evan" he laughs taking one of my hands and placing it on his crotch.

"Oh god what are you like, you're terrible," I laugh letting go. "Come on you idiot, take me to Buckingham Palace, you never know we might see the Queen."

I love Evan's mood today he seems so jovial and carefree and it's so nice spending time together just the two of us.

Arriving at Buckingham Palace I'm excited to see the Queen's official London residence. I take lots of photos on my mobile and some selfies of the two of us posing outside the Palace.

After spending some time looking around we begin to feel hungry again because it is way past lunchtime, we are also tired after all the walking we have been doing so Evan hails a cab and decides to take me for a bite to eat at Hamilton Tower, his hotel in Knightsbridge.

It's late afternoon when we walk through the hotel doors into the reception area and everything looks different from the last time I came here before our weekend away to Italy. Looking around the place it looks even more impressive in the daylight.

"Wow Evan your hotel really is stunning, you really do have great taste." I'm in awe of the place.

"I know" he smiles looking lovingly at me.

"Mr Hamilton, good day sir" the lady on the reception desk greets him as he walks over to her.

"Hi Felicity, is Curtis in today?"

"Yes sir, he is, would you like me to call him for you?"

"No, its okay, we'll go down to his office thanks Felicity."

"No problem sir."

"Come on we'll go and say hi to the big guy before we have dinner" Evan says taking hold of my hand and leading me down a corridor to a private area for staff.

Knocking on the door Evan waits for Curtis to say 'Come in' before we enter.

"Hey, my man," Curtis laughs "You daft sod knocking on the door that you own along with this hotel" he grins.

Evan walks over to him and they have a quick man hug consisting of back slapping.

"Kara" Curtis eyes light up when he sees me, and he gives me a kiss on both cheeks.

"Oi hands off" Evan laughs and Curtis winks at me and kisses me again.

"It's good to see you both I haven't seen you Kara since you were having a sneaky look around the Manor" he winks.

"Yes, and I told you not to tell him" I laugh.

"Well, it's a good job I did after hearing what happened with Ev's brother."

"I know I feel so thankful now I was being nosy that day and you turned up or who knows what could have happened."

I look at Evan, his face showing anger as he looks lost in thought. "Hey." I touch his arm snapping him out of his thoughts.

"Sorry it's just whenever I think about it and what he might have done to you I..."

"I know and he didn't okay..."

Evan pulls me closer to him and kisses the side of my head.

"So, what are we going to do about him then Ev have you decided?" Curtis asks leaning against his desk annoyed at the situation and wanting to help his best mate.

"I don't know I keep thinking about it all the time and coming up with beating him to a pulp so he never comes near me or Kara again but then I don't really fancy a prison sentence because it would take me away from this one," looking at me "or paying him the money which I really don't want to do because to be honest I don't think that would be the end of it, he would just keep coming back for more when he's lost it all."

"Evan violence isn't the answer" I state feeling concerned he will do something stupid and I will lose him again.

"I know babe I'm sorry for saying that he just makes me so mad that he is intent on ruining my life all the time and sometimes I can't help feeling that way."

"How about we just pay him a visit, give him a warning" Curtis suggests.

"We've done that before remember and he just laughed in our faces."

"You could just pay him the money, maybe he won't come back for more, maybe he will put it to good use and not waste it now he is older" I shrug.

"Yes, you're right, he is older, but I still think whatever I give him will never be enough."

"So, what do we do about him then because you can't carry on as you are?" Curtis says.

"I've thought about this long and hard and I think we should do nothing."

"Nothing but Ev he needs sorting" Curtis says not liking the sound of that idea.

"Curtis if he knows he is getting to me it will encourage him even more so I think we just carry on as normal and eventually when he realises he is not getting a reaction or anything from me he will give up, in the meantime though we need to be on our guard in case he tries something."

"I seriously think we need to visit him again," Curtis says looking frustrated. "What if he tries to go after Kara again?"

"He won't and Kara knows who he is now so she's aware and won't mistake us again. Anyway, I haven't come here to talk about him I promised my gorgeous girlfriend lunch, so we'll leave you to it."

Curtis sighs. "Okay dude but know I'm here if you need me man."

"I know mate, I appreciate it thanks" Evan says shaking his hand.

"Good to see you both" Curtis says kissing me on both cheeks and shaking Evan's hand.

We both say goodbye and Evan takes hold of my hand and we walk over to the door of the office and then Evan stops remembering something. "Oh, how did your date go with Stephanie last night?"

"It was good mate I'm seeing her again tonight as it happens."

"Great, did you get any action?" Evan asks looking at me smiling and I roll my eyes and laugh. It's quite funny listening to the two of them talking laddish to each other.

"Oh, you know they can't resist the Curtis charm."

"That means no then" Evan smirks.

Curtis laughs "Maybe it's my lucky night tonight I haven't had a good shag in months, sorry Kara" Curtis smiles.

I laugh. "It's okay."

"Well, have a good one!" Evan says opening the door for me.

"Oh, it will be more than once if I have my way" Curtis laughs.

"Bye mate and don't work for long, it's Saturday get off home and tart yourself up for your date tonight" Evan calls ushering me through the door.

"Will do, laters." Curtis calls.

Evan shows me to the private dining room where we ate last time we were here because it's more private than eating with the hotel guests. After Tony has looked after us once again, supplying us with drinks and delicious food we say goodbye and head back out the front of the hotel.

"So, what do you fancy doing now?" Evan asks.

"I fancy a nice walk after that big meal."

"Come on then we'll have a stroll through Hyde Park."

Walking through the park on a glorious sunny evening, we are joined by the many joggers, walkers and cyclists enjoying the open air. We walk past the Princess Diana Memorial Fountain. "I loved Princess Diana, it's such a shame she was taken so young" I say feeling nostalgic.

"I know she was such a good person doing so much good in the world and then there are people like my brother who cause nothing but misery."

"You wouldn't want anything to happen to him though would you? I know he's caused you a lot of upset but at the end of the day he is still your brother, he's your family?"

"I know of course not, I just wish he would realise he needs help, he is so bitter, and he's turned into someone I don't like, I don't recognise who he is anymore."

I stop walking and pull him to me for a kiss. I can see the sadness in his eyes, the torment on his face when he speaks about his twin brother, who he used to be such good friends with and are now enemies.

"Come on let's carry on enjoying this lovely sunshine" I smile holding his hand and pulling him along the path.

After having a leisurely stroll it's getting late and we are feeling weary after a full day out, so we hail a black taxicab to take us back to Evan's house.

Walking through the front door we kick off our shoes, go into the lounge and flop down onto one of the large sofas.

"God my feet are killing me." I can literally feel them throbbing.

"I know we've walked some miles today haven't we?"

"Yes, and all the other exercise we enjoyed last night I'm knackered" I sigh wearily.

"Fancy a nice soak in the bath?" Evan suggests.

"Yeah, sounds good, have you got any bubble bath?"

"Of course, I got some in especially for you."

"You got some in?" I smirk.

"Well, my housekeeper did, hope it's alright?" he laughs.

It's not long before the bath is ready so we both undress and step into the warm bubbly water. We both let out a contented sigh as we rest our aching muscles from a busy day of fun activities.

Resting my head against Evan's chest I close my eyes revelling in the feeling of being in love with the most amazing man I have ever met.

"So, I've been thinking about the job I could offer you," Evan says cuddling me to his warm body "and I think I could definitely do with some help in administration. When the Manor is up and running I will have vacancies in the office, on reception or if you want to stick to the catering side you could work on the restaurant side of things?"

"Really that's great. I quite like the sound of the office administration side of things though because I really want to move away from the catering side. I've been looking at courses I could do to learn the skills required for the job."

"You don't have to do a course baby; Curtis can teach you the basics to start with and I'm a great teacher too."

"Oh, okay. I do have one reservation though."

"Oh, what's that?" Evan asks.

"What if things don't work out between us and I'm working for you it would be awkward wouldn't it?"

Evan sounds serious. "Kara things not working out between us is not an option, things will work out because I love you and you love me so if we work together as a team then we will be okay. I know there will be bumps in the road along the way because relationships are never plain sailing but I can't lose you Kara not again."

I am beyond happy to hear his words. I turn around to face him and look into his big brown eyes. "I can't lose you either, I want to be with you for always." I smile.

"For always" he smiles kissing me.

After getting washed and dried the sky is turning dark outside so Evan shuts the bedroom curtains and feeling a bit peckish we go to the kitchen to get some snacks then watch some TV in bed.

Sitting in Evan's huge bed watching a romantic film Evan's mobile phone starts to ring. Picking it up and glancing at the screen he notices it's his mother calling and answers the call.

Evan

"Hello mother what can I do you for?" I answer sounding cheery.

"You sound happy, what have you got to be so happy about?"

I look at Kara and smile. "Just life in general."

"Oh, or could it be something to do with a special someone in your life, is it that girl you were taking out, what's her name, Sara."

"You mean Kara" I smile looking at her beautiful face sat in my bed smiling at me.

"Yes, that's it, well is it?" she enquires, and I can tell my mother is smiling on the other end of the line.

"Yes mother."

"Ooh I want to meet her, bring her to Monaco or I could come and visit you, I haven't been over in a while."

"I'm not sure mother."

"Why are you ashamed of me? Why not meet her?"

"Of course, I'm not ashamed of you and I'm sure you'll get to meet her one day."

"I tell you what I'll come over to you and then I can see what Sebastian's been up to as well."

"I can tell you what he's been up to, he's been pretending to be me to Kara and continuing to try and ruin my life."

"No, he wouldn't do that not Sebastian, he must have been playing a joke on you both."

"He would and it was no joke I can assure you."

"I'm sure he is only playing with you; you know how you both used to pretend being each other when you were little trying to confuse people and you were always winding each other up."

"This has gone beyond winding each other up, this is serious Mother, he's doing it so I will pay him the money, he is doing everything he can to make me which includes targeting Kara."

"I don't know why you don't just pay him" she sighs.

"You know why because of the way he treated me and whatever I pay him will never be enough."

"Well, he won't accept the money from me because I've tried believe me and I've more than enough to go around, he's stubborn just like your father. Oh, I wish your father were here to sort this mess out."

"Yes, and if he was, we wouldn't be in this mess would we."

"I'm sorry Son for everything, I'll talk to Sebastian make him understand what he is doing is wrong."

"I wouldn't waste your breath Mother, anyway, was there something you wanted, or did you just ring for a chat?"

"Well, there was something, I want to buy my lovely boyfriend Ace a present."

"Oh, you're still with him then."

"Of course, I am, I love him, I know he is a lot younger than me, but he is so good to me, he is a keeper and a true gentleman."

"I'm pleased for you, so what present?"

"Oh yes I want to buy him a Rolex watch and I wondered if you had the number of that friend of yours who owns that jewellery store in London?"

"Oh, you mean Alexander."

"Yes, that's him, there's a particular one I want to get him, and I thought he could source it for me."

"No problem I'll message you his number, just mention you are my mother, and he will look after you."

"Okay will do and thanks Son. I'll be in touch about coming over to visit soon. Love you, must go."

"Okay goodbye mother."

Evan ends the call and looks at me.

"So, you told your mum about me then?" I smile.

"I did and she wants to meet you."

"Are you okay with that?" I ask not sure how he feels even though he will be meeting my parents soon.

"Yes and no."

"Oh why?" I'm confused.

"Yes, I'm happy for you to meet her but no because my mother can be quite a handful sometimes."

"Don't worry I'm sure it will be fine and besides she can't be any worse than your brother" I laugh.

"No, you're right," he smiles walking over to me "are you ready for bed?" he asks looking at me with a twinkle in his eyes and climbing into bed.

"Yes, I am feeling a little tired" I reply.

"Oh, I didn't mean to go to sleep."

"Oh, what did you mean then?" I smile toying with him looking at his boxers that are now tenting from his arousal.

"I think you know what I mean" he says grabbing hold of my hand and pulling down his boxers at the front and placing it on his cock.

"I think you need to show me" I smile.

"Are you sure, if you're tired we can just go to sleep, I know we've had a busy day and I've had you plenty of times already" he says being caring but looking hopeful that I'll carry on.

"I'm fine babe so come here Big Evan and show me what you've got" I giggle.

"With pleasure" he grins.

Sixteen

Evan

I open my eyes and turn on my side to see Kara is fast asleep. After having sex numerous times since picking her up for the weekend I think I have well and truly worn her out. I can't help myself when I'm around her, she turns me on so much, the way she looks, her incredible body, her gorgeous breasts, her mouth, and those perfectly sweet soft lips of hers that I love to kiss so much.

Not wanting to wake her I creep out of bed quietly and go downstairs.

Checking the time on the clock on the mantelpiece in the lounge it's 7.00am, I feel wide awake as I scroll through my emails but as I look in the inbox all I can think about is my beautiful girlfriend fast asleep upstairs in my bed.

Now we are together all I want to do is make her the happiest girl in the world by being the best boyfriend I can be. She is so special to me, I have never felt this way about anyone before not even Julia, I thought I loved her once but the love I feel for Kara is something else.

The feelings I have for her scare me sometimes because she could so easily hurt me.

Our love is a rare and beautiful thing that you only find once in a lifetime and although we haven't been together for very long I am looking forward to making lots of memories and building a great future together.

Lost in thought and staring at his computer screen Evan doesn't hear or see me standing in the doorway watching him. 'I wonder what he's thinking about?'

I am so captivated by him, his hair is messy from sleep and sex, but he still looks gorgeous, his six-pack showing his toned physique, his tanned body, he looks divine and as I let out a sigh of appreciation for this fine specimen of a man Evan hears me and looks up.

"Hi beautiful" he says giving me one of his knockout smiles as he puts his laptop on the coffee table in front of him and holds out his arm for me to go to him.

"Hi, what are you doing?" I ask sitting down and nestling into his side.

"I woke up early so I was just checking my emails. I didn't want to disturb you because you looked so peaceful."

"Come back to bed, it's Sunday and you're supposed to have a lie in on a Sunday" I say looking at him.

"Well, there's an offer I can't refuse" he says turning off his laptop.

Evan picks me up in his arms and walks effortlessly with me up the stairs back to his bedroom.

Climbing into bed he takes me in his arms, and we cuddle each other both falling back to sleep again.

A couple of hours later I wake up to find Evan is not in bed again, so I grab a t-shirt from his drawers and go in search of him. As I walk downstairs I can hear him in the kitchen. "Hey, I woke up and you were gone again" I yawn perching onto a stool at the island in the centre of the kitchen.

"I haven't been up long, and I wanted to make my girlfriend breakfast as a surprise" he smiles taking some eggs out of the fridge.

"Oh sorry," I smile "I'm up now can I help?" I ask.

"No, it's okay I've got it all under control you just sit there while I look after you" he replies breaking some eggs into a jug. "Is scrambled egg on toast okay?"

"Perfect."

While Evan prepares my breakfast, I watch him thinking what a lucky girl I am not only to have a gorgeous boyfriend but a gorgeous boyfriend who can cook.

Evan sets two place settings at the island and then dishes up the scrambled egg on toast placing a plate in front of me.

"Wow this looks yummy, thank you" I smile taking hold of the knife and fork.

"Thanks tuck in before it gets cold" he says putting the kettle on ready for making a cup of tea afterwards then joining me at the island to eat his breakfast.

"Hmm this is so good so what are your plans for the week?" I ask before putting a forkful of egg and toast into my mouth.

"I'm at Hamilton Tower tomorrow then I've got a business trip to my hotel in Spain on Tuesday, I won't be back until Thursday, hey why don't you come with me?"

"I can't babe I've got work."

"Can't you take some time off?"

"Not at this short notice and I can't leave Sally on her own especially now she's pregnant."

"Sally's pregnant?" Evan asks surprised.

"Oh god didn't I tell you, yes Sally is pregnant."

"Oh, that's great, I like Sally she's a lovely lady. I guess you can't leave Sally in the lurch then."

"No, she's got really bad morning sickness at the minute."

"I see, have you taken your contraceptive pill?"

"Yes, don't worry you're not going to be a dad anytime soon."

Evan laughs nervously "Great." I know he's thinking he isn't ready for kids and neither am I for that matter.

"So, you go Tuesday and come back Thursday night."

"Yes, so I can come and see you on Friday when I get back if you like?"

"Yes, I would like that, will you be able to stay at mine for the weekend because don't forget we have a meet the parents' lunch on Sunday?"

"Just try and stop me" he grins.

By the time we have finished our breakfast and a cup of tea we both have a quick shower separately and then get dressed. It's late morning and we are just enjoying a cup of coffee sat in the kitchen when there is a loud knock at the door. Evan goes to answer the door and finds Curtis stood on the doorstep looking hungover and looking like he's wearing clothes from a night out last night.

"Hey dude got a cup of coffee for your best mate?" Curtis grins.

"Come on in mate we are just having one."

"We? Oh shit, I forgot Kara's here it doesn't matter I'll see you another time."

"Don't be stupid, get your arse in the kitchen and have a coffee."

"Okay boss" he grins slapping Evan on the back as he walks past him through the door on his way to the kitchen.

"Hi Kara" Curtis says giving me a kiss on both cheeks.

"I invited you for a coffee not a kiss with my girlfriend" Evan says smiling joining us.

"I was merely saying hello Ev, I can't help it if your girlfriend is gorgeous and kissable." He winks at me making me laugh.

Evan glares at Curtis "Relax dude I've got my own girlfriend to kiss now."

"What?" Evan says looking shocked.

"Well, she's not my girlfriend as such but I think it could lead to that, she's gorgeous Ev I really like her" Curtis sits down on one of the stools at the island.

"Is this Stephanie we're talking about?" Evan asks.

"The one and only I've just left hers now" he grins.

"So, you can't say you haven't had a shag in months anymore" Evan laughs pouring him a coffee and handing it to him.

"No I can't," Curtis grins "I think I'm in love" he says looking all gooey eyed.

"You're always in love I've lost count the number of times you've said that about a girl."

"Yeah alright, but this is different."

"We'll see" Evan smirks sitting down next to me and putting his hand on my leg.

"So, what does Stephanie do?" I ask.

"She's a hairdresser" Curtis smiles.

"Oh, so she's good with her hands then mate" Evan laughs.

"Oh yes and her mouth."

"Curtis." Evan apologises to me for his friend.

"Sorry Kara" Curtis laughs.

"Hey, it's fine don't mind me," I laugh "It's quite entertaining listening to you talking about boy stuff."

"So, when are you seeing her again?" Evan asks.

"I said I would call her to arrange something, we are going away on Tuesday aren't we so it will have to be when we get back."

"Oh, Curtis is going with you?" I say surprised.

"Yes, he is doing some staff interviews for me, I've been having some trouble with a staff member. Can you remember when I was talking to the manager in Spain that time when…" Evan smiles at me as an image of me on my knees sucking his cock must have popped into his head as I think the same thing.

"Oh yes" I blush smiling.

"Hey, am I missing something here?" Curtis says looking at our faces grinning at each other.

"No mate, yes well," Evan coughs clearing his throat. "We found out that a member of staff has been letting out vacant rooms to his friends for free, sneaking them in so as soon as we found out he is now unemployed hence why we are looking for a replacement."

"Do you speak Spanish then Curtis?" I ask.

"God no but anyone who can't speak English the manager translates for me so it's all good."

"Oh right."

"Speaking of work I've been discussing with Kara about a job at the Manor, she doesn't want to work at the coffee shop all her life and I thought it would be good to have her working in the office."

"Yes, sounds good mate," Curtis says liking the idea. "I would have thought you would want her working at Hamilton Tower so she can be close to you and live here."

I look at Evan and he looks at me and I think we both have the same thought; we have never discussed about where we would live when we decide to live together. If I'm working at the Manor and Evan is working at Hamilton Tower where will we live? I have always lived near my parents and Evan might not want to live in my hometown. We both look and feel slightly awkward after Curtis' comment. We have only just discussed marriage and children, for all I know Evan might want to move abroad and live in his villa in Italy. Sensing the awkwardness Curtis says, "Well whatever but I look forward to showing you the ropes Kara." smiling at me.

"Great yes I'll look forward to it" I smile.

"Anyway, thanks for the coffee Ev I'd best make tracks and get a shower and some kip because I didn't get much last night if you know what I mean" Curtis grins.

"Okay mate I'll see you out" Evan says getting up.

"Bye Kara." Curtis kisses me on both cheeks and then Evan shows him to the door.

"Are you okay?" Evan asks walking back into the kitchen seeing me deep in thought putting the dirty mugs in the sink.

"Yes, I'm fine" I smile.

We both go to say something at the same time and stop. Evan smiles and sits down at the island.

"What was you going to say?" I ask.

"I just wanted to talk about what Curtis said about living together."

"Okay."

"I haven't thought about living together have you?" Evan says looking awkward.

"To be honest no I haven't, how do you feel about it?" I ask wanting his view on it before I give him mine.

"Well, if I'm being perfectly honest, I think it's too soon" he says looking at me trying to gage my reaction.

"So do I." I sigh in relief. "I mean I love spending time with you, and I love staying with you but living together is different, it's a big step. I don't want to rush into moving in together because I don't think we are both ready for that."

"Yes, I agree" Evan replies.

"So, let's just take each day as it comes and when the time is right we can discuss it then, I love living with Jodie and I'm not ready to move out just yet."

"Yes, and I want things to be sorted with Sebastian before we start living together too."

"Yeah, so we are both on the same page."

"Yep, we are both on the same page," Evan agrees. "So now we have cleared that up what do you fancy doing for the rest of the day?"

"Absolutely nothing" I say stretching.

"Sounds good to me."

We spend the afternoon chilling on the sofa chatting about work, holidays and family and then decide to watch a film that's on the TV. When it's finished Evan looks at his watch. "It's 4.00pm babe I'd better take you home soon."

"Yes, I've got some ironing to do ready for work tomorrow and I'm sure you have stuff to do because you are going away this week."

"Uh huh I wish I didn't have to go to Spain, and I could see you instead" Evan sighs pulling me closer to him.

"Me too but just think how much more excited we'll be when we see each other again after not seeing each other for a few days."

"I don't think I could be any more excited than I am already when I see you, it's like all my Christmases have come at once" he smiles.

"I know me too, anyway I'll go and get my things together."

I give him a quick kiss and get up off the sofa.

"Okay beautiful."

Evan pulls up outside my flat and cuts the car engine. "So, I'll give you a call tomorrow okay."

"Okay."

"I'll be counting the days to Friday until I get to see you again" he smiles stroking my face with the back of his hand then moving it to around the back of my neck pulling me to him for a goodbye kiss. The kiss is slow and loving. While enjoying the pleasurable kiss Evan's mobile phone rings in his pocket.

"Great timing as always" he mutters taking it out of his pocket and seeing who is calling. "It's Julia" he sighs.

"Don't answer it" I huff.

"Babe if I don't answer it she will just keep calling me she can be very persistent when she wants to be."

"Okay answer it then" I sigh.

Evan

"Hi Julia, I thought I told you to stop calling me."

"Evan." I can hear her crying down the phone trying to get her breath as she says my name.

"Hey what's wrong?" I ask sounding concerned looking at Kara who is not impressed rolling her eyes at me. Although I'm not interested in her romantically anymore, I cared about her once, and she sounds really upset so I want to know why.

"Sebastian" she sobs.

"What about him, what's happened?"

"He, he...he came around to see me, Evan.... we argued and he grabbed me, he..."

"Shit did he hurt you?"

"I need you I'm sorry to ask please will you come I don't know who else to turn to, Jackie is not answering her phone and..." She sounds really distressed.

"Jesus, okay I'm on my way I'll be there as quick as I can."

"Okay but please hurry" she wails as I cut the call.

I look at Kara's face and it tells me everything I know already she is not happy, in fact happy doesn't cover it, she is fuming.

"Poor Julia what's happened now?" I say with sarcasm in my voice folding my arms defensively.

"Sebastian has been to her flat, apparently they argued, and he grabbed her, she sounds really distressed babe."

"That's awful but why do you have to be the one to go, can't she call her friends or her parents."

"She can't call her parents because they are both dead and she said she'd called her friends and couldn't get hold of anyone."

"Yeah right." I mutter.

"I'm sorry but what am I supposed to do when she sounds so upset tell her to go away."

"Yes…no… oh I don't know, I just don't like it Evan, I don't trust her."

"Look you have nothing to worry about and you trust me, don't you?"

"Yes."

"Look I'd better go, I'm sorry."

"Okay off you go then running to Julia" I huff grabbing the car door handle to get out of the car, but Evan grabs hold of my arm to stop me.

"Don't be like that please I'm stuck in the middle here."

"I'm sorry but I can't help how I feel, I'll speak to you tomorrow." I shrug out of his hold and get out the car. Evan gets out of the car too and I wonder why then realise my weekender bag is in the boot. He gets my bag and passes it to me. "Don't be mad at me, I'll call you, I love you Kara" he says looking guiltily at me as I walk off towards the flat. I don't say anything in reply and walk through the door not looking back.

Evan

Putting my foot down it doesn't take me long before I'm pulling up outside Julia's flat. I ring the doorbell feeling strange, I've not been here since that awful day when I found my brother in bed with her, the day my life fell apart. My heart is pounding in my chest while I wait for her to answer the door.

Minutes later Julia opens the door wearing a silky nightdress and dressing gown making me feel uncomfortable, her eyes are puffy from crying and as soon as she sees me she flings her arms around me and sobs. With her arms wrapped around me I feel awkward like I'm cheating on Kara or something even if it is an innocent consoling hug.

I peel her arms from around me and usher her to go inside. "You look like you could do with a stiff drink" I say walking into the kitchen and Julia follows. She sits down at the bistro style table while I open a cupboard remembering where she keeps the alcohol, take out a bottle of vodka and pour some into a glass. I pass it to her; her hands are shaking as she takes it from me.

"Thank you, you remember where I keep the alcohol then" she smiles before knocking back the vodka in one go.

"Yeah, so what happened?" I ask leaning against the kitchen worktop.

"Sebastian, he came here earlier, he had been drinking and when I opened the door he barged through it before I had the chance to shut the door on him."

"I told you not to open the door and to call the police."

"I know" she sobs.

"Okay so what happened?"

"He was pacing up and down continually saying I had ruined his life. He said I was a waste of space and couldn't even keep a child without losing it," Tears are falling down her cheeks as she continues. "He said I am selfish just like you and that we deserve each other, he looked so angry. Seb wanted to know if I had any money and started rummaging through my drawers frantically, I told him to leave and that I didn't have any money, but he wouldn't listen. I tried to stop him and then he grabbed me and pushed me away, I stumbled and fell to the floor. He then called me a stupid bitch, grabbed hold of my wrist, pulled me up and shoved me up against the wall, I thought he was going to hit me, but he just stared long and hard into my eyes then left."

"I'm sorry my brother treated you in that way."

"Why can't you just pay him the money Ev, he is just going to continue to make everyone's life a misery including mine?"

"You know why and I'm sorry, but I refuse to Julia, he needs counselling not money to solve his problems."

Julia gets up from the table and walks over to me. She cups my face with her hand. "Please Ev just pay him and then we can be free of him."

"Julia," I grab hold of her hand and pull it away. "Please don't, I've come here to make sure you are alright and that's all."

She steps back from me and I feel relieved until I see her take her silky dressing gown off and let it fall to the floor.

"Why can't we just go back to the way we were when we were both happy don't you remember Ev, can't you remember how good we are together, when we made love it was the most incredible thing, I miss you?"

"Julia stop, I'm with Kara now, we are not doing this, I'm leaving." I walk towards the kitchen door to leave but she steps in front of me blocking my path.

"I know you are with Kara, but she will never love you like I love you Ev." She goes to put her hands on me again, but I brush her off.

"Oh, you loved me when you were fucking my brother did you?" I seethe looking at her with disgust and moving out of her way leaning against the worktop again.

"You know I loved you, I still do so let's stop pretending because I know you still love me, I can tell" she smiles walking over to me.

I shake my head in disbelief. "You're deluded and I've heard enough of this bullshit, I'm going, please get out of my way." I go to walk around her, but she grabs hold of my arm. "Okay I'm sorry I shouldn't have made a pass at you but seeing you it brings back memories for me of what we had and what I lost. Please don't go I need you." Julia starts to cry again and slumps down onto the floor with her head in her hands sobbing. Seeing how distressed she is, her body is shaking I crouch down to her.

"Why won't you take me back Ev? I'm sorry, I'm so sorry" she cries.

"Julia, look at me." She looks at me with her teary eyes.

"You need to let this go, what we had we will never have again. I don't love you and what you did with Sebastian I can't forgive you. I will never forget how it felt finding you both that day so save yourself more pain and move on. I know Kara would prefer it if I didn't see you and to be honest I think it would be for the best."

Julia looks at me trying to convey to me how much she loves me but all I feel is sympathy. I stare at her for a few moments then get up and walk out the door.

Julia

I hear the front door slam and get up off the floor then look out of the kitchen window to see Evan leaving. I grab a tissue from a box on the worktop and wipe my eyes then pour myself another glass of vodka. I down it in one go feeling the burn on the back of my throat.

Picking up my dressing gown off the floor I put it on and walk into my bedroom. I lay down on top of my bed staring up at the ceiling thinking about what Evan has just said.

It must have been strange for him coming here after all this time and brought back lots of memories. We had some great times here in my flat before I had the affair with Sebastian.

After laying on my bed for a few moments I hear a loud knock on my front door startling me. I rush to answer it and fling the door open. "Evan..." Before I can say anymore I am taken into an embrace and kissed fiercely on the doorstep. I put my arms around his neck and kiss him passionately before pulling him inside and shutting the door. "Oh god I've missed you." He picks me up in his strong arms and carries me to my bedroom. "I've missed you too" he says putting me down as we quickly strip from our clothes while carrying on the ferocious kiss like we have been starved of each other for far too long until we are both naked. Picking me up again he lowers me to the bed "Evan..." I moan. "Shush" he says stopping me from talking by claiming my mouth again with his. He kisses me wildly, our tongues and teeth are colliding and clashing and then he takes me desperately claiming my body with his own, filling me deep making me scream out his name. He fucks me fiercely getting his fix of me, pounding into me thrust after thrust while I cling onto him digging my long fingernails into his back. I struggle to hold onto him from the force of his drives, our bodies are pressed together, our tongues are duelling and fighting from how turned on we are. "Fucking hell, so fucking good."

He pounds into me fast and precise; we can't get enough of each other. "OHHHH……YES" I scream, his cock hard and forceful rubbing me in just the right place, the friction causing me to moan loudly as my orgasm draws closer. "Aargh fuck…" Our sticky sweaty bodies enjoy every pound and every stroke until we come together in unison breathless and satisfied as our orgasms tear through us like a wild tornado.

"Oh my god, wow, just wow." I laugh as he rolls off breathing heavy and onto his back. The mind-blowing pleasure of our orgasms fogging our brain.

"Fucking hell," he smiles exhausted. "We are so fucking good together aren't we?"

"You know we are, god that was intense" I laugh trying to get my breath back.

"What was intense the sex or seeing my brother?" he laughs.

"Sebastian," I roll my eyes "the sex of course." I smile. "Evan fell for my story so easily he came like a shot when I rang him sobbing down the phone, he always was such a caring soul."

"You did amazing Liv (Julia Livingston – nicknamed Liv), you should have been an actress. Even when I was listening to you giving him the sob story on the phone before I left you, I even felt sorry for you and would have come running" he smiles leaning over and kissing me.

"Did you get the photos of us together when I opened the door to him in my nightwear?"

"Of course, I got some good ones and when you hugged him I didn't think he was going to touch you and then briefly he held you, my heart was pounding so much because I was desperate to get the shot and I knew I only had one chance."

"Great I was conscious you were watching us, but I didn't know where from, where was you hiding?" I laugh.

"I was crouched behind some fucking wheelie bin, as soon as I saw Evan's car pull up I was ready for him."

"You poor baby having to hide behind wheelie bins" I pout straddling him and kissing him.

"Well, you have to do what you've got to do" he grins holding my hips.

"I don't think we should send the photo to Kara just, yet we need to wait until the time is right, maybe try and get some more evidence so it's more believable that Evan is seeing me behind her back. Poor Evan will definitely be paying you the money when his precious relationship has ended because of us. He has made it so easy Seb, he told me he loves her so it's really going to hurt him when he loses her" I laugh.

"You're wicked I sometimes wonder whether you get a kick out of hurting my brother, first our affair and now this" he says with a smile on his face.

"I'm only doing it for you Seb so we can get our money."

"You mean my money."

"Yes, that's what I meant."

"Well, you did good tonight so I think I may have to reward you again" he says massaging my naked breasts and pinching my nipples hard sending a signal straight to my core.

"I like the sound of that.... OHHHHH shit Sebastian." He quickly flips me onto my back and sinks into me again making me moan with pleasure once more.

Evan

Arriving back home I'm so mad at myself for going to see Julia tonight, I honestly thought at the time I was doing the right thing because if my brother is causing her harm then I would never have forgiven myself if he had hurt her physically.

Seeing Julia at her flat brought lots of memories flooding back to me, some good but mostly how shit I felt finding them together when they had the affair. I don't care about any of that now, I'm over it but what I do care about is Kara's feelings and how upset she is that I was going to see my ex. I mean if it were the other way around and she was going to comfort her ex I don't know what I would have done.

I lock my front door then go and take a shower to try and destress after the night's events. I can't believe Julia tried to seduce me, why can't she just accept that we are over and move on. Then there is my brother he's still up to no good and why is he involving Julia in his games?

After getting showered and dressed I need to speak to Kara to explain what happened tonight, I can't stand that she is upset with me and if I don't sort things out with her I'm not going to be able to sleep tonight.

I sit on my bed and call her number and after a few rings she answers.

"Hello." Just the sound of her voice makes me smile even if she is mad with me.

"Hi baby."

"Hi" she huffs. 'God she really is mad.'

"Are you okay?"

"No, I'm not."

"Look I'm sorry I should never have gone to see her; I should have taken your feelings into account because I knew you weren't happy about it and I didn't. I just thought I was doing what was best, if you had spoken to her and heard how distressed she was on the phone I think you would have done the same."

"I'm sorry she was upset but you know how I feel about her, she's made it known she wants you back Evan and I just don't trust her. I mean how would you feel if I wanted to go and comfort my ex?"

"Like murdering someone."

"Exactly, are you sure you still don't have feelings for her because seeing the way you reacted when she rang you feeling upset makes me think that you do."

"No, I don't, please Kara you've got it all wrong, I love you."

"You say you do, and I want to believe you but ever since I've known you Julia has been ringing you all the time, how do I know you are not stringing us both along at the same time."

'Fuck is that what she really thinks?'

"That's bullshit and you know it?" I feel angry at her comment.

"I can't believe you just went running to her like that."

There is a long silent pause and then I can hear her crying down the phone. I feel like shit.

"Baby please don't cry I'm sorry it's just she really did sound upset, desperate even, I thought Sebastian had hurt her and she said she had tried phoning her friends and couldn't get hold of them."

"And you really believe that do you?"

"At the time I did yes, I just went to help someone in distress because that's the type of guy I am."

"I know you are but it's your ex-girlfriend the one you said you were going to ask to marry you, how do you think that makes me feel, she is going to come between us Evan?"

"I've told her that I love you and that she needs to move on, and I told her again tonight when she..."

"When she what? Did she come on to you?" Kara's sobs turn to anger.

"Yeah, she did, but I told her straight the only person I want is you, you need to trust me Kara and believe what I'm saying, I love you and only you."

"Yes, but you lied to me once before remember when you said you didn't care about me, when you left me, for all I know you could be lying to me now, oh god I'm so confused."

"That was different, and I've explained all that, I was trying to protect you from Sebastian. You can trust me, I would never do anything to hurt you because I love you so much, please Kara you have to believe me."

"Look I'm tired so I'm going to go to bed I'll speak to you tomorrow okay."

"Please don't overthink this Kara, you really have nothing to worry about."

"Bye."

Kara puts the phone down and I throw my phone onto my bed and flop down onto my back. Shit. Nice one Evan, you've fucked up big time.

Seventeen

I can't believe it's Monday again, I've had such a great weekend staying with Evan, well up to the point of my boyfriend going to see his ex-girlfriend last night.

I told Jodie about Evan going to see Julia and she thinks I should trust him, but I'm scared of getting hurt again, that's why I'm upset, and I can't think clearly. I didn't sleep very well last night thinking about things.

"Morning Kar, how are you feeling this morning?" Jodie asks as I walk into the kitchen to get some breakfast.

"Yeah, I'm okay I just wish Julia would do one, when it's just me and Evan it's amazing but then she always seems to pop up and spoil everything. We never argue normally and when we do it always seems to have something to do with her."

"I'd be annoyed if Matt's ex kept hanging around."

"Yeah, I know right and knowing she still loves him and wants him back, it's hard you know."

"I know but she's not having him," Jodie says sounding assertive making me laugh.

"I do believe he loves me it's just that we don't have history like he does with Julia because we haven't been together long enough."

"Yes but don't forget the history they have includes her having an affair with his brother."

"Yeah, you're right. Anyway, don't you need to get to work, you don't want to be late on your first day back at school, the summer holidays have flown by haven't they?" I say noticing the time.

"Oh my god yes I need to go," Jodie grabs her bag and finds her car keys. "I'll see you later, don't worry everything will be fine, love ya Kar."

"Love ya Jode."

After finishing getting ready myself I walk to work. It's cold today, there are lots of grey clouds in the sky and it looks like it could rain. Arriving at work I find Sally in the office looking and feeling nauseous.

"Morning Sal, you don't look good." I dump my bag on the floor and sit on the chair at the desk opposite her.

"I'm not feeling good" she groans.

"Are you sure you are okay to work, you should have stayed at home if you're feeling rough?"

"Yes, I'm fine, it comes and goes I'll be alright in a minute."

"Can I get you anything, a cup of tea, ginger biscuit?"

"That would be great thanks, I think if I move I'll be sick."

"Okay be back in a minute."

After making us a cuppa and getting some ginger biscuits for Sal I sit down again in the office for a chat.

"I've done the prep while I was waiting for the kettle to boil."

"Thanks Kara, you're a star."

"So, did you and Tim have a good weekend?" I ask taking a sip of tea.

"Yes, we did thanks, we just had a quiet one because I wasn't feeling too good. Oh, I rang the doctors when I got home on Friday and I've got an appointment with a midwife this week."

"Well, you definitely need one of those, how exciting, when do you go?"

"Wednesday after work, Tim is going to come with me."

"You should find out your due date then I should think."

"Yes, it will be nice to have an actual date anyway how was your weekend, you went to Evan's house didn't you?"

"Yes, it was really good we went on the London Eye, saw Big Ben, Buckingham Palace, it was really good spending time together."

"Oh wow, sounds like you had an amazing time."

"I did until Evan's ex spoilt it when she rang in tears when he dropped me off home last night."

"Oh no why, what did she want?"

I tell Sally about Evan visiting Julia and then it's time to open for the day.

The morning passes quickly and as lunchtime approaches a delivery man walks through the door holding a big bouquet of pink and yellow roses. "Delivery for Miss Kara Davis!"

"Yes, that's me" I smile taking the flowers from him and the customers in the shop all look at me and smile.

Feeling slightly embarrassed at the attention I'm receiving I quickly put them on the desk in the office while Sally mans the counter. I find the card and smile when I read it.

Hi gorgeous, sorry for upsetting you and for being an idiot, I shouldn't have gone, I hope you can forgive me. I really do love you Kara, Always. Evan xxxx

How can I stay mad at him when he does lovely gestures like this? I look for my phone in my bag with tears in my eyes and send him a text.

Hi thank you for the gorgeous flowers and no you shouldn't have gone but I forgive you. I know why you did because you are such a caring, amazing man and that's one of the reasons why I love you so much. I love you too and I can't wait until Friday when I can show you just how much. Kara xxxx

After pressing send I wipe the tears from my eyes feeling better about things and re-join Sally in the shop.

The end of the day comes quickly and after saying goodbye to Sally and waving to Tim I set off towards home with my flowers in my hand. I realise I haven't checked my phone since I text Evan earlier, so I retrieve my phone from my bag eager to see if he has sent me a message. I smile when I see he has.

I'm pleased you like the flowers I hate it when I upset you. I want to be the best boyfriend you have ever had. I can't wait to see you on Friday either. I love you Evan xxxx

Arriving home, I walk through the front door to find a tired Jodie sat in the kitchen drinking a cuppa.

"Hi Kar, the kettle has just boiled if you want one?" Jodie yawns then smiles when she sees that I'm carrying a big bunch of flowers in my hands.

"Bloody hell Kara more flowers, they're gorgeous, I take it they are an apology from Evan?"

"Yes, they are" I smile.

"I'm pleased you've sorted things out, I mean how can you stay mad at him when he sends you gorgeous flowers like that."

"I know our house is looking more and more like a florist since I've been seeing him."

"I know I think he needs to have a word with Matt I can't remember the last time he bought me flowers although he does bring me chocolate quite often."

"Yes, and we know why that is don't we" I laugh.

"Oh yeah but we won't talk about that" Jodie laughs blushing.

"Anyway, how was your first day back?" I ask placing the flowers that are already in water on the floor until I find somewhere to put them.

"Tiring" she smiles.

"What do you fancy for dinner, I'll make it?" I ask looking in the fridge.

"Oh, I don't mind, anything I'm not bothered."

"How about a stir fry?"

"Hmm... sounds good, I'll go and have a quick bath then while you're cooking it if you don't mind."

"Yeah sure" I smile.

After enjoying a nice dinner, we are both sat in the lounge watching TV when my mobile phone rings, Evan's calling me.

I go to my room for some privacy and answer the call.

"Hi."

"Hi beautiful."

"Thanks again for the flowers they are gorgeous."

"That's alright, are we okay now?" he asks checking to make sure after our argument last night.

"Yeah, we're fine babe."

"Good because I am truly sorry for what I did I never meant to upset you."

"I know it's okay. Anyway, I don't want to spend our time talking about her again so let's just forget about it."

"Me neither so how was your day?"

"Busy have you had a good day?"

"Yes, I have, and now I've got to pack a case because I'm leaving for Spain at 5am in the morning."

"Oh yes, is Curtis picking you up?"

"Yes, he's driving us to the airport, I wish I didn't have to go, and I could come and see you especially after upsetting you I want to make it up to you."

"Babe honestly we're fine so don't worry and you'll be back on Thursday so we can see each other Friday and spend the whole weekend together making up."

"Yes, I can't wait, anyway I'm really sorry but I'm going to have to go and sort my stuff out."

"Okay babe I'll see you Friday then, I hope everything goes okay in Spain."

"Yes, I'm sure it will, speak to you soon, love you."

"Love you, bye."

Eighteen

The rest of the week drags, Evan has spoken to me numerous times but it's not the same as seeing him in person, I'm desperate to see him again.

It's Thursday and Evan will be home from Spain tonight so this means tomorrow I will be seeing him again and I can't wait. Remembering that we are going to my parents for Sunday lunch I give my mum a call to arrange a time to go.

"Hi Mum" I say cheerily.

"Good morning daughter, this is an early call for you it's only 7.30am, is everything alright love?"

"Yes everything is fine Mum I just thought I would ring you about Sunday before I go to work."

"Oh yes you are definitely coming then."

"Yes Mum we are looking forward to it."

I'm bricking it; I haven't taken a boy home to meet my parents in such a long time and the fact that I love Evan so much I just hope my parents do too.

"Oh good," my mum squeals deafening me making me laugh "I can't wait to meet him Kara, is he a dreamboat."

"A dreamboat?" I laugh.

"Yes, you know an attractive man, a dreamboat."

"Yes Mum, he's a dreamboat."

"Oh, I remember the first time I met your father, I knew he was the one, do you think he could be the one Kara?"

Definitely! I knew from our very first encounter in the coffee shop and the strong connection we both felt but I'm not going to tell my mum that because I know what she's like she will just get overexcited and then she will be looking at wedding dresses next, so I play it down a bit.

"Mum…we really like each other but its early days."

"Okay love, well I've bought a lovely joint of beef for Sunday, I hope he likes roast beef?"

"He does what time would you like us to come?"

"Is 12 o'clock okay?"

"Yes, that will be great, what did dad say when you told him that I was seeing someone?"

"He said he is looking forward to giving him a good grilling."

"Oh no is he really going to grill him Mum?" I'm worried now, I don't want my dad to scare Evan off.

"No don't worry love relax he was only joking" she laughs.

"Okay well I'd better go because I need to be at work soon, so I'll see you both on Sunday then at 12 o'clock."

"Okay love, we'll look forward to seeing you both and don't worry Kara, it will be fine, bye love."

"Okay thanks Mum, bye."

I finish getting ready for work and arrive at the coffee shop slightly early because I'm keen to find out how Sally got on at the doctors last night.

"Morning Sal" I say chirpily walking through the door.

"Morning love."

"So how did it go then?" I ask smiling.

"How did what go?"

"The doctor's appointment last night, the day you found out when baby Jeffreys is due."

Sally laughs. "Oh yes it went great, the doctor is arranging an appointment to see a midwife and then I will get a date for my first scan."

"Great so did the doctor say when it is due then?"

"Yes, according to the date of my last period I'm due in April. I still can't believe I fell so quickly."

"Brilliant well from what you have been telling me about all the practising you and Tim have been doing I'm not surprised, I bet Tim will be glad of the rest now," I grin, Sally grins too.

"Bless him we've never had so much sex, I mean we did when we first got married but it kind of diminishes over time."

"I don't think that will be the case where Evan's concerned, he is up for it all the time."

"Oh really" Sally smirks.

I blush. "Anyway, enough about that," still blushing "It will be lovely having a baby in the summer you'll be able to go for nice walks. Have you told your dad yet?"

"No, we are waiting until my first scan before we tell my dad and the in-laws, we want to tell them and show them a baby scan photo."

"Aww that's lovely, they will be thrilled I'm sure. You never know Tim's mum might mellow a bit and you may find it brings you closer."

Sally laughs. "I doubt it, but it would be nice. I wish my mum were still alive she would have been a lovely Grandma."

"I know I wish she were too." I give her shoulder a rub because she looks a bit teary.

"Anyway, how are things with you and Evan?" she says wanting to move on because thinking about her mum always makes her feel sad.

"Great."

"Good to hear."

There's a steady flow of customers during the morning and as lunchtime approaches I'm just making some sandwiches for an elderly couple who often call in on a Thursday when they are doing their shopping when I hear a lady's voice at the counter asking Sally if she can speak to me. I turn to look to see who it is, and I can't believe my eyes when I see Julia stood at the counter.

'What the hell does she want and how does she know where I work?'

"Kara love I'll finish those off you have a visitor" Sally smiles not realising who my visitor is.

I put the butter knife down that is in my hand and walk over to the counter.

"Hi Kara, sorry to bother you while you are at work, what a quaint little place, is it possible to have a quick word?" Julia asks a fake smile plastered on her face.

"I haven't got long" I reply with a straight face ushering her through to the office giving Sally a sign to say I'll only be a few minutes and then closing the office door for some privacy.

"How do you know where I work?" I ask confused.

"Oh, Evan mentioned it once," 'He did?' "What a lovely little place have you worked here long?"

"A while so what can I do for you?" I ask with hostility in my voice.

"Well first of all I just wanted to apologise for the other night when we first met in the restaurant, I didn't mean for us to get off on the wrong foot" she smiles.

'Yeah right.'

"I do hope that we can be friends, I've known Evan a long time now and we have a lot of history together and so any friend of his is a friend of mine."

"Friends, you want us to be friends. I'm sorry but why would I want to be friends with you?"

"Well, if you are seeing Evan then I'm sure we will be bumping into each other again I mean I know you want me to stop seeing Evan because he told me, but I didn't get that impression that he wanted to stop seeing me the other night, quite the opposite in fact."

"What the hell is that supposed to mean?" I scowl.

"Let's just say he was very comforting when I was upset."

"That's not how I heard it, Evan has already told me you tried to seduce him, and he told you he's not interested."

"Not interested," Julia laughs "Well whatever he told you I can assure you he was extremely interested sweetheart."

"Get out, don't you dare come to my place of work and insinuate that you and Evan are getting it on, he doesn't want you Julia, he loves me so get that into that head of yours sweetheart, that ship has sailed and the sooner you start accepting that fact the better."

"I'm sorry I didn't want to upset you I was merely pointing out as a friend that you should know Evan does still care about me and coming to my rescue the other night proves it. I know he still loves me Kara and it's just a matter of time before he leaves you and we get back together."

"You think, I don't believe this, have you forgotten that you had an affair with his brother, you really think he still loves you after what you did?" I laugh sarcastically. "You are no friend of mine and you never will be and don't think for a second I don't know what game you are playing in order to try and get him back, ringing him all the time, crying down the phone, he is my boyfriend now Julia and he is not for the taking." I glare at her.

"Oh sweetheart you really don't know who you are dealing with here, I will get Evan back you mark my words."

I open the office door. "I think I've heard enough of your shit so please leave." I give her a dirty look.

"Okay," she smiles smugly "I have things to do anyway, have a nice day and Kara" she says walking through the door.

"What."

"Tell Evan I'll look forward to seeing him again soon."

Julia walks out and I'm seething as I return to the shop floor, the nerve of that woman coming to my workplace and saying what she did. I walk over to Sally who is getting a piece of cake out of the glass cabinet. "If that woman comes here again I do not wish to speak to her okay." I seethe.

"Oh, okay sorry who is she?" Sally asks confused.

"Julia, Evan's ex."

"Really oh god if I'd have known who she was Kara."

"Hey, its fine Sal she's just got me all worked up that's all, it's not your fault."

"What did she say to you?"

"I'll tell you later."

After serving the lunchtime rush I fill Sally in on the whole conversation with Julia and she's shocked. After stewing about it all afternoon I'm pleased when 5.00pm comes around and I can go home.

Arriving home to an empty house I go straight for a shower to destress. Feeling calmer after my shower I decide to send Evan a text.

Hi not sure what time you are home but I need to speak to you, had a visit from Julia today at the coffee shop, the nerve of that woman. I've missed you so much, can't wait to see you tomorrow K xxx

Taking my phone with me I go to the kitchen to see what I can prepare for dinner and see a note pinned to the fridge from Jodie that I didn't notice earlier when I got home.

Gone to see Mum and Dad, having dinner at their house, see you later Jode xx

"Meal for one it is then" I look in the fridge deciding I can't be bothered to prepare anything to cook so I find a pizza in the freezer and put it in the oven.

After eating the pizza I put the kettle on and make a cup of coffee and then sit down at the kitchen table again thinking about my day and the visit from Julia when my mobile rings. Evan is calling me.

"Hi babe" I answer sounding pleased to hear from him.

"Hi beautiful, I've just got home and got your text, I'm knackered, how are you?"

"I've been better, how was your trip?"

"Good but more importantly what's this about Julia coming to see you at work?"

"It's okay I can tell you another time. you're tired and you've just got back, I just wanted to tell you that's all."

"So, tell me, I want to know."

"Well, she turned up at work wanting a private word, she said she came to apologise for making me feel awkward when we first met the other day in the restaurant."

"Right and how does she know where you work?"

"That's what I thought so I asked her, and she said that you had told her."

"Really, I don't remember saying anything to her, that's weird so what else did she say?"

"She said she hoped that we could be friends because any friend of yours is a friend of hers."

Evan laughs. "You're joking she really said that?"

"Yep, she said if I'm seeing you then we will be bumping into each other again and that we should get along for your sake. She said she knows that I don't want you seeing her and then she said she didn't get that impression that you wanted to stop seeing her the other night quite the opposite."

"What the hell is that supposed to mean?"

"She told me you were very comforting when she was upset."

"Bullshit ignore her, she is just trying to wind you up and it's clearly worked by the sounds of it."

"She also said she knows you still love her and it's just a matter of time before you leave me and go back to her."

"What?" Evan laughs sounding shocked.

"Yes, and that I don't know who I am dealing with, that she will get you back and to mark her words and to tell you she will look forward to seeing you again soon."

"What the hell is she playing at I'll speak to her because I'm not having her upsetting you with the shit that comes out of her mouth."

"Yes I think you should I was so mad when she left, I've been reeling from our conversation all afternoon."

"I'm not surprised I'll sort it I'm not having her turning up at your work upsetting you and talking shit."

"I wish you were here I could really do with a cuddle."

"Me too baby, tomorrow I will give you lots of cuddles okay and a lot more besides" he says cheekily making me laugh.

"Good because I've got withdrawal symptoms and I need my fix of you."

"I know it's been hard not seeing you for a few days."

"Yes, and it's always hard when you do see me isn't it Mr H" I laugh.

"That's because you are sexy and turn me on so much."

"I feel better now having spoken to you, I've missed you."

"I've missed you too and I'm sorry you've had a bad day because of her. Don't worry about Julia I'll sort her okay."

"Okay."

"I'm going to go and unpack and get a shower, so I'll look forward to seeing you tomorrow babe, love you."

"Okay me too, love you, bye."

Evan

I end the call from Kara feeling angry and frustrated, I can't believe Julia visited her at work trying to cause trouble. How on earth does she know where Kara works anyway? Maybe Sebastian gloated to Julia about pretending to be me and told her?

Finding Julia's number on my phone I decide to give her a call. I'm so mad because Kara is upset again and yet again it's because of my ex.

"Evan hi it's lovely to hear from you I was just thinking about you" Julia says.

"Julia what the hell are you doing visiting Kara at work and why are you telling her I was very comforting the other night giving her the wrong impression, you know that wasn't the case?"

"Oh my god" she laughs" It wasn't like that she must have got the wrong end of the stick again. Look I'll explain, I'm in your neck of the woods I'll come around."

"Julia no." Before I can protest and say anymore she hangs up. 'Great Julia is coming here, fucking great that's all I need.'

After a short while there is a knock on my front door. I open the door and Julia walks through it.

"Julia you really didn't have to come here it could have been said on the phone."

"Well, I'm here now so put the kettle on, and I'll explain over a cuppa" she says walking past me towards the kitchen.

'Please, come in why don't you.'

I look around outside before I shut the door. I walk into the kitchen and she is sat on a stool at the island. I fill the kettle with water and put it on to boil.

'What the hell am I doing?'

"So how are you, you look tired?" Julia asks looking at my weary face.

"Well considering I've just got back from a business trip to Spain and I've not been home long I am tired so let's make this quick because I need to take a shower and get some sleep. So, go on then explain to me why you went to Kara's work to cause trouble?"

"I wasn't causing trouble Ev I merely visited her at work to apologise for getting off on the wrong foot when we first met at the Italian restaurant."

"Yes, but you didn't have to go to Kara's work to do that and how do you know where she works anyway?"

"You told me."

"I don't think I did." I frown.

"Well, it must have been your mother when I spoke to her on the phone or Sebastian may have mentioned it, but I thought it was you. Anyway, it doesn't matter who told me, but I didn't plan on going it was a spur of the moment thing."

"A spur of the moment thing, it's not like you live close by" I laugh.

"Well, it's the truth I was in the area."

"In the area I find that hard to believe how come?"

"Well, if you must know I actually came to look where your new hotel is, I've been reading about it so much in the paper recently and so I thought I would come and take a look."

"Oh right, well Kara didn't appreciate your little visit and neither did I especially hearing what you have been saying to her."

"All I said was it would be nice if we can be friends seeing as you two are seeing each other and that it would be good if we could get along for your sake so it's not awkward if we bump into each other."

"She doesn't want to be friends with you and why you think you could be friends is beyond me. Why did you tell her I was very comforting making her believe it was something else when I came to your flat the other night?"

Julia sighs. "I said you were gentlemanly and supportive I certainly didn't give her the impression that you were anything more than that."

"So, you didn't tell Kara that you want me back, that you will get me back and to mark your words. You didn't say to her that she doesn't know who she is dealing with?"

"No, I didn't say any of those things I was amicable and nice, can't you see what she is trying to do Evan she doesn't want us to be friends, so she is trying to stop you from having anything to do with me by making up these lies. You know me Evan you know I'm not like that."

"Oh Jesus, I don't know what to think, you say one thing and Kara says another and I'm stuck in the middle of you two."

"Evan I can assure you I wasn't trying to make trouble I promise."

I let out a big sigh and pour the drinks passing her a cup of coffee making it just the way she likes it and Julia notices that I have remembered.

"We may not have been together for a while, but you still remember how to make my coffee with lots of milk and half a sugar" she smiles.

"Yes, well I supposed you don't forget something like that when you are with someone for a while."

Julia smiles sexily at me and it turns my stomach.

After the coffee has cooled enough to drink we sip our drinks talking about what we have been doing in our working life since we parted ways. I briefly mention about the hotels and Julia tells me she has been busy at the clothing boutique she owns and it's doing well. It's nice catching up but the longer she is here the more uncomfortable I feel, and I want her to go. I don't want to be having chats with Julia over coffee I just want her to understand how I feel that I've moved on and I'm in love with Kara so she will take the hint and leave us alone. Kara doesn't deserve to have my ex hanging around, phoning me all the time, saying things to her that are not true like we will get back together, I need to make it clear that I will never take her back, it is NEVER going to happen.

"I don't suppose you've got any biscuits have you?" Julia asks smiling at me.

'Please will you just go already, just drink your coffee and go, if Kara could see us right now I would seriously be in deep shit.'

"Err I'll get the tin." 'What the fuck am I doing?'

I get up to get the biscuits and as I turn back around Julia squeals "Oh no." and has spilt coffee all down the front of her ruffled blouse that she is wearing with a black pencil skirt.

"Shit are you okay, is it hot?" I ask grabbing a cloth to give to Julia but there is no need because when I look at her again she has taken off her blouse to reveal her black silky bra underneath and the front of her skirt is soaked.

"Oh god I'm so sorry," she laughs "How careless of me, I don't know how on earth that happened" she says as I look and feel extremely uncomfortable quickly looking away.

"Err fine, umm do you want me to get you something to wear, yes I should get something, I'll be back in a minute." I go to walk out of the kitchen.

"I don't suppose I could have a quick shower could I? I stink of coffee now and yes if I could borrow something that would be great?"

"Err… a shower I'm not sure can't you just do that when you get home."

"Evan you can't expect me to get in my car like this I'm all sticky and covered in coffee" she laughs.

'Shit why the fuck didn't I just tell her to go when I opened the door earlier, this is turning out to be a complete nightmare, all I wanted to do was phone her and tell her to leave Kara alone. Then she turns up at my door, we have had a coffee and now she wants to take a shower, what the fuck.'

"Okay but be quick because I need to have a shower myself and time is getting on" I reply not looking at her because I feel awkward enough stood here talking to her with her boobs on display.

"You can always join me if you want to save water?" she says flirtatiously walking towards me.

"Julia don't." I snap.

"Okay, okay relax Ev I'm only joking" she laughs.

"I'll get a t-shirt for you to wear."

"It's okay I know where you keep them unless you've moved them from where they were before."

"Err no same place, okay go ahead." She walks past me, and I run my hands through my hair feeling stressed.

Julia

I walk upstairs to Evan's bedroom and take a quick shower in the en suite bathroom. I had forgotten how nice Evan's bathroom is, I miss being here with him.

Washing all the coffee remnants from my body I use Evan's shower gel; hmm I love that smell.

After getting washed I wrap myself into a towel and then walk back into the bedroom and over to the window. I can see Sebastian in the shadows in his hiding place waiting to get a photo of the two of us. I stand in the window for a few moments while Seb takes some photos of me stood naked dressed in just a towel then I call Evan from downstairs. "Evan."

"Yes" he shouts from the bottom of the stairs.

"Can you come here I need your help."

"Why?" he replies sounding stressed.

"Please Evan can you just come here" I stress.

"Shit." I hear him curse then hear his footsteps as he runs up the stairs to his bedroom.

"Sorry I can't seem to find something to wear, you have so many nice clothes I don't want to wear your decent stuff" I smile. The look of pure anguish on his face as he tries not to look at me stood naked in just a towel, poor man, how can you possibly resist this body?

Evan grabs an old t-shirt out of a drawer and passes it to me averting his eyes.

"Is that alright, do you need bottoms as well?" he asks.

"A t-shirt is fine it's quite long on me, so it'll cover me until I get home" I smile.

"Okay I'll be downstairs."

"Evan."

"Yes."

"Would you mind closing the curtains for me because I wouldn't want any of your neighbours seeing me naked?"

"Sure" Evan sighs and he walks over to the window.

Just as he is about to take hold of a curtain I walk up behind him so we are stood together so Sebastian can get his shot of the two of us looking cosy.

"Thanks," I say touching him on the arm "I'm sorry for being so stupid, I'll just get changed and then I'll leave you too it."

"Julia… it's fine but just hurry up will you" he says sounding flustered.

Evan looks out of the window giving Sebastian lots of opportunities to get more photos of us stood together in his bedroom.

I walk over to the bed where Evan has left the t-shirt and after Evan has shut the curtains he turns to leave the room so I can get changed and I drop my towel and stand naked in front of him.

"Julia for fuck's sake, what are you doing?" he snaps quickly looking away and walking over to the door.

"What's wrong it's not like you haven't seen me naked before" I smile calling after him.

Evan

'Shit, shit, fucking shit…'

I return to the kitchen and pace the floor feeling stressed. I am seriously pissed off at myself. I can't believe how stupid I am.

After a few minutes of pacing Julia appears wearing my t-shirt. "Hi," she says in a sexy voice "Look it fits perfectly." She runs her hands up and down her body making me feel even more awkward than I already do.

"Julia I…"

"It's okay I know, I apologise that you saw me naked my towel accidentally slipped" she smiles.

"I need to get on" I say hinting for her to leave and passing her a bag with her coffee-stained clothes in. I need you to get the fuck out of here that's what I need.

"Okay I'll leave you to it then, thanks for the shower and the coffee" she laughs accepting the bag.

"You're supposed to drink the damn thing not wear it" I say half smiling showing her to the door.

I open the front door and Julia pauses on the doorstep for a moment before flinging her arms around me and kissing me on the mouth. Before I know what's happening and have time to react she says "Bye Evan." then walks off down the road.

I look up and down the street nervously hoping that no-one saw before shutting the door feeling relieved that she has finally left.

Julia

Walking down the street looking for Sebastian he appears from behind a parked car making me jump.

"Sebastian you scared me you idiot" I laugh as he walks alongside me.

"Sorry baby," he says smacking me on the bum. "So, what happened then?"

"Well, I had a little accident and accidently spilt coffee all down my front, so I had to have a shower and a change of clothes."

"Oh dear, you are so clumsy" he laughs.

"I know" I smirk.

"You are so clever" he says stopping me and taking me in his arms kissing me wildly and passionately in the street while feeling my bum that is barely covered by Evan's t-shirt.

I pull away breathless. "So, did you take some good photos?" I ask.

"I did, put it this way if I saw the photos I've taken I would definitely think you two were having an affair."

"Fantastic, now take me home because after all the excitement I'm feeling extremely horny and turned on and I'd like you to fuck me." I smile walking towards his car.

"With pleasure" he grins opening the car door for me.

"Oh, it will definitely be pleasurable" I smile getting into the car joined by Sebastian and he speeds off down the road desperate to get me home.

Nineteen

Evan

I wake up in turmoil the next day, I need to tell Kara about what happened last night but how am I supposed to say "Oh by the way I rang Julia last night to tell her off for visiting you at work and talking shit and she came to my house, we had a coffee together and then she spilt coffee all down herself. Oh, and she ended up having a shower, I saw her naked and she went home wearing one of my t-shirts."

I was so looking forward to seeing Kara again after not being able to spend time together the last few days because I've been away on business and now I'm dreading it because I feel guilty although I haven't done anything wrong apart from letting Julia into my house and into my shower. I need to tell her because I don't want to keep things from her but then I don't want us to end up having another argument because of my ex and for it to spoil our weekend. I'm supposed to be meeting her parents on Sunday and once Kara knows what happened she is going to be angry and possibly not speaking to me and then I won't get to meet her parents and that's not going to be a great first impression because their daughter is upset because of me. As much as it pains me to keep quiet about Julia's visit, I think I am going to have to just for the time being to keep the peace, I will tell her next week, yes, I think that's for the best.

It's 7.00pm and I'm eagerly awaiting Evan's arrival, I'm so excited, if feels like it's been longer than a few days since I've seen him, and I can't wait to be in his arms again.

I'm wearing a short black denim skirt and a white cropped top after taking a shower and I've left my freshly washed hair down after blow drying it and put on minimal make up, I feel good. Jodie is out with Matt somewhere and I'm sat at the kitchen table waiting for him, I keep looking at my watch impatiently wishing he is here already. Evan told me he will be arriving about 7.00pm and true to his word I hear the roaring sound of a car engine outside, so I look out of the kitchen window and see him pull up outside.

'Oh my god he's here.'

I open the front door feeling excited and run down the path to greet him. Evan gets out of his car and picks me up so I'm straddling his waist and he kisses me like there's no tomorrow.

"Hi" I say breathless looking into his rich dark chocolate brown eyes that are looking at me with so much lust and love.

"Hi," he smiles. "Did you miss me?"

"No not really did you miss me?" I smile.

"No not one bit" he smirks. "Shall we go inside and get reacquainted properly?" he says putting me down.

"Yeah, come on then."

Evan gets his overnight bag out of the boot of the car and then we walk hand in hand to the front door closing it behind us. Dropping his bag at his feet he takes me in his arms and gives me the softest, slowest, tongue mingling kiss, his hands are in my hair, my arms are around his waist and we both moan with pleasure being reunited after days of being away from each other.

"Is Jodie here?" Evan whispers.

"No, she's staying at Matt's tonight, she thought it would be nice for us to have some alone time seeing as we haven't seen each other for a few days" I smile looking suggestively at him.

"Well in that case," he picks me up "it's time to get naked" and he carries me in his big strong arms to my bedroom.

I giggle loving how masterful he is and how keen he is to get me into bed. I'm not complaining though because I want him just as much as he wants me.

Lowering me onto the bed gently he kisses me giving me goose bumps all over my body as he massages my breast with his hand through my top.

"God I've missed you" he smiles.

"Hmm same here."

We help each other to undress as we kiss continuously only breaking apart when we need to. Now both naked I lay down on the bed and Evan sits next to me looking up and down my shapely body with hungry eyes. "What are you waiting for?" I ask expecting him to climb on top of me and have me straight away.

"I want to have a bit of fun first" he says looking at me grinning.

"Oh, what do you have in mind?" I smile wondering what he means.

"Have you ever been tied up before?" he asks with a smile.

"No, I haven't" I laugh blushing not expecting him to have come out with that.

"Would you mind if I tied you up?"

"Err no I wouldn't mind," Just the thought of it is making me excited. "Have you ever been tied up before?" I ask curious to know.

Evan laughs. "No, I can't say I have."

"What are you going to tie me up with?"

Evan looks around the room and notices my dressing gown hanging on the back of the door. "Perfect" he says standing up and walking over to it giving me an amazing view of his taut naked bum. He pulls out the belt from the dressing gown and then comes over to me, his erection standing tall, the tip glistening from his excitement.

I take a deep breath and clench my legs together because feelings are intensifying between them, I've not had an orgasm for days and just the thoughts of what Evan is going to do to me when I'm tied up has me wet and excited.

"Don't be nervous, trust me okay, you are going to enjoy this I guarantee it."

"Okay I trust you" I smile wondering what's to come.

"Give me your hands," I hold my hands out to him and he ties my wrists together with one end of the belt until it's secure. "How does that feel?" he asks checking to make sure it isn't too tight.

"It feels okay."

"Good now I'm going to secure it to your headboard with this end of the belt okay."

"Okay." I take in another deep breath letting it out slowly trying to calm myself because I am so turned on and Evan hasn't even touched me yet.

After tying the end of the belt to my headboard he stands back and looks at me.

"Do you realise how incredibly hot you look right now laid there naked and tied up?"

I smile squeezing my legs together to suppress the ache feeling moisture pooling between them.

"To make it even more intense I'm going to blindfold you as well, are you okay with that?" he asks smiling.

I love that Evan asks my permission instead of just doing what he wants, he wants me to feel comfortable and the way he is making me feel right now I am more than okay with that, I would let him do anything. I can't wait to have his hands on me, to feel him inside of me. I feel wanted and sexy tied to my bed waiting for my boyfriend to take me, the man who I love with all my heart, body and soul and can't get enough of.

"Do it blindfold me" I pant. Evan can see how turned on I am.

"Relax baby or you're not going to last very long" he says finding a scarf out of my drawer.

"Wait I've got an eye mask, it's in the bottom drawer on the right."

"Even better" he says finding it and placing it over my eyes.

Now in total darkness tied to my bed all I can rely on are my senses, my hearing, and his touch. Listening to Evan moving around my room I wonder what he's doing, and I don't have to wait long to find out because the first thing I feel are his lips on mine. I automatically want to put my arms around his neck and pull him closer, but I can't.

"Evan" I moan feeling exposed but loving how he makes me feel as I moan into his mouth returning the tongue mingling kiss.

"You are so beautiful" he says running light fingertips up and down my body but not touching me where I desperately want to be touched. "I'll be back in a minute" he says walking out the room making me panic slightly because there is no way I could free myself without Evan's help if he disappears. "Evan where are you going?" I call.

"Kitchen" Evan shouts and then moments later he is back, and I can hear him placing something on my bedside drawers beside me.

My breathing is erratic, and my heart is thumping fast in my chest from the anticipation. I wait for his next move and what feels like ages but is only minutes I feel something painfully cold touch my left nipple then my right making me jump.

"Oh shit, what is that? God that's cold but it feels kind of good.'

"Relax baby" Evan says doing it again. I realise the icy cold feeling is Evan teasing me with an ice cube.

"Oh Jesus, ohhhhh..." The pain soon turns to pleasure, the extreme coldness making my nipples protrude profusely. Evan then warms my nipple with his mouth.

"OHHHHH........" I moan writhing around, my body restricted by my hands tied to the headboard but needing to move from the sensations I'm feeling.

"Does that feel good baby?" he asks blowing hot air from his mouth onto my nipples.

"Yes…so good" I moan as he gives my breasts his full attention turning me on to the max.

"Hmm…you look so sexy; your nipples are so erect" he teases them with the ice cube then his tongue before moving down my torso and swirling his tongue around my navel.

"Evan please, I need you please." I wish I could grab a hold of him and place his head where I want him the most, my clit is throbbing and aching and I'm desperate for his tongue to touch me there.

"Shush, be patient all good things come to those who wait" he says. I hear him put the ice cube back in the glass then he trails kisses down my body bypassing my sensitive area and moving down my leg towards my feet.

"Oh god Evan I want you to taste me please" I cry as he sucks in one of my toes sending a signal straight to my aching core. I feel a rush of moisture between my legs as he circles his tongue around the instep of my foot, it tickles, and I can't help but giggle.

"Does that tickle?"

"Yes."

He makes his way back up my body. "Do you want me to tickle you somewhere else Kara" he teases. I know exactly where he is going next and as if he didn't need a big enough hint, I open my legs wide for him giving him easier access. "Yes please, please." I beg.

"Always so ready for me aren't you" he smiles plunging two fingers inside my wetness feeling how turned on I am then giving me some tongue action on my clit at the same time what I've desperately been craving for.

"Oh my fucking god" I cry out as he circles it gently, his skilled mouth working me up into a frenzy. I cry out his name as an orgasm sweeps through my body, my screams of pleasure sounding all around my room showing Evan what he does to me and how he makes me feel. I'm so thankful that we are home alone because there is no way that I would have been able to contain my screams as I enjoy the best feeling ever.

"Evan stop, please stop" I cry, and Evan moves his mouth away from me, I can't take any more of his tongue because it's too much, too sensitive as the most amazing sensation fills my brain giving me such a rush.

Evan pulls off the blindfold and my eyes adjust to the light to see Evan looking at me with a big smile on his face and so much love in his eyes.

"Wow," I laugh wanting to hug him, but I can't because my hands are still tied. "Will you untie me please I want to cuddle you" I ask.

Evan smiles and unties my hands and as soon as I'm untied I fling my arms around him bringing him to me for a kiss, a kiss that shows him how much I love him and for making me so happy.

"I told you that you would enjoy it" he says grinning at me with a smug look on his face.

"It was amazing the feeling was so much more intensified because I couldn't see you and I could only feel you."

"Hmm I'm pleased you enjoyed it" he says kissing me again.

I pull my mouth away from his and give him a cheeky grin. "It's my turn now."

"What to tie me up?" he laughs.

"Of course, and why not?"

"Okay go for it" he laughs holding his hands out for me to tie them together with the dressing gown belt.

After managing to tie the belt in a fashion around his wrists I then tie the belt to the headboard and put the eye mask on Evan making him laugh. "Well, this is a first for me."

"Are you ready?" I ask determined to give him the same treatment and feelings he has just given me.

"Always." Evan cock twitches with excitement as I think about what I am going to do to him.

"Back in a minute" I say making him laugh again leaving him on the bed and going to the kitchen.

I look in the fridge for some inspiration to tease Evan with and I can only find a pot of strawberry flavoured yoghurt, so I grab that. I don't want to use an ice cube like he had with me because I want there to be an element of surprise, so I take the yoghurt back to my bedroom with a smile on my face. I love strawberries and I know Evan loves them too.

"You've been a while" Evan says hearing me come back into the room.

"Aww was you getting lonely?" I say surprising him by running my tongue up the length of his shaft that is resting on his stomach making him jump before placing the yoghurt pot on my bedside drawers.

"Shit," he laughs "You certainly don't get any warning do you when you can't see" he grins.

"Yep." I push my breasts in his face and he happily accepts them sucking on my nipples which is one of his favourite things to do when it comes to my body and it's also one of my favourite things too.

"Hmm…I could suck your nipples and play with your breasts all day" he says as I fling my head back thinking I would love that too.

Feeling a tingling sensation in between my legs again I move away because I've had my turn and I need to concentrate on Evan's needs and not my own, so I pick up the pot of strawberry yoghurt.

Opening the yoghurt pot quietly tearing the strip of foil back I dip my fingers into the cold yoghurt. "Are you ready this is going to feel cold?" I say noticing Evan's chest rising and falling quickly because he probably thinks I've got an ice cube like he used on me and wondering what I'm going to do with it.

"Have you got an ice cube?" he asks bracing himself for the coldness.

"No this is something different" I smile.

"Okay… I'm ready."

Rather than go straight for his cock I want to give him some warning like he did with me, so I smear my yoghurt covered finger around his nipples making him gasp. I lick the yoghurt from him cleaning him with my tongue causing his nipples to harden making him moan." Oh Jesus Kara, what's that, is that custard?"

"No, it's not custard, do you want a taste?" I ask wiping some of the yoghurt on one of my nipples and holding it to his mouth. "Open your mouth" I whisper, and he does as I ask, and I push my yoghurt covered nipple inside letting him taste and suck the sweet strawberry flavoured yoghurt until I'm all clean.

"Hmm…you know how much I love strawberries," he says licking his lips "More."

I tip a small amount of the yoghurt into my mouth and then kiss him letting some of the yoghurt drip into his mouth and then kissing him our tongues come together as we taste the creamy yoghurt and each other.

"God Kara you're turning me on so much, I wish I could touch you."

"I know it's hard isn't it."

"Yes very."

"Speaking of hard" I reach for the pot of yoghurt again and dribble some of the cold, milky liquid along his length making him flinch as it touches his cock and spills onto his stomach.

"Aargh fuck…."

I start by licking the yoghurt off that has spilled onto his stomach swirling my tongue around and around his taut abs cleaning him. Once he is all clean I want him to watch my next move, so I remove the blindfold letting his eyes adjust to the light. "Oh hello" he smiles.

"I want you to watch" I grin as I move my mouth to his hardness making him draw breath.

"Oh wow" he moans as I take him fully in my mouth sucking and licking him clean from the strawberry yoghurt making Evan wild with desire. "Aargh…fuck."

I love pleasuring him in this way, so I give his cock plenty of attention sucking and licking along the full length until he is panting and almost to the point of his release.

"Oh wow baby, that's so good, but I'm desperate to be inside you, can you untie me please, oh shit stop… please baby please."

I stop and look at him with a big smile on my face because as much as I wanted to make him orgasm by doing this to him, I'm desperate for him to be inside me too so I untie him from the bed and as soon as he's free he soon has me flipped onto my back making me laugh and burying himself deep inside me with one swift move.

"OHHHH god." I cry as he thrusts into me deeply both of us turned on and ready for the ultimate ride of pleasure.

"Fuck you feel good" Evan says stilling and feeling my warm insides grab his length before pulling out of me and pushing into me slowly feeling our bodies connecting, the feeling is sublime.

I wrap my legs around his body. "Hold on baby I hope you're ready for me" he says powering into my body with force.

"OHHHHH god yes......" Evan fucks me hard and I struggle to keep my legs where they are, so I lower them again as he takes me fiercely driven by his love and passion for me.

"Oh fuck, you turn me on so much."

Evan gives me everything he has, a sexual need is driving him on as we enjoy the most amazing sex, our bodies craving this after being apart for a few days.

"Evan...I'm so close."

"Me too baby I'm with you" he pants and with a few more exhilarating thrusts he stills inside me and his orgasm takes over. He lets out a long, loud satisfying moan as he spills his seed into my insides filling me up as I come too, my body squeezing him for every drop of love he is giving me.

"Oh my god," I laugh "that was unbelievable, god I love you so much." I kiss him passionately before he pulls out of me exhausted flopping onto the bed on his back at the side of me.

"Fucking Hell," he laughs "I love you too baby" he says putting his arm around me so I can snuggle into his side, his body heavy from the fuzzy orgasmic feeling in his brain.

"Well, I wasn't expecting to be tied up tonight when I saw you, but we shall have to do it again" I smile looking at him.

"Me too that was awesome" he grins.

"You make me so happy; I can't wait to introduce you to my parents on Sunday."

"Oh yes the parents, do you think they will like me?"

I sit up and look at him serious for a moment. "Honestly no I don't think they will."

"Oh" Evan frowns "That's not good why do you think that?"

"I don't think they will like you; I think they will love you" I smile.

"Jesus Kara, I thought you were being serious for a moment, you little tease." He grabs hold of me then straddles me and tickles me.

"Oh god I'm sorry stop please" I giggle wriggling beneath him.

"I might stop, or I might not" he says with his fingers poised ready to tickle me again laughing at my scrunched-up face while I wait for him to decide. I look at him looking down on me. "Okay I'm sorry I shouldn't have said that because I guess you are probably nervous about meeting them aren't you?"

Evan climbs off me and lays down at the side of me again beckoning for another cuddle.

"I guess I am a little nervous, I just want them to like me. I love their daughter so much and well if your parents don't like me then that won't be great will it?"

"Honestly, babe they will love you, how can they not, you treat me so well, you are caring, considerate, loyal and honest you will be fine."

Evan

Now I feel guilty hearing the word honest when I'm keeping it from her about Julia's visit and the accident with the coffee. Thinking about it now I'm sure it wasn't an accident.

Maybe I should just tell Kara now and get it off my chest, but she looks so happy and we are both on such a high after the amazing sex we have just had. Telling her now will just ruin the moment but it's tormenting me from keeping it from her. No, I'm going to tell her. I'm just about to open my mouth to say the words when she says, "Are you hungry?"

"Err yes I am."

"Great do you fancy a pizza?"

"Yes babe, that would be lovely."

"Great because I'm starving, I'll go and put it in the oven" she says getting up and finding a nightie to slip on before going to the kitchen.

"Kara" I call, and she turns around in the doorway, her face beaming with happiness as she looks at me. I can't do it, I can't tell her now when she is looking at me like that, just mentioning Julia's name will make this moment turn sour so I change my mind. "I love you."

"I love you too" she smiles then skips off down the hallway.

Lying on Kara's bed for a few moments I feel stressed as I run my fingers through my hair thinking. When will it be the right time to tell Kara about Julia's visit, I mean whenever I tell her she is not going to be happy about it?

It's so frustrating because it's not like I invited Julia to come to my house, she just turned up. Yes I should have told her to go when she invited herself in, but it all happened so quickly, and I was tired from my trip to Spain and not thinking clearly. Then there is the fact that I let her use my shower, why the fuck did I do that? I am such an idiot.

Oh, and I saw her naked, but it wasn't intentional, I'm sure she will understand when I explain, god I hope she does. I'm so scared of losing her again especially after being without her for some time when I left before, I have never experienced such hurt and anguish in my whole life and I never want to go through pain like that again. Being with Kara now I know for sure she is 'the one' and I'm certain she feels the same from the things she says to me and the way she acts. I don't want anything or anyone jeopardising what we have whether it be Sebastian or Julia and I will do everything in my power for it not to happen.

"I thought you were coming to the kitchen." I say standing in the doorway of my bedroom seeing Evan still laid on the bed deep in thought.

"Sorry baby I was I am, I was just having a few moments" he grins getting up off the bed finding his boxers and jeans and putting them on choosing to leave his top off.

"Oh yes that's right while I'm slaving away in the kitchen like the good little wife, you're having a nap" I laugh. I'm suddenly aware that I said the wife word and feel awkward and embarrassed.

Evan clearly not bothered by my comment laughs.

"Well wifey you'd better get back to the kitchen and get your fella a drink because I'm parched" he says walking over to me.

"Come on then." As I walk off he smacks me on the bum while he follows behind.

"Ouch," I giggle. "What would you like to drink?" I ask as Evan takes a seat at the kitchen table looking divine being shirtless, his hair all mussed up from the wild sex we had earlier.

"I'd love a beer if you have one?"

"Yep, always got some beer, Matt keeps the fridge well stocked, here you go." I take a bottle out of the fridge and pass it to him.

"Hmm that tastes good, nice and cold" he says taking a sip of the bubbly liquid.

"The pizza won't be long."

"Okay thanks" he smiles.

I open a bottle of wine that has been chilling in the fridge and pour myself a glass then join Evan sat at the table while we wait for the pizza to be ready.

"Cheers" I say clinking Evan's bottle of beer with my glass.

"Cheers."

We sit and chat about Evan's business trip to Spain and I'm so engrossed in the conversation I forget about the pizza cooking in the oven.

The smell of burning hits my nostrils. "Oh god the pizza," I quickly grab the oven gloves and open the oven door.

"Oh," I laugh. "You like it well-done, don't you?" I giggle taking it out of the oven and placing it onto the cooker top.

Evan laughs "Well done is fine."

I dish up the overcooked pizza onto two plates and we sit at the table eating it. Just as we have finished eating Evan can hear his mobile phone ringing from my bedroom.

"I'll just see who it is" Evan says hurrying to my bedroom to get his phone.

"Hmm probably Julia." I mutter rolling my eyes.

Evan

I retrieve my phone and see it's my mother calling me, so I answer it.

"Hi darling" she says before I have a chance to speak.

"Hi mother is everything okay?"

"Yes, everything is great I'm just ringing to tell you I'm here."

"What do you mean you're here?" I ask confused.

"I'm here in London, I've brought Ace with me we've just checked in to Hamilton Tower, I'd forgotten what a gorgeous hotel you own Evan."

"What?"

"Well, I thought we weren't doing anything this weekend, so we hopped on a plane and here we are."

"I wish you had given me some notice you said you were going to let me know when you were coming."

"Sorry it was a spur of the moment thing I can't wait for you to meet Ace I think you will get on great."

'Probably seeing as we are nearly the same age.'

"So where are you, come and join us for drinks?" my mother says sounding eager.

"I can't I'm busy tonight and this weekend actually."

"Evan, I haven't come all this way for you to tell me you are too busy to see your mother, cancel your plans" she says sounding insistent.

"Great" I mutter. This is all I need an unexpected visit from my mother.

"Sorry, what did you say?"

"I said great I'll do that. I can see you tomorrow, but I can't see you Sunday, it's just not possible."

"Okay love that's alright I can go and visit Sebastian on Sunday and see what he's up to. Oh, and I want to see this new hotel of yours, it looks wonderful in the newspaper articles that Connie has been sending me."

"Okay I'm actually staying near there at the moment so if I give you directions you could come over tomorrow and I'll show you around then."

"That's sounds perfect we have hired a car from the airport, so transport isn't a problem. I can't wait to see you Son; will I be meeting Kara too while I'm here?"

"Yes, we will both look forward to seeing you tomorrow."

I smile and roll my eyes; my mother is so persistent.

"Oh good, me too, I'm looking forward to meeting her, until tomorrow then bye Son."

"Bye mother."

I walk back into the kitchen where I left Kara sat at the table. "For fuck's sake." I sit down opposite her.

"What's the matter, what's Julia done now?" she asks with a sigh.

"It's not Julia, you are not going to believe this it was my mother on the phone she has just checked into Hamilton Tower and is here for the weekend wanting to see me."

"Oh right" she smiles.

"Yes, that's my mother for you, hops on a plane and here she is. Oh, and she has brought her boyfriend with her, his name is Ace, and he is 32."

"32 wow he's only two years older than you."

"Yes, you don't have to say it I know what you are thinking because I thought the same when she told me, bit of an age gap huh."

"How old is your mother?"

"She's 50 but I must admit she does look good for her age; you would think she was younger to look at her."

"Oh, so does this mean I will get to meet her then?"

"Oh yes she wants to meet you and I need you with me for moral support" I laugh.

Kara laughs. "So, what's the plan then?"

"They are driving over tomorrow because mother would like to see the Manor and then I thought we could take them out for lunch somewhere if that's okay."

"Yeah great, what time are they coming?"

"I haven't sorted a time yet; I'll text mother tomorrow morning with the details she doesn't like to get up to early anyway."

"Okay so I guess it's a full weekend of meeting the parents then."

"Yes, you could say that I'm sorry baby I can't really get out of seeing my mother, I wanted to spend the weekend just the two of us apart from having dinner with your parents."

"It's okay I'm kind of excited to meet your mother."

"I wouldn't be, you will have had enough of her by the end of the day. Anyway, I'm ready for my dessert now."

"Oh, I've only got some ice cream or a biscuit" she says looking at me. I look at her with a twinkle in my eye. "Oh… okay come on then" she smirks running off to her bedroom laughing with me following close behind her.

Twenty

Evan

I wake up early Saturday morning, my mother's visit is praying on my mind as well as not telling Kara about Julia's visit. I look at my watch and it's 6.00am Kara is fast asleep at the side of me.

I creep out of bed quietly and go to use the toilet. I wash my hands and look in the mirror above the sink thinking about the last time I saw my mother. It was when things had come to light about Julia and Sebastian's affair, my mother had visited me, held me while I cried and told me everything will be okay and then she left. She had called me numerous times over the following months but although I know she loves me we are not as close as I was with my father, my mother is closer to Sebastian.

Thinking about my father I wonder if he were still alive today how things would be, maybe Sebastian wouldn't be so messed up and maybe we would all be great friends and spend time together.

I dry my hands on a towel at the side of the sink and then return to Kara's bedroom to see she is still asleep. I climb into bed and she stirs, I take her in my arms and cuddle her curvaceous body from behind and she moans softly. "Hmm…" I try to ignore the thoughts running through my head and the growing hardness of my cock as it rubs against her bum.

I wake slightly my eyes are still closed and I can feel Evan's growing cock against my bum. I open my eyes unbeknown to Evan because I'm facing away from him and I can't ignore the feelings he brings out in me. I smile and stretch pushing my backside into Evan's front causing him to draw breath and to grab my hips.

"You awake?" he whispers.

"Yes, and I want you" I whisper and that is all the words he needs to hear as he guides his cock to my entrance and pushes into me slowly. I arch my back accepting him and we both moan feeling the strong connection and bond between us when our bodies join as one.

Evan makes love to me, spooning me from behind, in and out, in and out, repeatedly and it's not long before we both come.

He pulls out of me and I turn around and kiss him.

"Good morning" he smiles.

"Good morning yourself" I smile looking into his captivating brown eyes.

"I love waking up to you."

"I love waking up to you too, especially when you give me orgasms like that first thing in the morning" I smile snuggling into him.

After getting showered and dressed I make us some breakfast and Evan calls his mum to say we will meet up at the Manor at 12.00 noon giving her the address. After relaxing in the lounge for a while it's soon time to leave.

We arrive at the Manor and Evan's mother and Ace haven't arrived yet. Although it still looks like a building site the new hotel is starting to take shape and I can see a big difference from the last time I was here snooping.

"Oh wow" I say getting out of the car looking around.

"It's looking good isn't it?" Evan says loving the look on my face and my reaction as to how impressed I am at what I am seeing.

"Yeah, I can't wait to see what you've done inside." I walk up to him and give him a hug.

"I wish we could have spent the day together on our own" he sighs thinking his mother will be arriving soon.

"I know but aren't you pleased that you are going to be seeing your mother and meet her new boyfriend you haven't seen her for a while have you?"

"I guess so, but I'd rather just spend time alone with you."

“Yeah, me too. Oh, is this them?” I notice a white car driving down the lane towards us.

“Yep, brace yourself you are about to meet my mother” He pulls a face and I playfully hit him on the arm.

“It will be fine” I smile standing next to him watching the car as it pulls up in front of us.

Evan’s mother’s boyfriend Ace is driving, and he immediately gets out of the car, smiles, and says hello. Evan’s mother waves at us and waits for Ace to open the car door for her.

She gets out wearing an elegant cream trouser suit, her hair is immaculately styled, brown waves flow around her shoulders and she has lovely chocolate brown eyes just like Evan’s, Evan is right she doesn’t look 50 at all. She has perfect tanned skin and as soon as she gets out the car she smiles and walks over to her son.

“My darling boy it’s so good to see you” she says as he kisses her on both cheeks.

“Mother, it’s nice to see you too, you look lovely, did you find it okay?”

“Oh, thank you and yes no problem at all, Ace just followed your directions and of course the Satnav helped. So, this must be the delightful Kara, I’ve been dying to meet you dear, I’m Annabelle but you can call me Anna” she says looking at me.

“Hi Anna, it’s a pleasure to meet you” I say holding my hand out to shake hers.

"Oh, come here dear" she says grabbing hold of me and giving me a hug and a squeeze.

"It's lovely to meet you," she says holding me at arm's length and looking me over. "Evan told me he had met someone and you're just beautiful" she smiles.

"Oh thanks" I blush not really knowing what to say.

"So, have you been seeing my son long?"

"Err a little while" I smile looking at Evan who is smirking.

"Oh, I'm so sorry how rude of me let me introduce both of you to my lovely young man, Evan, Kara this is Ace."

"Hi, it's good to meet you both" Ace smiles shaking both of our hands.

"Nice watch" Evan comments noticing the watch his mother had bought Ace after asking him for his friend's contact details who owns a jewellery store in London so he could source one for her.

"Thanks" Ace smiles.

Ace is the same height as Evan but has fair hair, he is tanned with perfect teeth and of a slim build. Evan looked slightly awkward when he shook his hand looking at the young man of a similar age to him who is dating his mother. I think he is trying to get his head around the fact that since his father died his mother has graduated towards younger men and although he likes to think of himself open minded and age shouldn't matter in a relationship, he still feels strange seeing his mother with someone almost 20 years younger than she is and it's taking some getting used to.

"So, this is your new hotel Evan it looks wonderful, are you going to show us around?" his mother asks looking at the building in front of her.

"Of course mother, if you would all care to follow me" Evan smiles.

After giving us all the grand tour of what the contractors have done so far and explaining what is yet to be done Evan's mother is suitably impressed as we walk through the front door ready to leave.

"Wow it really is a magnificent place, we will definitely be returning once it's finished and staying in one of those fancy suites you have told us about" Anna says smiling at her son.

"Yes, it looks amazing Evan" I agree.

"Thanks, it was such a great find not only because of how amazing the building is and the grounds, but I would never have met this beautiful girl if I hadn't have bought it" Evan says looking at me and putting his arm around me making me blush.

"Oh Evan, I'm so pleased to see you happy again, I was only speaking to Julia the other day and telling her how happy you are and that you have moved on."

'What Evan's mother still speaks to Julia? I didn't know this and after what that woman put him through.'

"Yes, Julia knows the situation, anyway, are you hungry I was going to take us all out for lunch?" Evan asks looking at everyone not wanting to dwell about Julia.

We all agree so I suggest eating at the new place on Bridge Street that people rave about and liking the idea we decide we will eat there.

Leaving the Manor in Evan's car Anna and Ace follow behind us in their car and we drive to the restaurant in town.

After parking the car in the car park at the back of the restaurant Evan's mother and Ace get out and just as I'm about to get out too Evan stops me by placing a hand on my leg. "Are you okay? It's not too awkward is it?" he asks looking at me.

"No relax I'm fine, they are really nice, don't worry."

"Okay I just wanted to check you are okay before we go into the restaurant."

"Thank you," I smile "I was a bit surprised to find out that your mother still speaks to Julia though after everything she put you through, are they friends then?"

"I wouldn't say they are friends, but they do still speak every now and again."

"Oh right" I frown feeling disappointed by that fact and Evan notices.

"Hey if it makes you feel any better my mother has never really been a big fan of hers and just tolerates her."

I smile "It does."

"Come on then we'd best go because they keep looking at us."

"Okay."

We are seated at a table by the window, a different table to where I sat last time when I came here with Sebastian which I don't want to think about.

A waiter comes over to take our order of drinks and then we sit and peruse the menus.

"So, Evan you never did tell me how you met Kara?"

"Didn't I well I met her in a coffee shop where she works in town, I called in for directions and there she was." He gives my leg a squeeze under the table and I place my hand on top of his.

"Oh, how lovely, have you worked there long?" Anna asks looking at me.

"About six years." I smile.

"Oh really, and do you enjoy it?"

"It's okay it pays the rent, it's not what I want to do for the rest of my life though."

"Oh, and what would you like to do?" Anna smiles.

"I'm not sure really, maybe more office type work."

"How old are you?" Anna asks obviously trying to get to know more about me.

"I'm 25."

"Such a sweet young thing you've no need to worry I'm sure Evan will look after you."

I don't know what to say to that comment, so I just smile.

"So, Ace what do you do?" Evan asks sensing I'm getting questioned by his mother and trying to take the conversation away from me.

"I'm looking for work at the moment, but your mother keeps telling me I don't need to work because she likes having me around, but I don't like your mother spending money on me I want to pay my own way."

I think Evan is impressed with his answer by the look on his face, his initial thought of 'is he sponging off his mother' is wrong because it sounds like he's not, I guess you shouldn't judge someone until you get to know them.

"I've told you Frederick left me so much money when he died, we'll have enough to live on for the rest of our days" Anna smiles looking at him adoringly.

"Yes, and like I told you it's your money not mine and I like to pay my own way."

"Oh, you are silly" she laughs.

"Are you ready to order?" the waitress asks arriving at our table.

"Yes, I believe we are" Evan smiles.

The waitress blushes looking at him and I know why because I had the same reaction when I first laid eyes on him because he is just so gorgeous.

We all place our orders and then the waitress leaves. While we are chatting and sipping our drinks waiting for the food Anna's mobile phone starts ringing.

"Will you excuse me for a moment" she says taking it out of her handbag and answering the call.

"Sebastian darling I've been trying to reach you" she says.

I look at Evan, his facial expression saying everything that I already know when he hears his name and it's the same as mine, torment.

We listen as Anna continues the conversation with Sebastian and Evan looks more agitated by the minute.

After chatting for a few minutes, she finishes the call. "That was Sebastian as you probably gathered, he was just returning my call about meeting up tomorrow."

"Right" Evan says the atmosphere around the table slightly tense.

"He said to say hi and he hopes you are keeping okay, oh and to give his regards to Kara too, see he is being friendly and nice, I think you should be the bigger man Evan and make the first move into making it up with him, he obviously wants to make it up with you."

"Oh my fucking god, you have no idea, can you not remember me telling you he was pretending to be me to use Kara to get to me."

"Oh, I asked him about that, and he said it was a joke and you took it the wrong way, you really need to stop acting so callous towards him you know."

"Seriously" Evan scowls standing up quickly and his chair scrapes across the wooden floor making a loud noise making people in the restaurant look.

"Evan where are you going?" his mother asks sounding upset as tears well in her eyes.

"The men's room." He walks off leaving me sat with his mother and Ace feeling awkward when his mother starts to cry, and Ace comforts her.

"Excuse me I'll be back in a minute." I get up from the table and make my way through the diners to the men's toilets, I stand outside and wait for Evan to come out.

After a few moments Evan appears not looking happy then seeing me stood waiting for me he smiles.

"Sorry about that are you okay?"

"I'm fine but you're clearly not" I say touching the side of his arm.

"I'm sorry she just pisses me off she can't see what Sebastian's like; it doesn't matter what I say she always sees the good in him."

"Babe try not to let it get to you we've got a meal to get through and your mother is already sat crying at the table."

"Fucking typical turns on the waterworks as usual."

"Listen just try and get through the next few hours, then we can go home" I smile.

"Yeah okay."

He pulls me to him for a kiss. I slip my tongue into his mouth and he pulls me closer pushing my body up against a nearby wall. We kiss passionately.

"Evan, we need to get back" I whisper feeling him getting aroused his body pressed up against mine.

Evan sighs. "If we must, come on then."

We walk back into the restaurant hand in hand and see Evan's mother wiping her eyes with a tissue.

"I apologise" Evan says with a serious face looking at his mother as we take our seats at the table again.

"I'm sorry Son" his mother sniffs and Evan takes a hold of her hand that is resting on the table and gives it a squeeze. "It's okay and I'm sorry if I upset you" Evan smiles.

"I hate that there is this animosity between you and your brother, I just wish it would all get sorted out and you could go back to being friends, it's been going on far too long" she sniffs.

"I know look let's just forget about it and enjoy our lunch because here it is now" Evan says letting go of her hand seeing the waitress from earlier coming over to our table with plates of food.

After enjoying the food it's time to leave. We say our goodbyes then Evan's mother and Ace get into the hire car and drive away.

"Well, that was eventful" I smile looking at Evan.

"Yes, I told you to brace yourself, thank fuck that's over with."

"She wasn't that bad, she's nice."

"Yeah, she's alright I was really looking forward to spending the weekend together alone and my mother visiting unexpectedly kind of spoilt it."

"Well, she goes back tomorrow and there is always next weekend."

"Yeah, there is…oh shit I forgot to tell you."

"What?"

"The trip to Paris I booked it for next weekend."

"Evan… how can you forget to tell me something as important as that? It's a bit short notice what if Jodie and Matt can't make it" I say looking cross at him.

"Sorry I've been busy, and it slipped my mind and if they can't go then it'll just be the two of us won't it" he smiles.

We arrive back at my flat to be greeted by Jodie and Matt in the kitchen having just finished eating a late lunch.

"Hi guys" I smile walking into the kitchen followed by Evan, and we sit down at the table joining them.

We tell them about Evan's mother's surprise visit and meeting her new boyfriend and that we have been out for lunch with them.

"Oh, that's nice," Jodie smiles. "I hear you are meeting Kara's parents' tomorrow Evan" Jodie smiles.

"Yes, I am, it seems to be the weekend for meeting the parents doesn't it babe" he says smiling at me.

"Yeah, it does" I smile.

"Do you fancy a beer mate?" Matt asks Evan getting up to get himself one out of the fridge.

"Yes, thanks mate" Evan replies.

"Are you staying tonight Matt?" I ask.

"I am if that's okay?"

"No, it's not, I think you should go home" I grin.

"Oh, so it's like that is it" he laughs.

"Only joking, oh we have some news" I smile.

"Ooh exciting what is it?" Jodie asks.

"Are you both free next weekend?" I ask.

"Yes, we are, why?" Jodie and Matt reply.

"Well Evan has booked for all of us to go to Paris and only just remembered to mention it."

"Sorry guys I've been away this week and been busy" Evan says holding his hands up in defence apologising.

"Yes of course it's okay we can't wait can we Matt?" Jodie smiles.

"Yes, and don't be sorry Evan when you are taking us away on a free trip, not that I agree with you paying for us" Matt smiles.

"No problem" Evan smiles pleased to see how happy they both are.

"Great anyway we'll see you guys in a bit because we need to go and have a shower."

"Oh yeah," Matt grins "together?" he laughs.

"Yeah, and is that a problem?" I laugh.

"Shut up Matthew and leave them alone" Jodie says.

"Care to join us?" Evan asks and we all look at him shocked. "Only joking, I'm really not into foursomes" he says, and we all laugh out loud stunned by Evan's comment.

Sebastian

"So, you are seeing your mother tomorrow, how lovely for you to spend your Sunday" Julia says sarcastically climbing into bed at my flat.

"Yeah, I know and if she knew we are still together you would be coming too so you got out of that one didn't you" I reply climbing into bed at the side of her.

"Did you say she's brought her boyfriend along with her?"

"Yes, and I can't wait to meet him, the sponger."

"What like you Seb, you still take money off your mother now and then" she smiles.

"Yeah, but she's got plenty and I'm her doting son" I laugh.

"Yeah right. Oh, I forgot to tell you with all the drama going on visiting Evan and the coffee spillage I went to see Kara at the coffee shop the other day."

"You did what, Liv you'd better not have ruined things and blown our cover I don't want her suspecting anything."

"Relax Sebastian everything is fine."

"Yes, but won't she find it strange that you know where she works."

"I told her that Evan told me, she's not going to know I know because of you."

"I hope not, what did you say to her?"

'For fucks sake Liv.'

"I suggested we should be friends and I dropped it in conversation that Evan was very comforting when he came to see me when I was upset after your so-called visit, you know when you grabbed me and said all those nasty things to me" she smiles wickedly.

"Julia Livingston you are such a bitch."

"I know I needed to get inside her head, so she starts questioning things wondering if Evan is for real or if he does still have feelings for me, so she believes we are having an affair."

"Well as long as she didn't suspect anything about us then I suppose it was a good idea. So, when do you think we should send Kara the photos and destroy their relationship, so Evan sees sense and pays me my money?"

"Oh, I think we should wait a bit longer and get more evidence first. By the time we are finished Evan will definitely be paying you your money Seb I'm sure of it."

"I hope you're right because this is getting exhausting, I mean it was fun to start playing these games but it's all becoming a bit tedious."

"Oh, I don't know I'm enjoying our little game seeing Evan squirm and getting Kara all worked up and when your bank account is so much richer just think how much nicer our life will be. I can just picture us now jetting off to lots of exotic places living the high life, what do you think?"

"Yeah, maybe, but I was thinking I could set up a business and do something more with my life."

"Oh, but why work when you can just have fun?"

"Speaking of fun, I think it's time we stopped talking and had a bit of fun of our own."

"Oh yeah and what do you have in mind?" she grins.

"Well first of all I'm going to tie you up and explore every inch of your naked body with my tongue until you are begging me to fuck you, then I'm going to make you come over and over again until you see stars and are begging me to stop, how does that sound?"

"It sounds like you should go and get the handcuffs because I'm already getting wet just thinking about it."

"I'm on my way."

Twenty One

"Morning beautiful" Evan says stretching looking at me staring at him with a smile on my face.

"Morning babe, did you sleep well?"

"The best, did you?"

"Hmm really well, are you nervous about today?" I ask. Today is the day Evan will be meeting my parents.

"I am a little I haven't met any girl's parents in a very long time, I didn't meet Julia's because they have been dead for a long time, they both died in a car accident when she was ten."

"That's really sad they died when she was so young, who brought her up then?"

"Her grandparents on Julia's mum's side but they have both passed away now too."

"Oh, and does she have any brothers and sisters or any other grandparents who are alive?"

"No, she is an only child. When her grandparents died they left her the house and some money and that's when she moved to London."

"So, she's not originally from London then?"

"No, she lived on the South Coast somewhere in a small village, she said she wanted to experience what it was like living in London and that's why she moved."

"Oh, I see. How did you two meet then?"

"Kara, do you really want to know this?" Evan asks knowing that every time we talk about Julia it always ends up with us arguing.

"Yes, I'm curious."

"Are you sure because I don't want to talk about this if it's going to upset you?"

"No, it won't I promise, so how did you two meet?"

"We met in a park, I was going for a morning run and I ran past her and she called out to me. She was sat on a bench, so I stopped running and walked over to her. She asked me if I knew where this place was, apparently she was supposed to be meeting someone there, she was going on a date and because she didn't know London very well she was unsure where it was."

"She was going on a date?"

"Yes, with some guy she had met in a bar apparently, they had arranged to go out for lunch that day."

"Oh, so how come you started dating then?"

"Well after explaining to her where this place was, we started talking and after about 10 minutes she said, "Do you fancy going out for lunch with me instead?"

"Really oh my god she ditched the other guy, she was brave asking you that."

"Yeah, I was a bit shocked to be honest, but I thought okay why not because we seemed to get on quite well and then after that we started dating."

"Oh." I hate thinking about the two of them together it makes me feel jealous but then I did ask so it's my own fault.

"Kara."

"Uh-huh."

"Stop it."

"Stop what?"

"Stop thinking about Julia and I being together, I know what you're thinking."

"Sorry I can't help it" I smile.

"Well don't because when I met Julia it was nothing compared to the spark I felt when I first saw you."

"Really?"

"Yes, so let's leave it there and talk about something else."

"Okay, listen don't be nervous about meeting my parents today because they are really down to earth and I'm sure you will get on great."

"I'm not nervous about meeting your mum it's just your dad I want him to approve, I want him to know how much I care about his daughter and how much I love her and will take care of her." He kisses me on the top of my head and wraps his arms around me.

"Don't worry, my dad will approve but I wouldn't mention to them that you love me just yet because they need to get their heads around the fact that I have a boyfriend first before telling them you love their daughter."

"Kara I'm not going to declare my love for you at the dinner table" he laughs.

"Alright just saying" I laugh as we look at each other before kissing each other softly.

"Shall we get up then and get some breakfast, we'd better just have some cereal though because my mother will have gone all out, and we will be having a big meal in a few hours" I smile.

"Okay come on then."

I go to move to get out of bed but before I have a chance to go anywhere Evan grabs hold of me making me squeal and pulls me on top of him, I look into his chocolate brown eyes.

"Hello" I giggle as he holds me in place.

"Hello" he smiles nuzzling his nose against mine.

"I thought we were getting up?" I giggle.

"We are but I want another kiss first before we do."

I smile then kiss him encased in his arms feeling happy. Today I will be introducing Evan to my parents and I feel so proud to call him my boyfriend. I already know that my parents are going to love him, he is financially stable, he owns his own house, drives a fantastic car and he makes their daughter so unbelievably happy so what's not to love.

"Come on then let's get up because I can feel something else getting up and we haven't got time" I giggle getting up off the bed.

We both get dressed, I'm wearing some tight-fitting black jeggings and a multi coloured blue and white patterned tie front shirt showing a bit of cleavage and Evan's wearing some blue jeans and a casual white shirt. We go to the kitchen and have some cereal followed by a cup of tea. After chilling in the lounge talking to Jodie and Matt for a while it's time to go.

"Right, we'd best go babe because we don't want to be late" I say looking at Evan.

"Yes, I need to make a good impression, so we'd better not keep them waiting" Evan agrees.

Deciding to walk to my mum and dad's which isn't far we set off walking in the sunshine hand in hand.

"I'd like to buy your mum some flowers" Evan says as we walk by a shop with them displayed in buckets outside. "Okay she would like that" I smile.

We pick a few bunches of carnations, pay the lady then continue our walk. It's only a short walk to my mum and dad's bungalow and turning into the road where they live Evan's mobile starts ringing. He looks at the screen, it's Julia.

"Why the fuck can't she leave me alone, this is getting beyond a joke now" Evan says looking angrily at his phone.

"Hmm Julia what a surprise" I huff rolling my eyes.

"I'm not answering it" Evan says putting his phone back into his pocket.

The call stops and then immediately starts ringing again.

"For fuck's sake go away will you?" Evan says running his hands through his hair looking agitated.

"Just answer the bloody thing she will only keep ringing otherwise."

"I'm really sorry babe, here can you hold these a moment?" Evan says passing me the flowers.

"Fine." I grab hold of them and lean against a nearby lamp post feeling really annoyed.

Evan

I answer the call sounding displeased. "Julia what do you want I thought I told you to stop calling me all the time?"

"Evan hi that's not a very nice way to greet someone."

"I'm sorry for being rude but…"

"I need to see you" she says interrupting me.

"What no I'm sorry but that's not going to happen."

"Evan please it's important."

"Why what's so important Julia?"

"It's Sebastian he threatened me again… look I don't want to tell you all the details over the phone, but it was worse than last time, will you meet me somewhere later?"

"I don't think that's a good idea and I can't I'm busy."

"Oh, I'm guessing she's there," there's a long pause I don't say anything and remain silent.

"It's okay I understand you can't talk, tomorrow then, how about I call to see you at Hamilton Tower, I really need to tell you what happened" Julia says sounding tearful.

I think for a moment, I want to say no because I don't want to get involved but I find myself saying "Okay come to the hotel at 10am." If I have to meet with her then my hotel is the best place, so she won't be able to try anything like last time. Plus, if my brother is up to no good I need to know in case Kara is going to be a target again.

"Perfect thanks Ev I'll look forward to seeing you then and thank you."

"Goodbye Julia."

"Goodbye Evan."

Evan ends the call and I'm fuming. "So, you're meeting her again tomorrow?" I shove the flowers into his chest and cross my arms defensively.

"Yes, it looks that way, I'm sorry but she said Sebastian has threatened her again and it was worse this time, I need to know what he's up to in case he comes after you and threatens you."

I roll my eyes. "Yes, but is she just saying that Evan so you will see her?"

"No, I don't think so, she started to get upset again and she did sound genuine."

"So why did he threaten her, what happened this time?"

"I don't know that's why I'm meeting with her tomorrow she wouldn't tell me over the phone so she's coming to Hamilton Tower at 10am to give me the details."

"Evan how much longer is this going to go on for, the ex, the meddling twin brother, are they always going to be interfering in our lives?"

"I know I'm sorry and I'm going to sort it I promise."

"Yes, but you keep saying that and nothing has changed."

"I know look I've decided after I've heard what she has to say I'm going to tell her that this is the last time and not to contact me anymore and if she does I will ignore her, I'll change my mobile number if I have to. If Sebastian is doing these things that she says he is then it's their problem not mine, I've moved on now and she can't expect me to keep being involved in their business. I am not having her destroy what we have by her being in the background all the time."

I smile. Evan moves towards me and puts an arm around me. "Don't be mad at me please I didn't ask her to phone me, it's not my fault" he says looking at me with a sad face.

How can I be mad at him because what he is saying is true? It's not like he is phoning her, it's Julia who is the one who seems to be contacting him all the time.

"I know she just makes me mad that's all."

"I know she does, come here" he says pulling me closer to his body and kissing me like there is no tomorrow. I pull away breathless.

"Come on let's forget about her and go and see my mum and dad because we're running late now."

"Sorry, come on then beautiful."

We walk quickly up the road to my parent's bungalow, and I see my mum looking through the kitchen window waiting for us to arrive. When she sees us, she opens the front door, and she shouts to my dad "Graham they're here." I walk up to her and she flings her arms around me giving me a big hug like she hasn't seen me for weeks; I think she is overexcited about meeting Evan. My dad appears in the doorway.

I let go of my mum and do the introductions. "Mum, Dad this is Evan, Evan this is my Mum and Dad Jules and Graham."

"Hi, it's a pleasure to meet you both" Evan says shaking hands with them and presenting my mum with the bouquet of flowers. "Oh, these are lovely thank you Evan" my mum says with a big smile of her face.

"Sorry we're a bit late." I smile.

"Oh no it's fine dinner's not ready for a little while yet I thought we could have a cuppa and a chat first, come on in then" my mum says ushering us through the door and towards the lounge.

"Dinner smells good Mum" I say walking past the kitchen.

"Thanks, it was a lovely joint of beef I bought from the butchers" she smiles.

Taking a seat next to each other on the sofa there is a slight awkwardness in the room at first. My dad keeps glancing at Evan as well as my mother because I haven't introduced a boyfriend to them in a long time.

"So, what do you do Evan?" my dad asks all serious.

"I own and run six hotels, my sixth hotel is being renovated at the moment I don't know if Kara told you, but I bought the Manor on Danes Avenue and I'm having it turned into a hotel."

"Oh, that's you is it?" my dad Graham says sounding impressed "I've been reading all about it in the local paper."

"Yes, that's me" Evan smiles.

"It's going to be magnificent when it's finished Dad" I say feeling proud of Evan and what he has achieved in his life so far.

"I thought it looked very impressive from the photos I keep seeing" Dad says.

"Thanks, you will have to come and have a look when it's open" Evan says.

"Oh, we'd like that wouldn't we Graham?" Mum says not taking her eyes off Evan and swooning at how handsome he is.

"Yes dear, tell me how did you meet my daughter?" Dad asks.

Evan tells my dad about his Satnav not working and calling into Walt's Coffee Shop looking for directions and then bumping into me later that day.

"So, if you were visiting the area where do you live?" my dad asks continuing with the questions.

"I live in London" Evan replies.

"Oh right, not too far away then."

"Evan also owns his own villa in Italy as well" I smile.

"Oh wow, sounds like you are doing well for yourself then, I've always wanted to go to Italy" my mother gushes.

"Well, you are welcome to stay at my villa anytime Mrs Davis" Evan states.

"Oh, thank you and please call me Jules" my mother blushes.

"Yes, thank you Evan, that's very kind of you to offer," Dad smiles.

"Oh Graham, we haven't even got them a drink yet what sort of hosts are we?" Mum laughs. "Would you like a beer, or a cup of tea or coffee Evan?"

"I would love a beer thank you Jules."

"Okay great, Graham get the man a drink will you, Kara would you like a glass of wine?"

"Yes please Mum."

I watch my parents scurry off out of the room like a couple of excited children.

"So how do you think it's going, do you think they like me?" Evan whispers.

"It's going great they love you I can tell."

"Hope so" he smiles giving me a quick kiss on the lips before my parents return.

After drinking our drinks my parents ask Evan some more questions about his life, where did he grow up, schooling, holidays that sort of thing and then it's time for dinner.

Sitting at the kitchen table mum dishes up a lovely roast beef dinner with all the trimmings and I feel happy because my parents and Evan are getting on well.

"Jules this looks lovely, thank you" Evan smiles making my mum blush. That's who I get it from because he always makes me blush too.

"Oh, thank you and it's my pleasure Evan, it's so lovely to meet you I think we should have a toast, Graham" Mum says looking at my Dad for him to say something as we all pick up our glasses.

"Oh right, well I'll admit I was a little apprehensive when Jules told me that Kara was bringing her boyfriend home to introduce you to us and as her father I had high expectations. Kara is our only child, our beautiful daughter who we love with all our hearts and we only want the best for her, and Evan I can honestly say you have surprised me. I know from meeting you that I can tell you are a good person and I think you will do right by my daughter and we welcome you into our family home anytime. So, a toast to both of you wherever life may take you and of course to my gorgeous wife Jules for cooking this wonderful meal. Cheers." We all smile and chink glasses. My dad's words bring tears to my eyes, I love my mum and dad so much and it means the world to me to know that they approve of Evan and love him just as much as I do.

"Cheers" we all say and then we tuck into the lovely meal.

After eating the roast followed by homemade apple pie and custard, we sit in the lounge with full tummies with a cup of tea talking some more until it's getting late and time to leave.

"We'd better go Evan because you've got to drive back to London tonight and I've got some ironing to do."

"Oh right, yes okay" Evan says looking at his watch and seeing it's 4.30pm.

We say our goodbyes and my parents tell Evan he is welcome to come around again sometime soon and then we leave.

Walking back to the flat hand in hand I think what a great day and weekend it's been, even though most of it has been taken up with meeting the parents I have enjoyed every minute of it, spending time with Evan and being a couple.

We arrive back at the flat and go to see Jodie and Matt who are sat in the lounge watching television. After letting them know how lunch went Evan and I go to my room so he can pack his overnight bag in readiness for leaving.

"I wish you didn't have to go" I sigh closing the bedroom door.

"Me too, come here" he says sitting on the bed beckoning me over to sit next to him.

Pushing my hair back from my face and sweeping it behind my shoulder he takes me in his strong muscly arms and kisses me then forcing me gently to lie back onto the bed we carry on the tongue mingling kiss.

"Hmm... please can you stay?" I whisper feeling for the belt on his jeans and undoing it.

"Kara," he smiles "I can't baby, and besides haven't you got some ironing you need to do" he says placing his hand on top of mine stopping me from undressing him any further.

"Yes, but I need to do you more, you know you want to" I smile teasing him taking hold of his hand and placing it on my breast as my hand returns to his jeans opening the fly and he doesn't stop me this time. He never can resist me, and I love that he can't. I slide my hand into his boxers finding his erection and take his hard length in my hand stroking it up and down.

"Aargh Jesus Kara I don't think I could ever say no to you" he moans massaging my breast through my top while I continue to stroke up and down his length feeling how turned on he is feeling the wet tip around the end of his cock and rubbing it with my thumb.

"That's because you love me, and you want me just as much as I want you." I kiss his neck and face "Kara …" I stop him from saying any more words finding his mouth again and carry on the kiss turning him on more and more.

"Make love to me" I whisper the kiss becoming more urgent "Oh fuck that's good" he says as I stroke his cock while he fumbles with the button and zip on my jeans then sliding his hand into my knickers finding me soaked as he pushes two fingers inside.

"Kara you're so wet" Evan says pulling his fingers out so he can help take off my jeans and knickers. Pulling off his own jeans both of us naked from the waist down I'm expecting him to sink his cock into me straight away, but he doesn't he encourages me to lay down on the bed and surprises me by lowering his head in between my legs and placing his mouth onto my clit sucking gently causing me to cry out.

"OOOOHHH……shit." I forget that Jodie and Matt are down the hallway when I let out a loud moan as he circles his tongue around my sensitive spot turning me on to the extreme. We are completely consumed in the moment when there is a knock on my bedroom door.

"Kar." Jodie calls.

"Fuck" Evan mutters getting up quickly and grabbing his boxers and jeans to put them on. "Hang on a minute" I call to Jodie who is stood waiting outside the door. The pair of us run around my bedroom trying to get dressed like a couple of teenagers who are up to no good and have nearly been discovered by their parents.

"Did you call me?" Jodie says as I open the door ajar.

"No why?"

"Oh, I thought you shouted Joooode."

"No, I didn't" I smirk trying not to giggle because I definitely called out, but it wasn't Jodie's name I was shouting it was more like "OOOOHHHH...." a long moan.

"Okay no worries I'll leave you too it then whatever you are up to in there" Jodie grins.

"I'm just getting changed that's all and Evan is packing his stuff getting ready to go home" I smile turning around to look at Evan's cheeky face smiling at me.

"Okay I'll leave you to get changed then" Jodie winks walking off back to the lounge and I close the door.

"That was close" I giggle looking at Evan.

"It was I'd best go then" he says.

"Oh no you can't leave me like this when I'm turned on, I want you...badly" I pout.

"Well, if you put it like that" he laughs undoing his jeans again.

"Where were we?" I smile walking over to him.

Pulling off my jeans and knickers again Evan leaves his on this time but just pulls them down at the front as well as his boxers revealing his massive erection.

"Come here," he says picking me up so I'm straddling him as he walks over to the wall by the window.

Pulling the curtains shut with one hand he smirks. "You need to be quiet this time okay."

"I'll try" I giggle as he pushes me up against the wall and enters me "Oh god Evan" I moan trying to be quiet as he plunges his cock into me.

"Shush," he smirks "This is going to be quick, hold on to me" he says as I cling onto his back and he starts to pick up the pace.

Evan fucks me against my bedroom wall and with every thrust it sends me to a place of pure pleasure.

"Fuck that's good" he pants holding me up as he takes me forcefully both of us desperate for one another.

In and out, in and out he pounds into me and Evan is right it is quick because we are so turned on we reach our explosive orgasms quickly. He fills me with his come while I clench around him burying my face into his neck trying to contain the scream that I so desperately want to let go.

The feeling is incredible and it's hard to suppress how I really feel when Jodie and Matt are just down the hallway and have heard me once already. I need to be quiet as the amazing feeling fills my brain. Evan is breathless and hangs his head on my shoulder while we come down from our orgasms that are spiralling throughout our bodies.

“I feel like a naughty teenager” Evan laughs.

“I know sorry, I can’t believe Jodie thought I was calling her earlier” I giggle.

“Oh Joooooode, oh god it’s sooooo good Jooodee…” Evan jokes laughing, and I playfully hit him,

“Shush you I was enjoying myself” I laugh.

“Yes, I could tell, and you were being very vocal as well.”

“I wasn’t that loud, was I?”

“Well, if Jodie could hear you from the lounge I would say yeah pretty much” he laughs.

“I forgot for a moment they were here” I giggle.

“I apologise that my cock makes you scream” Evan grins.

“Alright big head.”

“Hmm it is big isn’t it?” Evan says still inside me moving his hips around making me laugh at his jovial ways.

“Well big boy do you think you could free me now or are you going to keep me impaled on your big cock for the rest of the night?” I smile.

“There’s an idea yes I think I will keep you on here all night” he smiles kissing me, my legs still wrapped around him.

“Evan” I laugh.

“Yes baby.”

"Are you going to let me down then or what?"

"I might do, or I might just go for round two" he laughs.

"Seriously?"

"I'm joking" he laughs pulling out of me and helping me down to the floor, my legs feeling like jelly. I walk over to the bedside drawers to get a tissue to clean ourselves with.

"Thank you for making me so happy" I smile.

"You don't have to thank me, you make me happy too, I love you more than anything or anyone in this world."

"Do you love me more than your car and your precious boat and motorbikes?" I smirk.

"Well… maybe not quite as much as them" he laughs.

After both getting dressed Evan packs up the rest of his things and then we make our way down the hallway passing the lounge. "I thought you were getting changed?" Jodie says walking into the hall with a cheeky look on her face.

"I was and then I thought there is no point now because I'll be getting my pyjamas on soon." I blush.

God that was such a lame thing to say Jodie knows exactly what we were doing, she's not stupid.

"Evan's going now" I say wanting to change the subject in case she mentions hearing me moaning while having sex, god how embarrassing.

"Oh, okay bye Evan" Jodie and Matt call.

“I’ll walk out with you” I say as Evan says goodbye and then we walk down the path towards his car.

Evan puts his overnight bag in the boot and then walks over to me for a goodbye kiss.

“I’ll give you a call tomorrow okay.”

“Okay and I hope your meeting goes alright with Julia tomorrow.”

“Oh yes don’t remind me” he grimaces before taking me in his arms and kissing me again.

Watching him drive away I feel sad, I love being with Evan and when we are apart I hate it.

I think because Julia is hanging around it makes me paranoid when we are not together because I don’t trust her and what she might do.

Knowing she is going to see him at Hamilton Tower tomorrow makes me anxious. I would love to be a fly on the wall in that meeting, not only to hear what she has to say but to see Evan telling her that she is not to contact him anymore, their so-called friendship is over.

Good riddance that’s what I say.

Twenty Two

Evan

It's five minutes to 10am and I'm waiting anxiously for Julia to arrive. I look at my watch while I pace the floor of my office at Hamilton Tower feeling edgy because Julia will be arriving any moment. I keep going over in my mind what I'm going to say to her, what is the best way to tell someone I don't want you in my life anymore not even as friends. I jump when there is a knock on the door.

"Come in" I call, and Tony enters announcing Julia's arrival. I thank him and he shows Julia in then shuts the door leaving me alone with her in my office.

"Evan hi" she smiles.

"Hi Julia please take a seat, would you like anything to drink, tea, coffee, water perhaps?"

"No, I'm fine thank you and I'd probably better not risk having a coffee because we both know what happened last time" she smiles taking off her long black wool stylish coat and laying it across the back of the chair. Julia is wearing a knee length red pencil skirt with some high heeled black shoes and a black blouse tucked in at the waist, I must admit she looks nice. I can't help noticing she is showing some cleavage her lips are painted a deep red and I think she has dressed to impress for the occasion.

"Oh, that reminds me here's your t-shirt I borrowed thank you" she says getting it out of her handbag and passing it to me which smells of her perfume, which I'm sure she has sprayed on purpose so it will remind me of her.

"Thanks." I accept it and put it on my desk.

"So how have you been since I last saw you at your house?" Julia asks with a smile.

"Good but I should be asking you that question seeing as that's why you're here isn't it, so… what happened this time, why did Sebastian threaten you?"

"Oh Evan, every time I think about it I feel upset," she says taking a moment making herself sound tearful before continuing. "It was awful, I was out in London with my friend Jackie and we were having a lovely night until we saw Sebastian. He came to the Wine Bar where we frequently hang out, it was that one where I saw you not so long ago when you were out with Curtis anyway he spotted me and came straight over to me. I told him I didn't want to talk to him and that we were leaving but he said he wanted to apologise for turning up at my flat that time when he was ranting about you and me and so because he seemed sincere I thought I would listen to what he had to say."

"Okay."

"Anyway, he said he didn't want to talk in front of my friend he wanted to apologise in private, so we went to a quiet area near the toilets. He started to apologise saying that he was sorry but then he followed it with he was sorry he ever laid eyes on me, he said I was always so needy and that he only slept with me because he needed a good shag, and I was easy and offering it to him on a plate. I swear Evan it was him that came on to me."

"Yes, so you've said hundreds of times before so what happened next?"

"He kept saying nasty things to me so I tried to walk away but he grabbed me around the throat and pushed me up against the wall." Tears roll down her cheeks.

"Here." I pass her a tissue from the box on my desk.

"Thanks" she sniffs before carrying on. "He said if I saw you to tell you that if you don't pay him the money then you will regret it, and he will do something to make you pay. He said you'd better watch your back and I was to give you his warning."

"It's just words Julia" I sigh.

"Yes, but his hands around my throat wasn't just words was it, you didn't see him Evan I seriously think he will do something; I think he is getting desperate now. I had marks around my throat he grabbed me that tight. I thought he was going to strangle me there and then; I was so scared I honestly think he's going to hurt me or you."

Julia starts to cry even more. "He also said don't bother going to the police because they can't protect us."

"I didn't realise he was that bad, name calling is one thing but if he is getting physical and threatening you then you definitely need to go to the police."

"Didn't you hear what I just said Sebastian said that..."

"I know what he said and it's bullshit, did you go to the police and show them the marks he had left on your neck?"

"No, I didn't because I was scared of what Sebastian might do if I did, that's why I wanted to talk to you about it."

I get up from my desk feeling annoyed and stressed and pace the floor of my office.

"Evan, I feel like his anger and bitterness has increased tenfold and that if he doesn't get his money he is going to seriously do some harm like even kill someone most likely you or me" she sobs.

"It must be the drink making him act this way unless he's doing drugs" I say walking to the front of my desk and leaning on it offering her another tissue.

"Thank you I don't know but you should have seen his eyes, they definitely weren't normal." Julia seems genuinely upset; her head is bent down as she wipes the flowing tears from her eyes.

"I really think you need to go to the police and report this then if he does do something they will have a record of it which will go towards any evidence they might need" I stress.

"Oh god, I'm so scared Evan please just pay Sebastian the money please" she begs looking up at me shaking and scared.

"I'm sorry Julia but paying him the money isn't the answer, he needs professional help. I'm sure he was just trying to scare you so you would tell me, and I will pay him, I don't think he will carry out his threats."

"Yes but he might Evan and what then it will be too late, please just pay him" she pleads.

"I'm sorry I can't do that. I won't have my brother threatening us to get his own way."

"Why do you have to be so bloody stubborn, surely you can see how scared I am?" she snaps getting angry.

"My brother is a lot of things, but he wouldn't physically hurt someone or resort to murder."

"Yes but how do you know that for sure, he was like a man possessed?"

"Look I'm sorry that he seems to be targeting you and I'm not sure why because what we had was a long time ago now."

"He's targeting me because he always goes after those you care about just like he targeted Kara."

"You know about that?" I say looking surprised.

"Yes your mother mentioned something when I spoke to her on the phone. I know we're not together anymore Evan, but I still care about you and what happens to you, I'm scared that he's going to hurt you or me. As far as Sebastian is concerned he knows we have history and I think because of what happened in the past between the three of us and me losing his child, it's like he can't let go of the anger."

"It should be me who is angry not Seb after all you are the ones who betrayed me by having an affair for months."

"Yes, I know but Seb is angry because he can't have me, he wanted to make a go of things when you discovered our affair, he said he loved me, but I just couldn't be with him, I was still in love you and I still am now." Julia stands up and walks towards me.

"Julia please don't." I freeze when she places her hands on my chest.

"Evan, I love you, you must know that I have always loved you and will continue loving you until the day I die."

"Julia stop." I remove her hands from me and move out of her way. "I'm with Kara now how much clearer can I be, I don't love you anymore, I love Kara and you need to stop this. Being friends is clearly not working so we need to cut all ties, you need to stop calling me and you need to leave me alone." I walk back to behind my desk and sit down.

"I don't believe you; you must still feel something for me Evan you were going to ask me to marry you for god's sake" she says thumping the desk making me jump.

"I'm sorry but it's the truth I feel nothing for you people change, I've changed, I'm not that man anymore, you need to move on and forget about me."

Julia slumps down in the chair opposite me again and starts to sob. "Why can't you just forgive me, why can't you love me like you used to, I'm sorry for what I did, I'm so sorry?"

"I will never forgive you Julia, I've accepted it, but I will never forgive you. I love Kara, there is no one else for me now."

"I honestly don't know what you see in her she is the opposite of me Evan, yes she's got big tits and a curvy body but she's not as clever as me, she works in a coffee shop for god's sake," she laughs "I know she won't be able to please you in the bedroom like I can."

"Don't you dare say anything derogatory about her because I won't stand for it do you hear me. I think it's time you left." I get up and walk over to the office door and open it.

Julia turns to look at me and stares at me for a moment in silence then continues with the crying.

"I'm sorry I didn't mean to upset you, but I can't help how I feel, and I didn't come here to argue with you I came here to discuss what to do about Sebastian."

I stand thinking for a moment then close the door again. "What a fucking mess." I run my hands through my hair and sit down behind my desk again.

"Please don't push me away, please don't cut me out of your life, I'm sorry, I'll stop saying these things that upset you, please Evan please be my friend, I can't stand the thought of not having you in my life at all, it doesn't need to be that way."

"It does Julia, we need closure, you keep telling me that you love me, and you want me back so if you love me like you say you do then you need to let me go, you need to let me be with Kara and be happy and that means stopping contact, you can't be calling me all the time."

"Okay I'll stop calling you and leave you alone if you'll still be my friend" she smiles.

I sigh. "Look I..."

"Anyway, can we please discuss what we are going to do about Sebastian? I can't live like this Evan. I don't want to be scared wondering if he is going to hurt me or even kill me. Oh god I think I'm having a panic attack." Julia slumps over her knees breathing heavily and fast.

"Jesus, are you okay?" I ask jumping up from my chair checking to see if she is alright.

"I'm sorry, this whole situation of you wanting me out of your life, Sebastian hurting me and possibly wanting to kill me has upset me so much I really don't feel well." Julia gasps for breath holding her chest.

"Julia do you need me to call you a doctor, yes I'll call a doctor, shit?" I go to pick up the phone.

"Evan no I'll be fine in a minute" she says gasping for air.

"Seriously I insist let me call you a doctor." I go to dial a number.

"No Evan," she says firmly "I said I'll be fine, I've had panic attacks like this before. I don't need a doctor I just need somewhere to lie down for a few minutes to calm myself down, have you got a room I could go to just until I feel better?"

"Yes of course if you're sure you'll be okay?"

"I'm sure" she smiles.

"Okay I'll just make a call to reception to see which room you can use?"

"Thank you" Julia smiles fanning her face looking distressed.

I call reception and explain the situation then ask Julia to follow me so I can show her to a vacant room. As we are walking out of my office she grabs hold of my arm. "Please can you put your arm around me because I feel really unsteady on my feet. I feel like I might fall over?" she asks.

I don't want to but being a gentleman, I reply "Sure."

We walk into reception to obtain the room key and I feel uncomfortable especially when I see Curtis come out of his office and make his way over to us. With my arm wrapped around Julia's waist Curtis looks at me confused. "Evan?"

"Curtis hi, Julia is not feeling well so I'm just taking her to a room so she can have a lie down for a bit."

"Oh, I see" he frowns looking at me then Julia.

"I'm sorry to hear that, I hope you feel better soon" Curtis says with a serious face not taking his eyes off her.

"Thank you, can we go now please?" she says holding onto me tightly.

"Yeah sure." I hate the look my best friend is giving me right now, he thinks I'm up to no good with my ex and he couldn't be any more wrong.

The lift arrives on the third floor and I escort Julia to the vacant hotel room. I open the door for her and help her inside.

"Thank you Evan, oh what a lovely room, will you stay with me for a while?"

"Julia, I need to get back to work" I stress.

"Please Evan I really don't want to be left alone while I'm feeling like this" she pleads.

'Great here's wanting to get away from her as soon possible.' "Okay I'll stay but just for a few minutes."

I help her to the bed and Julia lays down then pats the bed at the side of her for me to join her.

"Err no it's okay… I'll sit over here" I say pointing to a chair in the corner of the room.

"I won't bite Evan" she smiles as I sit down.

'No, you wouldn't bite you would just try to swallow me up whole wouldn't you.'

I sit awkwardly on the chair for a few moments and then my mobile phone starts ringing in my jacket pocket. I take it out and look at the screen and Kara is calling me. Shit. This is awkward when I'm sat in a hotel room with my ex. I'll call her back.

"Who's that?" Julia enquires.

"Oh, it's nothing I'll speak to them later."

"It's Kara isn't it, just answer it I'll be quiet if you don't want her knowing you are with me, I know it would make things awkward for you" she smiles.

'Do I answer the call or not?' I can't ignore her, so I press accept.

"Hi babe" I say sounding happy trying to sound normal.

"Hi babe I was just ringing to see how your meeting went with Julia?"

"Oh right, are you not at work today?" I ask. I'm surprised she is calling me at this time and not serving customers.

"Yes I'm at work but I've been stressing all morning about you and her so Sally said I could give you a quick call, I'm in the office. So how did it go what did she say?"

"Oh right, well I can't really talk right now so can I call you later?"

"Yes of course sorry are you in a meeting?"

"Err yes I am."

"Oh, you should have said, here am I interrupting you when you're a busy man."

"It's okay."

During the conversation Julia coughs on purpose.

"Who's that is that a woman in the background I thought you meant you were with Curtis sorry?"

"No, I'm not with Curtis it's a member of staff" I say hating that I just lied to her but it's easier than trying to explain the predicament I'm in.

Julia giggles and I give her an evil stare.

"Well, it sounds like you are having fun in your meeting I'm sorry to have bothered you, I'll let you get back to her" Kara says sarcastically, she sounds pissed off.

"Kara don't be like that."

"Like what, you sound strange like you don't really want to talk to me and there is clearly a woman giggling in the background, so I'd best not keep you and let you get back to whatever you were meeting her about."

"You just caught me at an awkward time that's all I'll speak to you later okay."

"Okay well sorry for disturbing you" she huffs.

"Kara...I..." and before I say anymore Julia laughs and says "Awkward" loud enough for Kara to hear her, so she knows who I'm with.

"What the hell is that Julia, are you with Julia Evan?"

"Yes, Kara listen..."

"Jeez you're having a long meeting aren't you, well it seems you have a lot to talk about, so I best not keep you."

"Kara wait…" She puts the phone down on me.

'Fuck!' I'm fucking fuming.

"What the hell are you playing at you did that on purpose, that was uncalled for Julia I thought you said you would be quiet."

"Sorry I forgot" she smirks.

"Well, you are clearly feeling better, so I think it's time you went." Kara sounded so mad and now I'm in trouble because of Julia yet again.

"Oh Evan, don't be so dramatic and yes I'm feeling much better thank you so why don't you stay and have a drink with me before you go?"

"I can't I've got to go," I snap striding over to the door "Let yourself out."

"Oh, come on Evan, just one drink please, for old time's sake."

"Goodbye Julia."

Julia

Evan closes the door behind him leaving me in the hotel room alone.

"Great." My mission has failed, I've got a tablet in my handbag I was going to drug Evan with that Sebastian got me from some guy in a bar. I was going to pop it in his drink, strip him of his clothes and take some photos of the two of us pretending we were in bed together, but that plan is now ruined.

Hmm maybe my mission isn't a complete disaster because first Curtis saw us, and Evan had his arms around me and then Kara called Evan and knows that he was with me. Yes, thinking about it I think it could work in our favour.

I sit on the bed thinking for a moment. I thought now some time has passed Evan would have forgiven me for having an affair with his brother and we could rekindle what we had, I'm just going to have to prove to him how sorry I am, so he does forgive me.

I really do love Evan and after having the affair with Sebastian it made me realise just what I had, what I lost. I had security, a man who would have given me a great life, a man who was going to ask me to marry him and unbeknown to Sebastian I still have feelings for.

Yes, I love Sebastian, but Evan is my one true love and although I'm with his twin brother and they look the same it isn't the same because he's not Evan.

If I could turn back the clock I would, I wish I had never fallen for Sebastian's charm, but I did and now I am paying the price for it. I am with a man who is the double of Evan in looks but so different in personality, but my heart belongs to Evan and always will.

It's heart-breaking that Evan won't forgive me and take me back so if I can't have him I will make his life a misery and any girl he hooks up with until he changes his mind.

Evan

No sooner have I returned to my office feeling flustered and angry because of Julia and now I'm in Kara's bad books again there is a knock on my office door.

"Yes" I call knowing exactly who it will be.

"Ev have you got a minute?" Curtis says walking into my office, shutting the door and plonking himself down on the chair opposite my desk.

"Don't" I say looking at him seriously.

"What the fuck do you think you're doing?"

"I'm getting myself into all kinds of shit unintentionally that's what I'm doing."

I explain to Curtis what happened in the meeting.

"Julia is coming between me and Kara. She keeps calling me and Kara is not happy about it and if it continues it's going to break up my relationship."

"Just don't answer her calls mate she'll soon get the message."

"I've tried that, and she just keeps ringing until I answer, or she rings my house phone."

"You'll have to block her then or change your number."

"Yeah, I thought speaking to her and hearing what she has to say about Sebastian would do me a favour because then I would be able to keep tabs on him but every time she rings, or I see her she always moves the conversation away from Seb and starts saying things about how much she wants me back and how she still loves me."

"I know what you're saying about keeping tabs on Sebastian but if Julia is coming between you and Kara then you seriously need to cut ties with her, you can't trust her man."

"Yeah, I know you're right. Kara has just called me to find out how the meeting went, and I was in the hotel room with Julia and she was giggling in the background. I should have just called her back and not answered because now Kara is going to think I was up to no good with her, she wasn't too happy when we ended the call I can tell you."

"I can imagine that's not good."

"No and that's not all."

"Oh mate, what?" Curtis says not liking the sound of what I'm going to say next.

"Something happened the other night as well."

"What do you mean something happened? Shit Evan what have you done? You haven't..."

"No nothing like that I wouldn't do that to Kara but when I got back from our business trip to Spain Julia came around to my house."

"Why what for?"

"Well, I called her because Julia had paid Kara a visit at work and had been saying all kinds of shit to her, so I rang her to let her know I wasn't happy and then the next thing I knew she had cut the call and was at my door."

"Jeez man, you didn't let her in did you."

"I'm afraid so, she barged past me when I opened the door."

"So why didn't you stop her? You should have just told her to leave."

"I know and I wish I had now I can tell you."

"Why what did you do Ev?" Curtis frowns.

"Not what you're thinking mate. I made her a coffee while she explained why she visited Kara at work and then Julia accidently spilt coffee all down herself, well she said it was an accident, but I don't think it was."

"No, I'm guessing not."

"So anyway, she insisted on having a shower because she was drenched in coffee and begrudgingly I let her."

"Evan, man what were you thinking?"

"I know I wasn't thinking obviously, I'm such a fucking idiot, I was tired from the trip and it all happened so fast."

"So, what happened then?"

"She had a shower and wanted to borrow one of my t-shirts, she called me to my bedroom because she didn't want to borrow one of my best ones, so I went to find her one and as I was leaving the room she dropped her towel and I saw her naked."

"What the fuck, does Kara know about any of this?"

I sigh feeling like I've got the whole world on my shoulders. "No, I haven't told her yet and the thing is I feel guilty like I've done something wrong, but I've not done anything. I didn't ask for this to happen it's Julia she won't leave me alone she's always seems to be there. What do I tell Kara? She is going to flip when I tell her what happened especially the part where I let Julia have a shower and I saw her naked."

"Shit man it doesn't sound good if I'm honest, but you do need to tell her, explain what happened."

"I know I do but I'm scared that she won't understand, I'm scared I'm going to lose her again."

"I know mate, but you can't keep this from her man because if she finds out any other way it's going to be worse I can tell you, what if Julia says something to her?"

"Yeah, I'll tell her tonight, you're right she needs to hear it from me."

"Just be honest and explain what Julia is up to and I'm sure everything will be fine."

"What if it isn't fine though and she leaves me?"

"She won't Ev she loves you and yes she might be mad, and you might have to give her a few days to calm down but if she really trusts you she will know you are telling the truth."

"I hope so mate, I really hope you're right."

"Anyway, I'd best get on I've got a ton of paperwork to do" Curtis says standing up to leave.

"Yes, I don't pay you to sit and talk to the boss about his problems" I grin.

"If you did I would definitely be asking for more money with the shit you've got going on mate."

"Alright big guy oh have you seen anymore of Stephanie?"

"No, I haven't, it's not happening mate."

"Oh why, you seemed so in love the other day?"

"Well, she's done the old 'It's not you it's me' speech so this man is back on the market" Curtis laughs.

"One day mate you'll meet the woman of your dreams" I smile.

"Already have mate but she's with you."

"Hey, fuck off and don't you even think about..."

"Your face..." Curtis laughs walking towards the door.

"Goodbye Curtis" I say smiling sarcastically.

"Later dude." and he leaves my office laughing.

He's a good mate and he's right I do need to tell Kara what's been going on with Julia, I just hope she understands, she means everything to me and I'm just going to have to make sure she knows that.

Twenty Three

It's Monday evening and I'm tired after a long day at work not only from serving customers all day long but constantly thinking about Evan and why he was acting strange on the phone this morning when I called him. Why was Julia still there I thought it was going to be a quick meeting and why was she giggling in the background and why did she say 'Awkward'?

My head is pounding from thinking about it, so I get a glass of water and some headache tablets and sit at the kitchen table pondering in silence. Jodie has gone out with Matt so I'm home alone.

I swallow the tablets contemplating ringing Evan because I haven't heard from him all day since the phone call.

I admit I wasn't very happy when I spoke to him, but I had every right to feel that way. I mean anyone would be upset when they ring their boyfriend who is with their ex and he is supposed to be telling her that he doesn't want her contacting him anymore and that their friendship is over, and she is laughing and giggling in the background.

The doorbell rings so I get up from the table to answer it and glancing out of the window I see Evan's car parked outside.

I open the door with a straight face "Hi."

"Hey beautiful, surprise," Evan says smiling walking into the hallway "How are you?" he asks looking cagey trying to gage my mood.

"I'm not great I've got a headache." Evans walks in closing the door behind him and follows me into the kitchen. I put the kettle on, and Evan sits down at the kitchen table.

"What are you doing here? I wasn't expecting to see you tonight?" I sit down at the table and there is tension between us, and I don't like it. Evan looks like he has something to say. I'm nervous.

"I wanted to apologise for acting strange when you rang me this morning when I was with Julia, our conversation was awkward, and I know you are upset with me. I need to explain what happened at the meeting and why Julia was giggling in the background."

"Yes, it was awkward I thought your meeting would have finished after you had told her to leave you alone I wasn't expecting her to still be there and giggling in the background and why did I hear her say 'Awkward' and laugh?"

Evan takes a deep breath "Yes I'm sorry about that, the meeting it was quite eventful."

"Why what happened?" I frown.

He tells me about the meeting and what Julia had to say.

"After Julia told me about Seb she declared her love for me again so I told her we should cut all ties and not be friends and she was sobbing uncontrollably begging for me not to do that, then she started having a panic attack. She was gasping for breath and I was quite worried about her I've never seen her like that before."

"Oh my god."

"Yeah, so I offered to call her a doctor, but she said she would be fine and just needed a lie down."

"Oh, don't tell me you took her to one of the hotel rooms?" I scowl.

"Yes, I'm afraid I did. After refusing to see a doctor and telling me she would feel better once she'd had a lie down I located a vacant hotel room so she could rest for a while and escorted her there."

"What do you mean you escorted her there?"

"She said she was feeling dizzy and sick and unsteady on her feet, so she held onto me and…"

"Evan…oh my god you kissed her didn't you?"

"No, I didn't."

"Oh no please don't tell me you slept with her?"

Tears spring in my eyes as I get a vision of the two of them together and I get up from the table and walk over to look out of the window. Evan stands up and comes over to me, I can feel him stood behind me. "Kara look at me." He takes hold of the sides of my arms and turns me so I'm facing him.

"I didn't sleep with her, I didn't kiss her, I didn't do anything with her all I did was sit on a chair in the corner of the room to keep her company while she felt better because she didn't want to be left on her own while she wasn't feeling well."

"Honestly, nothing happened between the two of you?" Tears are rolling down my cheeks.

"No, honestly nothing happened," Evan wipes my tears with his fingers. "I wouldn't do that to you and that's the reason why I sounded strange this morning when you called because I was in the hotel room with her and I felt awkward. Julia said she would be quiet while I spoke to you because I knew you wouldn't be happy knowing I was still with her but as you know she wasn't quiet. I also said I was in a meeting because I didn't want to tell you what was happening at the time because Julia was listening to our conversation, I'm sorry for not telling you."

"So why did she giggle then, what was you doing for her to say 'Awkward'?"

"I wasn't doing anything she knew it was you on the phone and so she obviously said that on purpose so you could hear her in the background to make you think I was up to no good with her."

"What a bitch" I mutter under my breath.

"I'm so sorry, I honestly thought we were having a meeting about Sebastian and that's all, I didn't expect our meeting to turn out the way it did."

"I didn't know what to think and when I heard Julia in the background giggling..."

"Baby I'm sorry. I assure you nothing happened, and Julia will never get me back because I have found my soul mate, I've found the woman I want to be with for the rest of my life."

"Really" I look at him with teary eyes.

"Really" he smiles cuddling me.

I put my arms around him. "Thank you."

"What for?" he says looking at me.

"For telling me, for being honest."

"Talking of being honest there is something else I need to tell you as well" Evan says looking serious.

'Oh god what now.'

"What?" I let go of him and go to make us both a hot drink.

Evan takes a seat at the table and sits looking at me with a serious face as I fill two mugs with coffee. I don't like this, what is he going to say now?

"Come and sit down."

"I will in a minute once I've made the drinks."

"No leave that come and sit down" Evan persists.

"No why, why do I need to sit down, is it bad?"

"Just come and sit down and I'll explain."

"Evan you're scaring me just tell me."

"I will when you've sat down."

I take a seat at the kitchen table feeling anxious. Evan stays silent for a few moments looking like he's trying to find the right words.

"Look you've obviously got something on your mind so just say it."

"Something else happened with Julia that I need to talk to you about, but I don't want you to freak out."

"I don't like this Evan you have slept with her haven't you, just be honest and don't lie to me I need to know."

Tears spring in my eyes again.

"No, I haven't slept with her honestly" he says grabbing hold of my hand that's resting on the table. I take my hand away from his because I'm not sure whether I want to hold it until I've heard what he has to say.

"Then what then? Please just tell me, just say it."

"I need you to promise to listen and to not freak out."

"How can I promise not to freak out when I don't know what you are going to tell me?"

"Right well you know when I got back from my work trip to Spain the other night and you told me Julia had visited you at work."

"Yeah..."

"Well, I rang Julia because it really annoyed me that she had done that and upset you with the things she said."

"Okay."

"Yeah, so I rang her, and she told me that she was trying to be your friend and that you had took things the wrong way and that she would explain."

"Okay well that's a lie, there was no other way of taking it she was being a bitch to me not a friend."

"Anyway, the next thing I knew she said she was in the area and she was coming around to see me and before I could put her off she put the phone down on me and turned up at my house."

"Evan, I don't like the sound of this," I fidget in my seat with nerves. "Go on" I frown.

"Well, she arrived at my house and more or less barged her way in and said to put the kettle on."

"And…"

"I wish I had told her to leave but I was tired from my trip and not thinking clearly I made her a cup of coffee. While she was explaining what she had apparently said to you she asked for a biscuit, so I went to get the biscuit tin and that's when she claimed she accidently spilt coffee all down her front, her blouse was soaked."

"What she must be very clumsy then, did it burn her did you have to take her to hospital?"

"No nothing like that we had been talking so the coffee had cooled and was not scolding hot but because she was all sticky and her clothes were soaked in coffee she asked…" Evan pauses.

"What she asked what?"

Evan takes a nervous deep breath "She asked if I would mind if she took a shower."

"Oh my god you didn't let her did you?"

"It all happened so fast and before I knew it she was in my shower."

"What so are you trying to tell me you ended up in the shower with her?"

"No of course not and it pisses me off to think you think I would do that to you."

"Well, I'm sorry but it pisses me off the fact that you let your ex-girlfriend take a shower in the first place whether she is soaked in coffee or not, you should have told her to go home."

"I did and she was like 'you can't expect me to get in my car like this'."

"Oh, poor Julia, I don't believe this, so you just let her take a shower?" I roll my eyes and fold my arms defensively "Anything else, she was tired, so you let her get into your bed? She was feeling horny, so you fucked her."

"Kara if you're going to be like that I'm not discussing this anymore until you are thinking rationally and calmed down."

"Calmed down how on earth do you expect me to react when you are telling me shit like this?"

"She didn't sleep in my bed and I didn't fuck her," he snaps "but she did ask to borrow one of my t-shirts because she couldn't wear her top because it was soaked in coffee so I went to get her one out of my drawers and as I passed it to her she dropped her towel and I saw her naked and that's everything that happened I swear."

"Oh... my... god... Evan" I shout getting up from the table and pacing the kitchen floor in anger.

"It's not like I told her to do it I passed her the t-shirt, and she dropped her towel, I only saw her naked for a split second because I was out the room like a shot I can tell you."

"Yes, but you saw her naked Evan" I yell.

"I know and it repulsed me if that makes you feel any better" Evan shouts back.

"It doesn't," I scream. "Why are you only telling me this now, why didn't you tell me the other night when it happened?"

"Ever since it happened I've been worrying about telling you in case you thought there was more to it which there isn't."

"Evan you know how I feel about the two of you and you know she did this on purpose to try and get you back right."

"Yes, I know you're right I can see that now and I should have been more assertive in telling her to leave me alone, I'm sorry baby please don't let this ruin what we have" he says getting up from the table and walking over to me.

"Don't" I say stopping him in his tracks. "I am so mad at you for being so naïve when it comes to her it was definitely not an accident spilling her coffee down her front."

"At the time I thought it was but now I know you're right especially after she declared her love for me again today."

"So that's it are you sure there isn't anything else I need to know?" I glare at him.

"No, I promise you that's everything" he says edging closer to me.

"Evan please," I hold my hands up to tell him to back off. "I'm so pissed off with you right now."

"I know baby and I'm so sorry for not telling you sooner" he says looking down to the floor looking regretful.

'I can't believe what he's just told me, I'm in shock, what the fuck?'

"I can't do this, I need you to go, I need to be on my own for a while to think about things." I walk to the front door and open it.

"Baby no please I'm sorry," he says panicking taking me in his arms and hugging me "Please don't say that I don't want to go, we need to talk, we need to make friends."

"Evan I'm sorry but it's how I feel, I want you to go" I shrug him off.

"What do you mean you need to be on your own for a while? What just tonight or are you saying you're ending it with me, are we over?" he asks in a panicked voice.

I look at him seeing the pain on his face. "No, I'm not ending it with you I mean I need some time tonight to think to process everything what you've just told me because I'm so pissed off right now and I don't want to say something I will regret."

"Please don't make me go, I'm so sorry" he says looking at me with pleading eyes.

"Julia is coming between us Evan; I can't stop you from seeing her but if you carry on and these things keep happening then we will end up splitting up."

"Kara I will I'll stop seeing her, please don't say we will split up, I can't lose you not again." He holds me at arm's length looking into my teary eyes. "Kara please baby I don't want her I want you, always. I love you."

"Then prove it, prove how much you love me and what I mean to you, every time she rings you or wants to see you tell her NO."

"I will I promise."

"Get rid of her Evan or you WILL lose me."

He pulls me to him and crushes his body to mine and hugs me tightly like he's never going to see me again and I let him. I'm so mad with him but I can't stop myself from wanting him.

"I'm so sorry I love you so much" he says taking my face in his hands watching tears run down my face and wiping them away with his fingers. "Please don't cry baby." He looks distressed knowing how upset I am.

He pulls me to him again and feeling calmer now I want to reassure him that although I'm upset with him, I love him too. I look at him. "I know you're sorry and I don't want to lose you either because I'm so in love with you Evan so please don't let that woman come between us anymore, she is your past and I'm your future so let's keep it that way okay."

"Okay, there's no one else for me now, you're it for me, I love you Kara" he says placing his mouth on mine and kissing me sealing our love for each other tasting my tears on his lips. "So, does this mean I can stay?"

"Yes, you can stay" I smile then kiss him again.

"I don't want to fall out with you, I hate upsetting you." Evan holds me tightly and I snuggle into Evan's chest, I can hear his heart beating fast in his chest from how anxious he must have been telling me. I know it must have been hard and wanting to reassure him that things are okay between us I know the best way and that's to show him.

"I don't want to fall out with you either so you can make it up to me by taking me to bed" I smile looking into brown eyes filled with love.

"I'd love to" he smiles.

I grab hold of his hand and drag him to my bedroom kicking the door shut behind us.

Sebastian

"I've been thinking about the plan and I think we need to forget about drugging Evan now because it's not going to work" I say getting into Julia's bed.

"It's not my fault he wouldn't have a drink with me" she pouts brushing her hair sat at the dressing table in her bedroom.

"I know Liv I'm not saying it is I just think we have enough evidence now of your so-called affair. I also don't think we should bother arranging a meeting with Evan like we planned because I don't think he will pay up anyway. You said you got that impression from the meeting you had with him so I think we should just send Kara the photo evidence and take it from there."

"Yes, but how will that get Evan to pay us the money Seb, surely we need to blackmail him with the photos and say pay up or we will send them to Kara. I mean if she sees the photos she will definitely think there is something going on between us because you got some great pics." Julia finishes brushing her hair and then gets into bed at the side of me.

"I think we should deliver the photos to Kara then she will question Evan about it, they will have an argument then Kara will break up with him and then when his life is falling apart, and he is heartbroken we pay him a visit and say if he pays the money we will put everything right and leave him alone."

"I'm not sure Seb it's not that simple" Julia says deep in thought.

"Like you said you think Kara doesn't trust Evan and is jealous of you so once she sees the photo evidence what else if there to think other than you two are having an affair."

"I know it just needs to be done right, we don't want to rush this and not get the result we want."

"I know but surely Evan will pay up, he loves this girl so surely he won't stand anymore of me interfering in his life and he knows the only way I will stop is when he pays me the money."

"Okay so what's the new plan then?"

"The plan is to send the photos to Kara like I said, we'll deliver them to her house then you pay her a visit again and confirm the affair then we'll pay Evan a visit and he will pay us the money. I think sending the photos to Kara will have more impact than sending them to Evan because he will just hide them if we send them to him."

"Okay so when do we do this?"

"How about we deliver them tomorrow?"

"Tomorrow, I think we should wait until Friday night then she can wake up on Saturday morning and find them and I'm not working on Saturday so I can pay her a visit then."

"Okay sounds good."

"I hope this plan works, I mean how much more can a man take, he's got plenty of money, so he isn't going to miss a few millions is he?" she smiles.

Twenty Four

It's Friday the day that we all jet off to Paris for the weekend and I can't bloody wait.

"Oh my god I'm so excited Kar" Jodie says looking at the clock in the kitchen seeing it's nearly 6.00pm.

"Yeah, so am I," I squeal. "Paris here we come."

"Have you got everything?" I ask looking out of the window waiting for Evan's car to pull up outside.

"I'll just have a quick check around to see if we have forgotten anything" Jodie says walking in and out every room.

"He's here" I squeal seeing him pull up outside as Jodie runs back into the kitchen and looks out the window.

Evan walks up the path to the front door. I open it with a big smile on my face.

"Hi babe" he says giving me a kiss.

"Hi" I smile pleased to see him.

"Are you guys ready for our trip?" Evan asks.

"We are so ready" Jodie squeals making him laugh.

We arrive at London Heathrow Airport happy and excited to be going away for the weekend.

"I've never flown on a private jet before" Jodie says sounding excited and nervous.

"I have" I grin, and Jodie pulls a face at me.

We get out of the car ready to board the plane waiting for us on the tarmac feeling giddy with excitement. With the luggage on board, passports checked we take our seats and then Evan orders everyone a round of drinks to settle the nerves and to start our holiday in good spirits.

"Are you feeling nervous this time?" Evan asks holding my hand knowing I was nervous the last time we flew.

"No, I'm fine," I smile "Is there a private bedroom on this plane like the other one?"

"Why are you feeling frisky?" Evan asks grinning at me.

"No" I blush "I was just wondering that's all."

"No there isn't so I'm afraid you'll have to wait until later to have your wicked way with me unless you want to have me in the toilets" he laughs.

"I can wait" I laugh shaking my head and rolling my eyes at him.

"What did you say the toilets are wicked, I should imagine they are being in a posh plane like this?" Jodie says catching a snippet of our conversation.

"Yeah, something like that, are you okay Matt you're very quiet, are you nervous?" I ask with a smile.

"No not at all I'm just listening to you lot" he smiles clearly looking uncomfortable.

"It's okay babe I'll hold your hand" Jodie laughs.

"I'm not nervous alright" Matt says raising his voice slightly.

"Okay babe" Jodie looks at me mouthing 'he is' as Matt looks out of the window.

It's not long before the pilot is announcing we're ready for take-off and after a good flight and numerous alcoholic drinks we are soon landing.

"Welcome to Paris!" the pilot announces, and we all smile pleased to have arrived at our destination.

A taxi ride takes us to an exquisite hotel situated on a tree-lined boulevard.

"Wow" we say as we arrive clearly impressed with Evan's choice of accommodation.

"I've booked us both a suite near each other I'm sure you'll like it, and it will be comfortable for the next two nights" Evan says obviously knowing how gorgeous the suites are and loving the looks on Jodie and Matt's faces when he told them he had booked them a suite.

"Oh really, thank you Evan, I can't believe this" Jodie says hugging him making Evan laugh.

"Yeah, thanks mate" Matt says shaking Evan's hand.

"You're welcome. Come on then let's get checked in and then we can all go for a drink if you fancy?" Evan says ushering us towards the magnificent reception area.
"Sounds good" we all agree.

Once we are settled in our rooms or should I say luxurious suites we head down to one of the hotel bars for a drink.

"So, what's the plan for tomorrow Evan?" Matt asks taking a sip of his beer.

"Well, I thought we could spend the day seeing the sights I know the girls want to visit the Eiffel Tower."

"Yes, we do" Jodie and I agree.

"Then we can have a nice lunch somewhere and if everyone fancies it I thought we could go and see the Moulin Rouge?"

"Oh my god yes we would love that" I say and Jodie smiles agreeing.

"I'm pleased you said that because I've already booked us dinner and the show."

"Oh my god, have you?" Jodie says and we both squeal forgetting that we are in a posh hotel for a moment then looking around at the other hotel guests who are looking at us. They can look all they like because we are going to see the Moulin Rouge in Paris and we are beyond excited.

"Thank you so much babe" I say giving Evan a kiss.

"That's okay, I love making you happy" Evan smiles pulling me to him and giving me a slow, lingering kiss.

"Alright guys get a room" Matt laughs.

"Good idea. I don't know about everyone else, but it's been a long day and I'm ready for bed" Evan says.

Matt smirks "I bet you are," making Evan smile and me blush. "Come on then ladies us gentlemen will escort you back to your suites because you've pulled" he grins.

"Ooh I think we could be on a promise here Jode" I laugh having drunk far too much wine.

"Good because we've never had sex in a posh hotel before have we Matt?" Jodie smirks as the two men high five each other at the thoughts of what's to come.

We say goodnight to each other and arrange to meet for breakfast at 8.00am in the morning then we go back to our suites.

After enjoying incredible sex with the best boyfriend I could ever have wished for I walk my weary body into the en suite bathroom followed by Evan. "I'm so tired now" I yawn feeling in a contented, post orgasmic state.

"Yeah, me too" Evan smiles as we both get into the shower to freshen up.

"I wonder if Jodie and Matt are still up?"

"Don't you mean I wonder if Matt is still up Jodie?" Evan laughs.

"Oh yeah bless them they both seemed excited about going to bed in their suite didn't they?"

"You could say that I think that wine you both had got Jodie well and truly in the mood."

"Yes, well Paris is called 'the city of love' as they say."

"It certainly is" he smiles.

Evan

After getting ready for bed Kara climbs into bed and I quickly check my phone for any messages. I have one unread text message from Julia. I open the message with a frown.

I hope Kara didn't hear me in the background when we were in the hotel room together the other day. Julia xx

"Is your message about work or is it from Julia by any chance?" Kara asks seeing my serious face.

"What do you think?" I reply putting my phone down and climbing into bed at the side of her taking her into my arms for a cuddle.

"Hmm... let me guess Julia?"

"Yep, the one and only."

"What did it say?"

"She's shit stirring again she said she hoped you didn't hear her in the background when I was in the hotel room with her the other day."

"God that woman is such a scheming bitch...aargh..."

"Don't let her upset you, forget about it, I've deleted her message."

"Good" I huff.

"Kara you do trust me don't you?"

"Yes, I trust you I just don't trust her, why do you ask?"

"I just wanted to know because I would never do anything to hurt you, you do know that don't you."

"I know, are you still stressing about not telling me about Julia?"

"Yes, I am a bit, I'm also a bit anxious because Sebastian has been quiet recently and I'm wondering what he's up to."

"I was thinking the same thing, we haven't heard from him for a while have we and it makes me nervous."

"I know, you do know that Julia means nothing to me don't you, you know I wouldn't go there again however much she tries to coax me back; it won't work."

"Yes, don't worry, I'm over it, now go to sleep."

"Okay goodnight beautiful. Love you."

"Good night babe, love you."

Sebastian

It's late Friday night and my heart is beating fast in my chest because I've just pulled up outside Kara's flat in Julia's car. I'm here to deliver the photos of Julia and Evan that I took making it look like they are having an affair and I'm nervous in case I'm spotted.

Julia decided to stay at home because she didn't want to risk being seen together because this will ruin our plan to get Evan to pay me my money.

It's 11.30pm, I cut the engine and grab hold of the brown envelope that's on the passenger seat and get out of the car, quietly shutting the car door behind me. A dog barks in the distance making me jump, shit the sooner I get out of here the better.

I take the path up to the flat. The lights are out so I'm hoping everyone is in bed asleep.

Arriving at the front door I open the letterbox quietly and push the envelope through hearing it drop loudly on the floor. Shit. I flinch when I hear the clatter and quickly scurry back to my car feeling concerned in case I've woken anyone, and I'm spotted.

I sit in my car for a few moments and no lights come on in the flat so I must have got away with it.

I drive away with a smug grin on my face pleased to have delivered the photos without being caught.

Twenty Five

It's a lovely sunny morning in Paris and after enjoying an early cooked breakfast courtesy of the hotel restaurant we make our way around the sights of Paris starting at the Eiffel Tower.

"Wow I can't believe we are here" I say craning my neck as I look up at the tower stood with my best friend as we take photos on our mobile phones.

"Yes, it's an amazing view from here" Matt says, and we turn around to see the men are looking at our bottoms dressed in some skintight jean shorts.

"Come on you two I think you've seen enough" Jodie laughs taking Matt's hand and I take Evan's and we walk away looking forward to the next tourist attraction on our list of places to visit.

After taking a bus and visiting the Louvre Museum we are starting to feel hungry, so we decide to have a late lunch. Choosing a little cafe situated on a tree lined street, we choose to sit at a table outside and peruse the menu.

"What are you having Matt?" Jodie asks checking her hair and make-up in a compact mirror from her bag.

"I'm going to have the Club Sandwich" Matt says looking at the menu.

"Yeah, me too," I agree "It sounds good" I say sharing a menu with Evan.

"Me three" Evan smiles.

"What's in it?" Jodie asks still looking in the compact mirror preening.

"It's got frog's legs, snails, sautéed onion and brie cheese" Matt says winking at us.

"Urgh really that sounds disgusting, are you really having that? Yuck just the thought of eating that makes me feel sick" Jodie says pulling a face looking at him.

"I'm only joking," Matt laughs. Evan and I are laughing too. "It's slightly toasted homemade French bread with roast chicken, bacon, tomato, green salad and mayonnaise."

"Matt you sod I thought you were being serious," Jodie says hitting him playfully on the arm feeling embarrassed that she fell for his joke "well in that case I'll have one of those too" she smiles, and we all laugh.

"I'm paying Evan and no arguments because you've treated us to a top suite in a gorgeous hotel and got us here so the least I can do is buy us lunch" Matt says looking at Evan before he has a chance to say that he is.

"Okay thank you." Evan smiles.

"Thanks guys" I smile.

The lunch is delicious and after seeing a few more of the sights we make our way back to the hotel.

We decide to go to our rooms to rest for a while and arrange to meet in the hotel bar at 6.30pm. Tonight we are going to see the Moulin Rouge and we are having dinner beforehand which I'm excited about.

"Thank you so much for this weekend I'm having a lovely time, I can honestly say I'm the happiest I have ever been in my entire life." I smile cuddling Evan on the bed.

"Me too." Evan smiles pulling me closer to him.

"I do worry sometimes though because everything is so perfect that it's all going to go wrong."

"Hey nothing is going to go wrong I promise you" Evan says looking at me seriously trying to reassure me.

"Yes, but what if Julia does get around you and you change your mind and realise that you do still love her?"

"Babe I can assure you that's never going to happen."

"Yes, but how do you know?"

"I know because my heart is so full of love for you, I wish I could explain to you just how I feel about you" he smiles.

"I think I know because that's how I feel, I'm sorry for doubting us, it's just with Julia and Sebastian in the background all the time I worry that …"

"I know, please try not to worry, I'm not going anywhere" he smiles. "We had better start getting ready" he says looking at his watch.

"Okay, I'm so excited" I smile feeling happy.

After getting ready and having a quick drink in the hotel bar we get in a taxi and head out for the evening. On route to the venue Evan's mobile phone rings.

"Who is that Julia?" I ask.

"Yep, and I'm ignoring her" Evan says rejecting the call.

"What is her problem Evan why is she constantly ringing you all the time? You're with Kara now so why can't she accept that and leave you alone?" Jodie asks hearing our conversation looking at me and rolling her eyes.

"I know she is being a real pain in the ass, she wants me back, but she can't have me because I'm totally in love with this woman right here" he says rubbing my leg with his hand.

"Aww you two are so cute together" Jodie gushes.

"Thanks" I blush.

The Moulin Rouge is everything I imagined it to be, a magical world of singing and dancing with shining costumes, the amazing performers especially the Cancan dancers and we all have an amazing time.

Before we know it the show is over, and we are heading back in the taxi to the hotel.

"Wow what a fantastic night it was utterly brilliant," Jodie says, "Did you enjoy it Matt?"

"I did actually it was great."

"I thought you might say that with all those pretty girls dancing and strutting about the stage."

"Hey, I can look but it's you I get to touch" Matt grins pulling her to him for a kiss and grabbing her boob.

"Matt," Jodie laughs "Wait until we get back to the hotel, we do have company you know."

"Sorry guys" Matt smiles making us all laugh.

"Thank you so much I've had a wonderful night" I say cuddling up to Evan in the back of the taxi.

"Your welcome babe" he smiles.

"What are we doing tomorrow?" Jodie asks.

"I thought we could enjoy the hotel facilities in the morning then our flight back is in the afternoon."

"Sounds good" we all agree.

After a good night's sleep, a morning swim and being pampered in the spa we pack our suitcases after enjoying a fun packed weekend in Paris and catch the flight back home to England.

Pulling up outside the flat we are all tired and happy to be home.

"I'll give you a hand with the cases Evan," Matt says, "You girls go in and get the kettle on I don't know about you, but I'm parched and could do with a coffee."

"Okay will do" Jodie and I reply walking off arm in arm to the front door leaving the men getting the luggage out of the car boot.

Jodie unlocks the door, picks up the post and puts it on the kitchen table while I fill the kettle and switch it on.

"Where do you want these suitcases putting?" Evan calls from the hallway.

"Oh, can you put them in our bedrooms please, thanks babe" I reply.

The men join us in the kitchen, and we all sit at the table and enjoy a nice cup of coffee.

"Right let's have a look and see what the postman has brought us" I say picking up the pile of letters.

"Is there anything for me?" Jodie asks as I sift through the mail.

"Yes, these are for you and these are for me" I pass some letters to her.

We open our mail and the last thing I come across is a mysterious brown envelope with my name handwritten on the front.

"I wonder what this is?" I frown opening the seal.

"I'm just going to pop to the loo" Evan says getting up from the table and leaving the three of us.

"Okay," I smile "Hmm this is weird." I take the contents out of the envelope.

"What is it?" Jodie asks.

"I'm not sure it looks like photos and they've been hand delivered because there is no stamp on the envelope just my name," I take the photos out of the plastic sleeve they are in. "There's a note as well."

"That's strange, read it out then" Jodie says sounding impatient.

"It says 'I thought you would like to know that things are not always as they seem, you can't always trust those closest to you, Evan Hamilton is a liar and a cheat.'"

"Who's a liar and a cheat?" Evan asks walking back into the room.

"It says you are" I frown looking at him confused.

"What? What are you talking about?"

"I got this note, look." I pass it to him so he can read it. While Evan is reading the note I begin looking through the photos.

"Oh my god..." I whisper.

"Are you alright Kara you've gone really pale?" Jodie asks concerned "What are the photos of?"

I feel tears roll down my cheeks and they keep on coming, I'm in shock and so angry I can hardly speak.

"What are they of?" I laugh "They are photos of Evan and Julia... together" I seethe.

"What?" Evan says surprised "Let me see those." I pass him the selection of photos.

The photos show Evan hugging Julia on her doorstep with her dressed in a silky nightie, there is another photo of them stood together in Evan's bedroom window, Julia is dressed in just a towel and Evan is shutting the curtains. Another shows Evan stood on the doorstep of his house looking around and Julia looks like she is just leaving. Another looks like they are kissing.

I can't believe what I'm seeing, Evan has told me his version of what happened when he saw Julia, but these photos say a different story. He's been lying to me. It looks like he's been seeing both of us at the same time. Is he in love with me but also still in love with Julia and can't decide who he wants?

I feel sick to the stomach.

"What the fuck are these?" Evan says angrily.

"I should be asking you that, how could you?" I scream sobbing.

"What you seriously think there is something going on with me and Julia? Baby this is not what it looks like."

"Oh, and where have I heard those words before?" I scoff. "Not what it looks like, how else can it look Evan, the photos prove it there is obviously something going on?" I cry.

"No, you have to believe me this is Sebastian he's trying to set me up, he must have taken them and…"

"No Evan it's not Sebastian this is all you," I scream in anger. Evan tries to come near me to console me, but I shrug him off standing up from the table and moving away from him.

"All those times Julia has been ringing you, then you rushed to see her after you left me, her visiting you at your house and having a shower, god I've been so stupid." I laugh "It's obvious you've been stringing me along and you've been seeing her too, how could you do this to me? I believed you when you said fidelity was important to you, you're such a LIAR." I shout.

"No, I haven't baby it's not true and fidelity is important to me, I've been on the receiving end remember, affairs are the worst thing you have to believe me, I'm telling the truth."

"Don't call me baby, you've been lying to me and having an affair with your ex. I was just to blind to see it, you can't decide which one of us you want can you?"

"FUCK..." Evan shouts making us all jump "I haven't I'm telling you you've got it all wrong, I know it looks like that from these photos but it's a lie, it's all bullshit it's Sebastian trying to set me up. Can't you see he is trying to ruin things between us Kara, he's trying to hurt me, and he knows the best way to hurt me is through you?"

Jodie and Matt sit stunned at the kitchen table not knowing what to say or think.

"The meeting you had with Julia at your hotel, I even rang you and you were with her in a hotel room and she was giggling in the background, awkward she said, I bet it was awkward when I phoned wasn't it, what was you doing eh, having sex at the time? Oh my god it all makes sense now." Tears continue to fall down my cheeks.

"No Kara I haven't, please you have to believe, I wouldn't do that to you." Evan comes to stand in front of me and grabs hold of me by the shoulders trying to make me understand.

"Get off me, don't you dare touch me, you never get to touch me again do you hear me, NEVER" I scream.

"Kara please… it's all lies" Evan pleads looking distressed pacing the floor with tears in his eyes not knowing what to do or say to me to make it better.

I'm devastated, seeing the love of my life with his ex in those photos has destroyed me.

Jodie and Matt remain quiet watching the anguish play out in front of them.

"Lies you say, the only lies are the ones you have been telling me all along and what you are telling me right now," I scoff. "Julia said she wanted you back, but she already has you doesn't she, you were just playing me again, using me, why?"

"I wasn't using you I love you."

"Bullshit, you love playing games, you, Sebastian, Julia you are all sick."

"If that's what you think of me then you really don't know me at all," Evan says angrily "You say you love me, you say you trust me, but you obviously don't, I'm telling you this is not true, but you choose to believe my twisted, fucked up brother."

"What else am I supposed to think, what would you think if you were sent photos of me looking like that?"

Evan doesn't say anything.

"Kara," Jodie says. "Let's just think about this for a moment I honestly don't think Evan would do that to you I think he's telling the truth."

"What? You've seen the photos Jodie what else is there to think oh they are just friends. I thought you were supposed to be my friend and have my back not his so why are you taking his side?" I shout.

"I think we all need to calm down, we're all tired" Matt says trying to help.

"Shut up Matt" Jodie and I shout.

Matt holds up his hands and then keeps his mouth well and truly shut.

"Go on then explain your theory Jodie because you obviously know better than me" I huff giving my best friend a dirty look.

"All I'm saying is you should think about things before you do or say anything you might regret; I think Evan is telling the truth and once you have calmed down you may think differently."

"Oh, so go on then let's hear what you've got to say, you said its lies so explain it then, explain these photos to me Evan" I say picking them up off the table and throwing them at him with hatred in my eyes as they all scatter on the floor at his feet.

Evan glares at me. "I have told you everything, what happened when Julia turned up at my house, the meeting at the hotel and I've told Julia to stop contacting me but obviously my brother has been taking photos of me and Julia in secret or he's hired someone to take them. He is trying to make it look like something is going on between us to cause trouble because he is trying to ruin my fucking life."

"Ruin your fucking life, what about my fucking life, ever since I met you I have had to put up with your interfering ex-girlfriend constantly wanting your attention, your meddling twin brother pretending to be you, I'm beginning to wonder if this, US, is all just 'Two Much Trouble'.

"Don't say that you don't mean that" Evan says glaring at me.

"Don't I." I glare back at him.

"FUUCCCKKK it doesn't matter what I say you're not going to believe me so what's the point" Evan shouts throwing his hands up in the air. "Well, I know one thing for sure and that is he is not doing this to me anymore...." Evan storms out of the kitchen and to the front door enraged.

I follow him and Jodie and Matt are close behind me.

"That's it run away, where are you going?" I shout after him. "Let me guess to see Julia."

Evan stops, turns around and glares at me halfway down the path. The anger and hurt written all over his face is clear to see. "I'm going to see Sebastian that's where and I'm going to fucking kill him" he seethes, and he walks off towards his car.

"Evan no." I panic hearing his words and run down the path towards him, he is upset, too upset to be driving a car and to think rationally. I'm scared that he is going to do something stupid. "Evan STOP please" I shout but he ignores me, gets in his car, and drives away.

"Shit," I'm shaking and crying uncontrollably as I run back to the house. Jodie and Matt are stood on the front doorstep. "He's gone Jode, what if he does something stupid? What the hell just happened?" I sob as Jodie takes me in her arms and hugs me.

"I'm sure Evan won't do anything stupid Kar, he's angry and just needs to find out what's going on" Matt says trying to make me feel better.

"Yes, but he said he was going to kill his brother, I need to go after him I need to find him to stop him."

I let go of Jodie and go into the kitchen to grab my car keys from the hook at the side of the fridge.

"Kara no you're not going anywhere, you're in no fit state to drive, you could have an accident and I'd never forgive myself if I let you go" Jodie says stopping me.

"Please Jodie let me go, please" I sob as everything becomes too much and I sink down onto the kitchen floor with my head in my hands crying a river as Jodie kneels next to me hugging me.

"Shush it's okay Kar, everything will be okay."

"Jesus" Matt says running his hands through his hair clearly stressed and feeling useless not knowing what to do.

"Does he know where Sebastian lives?" Jodie asks.

"No, I, I… d… d…don't think so, I don't know" I cry trying to get my words out.

"Where do you think he's gone?" Matt asks.

"I'm n… not sure. I need to ring Curtis, I need m...my phone" I try to get up.

"Matt get Kara's phone" Jodie says.

"Where is it?"

"It's, it's in m… my bag" I answer.

Matt gets my phone and passes it to me. I find Curtis' number and after a few rings he answers the call.

"Hey Kara, this is a surprise, did you guys have a good weekend in Paris?" he says sounding happy and cheerful.

"I'm…I…" I can't speak because I'm crying so much, I'm too upset to talk so Jodie takes my phone from me.

"Hi Curtis, it's Jodie, Kara's friend."

"Oh, hi is Kara alright she sounds really upset?"

"No, she isn't, it's Evan."

"Shit is he okay, is he hurt?"

"No nothing like that, we just got back from our trip to Paris and Kara received some photos of Evan and Julia together, they were put through the door with a note suggesting they are having an affair."

"What that's crazy."

"I know look you're Evan's best friend do you know anything about this, is he having an affair with Julia?"

"What no way I can assure you he is definitely not having an affair with Julia he's in love with Kara."

"Yes, but if you saw the photos they do look pretty incriminating."

"I don't know anything about any photos but all I know is that Julia wants Evan back and she has been coming on to him every chance she gets. I know my friend and he would never go there again not after what she did with his brother. He loves Kara I've never seen him with any woman like the way he is with her he truly does love her."

"Okay" Jodie sighs.

"Where is Evan now?" Curtis asks.

"We don't know he was really angry, and he said he was going to kill Sebastian and then he took off in his car."

"Jesus that bad huh okay thanks for letting me know, I'll go and look for him I think I know where he will have gone."

"Thanks Curtis, will you let us know when you find him, I know Kara's hurting right now but she's really worried about him, she really does love him and would hate for anything bad to happen to him."

"Okay will do, I'll give you a call later."

Evan

I'm driving down the road at lightning speed towards London on the M25 and all I can think of is Kara's distraught face. Why doesn't she believe me when I tell her that Julia means nothing to me, and I love her? I have never loved anyone like I love Kara in my entire life. The look of devastation on her face when she saw those photos of Julia and me, I can't get that image out of my head.

So, Sebastian has been taking photos of me to make it look like I'm having an affair with Julia, I am fucking raging right now and when I see my brother he is going to pay for hurting me, hurting Kara and this will be the last time he ever does.

"Shit that's all I fucking need." I don't see the police car parked on the slip road when I drive past. All I am concentrating on is finding my brother. I need to see Julia to find out what she knows and if she knows where Sebastian is but first I need to deal with the policeman who is tailing me with blue flashing lights.

"FUUUCCCKKK……"

The police car flashes me to pull over so I pull onto the hard shoulder looking at the police car in my rear-view mirror. I cut the car engine and punch the steering wheel in frustration because the longer I'm here the longer I am from dealing with my fucked-up brother.

There is a tap on the window, and I open it to see a 6ft burly police officer looking down on me. "Good evening sir could you please step out of the vehicle for a moment?"

I get out of the car and the policeman explains why he has stopped me, apparently I was doing speeds in excess of 90mph. The policeman then asks me to join him in his car where his colleague is sat waiting in the passenger seat.

After showing me the footage on his dashcam the policeman says, "So can you tell me why you think driving at speeds of over 90mph is acceptable to you?"

"Look I'm sorry I've just had an argument with my girlfriend, and I need to be somewhere I didn't realise I was driving so fast" I huff.

"Okay but do you do realise why we have these speed limits in place?"

"Of course, I'm not fucking stupid." I don't need this shit right now, don't be cocky with me just let me go and then you can get on with your job of catching actual fucking criminals because I'm not one of them, well not yet anyway I might be after seeing my brother.

"You seem agitated sir, calm down and I would like to remind you that you are speaking to a police officer and if you carry on speaking to me in that way you are going to land yourself in more trouble and will be accompanying me down the station."

"Yeah, whatever, either fine me or let me go because I really need to be somewhere, and I haven't got all fucking night" I snap.

"Can I have your driving licence please?"

I sigh and get my wallet out of my jacket and pass it to the police officer. "Is this your car sir?"

'Oh great, now he thinks I've stolen this car.'

"Yes it's my car, do you see anyone else driving it?"

The police officer checks my licence and then satisfied that I own the car he checks on their system to make sure I have valid insurance and I'm not wanted for any other criminal offences.

"Can you please hurry the fuck up, this is taking longer than it fucking needs to be" I say feeling agitated.

The officer passes me back my licence and I put it back into my wallet.

"So, what's got you so angry you said you've had an argument with your girlfriend, it must have been a pretty bad one to put you in this state?" the policeman says.

"None of your fucking business now are you going to let me go or what?"

"I think you need to calm down sir that's what I think it's not safe for you to be driving a vehicle when you are in this frame of mind."

"This is ridiculous yes I'm angry, but I can still drive a fucking car."

"Have you been drinking this evening at all?"

"No, I haven't been drinking but I am pissed…pissed off."

"I would like you to take a breathalyser test."

"Oh you have got to be fucking kidding me I've just told you I haven't been drinking I was speeding that is all."

If this police officer keeps on at me then he is not going to be seeing me calm down anytime soon.

"Right so are you telling me you are refusing to take a breathalyser test?"

"Yes, I fucking am."

"Okay so to clarify you are refusing to take the test."

"Are you fucking deaf, that's what I just said didn't I."

"For refusing to take a breathalyser test you need to accompany us down to the station."

"What you're kidding me? No, I'm not doing that."

"I can assure you sir I do not kid anyone."

"Right well I'll take a test then, give it here."

"I think we'll do it back at the station. You are very agitated in my opinion; you are not fit to drive in this state, and I think you need to take some time to calm down."

"What? I would be calm if you stop wasting my time and just let me go" I shout in anger. I've had enough of this shit. I try to get out of the car pulling at the door handle, but the doors are locked. "Let me out of this god damn car, this is harassment" I shout hitting the glass with the palm of my hand.

The next thing I know the police officers have handcuffed me and I'm being driven to the police station. "What about my car, if that gets stolen I swear to fucking god…"

"Relax sir it will be recovered so just try and relax because the sooner you do so the sooner you can go."

After causing more commotion when we arrive at the police station it is decided that I will be staying the night in a cell because I am a danger to myself and others.

What a joke the only person in danger of me right now is Sebastian.

After being booked in and carrying out a breathalyser test and a drugs test which of course are both negative I'm stripped of my personal belongings including my mobile phone and escorted to a cell.

"Is there anyone you would like us to call so they know your whereabouts?" the police officer asks.

"No no-one thanks." I reply. The last thing I need is anyone knowing I'm in a police cell for the night for speeding, resisting arrest and swearing at a police officer. The police officer is right I do need to calm down and I do understand his decision after the way I was acting earlier. This is just great; it's going to be a long fucking night.

Curtis

I arrive at Julia's flat, but I can't see Evan's car parked anywhere. I walk up the steps to her front door knock loudly and wait for her to answer. When Julia opens the door she looks shocked to see me.

"Curtis what are you doing here?" she asks surprised.

"Hi Julia, is Evan here?"

"Evan? No why I haven't seen him since our meeting at the hotel is everything okay?" she asks sounding worried.

"Everything is fine but if you do see him can you tell him to call me?"

"Of course, has something happened?" Julia's expression changes from concern to a smug grin, does she know something? I don't like her, never have and never will.

"Just tell him to call me please" I say walking off.

"Okay sure" she calls shutting the door.

Julia

"Who was that?" Sebastian calls from the lounge.

"That was Curtis looking for Evan" I smile.

"Oh, I take it Kara has seen the photos and Evan is on the rampage."

"Yes, sounds like it, but I'm surprised we haven't had a call or a visit from him though? I wonder where he can be?"

"Hey, you're not worried about my brother are you Liv?"

"Of course not, I'm just intrigued as to where he is that's all."

'Oh god I hope he's alright, I hope he's not hurt, I would hate it if anything has happened to him.'

"Fancy a cuppa Seb?" I ask trying to act normal and hide the fact that I'm worried.

"Yeah, go on then."

Curtis

"Shit" I get into my car feeling deeply concerned for my best friend. Where are you buddy? Why aren't you answering your phone? God, I hope nothing serious has happened to you. I have already called around a few places and no-one has seen him, this is so unlike him.

I take my phone out of my pocket and call Kara's number to give her an update. Jodie answers.

"Hey Jodie."

"Hi Curtis, any news?"

"Nothing I'm afraid, I've looked everywhere but no-one has seen him. He's not answering his phone either because it's switched off. I've just been to Julia's and she says she hasn't seen him either. How's Kara?"

"Not good at all, she's really distraught."

"Listen I'll keep looking someone has got to have seen him, I'll try the bar where we go and see if he's in there, you never know he might have turned up."

"Okay, thanks for calling I'll let Kara know you've phoned and let us know if you find him."

"Okay will do, bye Jodie."

"Bye Curtis."

Twenty Six

Evan

It's 6.00am in the morning, the cell door opens and the burly police officer from last night walks in carrying a mug of tea. It's been a long, rough night, the bed in the cell wasn't exactly the most comfortable bed I've slept on, not that I got much sleep.

"Good morning sir are you feeling better today?" the policeman asks with a smile as I sit up on the bed.

"Yes, much better thanks, I must apologise for my terrible behaviour last night, I'd had a shock and an argument with the love of my life and well I was upset."

I accept the mug of tea.

"I know sir, don't be too hard on yourself we've all been there, we're all human at the end of the day we just have our job to do you know."

"I know and I understand thank you." I hold out my spare hand and the officer shakes my hand to say no problem.

"When you've had your tea we'll assign you back your belongings and then you're free to go."

"Okay thanks what about the speeding and the insults am I being charged?"

"Just a speeding ticket and a warning that's all, we could see you just needed a break, don't let me catch you speeding or insulting a police office again or it will be more severe next time" he smiles.

"Don't worry I don't want to spend another night here again that's for sure and thanks I appreciate it."

Once I'm allowed to leave I get into my car but before I set off I turn on my mobile phone knowing that I will have a lot of missed calls and messages. There are lots of missed calls from Kara and Curtis and deciding I will deal with them later because I need to get home and have a shower, I head off home.

After having a shower I call Curtis to let him know I'm okay.

"Evan jeez man I've been worried sick about you, where have you been I've been looking for you everywhere, it was like you had vanished into thin air?"

"Curtis relax I'm okay mate and I'm sorry I worried you. The reason you couldn't find me was because I was in a police cell for the night."

"Jesus mate what have you done, have you hurt Sebastian?"

"No not yet."

"Evan violence isn't the answer mate, I know what's happened because Jodie told me."

"Jodie?"

"Yeah Kara called me and tried to explain but she was too upset to speak so Jodie came on the phone and explained everything."

"He's gone too far this time mate; Kara hates me and thinks I'm having an affair with Julia for fuck's sake."

"I know" Curtis replies understanding my anguish.

"Have you spoken to her?" I ask.

"Spoken to who Kara or Julia?"

"Kara, have you spoken to her since she called you last night?"

"Yes, she called me early this morning to see if I'd heard from you, but I couldn't tell her anything because I didn't know where you were, she's in bits man."

"Yeah well, so am I. She doesn't believe that I'm not having an affair, she just saw the photos and automatically thought I was guilty."

"I know but from what Jodie told me the photos are pretty incriminating."

"Yeah, I suppose they are but it's bullshit mate, I wouldn't go back to Julia even if you paid me."

"I know mate."

"Everything was going great, I thought it was strange I hadn't heard from Seb for a while, he was obviously biding his time before dropping this bombshell wasn't he."

“Yeah, I went to Julia’s house last night I thought you might have gone there to have it out with her.”

“I was heading there when I got pulled over for speeding and that’s when I got locked up for the night, did she say anything, did you mention the photos?”

“No, I didn’t mention them, just said I was looking for you. Hang on a minute you got locked up for speeding?”

“No not just speeding, swearing at police officers, punching the car trying to get out because they had locked me in, refusing to do a breathalyser test because they thought I had been drinking.”

Curtis laughs “Jesus mate you have had a shit night haven’t you.”

“Yes, you could say that, anyway what did Julia say when you called at hers?”

“Nothing much she said she hadn’t seen you and acted worried.”

“Oh right, well I’m going to her house now to see if she knows what the hell is going on and I wondered if you’d come with me, I don’t trust that woman and I certainly don’t want to be alone with her.”

“Yeah sure, are you picking me up?”

“Yeah, are you at Hamilton Tower?”

“Yes mate.”

“Okay I’ll be there soon.”

“I think you should call Kara to let her know you are alright, she’s really distraught.”

“Okay mate, will do.”

I haven't slept all night, I've been so worried about Evan, where is he? Why can't Curtis find him? Maybe he is in a hospital somewhere? Or is he with Julia? Curtis said he isn't or was he lying and covering for his friend? I don't know what to think.

My eyes are bloodshot from crying and tiredness. Although I'm mad with Evan I just want to know he is alright. I'm so scared that something terrible has happened to him, he was so angry and upset when he left last night, he was capable of anything.

I'm lying on my bed when my phone signals a text message making me jump. I sit up, grab my phone off the bedside drawers and feel relieved when I see the message is from Evan.

Hi, just wanted to let you know I'm alright, I know you are upset but so am I. I didn't have an affair with Julia I promise you and I hate it that you think I did. I am going to get some answers today and prove to you that I am telling you the truth. Evan

I hold my phone in my shaky hand contemplating what to put. I send a text back.

Hi, I'm so relieved to know you are alright. I'm so confused about everything, please don't do anything stupid. Kara

I don't feel like work today, but I don't want to let Sally down, so I drag my weary body out of bed. While I'm getting ready I think about everything that's happened.

'If Evan is having an affair with Julia and knowing that she wants him back why would he still be with me? Maybe he loves both of us? How did Sebastian know when Evan was going to be at Julia's house so he could take the photos?

Something else that has been bugging me is how did Julia know where I work because I'm sure Evan wouldn't have told her? Julia claims he did but then when he asked her how she knew she told him it was his mother that had told her. His mother can't have told Julia because when I met his mother for the first time she had said to Evan 'You never did tell me how you met Kara' then Evan told his mother that I worked in a coffee shop, he didn't actually say Walt's Coffee Shop.'

"Oh my god, surely not."

The realisation dawns on me as a thought comes to mind. I need to speak to Evan, how could I have been so stupid, shit what time is it? I look at my watch and it's 7.15am. I really need to get ready for work.

I grab my mobile phone and call Evan's number. It just rings and rings. "Evan answer your bloody phone… please baby, please pick up." Eventually it goes to answer phone. Shit. I leave him a message.

Evan baby it's me, I'm so sorry for not trusting you, for not believing you, I realise now that you are telling the truth and I should never have doubted you. I've just been thinking about Sebastian and Julia and everything they have said and done, and I've worked it out. Sebastian and Julia are together, they are working together to try and destroy us babe, think about it. I'll explain everything when I speak to you. Listen if you see them don't let on what I've said until I've spoken to you. I've got to go to work now but please call me, I love you and I'm so sorry.

Evan

I arrive at Hamilton Tower and as soon as Curtis sees me he gives me a man hug relieved that I'm alive and well. I check my phone and it says I have a voice message, but I haven't got time to listen to it now because I need to see Julia, I'll check it later.

I know Julia won't be at home she will be at work, so I drive to Julia's boutique in Knightsbridge.

Walking into the posh ladies clothing boutique the shop assistant looks up from behind the counter and smiles "Hi Sebastian she's in her office go on through."

"Okay thanks" I smile looking at Curtis who looks at me and we both frown confused.

"That was weird don't you think thinking you were Sebastian; I mean they are supposed to be on bad terms aren't they?" Curtis whispers.

"Yeah, that's what I thought" I whisper back.

I knock on the office door and Julia shouts, 'Come in.' and we walk into her office and Julia's face is a picture, shocked doesn't cover it.

"Evan, Curtis what a lovely surprise come in" she says standing up and offering us a chair to sit in then closing the office door.

"You found him then," Julia says looking at Curtis "apparently you went AWOL last night."

"Yes, something like that" I smile.

"What are you both doing here?" Julia asks surprised.

"Come on Julia I think you know" I reply.

"No, I'm afraid I don't you'll have to enlighten me" she grins.

"Kara received some photos of me and you yesterday in compromising positions with a note suggesting we are having an affair."

Julia laughs "Really?" fidgeting in her seat seeming uncomfortable. "And you think I sent them?"

"Well did you?"

"How absurd I've never heard anything so ridiculous in all my life."

"Why would your shop assistant think I'm Sebastian?"

"What I haven't got a clue. She's obviously got your names mixed up from when we were together. Anyway, is that all you came here for to accuse me of sending some stupid photos?"

"So, you honestly know nothing about them?"

"No Evan I don't" she says looking seriously at me.

"Have you heard from Sebastian?"

"No, I haven't thank god not since he nearly strangled me."

"Are you sure about that?" Curtis says glaring at her.

"Look I don't appreciate you coming here accusing me of doing things I have no clue what you're talking about and making me out to be a liar."

"Okay well sorry to have bothered you about this, we'll leave you to get on," I smile standing up "come on Curtis." Curtis stands too and we walk towards the door.

"Evan" she calls.

"Yes" I turn to look at her.

"I really don't know anything. Have a nice day sweetie and I'll see you soon" she smiles.

I nod and then we walk out of the boutique.

"Do you believe her?" Curtis asks as we get outside.

"Not a chance, come on."

We arrive back at Hamilton Tower and the first thing I do is listen to the voice mail on my phone. I'm nervous as I wait for Kara's message to be played because I've no clue what she is going to say to me.

I listen carefully as the message plays and the relief I feel is immense when I hear she has come to the same conclusion I have that Sebastian and Julia are together.

I go to find Curtis in his office and inform him what Kara had to say and then after having a chat about it I get into my car and make my way to Kara's hometown.

I'm desperate to see Kara because the last time we saw each other I was leaving her flat angry after being accused of having an affair and she was so distraught because she thought I had been unfaithful to her. I need to make things right between us.

I walk through the door of Walt's coffee shop and Kara looks up to see me walking towards her.

"Hi" I smile.

"Hi" she smiles.

I turn to Sally. "Please can I have a quick word with Kara?"

Sally smiles "Yes of course, go into the office."

"Thanks Sally" I smile.

Kara finishes serving a customer and then we go into the office. Once she has closed the door she says "Did you get my message I left on your mobile? I'm so sorry I should have trusted you I should never have…"

I take her in my arms and place my mouth over hers stopping her from speaking and kiss her.

After a few seconds she pulls away. "Evan, I need to apologise I…"

"No, you don't, I need to apologise for taking off like that, for being so angry and for upsetting you with my stupidity of giving Julia the time of day."

"Where were you? Where did you go when you left? I've been so worried I called you so many times and I called Curtis, and no-one could find you."

"I know and I'm sorry for worrying you, but I couldn't reply to any messages because I didn't have my phone I was locked up in a police cell for the night."

"Oh my god Evan what have you done, have you done something to Sebastian?"

"No nothing like that I just got caught for speeding, insulting a police officer oh and refusing to take a breathalyser test, that sort of thing" I smile.

"Oh god, are you in trouble?" she asks looking concerned.

"No, I just got a speeding ticket and a caution that's all."

"Thank god. So, did you listen to my message then?"

"Yes, I did, and I agree with you 100%, I also paid Julia a visit with Curtis."

"You didn't say anything to her about being with Sebastian did you?"

"No because when we visited her I hadn't listened to your message, so I didn't know. Our little meeting was quite enlightening actually."

"Enlightening in what way?" Kara asks.

"When we walked into her boutique her assistant thought I was Sebastian and told me to go through to her office like it was a normal thing."

"Really that just confirms it then."

"Yes, I must admit the two of them together hadn't even crossed my mind until I went to pay Julia a visit today and the lady mistook me for Sebastian and then it got me thinking too. Considering Seb is supposed to be threatening her why would he be calling to see her at work and be welcomed by her staff. Then when I listened to your message you left on my mobile it all made sense."

"So, what are we going to do about them?"

"I have an idea. Listen you need to act like we are finished, we can't let them know that we know their little game okay."

"Okay but for how long I don't want to be apart from you?"

"Don't worry it won't be for long. I'm going to enjoy exposing them and their little game."

"Okay" she smiles.

I love her smile. I bend my head and kiss those sweet soft lips of hers again. I kiss her with so much passion, I hold her close to me, I love her so much, she is everything to me and I will do everything in my power to protect her and our relationship from the likes of my conniving brother and my bitter ex.

"I've got to go," I say breaking the kiss and looking at my watch "I've got a meeting at the Manor which I'm running late for."

"Okay when will I see you again?"

"The weekend. I need to sort something out and you need to trust me okay."

"Okay I do trust you Evan and I really am sorry for not believing you." A tear rolls down her cheek.

"Hey, it's okay," I wipe away her tear then take her face in my hands and kiss her softly. "Don't cry I love you."

"I love you too."

I leave the coffee shop feeling relieved and happier knowing that we are okay.

After a quiet afternoon I fill Sally in on what's been happening with Julia and Sebastian and their plans to split up Evan and I, I also explain that Evan and I are pretending that we have broken up and she can't believe what's been going on.

I'm pleased when home time comes around because after not getting much sleep last night worrying about Evan I'm exhausted.

I arrive home and Jodie and Matt are sat in the kitchen talking when I walk in.

"Hi guys."

"Hi Kar, how are you?"

"I'm knackered" I sigh slumping down onto a chair.

"Have you heard from Evan at all?" Jodie asks.

"Yeah, he came to see me at the coffee shop today and we've made up except we're pretending that we haven't, and we have broken up."

"What I'm confused, why?" Jodie asks surprised.

I explain everything to Jodie and Matt, and they react angrily at the nerve of Julia and Sebastian's plans to try and break us up, trying to ruin Evan's life so he will pay Sebastian the money.

"Oh my god I can't believe it, they are just vile, they do say the love of money is the root of all evil" Jodie says shaking her head looking angry.

"I know the things people will do for a few quid eh" Matt says looking just as mad.

"Yep, seems that way, I'm not seeing Evan until the weekend now, he's got an idea to play them at their own game and then he is going to expose them for what they really are."

"Liars that's what" Jodie says.

"Yeah, and troublemakers, greedy bastards" Matt says.

"They certainly are" I agree.

"I can't believe they would stoop so low like that, trying to set Evan up to look like he is having an affair just so they can get some money out of him."

"I know."

"And the only way they can hurt him the most is to ruin your relationship" Jodie says.

"I know I bet Evan sometimes regrets getting mixed up with me."

"Don't be stupid Kara you are the best thing that has ever happened to him."

"Yes, but if we had kept things casual like he wanted to then he wouldn't be going through what he is now and giving them an opportunity to hurt him."

"Things were never going to be casual between you, you clicked, the earth stood still, you both found your soul mate that day when you met in the coffee shop, everyone can see how you are meant to be together and if it weren't you it would have been some other girl. I mean his brother has already ruined his previous relationship hasn't he."

"Yeah, you're right and I wouldn't want it to be some other girl, all this shit we are going through I suppose it will make us stronger and it proves that our love is strong enough to get through anything, we just have to get over this and then hopefully everything will be good. I just don't want Evan to get hurt."

"I'm sure Evan can handle them I mean the Evan I know is super confident and he will do anything to protect you Kara."

"I know thanks Jode you always make me feel better."

"I know what would make you feel even better" she smiles.

"What's that?"

Jodie gets up from the kitchen table, opens the freezer door and gets out my favourite Strawberry Cheesecake flavoured ice cream. "This" she says with a big grin on

her face. “I thought you might need cheering up after the weekend you’ve just had. Well not the going to Paris part but once we came back.”
“Thanks Jode, you really are the best.”

Julia

“Liv” Sebastian calls as he walks through the front door of my flat closing it behind him.
“I’m in the bedroom” I call. I’m sat at the dressing table taking off my make up.
“Hi babe how was your day?” he asks kissing me on the cheek then laying down on my bed.
“Good and you?” I turn to look at him.
“It was okay, so have you heard anything from Kara or Evan today after receiving the photos?”
“I’ve not heard from Kara, but I did have a visit from Evan at my shop today.”
“Oh really, that’s interesting, what did he want?”
I explain to Sebastian what happened and that my assistant mistook Evan for Sebastian and he is not happy.
“For fuck’s sake Liv I hope she hasn’t dropped us in it, we are so close to getting my money now and I don’t want anyone messing up our plan.”
“I know honey, relax everything is fine.”
“I hope you’re right.”

"I was thinking of contacting Kara what do you think? I walk over to the bed and sit down at the side of him.

"Okay sounds good you definitely need to back up the photos to her so she doesn't forgive Evan, you need to tell her it's true so it will mess with her head and to confirm what she must be thinking. Once you have confirmed it there is no way she will take him back after that. Have you got her mobile number?"

"No, I haven't, can you give it to me."

"Here you go."

Sebastian reads out Kara's number and then I call the number. After a few rings she answers.

"Hello."

"Kara it's Julia don't hang up."

"You've got some nerve."

"Listen Evan told me you've seen the photos of us together and I'm sorry you found out that way that we are seeing each other but I did try to warn you. I told you Evan and I still love each other, and he would come back to me eventually, I told you that you would end up getting hurt."

"Well obviously I should have listened to you shouldn't I. You two are welcome to each other I don't ever want to see Evan Hamilton or you again."

"Evan was kidding himself trying to move on with you but I'm afraid he just can't help himself when it comes to me, we have a special connection you see that no one else has, we're soul mates."

"I get it Julia, you don't need to say anymore, have a nice life." Kara puts the phone down.

"Well, that went well," I laugh. "she never wants to see me or Evan again, apparently we are welcome to each other."

"Fantastic well done gorgeous you were very convincing anyone would think that you do still love my brother."

'If only you knew.'

"Yes, well that's phase one complete to split them up" I smile.

"So, we are now ready for phase two, arrange to meet with Evan and tell him if he pays me my money we will confess to Kara that we set him up and put things right. I think he really loves this girl, so I think he is going to pay this time Liv."

"Well, if he doesn't then we will just continue to ruin his life until he does."

"You really are wicked Liv, are you sure it's just about the money, all these plans you come up with to try and hurt my brother it's like you enjoy it or something."

"What do you mean?"

"Well, you seem like you are enjoying this more than I am, yes I want my money, but I never wanted to completely destroy my brother in the process."

"Evan hurt me Seb yes I had an affair with you which was wrong, but I really love, loved him, we had something special and… never mind."

"What."

"I don't want to talk about it anymore, anyway, are you staying tonight or what?" I snap.

"I will if you want me to" he says looking seriously at me.

"Why wouldn't I want you to?" I reply sounding offish.

"I don't know I sometimes get the impression that you wish it were Evan in your bed rather than me I mean you just said you love him before you corrected yourself."

"I said loved as in the past oh don't be ridiculous now you're just being stupid and jealous."

"Yes, but do I have a reason to be jealous Liv?"

"Seb I love you not Evan now if you'll stop being such an arse I'll show you just how much." I climb on top of him and straddle him.

We stare at each other intensely and I move down his body unzip his jeans then pull his boxers down at the front. I take his cock in my hand and stroke him up and down a few times until he is fully hard then I put his cock into my mouth and suck him hard.

"Oh, fuck Liv" he moans grabbing hold of my head with his hands.

While I'm pleasuring Sebastian his mobile phone rings in his jacket pocket.

"Oh fuck, who's that?" he says moaning in pleasure.

"Leave it Seb" I say before continuing.

"Fuck Liv" Seb gets his mobile out of his pocket to see who it is. "Shit it's Evan" he says breathless.

I stop what I'm doing and smile. "Well, you had better answer it then." I take his cock in my mouth again and start to tease him with my tongue.

"Liv I will but you need to stop doing that, aargh Jesus Liv seriously stop I can't talk to him while you are sucking my cock." He pulls out of my mouth and moves away from me making me laugh then takes a few deep breaths and answers the call.

Sebastian

"Hello, my dear brother, what a lovely surprise what can I do for you?" I smile.

"You devious bastard, enough is enough you win I can't do this anymore."

"You can't do what?" I ask with a smug grin.

"You know damn well what, I'm not playing your games anymore Seb, I know you took photos of me and Julia and sent them to Kara making it look like we are having an affair which is a complete lie."

"Oh yes I took some great photos didn't I so I thought Kara would like to see them. You played right into my hands dear brother, you made it so easy for me?"

"Well congratulations you got what you wanted Kara and I have split up, she wants nothing more to do with me, she hates me so you win I can't take this anymore,

I'll pay you your money." Evan sounds so angry and frustrated.

"I knew you would see sense eventually and I'm sorry it's taken you so long to realise that I would do whatever it took. Don't worry though Ev there's plenty more fish in the sea."

"You really are a heartless bastard aren't you?"

"I wouldn't say that I just want what is mine that's all."

"Okay meet me at my new hotel The Manor on Saturday morning at 10am and I'll give you your money then. I'll send you directions, it will be quiet there so we can discuss everything in private."

"Okay I'll be there and Evan."

"What?"

"I want cash and if I find out you have duped me when I have counted it then..."

"I won't it will all be there, see you Saturday."

Evan cuts the call.

"Well, well, well it appears our plan has worked. He wants to meet on Saturday, and he is bringing the cash" I grin.

"Oh Seb, that's fantastic, we'll be rich" Julia laughs.

"Certainly will baby, now, where were we?" and before Julia can say anything else my cock is back in her mouth so she can finish what she started.

Evan

I put the phone down from Sebastian and call Kara to let her know what's happening.

"Hi baby it's me."

"Hi, is everything okay, is it alright for you to ring me?"

"Everything is great and I'm sure they haven't bugged my phone babe" I laugh.

"I know sorry I'm being stupid I just don't know what to do with myself."

"I know babe it's okay."

"I had a call from Julia earlier."

"Really what did she want?

"The usual to shit stir, I told her that I never want to see you or her again and that you are welcome to each other."

"Good thinking then she won't suspect anything. Well, I've just spoken to my brother and he has agreed to meet me on Saturday at the Manor, he thinks I'm going to pay him the money, so we just need to keep away from each other until then."

"Okay but what are you going to do about Julia?"

"Don't worry Julia has got it coming to her, I'm going make her think once everything is sorted we can get back together, which of course is a complete lie. I'm going to ask her to come with me on Saturday for moral support and then I'm going to expose them both about their game. I can't wait to see both their faces when they realise we are still together and he's not getting a penny from me."

"Oh god he's going to be so mad and Julia is too."

"I know I want you to be there on Saturday but not straight away, after I've exposed them I want you to turn up so we can show them that they haven't won and that we are as strong as ever. I'll arrange a time for Curtis to bring you."

"Oh okay."

"You need to trust me Kara because I'm going to have to get Julia on side this week so she will come with me on Saturday."

"I trust you; I just don't trust her; I don't want her touching you Evan."

"Baby don't worry I'll be keeping her at arm's length I promise."

"Are you sure you know what you are doing?"

"Yes, I'm going to end things once and for all so they will never come near us again."

"Okay, let's do this."

Twenty Seven

Evan

It's Tuesday evening and after a long tiring day at work I arrive home, shower and get changed into some blue jeans and a white t-shirt.

After having a shave, I put on my favourite aftershave and I'm ready to pay Julia a visit. I texted her earlier in the day and asked if it were possible to go and see her tonight and of course she replied saying she would be delighted to see me.

I arrive at Julia's flat and knock on the door, it's almost 7.30pm and I'm anxious as I wait for her to answer the door.

"Evan hi please come in" Julia says gesturing for me to go inside.

"Thank you" I smile walking into the lounge as she offers for me to take a seat.

"Can I get you a drink?"

"A coffee would be great thanks."

I could really do with something stronger the way I'm feeling right now but I need to keep my wits about me in case she tries anything, so a coffee is the only option.

Julia goes to the kitchen to make the coffees while I stay sat on the sofa looking around the room for any signs that Sebastian has been here but there's nothing.

"There you go" she says returning with two cups of coffee and placing them on the coffee table in front of me.

"Great thanks."

"You're welcome, I'll try not to spill mine this time" she laughs.

"Oh yes" I laugh.

"So why are you here?" Julia asks batting her eyelashes at me.

'It's definitely not that if that's what you're thinking.' The way she is looking at me is turning my stomach and it's already in knots.

"Well, I would like to apologise for accusing you the other day of knowing anything about the photos sent to Kara when I visited you in your shop."

"Oh, that's okay I've forgotten about that now" she smiles.

"No, it's not okay I was angry, and I have spoken to Sebastian and he has admitted he was responsible for taking the photos and sending them to Kara. Anyway, Kara has ended things with me because of them, she never wants to see me again and I took my anger out on you and that's not fair."

"I understand that you were upset, and I can't believe Sebastian has done that. I promise you Evan I didn't know what he was planning. So, Kara has ended things has she?"

"Yes, she has, but thinking about it now I think Sebastian has done me a favour."

"Oh, why do you say that?"

"Because Kara doesn't trust me, she accuses me all the time of having an affair with you, she tells me not to see you or speak to you and I'm not having some woman dictate to me who I can and can't see. I lost my way for a while because I thought I had strong feelings for her but after she found the photos of the two of us and reacted the way she did without giving me a chance to explain it kind of confirmed it for me, we wouldn't have worked anyway." I pick up my coffee and take a sip.

"I'm sorry things haven't worked out for you, but they do say things happen for a reason and maybe that reason is that we are still meant to be together Ev." She changes seats and comes and sits down next to me.

"Maybe but I need to sort my brother out first before I can even start to think about us which is another reason why I'm here."

"Oh?" Julia takes a sip of her coffee.

“Yes, I’ve arranged to meet Sebastian on Saturday at my new hotel so we can talk about what he’s been doing, I want it to stop so I’m going to pay him the money.”

“You are, really?” Julia says sounding a little too pleased and excited then realising trying to play it down “I think it’s for the best I mean if you pay him the money then you can get on with your life and he won’t be trying to ruin it or mine for that matter.”

“Yes, it’s been going on far too long and I can’t do it anymore after everything he’s done, threatening you, trying to use Kara to get to me, I’ve had enough so I’m going to pay him, so we are free of him once and for all.”

“I’m here for you Evan and I always will be if you’ll let me” Julia smiles touching my arm.

“Thanks. I’m sorry for pushing you away when you told me how you still feel about me, I think if I’m honest I didn’t want to admit to myself that I still have feelings for you too. I just don’t know what those feelings are and how to deal with them.”

“Really?” Julia says sounding surprised but grinning from ear to ear moving closer to me.

“Yes, I think so.”

“You’re not just saying that?”

“Since we’ve reconnected again every time I see you I feel something but I’m not sure if that feeling can develop into anything more. When you had the affair with Seb I was crushed, my whole world fell apart, but I think deep down I’ve never stopped loving you. I hated you for a while for what you did to me, to us but as time has gone by I can see past that now. I know how manipulative Sebastian can be so I can imagine it must have been hard to reject him, after all we do look the same so I guess you would be attracted to him wouldn't you."

"Yes, but what I thought I felt for Sebastian doesn't come close to how I feel about you."

"I tried to suppress my feelings for you because of what you did and being with Kara I was trying to move on but the connection we have is so strong, I was kidding myself to think I was over you."

"Oh, Evan, I don't know what to say, all this time you have told me you would never take me back and now you are saying what I have wanted to hear for so long." Tears fall down her cheeks.

"Don't cry." I wipe her tears away with my thumb.

"I'm sorry, I'm so sorry for everything I ever did to hurt you, for the affair, for..."

"Shush, it's okay Julia, I know you are," I begrudgingly hold her hand. "I forgive you."

Julia moves towards me for a kiss, but I stop her.

"Wait."

"What but I thought..."

"I can't not yet."

"Why not?"

"It would be so easy for me to kiss you right now, but I need to sort Sebastian out first, if he knows that we still have feelings for each other and we get back together he will come after you again like he did with Kara and I can't take that risk."

"But Evan surely we can just be together tonight, Sebastian won't know and how will he find out if we keep it between us?"

"I'm sorry I just can't which brings me back to why I'm here."

"Yes, why are you here?" she huffs. Julia's not happy now because I have rejected her advances.

"Like I said I came to apologise to you, but I also wanted to ask you if you would come with me when I meet Sebastian on Saturday. I thought we could face him together as a united front. I going to make it clear he is not to threaten you anymore or go near you again, he is not to play anymore of his games and if he agrees then I will give him the cash and then we can put all this behind us and start a fresh."

"I think that's sounds perfect, of course I'll come with you" she smiles.

"Great he will think he has won but when we tell him we are still in love it will be us having the last laugh, unbreakable." I smile stroking her cheek with the back of my hand.

"Unbreakable" she smiles looking adoringly at me. "Evan if Sebastian starts saying things to you about me you need to ignore him, he is bitter and will do or say anything okay."

“Okay don’t worry I don’t believe anything that comes out of my brother’s mouth.”

“Oh god, are we really doing this?” Julia asks.

“Yes, we are really doing this,” I smile. “Anyway, I’d better go.”

“I wish you didn’t have too; can’t you stay a bit longer?” she says rubbing her leg up against mine.

“I’m sorry, I can’t.”

“Okay I’ll see you out” she says showing me to the front door.

“I’ll see you on Saturday then.” I kiss her on both cheeks holding her upper arms and linger for a few seconds as I kiss her.

“Oh god Evan I’ve missed you so much.”

“Me too, see you Saturday.”

“Bye.”

Julia watches me leave and I get in my car feeling guilty that I’ve made her think we have a chance again. I had to do it to get her on side but let’s face it after everything she has done she deserves everything she gets.

Twenty Eight

Julia

It's Friday evening and I'm feeling nervous about tomorrow, Sebastian will be here any minute and he doesn't have a clue that tomorrow I'm going to tell him things are over between us. Evan wants me back and I can't wait to be with him again, to be in his arms and for him to make love to me like he used to.

"Hi Liv, it's me" Sebastian calls walking into my flat closing the door behind him.

"Hi" I call from the kitchen.

"Pleased to see me?" Sebastian asks walking over to me and giving me a kiss.

I frown. "Yes, why wouldn't I be?"

"Just asking," he smiles helping himself to a bottle of beer from the fridge. "Have you heard anymore from Evan or Kara?"

"No why?" I snap. I feel so on edge.

"Hey what's wrong with you?"

"Nothing I guess I'm just anxious about tomorrow that's all."

'I'm anxious about telling you we're over and I'm going back to your brother.'

"I can relieve some of your tension if you like?" Sebastian says coming up behind me moving my hair to one side and kissing my neck up to my ear and massaging my breasts in his hands.

"Sebastian it's not always about sex you know, can't we just have a conversation without you groping me all the time" I say shrugging him off.

"Hey why are you being such a bitch I was just trying to relax you because you're wound up like a tight spring, it'll be fine tomorrow we'll get our money and then everything will be good… yes" he says turning me to face him and cupping my face in his hands looking at me intensely.

"I'm sorry I'm just not feeling horny at the moment, I can't just drop my knickers because you are."

"Hey, fuck off Liv you're talking shit" Sebastian snaps moving away from me.

"What do you mean I'm talking shit?"

"You always want it as much as I do, you never normally refuse me so what's wrong is it just about tomorrow or do you have something else on your mind?"

"No just because I don't want to have sex with you at this moment in time you think something is wrong."

"You seem distant from me all of a sudden, you certainly weren't complaining last night when I was fucking your brains out and you were screaming my name, so what is it, what have I done?"

"Oh, do you have to be so crude all the time Sebastian why can't you be more like…"

"What, why can't I be what more like my brother you mean, fuck you Liv."

"Oh, fuck off Sebastian, in fact you can just leave, get out" I shout.

"No, I'm not going anywhere until you tell me what your problem is."

"You are, you are my fucking problem, get out, just go" I scream.

"I said NO" he shouts and then he walks straight over to me grabs hold of me and kisses me fiercely. I shove him off and slap him hard across the face and glare at him.

"What the hell are you doing Seb?" I'm breathing fast and my heart is pumping.

"You bitch," he holds his face rubbing the sting. "What the fuck is wrong with you?" he shouts.

"NOTHING…" I scream and he lunges at me again but this time I don't refuse him.

Having sex will make me forget about this mess I'm in for a while. I do love Sebastian but just not in the same way that I love Evan. I have tried to put Evan out of my mind for so long, but I just can't, I love him, he captured my heart first and the love I felt for him has never gone away.

I am so stressed and having sex with Sebastian will destress me when he fucks me into oblivion.

I kiss him hard and help him to take off his shirt. Our mouths and teeth are clashing, we are desperate for one another. Sebastian picks me up and carries me to the bedroom then throws me on the bed. "I think you need to calm the fuck down and forget about tomorrow for a while and I know just what you need" he says his eyes hooded and focussed on me, the look on his face is hot and fierce and he has me captivated when he stalks over to me. Sebastian and I have always enjoyed fierce and intense sex.

Once we are both naked Sebastian gets the handcuffs out of the bedside drawer and ties me to the bed. "Look at you, you angry bitch I'm going to give you just what you need, I always know what you need Liv and that's me. I know seeing my brother again has confused your mind I'm not stupid, but you are mine now Liv, not his and I want you to remember that when I fuck you and make you come so hard repeatedly. I fucking own you Liv, you need to remember that, and you own me" he says.

"Sebastian…" I pant. He sure does know how to turn me on, I'm so aroused.

"What you want me now do you Liv? Do you want me to fuck you, is that what you want?"

"Yes, fuck me you bastard" I rage.

Sebastian strokes himself up and down in front of me looking at me intensely. "Do you want this do you?" he says taunting me with his hard length in front of my face, I can see how excited he is.

"Yes," I scream "yes."

He takes his cock and wipes the glistening tip along my lips, my tongue immediately darts out of my mouth and I taste him. I open my mouth wide for him and Sebastian starts to fuck my mouth.

"Don't you forget who fucking owns you Liv" he moans as he enjoys thrusting in and out of my greedy mouth making us both more and more aroused. After a few minutes he pulls away leaving me breathless and then goes down on me.

"OHHHH fuck…Seb………" I cry out when I feel his soft, wet tongue lick and suck my pulsating clit.

"Who turns you on like no other man has?" he says stopping and looking up at me.

"You do."

"Say my name Liv, who turns you on like no other man."

"You do Sebastian…, you turn me on" I cry.

"Whose cock do you want inside you Liv?"

"Your cock, I want yours," I pant. "Sebastian please."

He is driving me crazy and it's not long before I'm screaming his name as an orgasm so powerful and intense rushes through my body.

My face is flushed and I'm seeing stars when Sebastian unties me, and I grab hold of him and kiss him hard. He has made me desperate for him and manoeuvring him onto his back I straddle him and sit on his hard cock and begin riding him up and down repeatedly. We stare at each other until we both come feeling exhilarated.

I climb off him exhausted and flop down on the bed at the side of him and then all the emotions that I'm dealing with, loving Evan, loving Sebastian, not wanting to hurt him come rushing to the surface and I sob.

"Liv baby what's wrong, I'm sorry for earlier please don't cry, I'm sorry" he says holding me as tears run down my face.

"No, I'm sorry…" I snuggle into his side and hold him tightly.

"What for baby?"

"For everything."

Twenty Nine

Evan

It's Saturday a normal day to most people who are having a day off from work, but this day isn't a normal day for me because this is the day I get to confront my twin brother and my ex-girlfriend, to make it clear that I will not take any more of their shit, this is the day I'm going to sort them out once and for all.

I awake with a startle drenched in sweat, I have been dreaming about the day ahead of me and in my dream Kara is stood outside the Manor listening to what Sebastian and Julia have to say about everything and she believes their lies. Kara stands looking at me with so much hatred in her eyes calling me a liar and a cheat and she tells me it's over between us for good this time and never wants to see me again.

"Shit." I rub my eyes with the back of my hands, I haven't had much sleep and my head feels fuzzy. I sit up and run my fingers through my hair then look at my watch, it's 6.00am. I need to speak to Kara; I need to check that she's okay and to tell her if Sebastian and Julia try to fill her head with more lies she is not to believe them. I reach for my mobile phone and desperate to talk to her I call her number.

After ringing for a while, a sleepy, tired voice answers.

"Hello, Evan are you okay?"

"Kara."

"What's wrong you sound weird?" she yawns trying to wake up.

"Sorry to wake you, I had a nightmare it was awful babe you took Seb and Julia's side and told me you never wanted to see me again, you told me we were over."

"Evan calm down it was just a nightmare, relax that's never going to happen."

"I can't lose you again Kara, what if...?"

"You're not going to lose me okay."

"You swear because it will crush me Kara, I love you so much, I don't know what I would do…"

"I swear to you listen to me, you need to try and relax because you can't meet your brother in this state, you need to be strong. Plus, Julia might suspect something is wrong when you see her if you're all agitated, so go and take a shower and have a coffee and try not to worry."

"You're right, it's just the nightmare seemed so real you know and the way you reacted when you saw those photos of Julia and I, how do I know that you won't change your mind when you start listening to what they've got to say because they will try and turn you against me Kara, I know they will."

"It's not going to happen I admit I did jump to conclusions before but that was because I was confused, I didn't know what to think, I'm sorry, I regret it now."

"I don't blame you for reacting the way you did but how do you know you won't start thinking that way again?"

"Evan stop don't do this I'm not going to think like that okay."

"Okay I'm sorry." I take some deep breaths to calm myself, the stress of seeing my brother is getting to me and I need to sort my shit out.

"You always say to me that I need to trust you, so you need to trust me" Kara says reassuring me.

"I do trust you."

"So, believe me when I say I won't change my mind, I won't leave you."

"Okay I'm sorry these past few days it's been torture not being able to see your face, to hold you."

"I know I feel the same, but we'll be together later once it's all over, but you need to be strong for now so go and get in the shower and I'll see you soon."

"Okay baby I will, I love you."

"I love you too."

Julia is ready and waiting for me when I arrive. I greet her with a peck on the cheek and she seems excited to see me.

"Hi, are you okay?" she asks grabbing hold of my hand as we walk to my car.

"I will be once I've sorted my brother out" I smile.

"Have you brought the money?"

"Yes, it's in the car boot."

We arrive at the Manor and we don't have to wait long before Sebastian's blue Audi R8 drives down the lane at speed.

"Here he is" I say taking a deep breath to calm my nerves and get out of the car. Julia stands at the side of me and we watch the car pull to a stop in front of us.

Sebastian gets out of the car. "Well, this is nice hello dear brother, Julia, how lovely to see you" he grins.

"I wish I could say the same but then I would be lying but you know all about lying don't you" I seethe.

"I don't know what you mean," he laughs. "Anyway, why is she here?" he says looking at Julia who is looking edgy.

"Julia is here because I asked her to come here" I answer.

"Oh, really and why is that don't you trust being on your own with me bruv?"

"I don't trust you full stop."

"So, have you brought my money?"

"Always eager aren't you Sebastian when it comes to money."

"Of course, when it's my money and should have always been my money, you should never have accepted what was not yours."

"I agree Father should never have done what he did but after everything you have done to me, the things you have said you need to know you will never get a penny of it."

"What do you mean so you haven't brought me the cash?" Sebastian says looking shocked and angry.

"No I haven't" I smile.

"You bastard, you tricked me" Sebastian moves towards me in a rage, but Julia stands in front of me blocking his path.

"Julia what are you doing? Get out of my way" Sebastian snarls.

"No Seb I won't let you hurt him" she replies shielding me from him.

"Oh my god this is hilarious" Sebastian laughs standing back looking at us both "What are you going to do? You can drop the act now Liv?"

"I'm sorry Seb but Evan and I are getting back together, I love him" Julia says looking at me then back to Sebastian.

Sebastian laughs and continues to laugh. "Julia you don't have to pretend anymore, come here babe" he says beckoning her over to him with open arms.

"What act?" I ask looking between them both.

"I'm serious Seb, Evan has told me he still loves me, and I still love him, so we are getting back together."

Sebastian smiles. "Come on Julia I think we can tell him now don't you."

"Tell me what?" I say backing away from them both, but I already know.

"Julia and I are together, and we have been together since you found us that day, you know when I was fucking your girlfriend in her bed."

"Julia?" I question looking shocked.

Julia looks awkward "It's true Evan but I have never loved Seb like I love you."

"What?" Sebastian says angrily. "Julia babe please you can stop this, come here" he says looking at her with pleading eyes.

"No Seb, Evan has admitted he still has feelings for me and we're going to try again so I'm sorry, but I choose Evan."

"You have got to be fucking kidding me." Sebastian paces up and down raging and shaking his head in disbelief.

"No, I'm not kidding I love him. I've always loved him." Julia walks over to me and grabs hold of my hand.

"No, you don't Liv, you love me, you tell me all the time, you love me, you're just confused." Sebastian looks, angry, hurt and confused.

"I do love you Seb but it's not the same love that I feel for Evan. I've always preferred him can't you see; I've always loved him ever since the first day we met, being with you was a mistake, I should never have let you charm your way around me like that. I lost the man I love, who I still love and yes you and I have been together for a long time now and I care about you I really do but what we have could never compare to what I had with Evan."

"You fucking bitch," Sebastian snarls moving towards her and she goes to hide behind my back. "After everything we have been through and you still prefer him."

"Sebastian," I say holding my hands up blocking his path "Stay where you are." He stops in his tracks.

"What you would seriously take her back after everything she has done to you, she had an affair with me, your brother remember. I was fucking her behind your back and I've been fucking her for some time now and you still want her, you must be fucking desperate or something" Seb seethes bunching his fists together still pacing up and down looking more and more upset.

"You fucking asshole" Julia screams crying.

"Julia go inside the Manor until he's calmed down" I'm concerned he might do something from the look on his face.

"Evan, I don't want to leave you with him" she sobs.

"Go I'll be fine," I say assertively passing her the keys to the Manor "I need to talk to my brother."

"Yeah, fuck off Julia, do as he says I can't bear the sight of you right now, you know what you are don't you you're a fucking whore" Sebastian shouts.

"Fuck off Seb I can't help it if your brother is better in bed than you are of course I'm going to prefer him."

"You fucking bitch" he shouts lunging forward towards her and I hold him back while Julia runs off unlocking the door of the Manor quickly and taking retreat inside. I hold onto my brother until she's gone stopping him from doing something he will regret.

"Get the fuck off me" he shouts shrugging me off and walking away running his hands through his hair.

"Sebastian listen you need to calm down."

"Calm down don't tell me to calm down, I fucking love that woman and she loves me, she doesn't know what she's saying" he says clearly hurt by her words.

"Seb she's been using you can't you see? She's only with you because she couldn't have me; I've lost count the number of times she has asked for my forgiveness begging for me to take her back."

"Yes, but that was all part of the plan, we have been working together she was supposed to say those things like that until we got the money."

"I know" I sigh.

"What do you mean you know?" he says looking at me shocked.

"I worked it out I know you and Julia are together."

"What how? We have been so careful" Sebastian frowns.

"I guess it all fell into place that day I paid Julia a visit at her boutique, her assistant thinking I was you and…"

"Everything would have been okay if it wasn't for her ruining everything."

"You can't blame Julia's assistant the only person to blame here is you. I can't believe you have been continually trying to ruin my life because of money. Money isn't everything Seb."

"It is when you are entitled to some of the millions that your father left you and you got pittance."

"I know Father wronged you and he should never have done that but it's not my fault Seb, when he died you were in a bad place, gambling, drinking, wasting money on holidays, your friends, there was a moment when I was going to give you that money, but I didn't because I knew it wouldn't have meant anything. You would have been in the same position as you are now, can't you see you would have spent it all, wasted it and been penniless."

"You had no right it was mine and it's up to me how I decide to spend my money."

"I made a decision at the time and unfortunately you have proved me right" I stare at him seriously.

"You sound just like Father you two always thought you were better than me."

"That's not true we were trying to help you."

"Help me, don't make me laugh."

"Look I don't want to argue with you, but this ends now do you hear me, you won't be getting any money and you will leave me alone, leave Kara alone and stay the hell out of my life. I never want to see your face again and if you don't do as I ask then I will go to the police and have you charged for harassment; I have evidence Seb that I can use against you for things you have done to me in the past."

"Evidence, what evidence? You have nothing on me and leave Kara alone I thought you two had finished?" Seb laughs.

"Well, I guess you thought wrong you see your little plan to break us up didn't work either we're still together."

"So, you don't want to get back with Julia?"

"No, I don't."

"So where is your little bitch now then eh?"

"She'll be here soon."

Just as I say the words I look up and see Curtis' red Audi TT driving down the lane towards us. "And here she is now" I smile.

"Whatever I don't give a fuck about your relationship so what if you're still together all I want is my money and Julia and then I'll leave you alone."

"You're not getting any money from me Seb."

"Evan you pay me my money, or I swear to fucking god you will regret it" he scowls.

"You can't hurt me anymore Seb" I smile.

"Do you want to bet?"

Sebastian walks towards me and takes a stance in readiness to fight.

"I don't want to fight with you Seb" I say calmly.

Sebastian stands in front of me and we are almost nose to nose. I glare at him. "This is not over dear brother" he then walks off towards the Manor.

"Where are you going?" I call after him.

"I need to talk to Julia."

"Don't you dare hurt her Seb."

"Why would I hurt her I fucking love her" he shouts walking into the building.

I walk over to Curtis' car just as Curtis and Kara are getting out.

"Oh god is everything okay?" Kara asks running over to me and hugging me. God I've missed her.

"You okay buddy?" Curtis asks coming to stand at the side of us.

"Yeah, I'm fine but I'm so pleased you're both here, god that was intense."

"So, what happened then?" Kara asks.

I tell them everything that was said and explain that Sebastian has gone into the Manor to talk to Julia.

"What happens now?" Kara asks.

"We'll just wait out here for a while until they come out and if they haven't come out after 10 minutes or so then we'll go and find them."

After 10 minutes has passed and there is still no sign of Sebastian or Julia I decide we need to see what's happening. "I think they've had long enough to talk now, come on let's go and see what they are up to."

I walk up to the front door of the Manor followed by Kara and Curtis. As I place my hand on the door handle and turn it the doors locked.

"That's strange the door's locked," I try the handle again "They must have locked it from the inside."

"How come, where are your keys?" Curtis asks.

"I gave them to Julia when Seb lunged at her, I needed to get her away quickly because I didn't know what Seb was going to do, he was so angry when Julia told him she is still in love with me and wants me not him."

"Why would they have locked the door though?" Kara asks.

"I don't know babe?"

I open the letter box and shout through it, Julia…Sebastian…open the door" and that's when I smell it… smoke.

Peering through the tiny gap in the door I can smell and see smoke and flames coming from one of the rooms down the long hallway.

"Shit, the Manor's on fire."

"What?" Kara and Curtis reply shocked.

"The Manor it's on fire" I say sounding panicked.

"Oh fuck," Curtis says, "What shall we do?"

"Quick we need to get this door open and find Seb and Julia before the fire escalates, the sprinkler system should give us a bit of time. Have you got your keys on you Curtis?"

"Yes, sorry mate." Curtis fumbles around in his jeans pocket and locates his keys then passes them to me to unlock the door.

As I open the door the smoke is getting thicker and the flames are getting stronger by the second.

"Sebastian…Julia…" I shout feeling the heat from the fire, the smoke making me cough. There is no reply.

"We need to go and find them we need to get them out" I say to Curtis.

"Evan no please don't go in there please" Kara cries holding onto my arm to try and stop me.

"Baby I'll be fine," I look seriously at her. "I need to find Seb and Julia before the fire gets worse and you need to stand back from the building and call the fire brigade for me okay, can you do that for me?" I say calmly.

"Please don't go in there Evan, please" she begs.

"Kara listen I haven't got time to argue, can you do that for me?"

Kara is crying, I know she's scared but I need to do this and quickly before the fire really takes hold and it's too late. The fire is starting to light up the windows of the old building and I need to act now.

"Okay but please be careful I can't lose you" she cries.

"You're not going to lose me" I smile.

I take one last look at her face full of anguish and then Curtis and I enter the building disappearing amongst the smoke, covering our mouths with our hands trying not to breathe it in.

My twin brother and my ex-girlfriend are inside and as much as I hate them for what they have done to me I am human at the end of the day and I don't want them to get hurt.

The fire has spread quickly in the old building and the rooms are already engulfed in smoke and flames.

"Why isn't the sprinkler system working?" I ask Curtis.

"No idea mate but it should be, maybe one of the workmen turned it off on Friday I know they found a serious water leak that they were trying to fix so they may have turned the water off and forgot to turn it back on again?"

'Oh, great, of all the times to have a serious fucking fire and someone has turned the fucking water off, so the sprinklers are not working, unbelievable.'

"Someone's going to be in serious fucking trouble if that's the case."

I walk further into the building and shout as loud as I can whilst trying to cover my mouth from the fumes.

"Seb, Julia..." but nothing comes back. We make our way down the long corridor.

"Jesus... where the hell are they? Sebastian...Julia?" I cough desperate to find them.

"Evan look over there" Curtis shouts and we see Julia laid down on the ground in the distance.

We rush over to her and she is hysterical and crying.

"Where's Sebastian?" she screams.

"Julia what happened?" I ask crouching down beside her.

"We argued, he's really upset, he's so mad at me, he told me you lied to me that you don't want me back, is that true?" she sobs.

"I'm sorry yes it's true but I haven't got time for this right now we need to get you out, where's Seb?"

"I believed you" she cries.

"Julia" I shout.

"Sebastian said he hates me, he said if he can't have me then nobody can and then he set fire to the building" she sobs.

"Which way did he go?" I ask.

"I don't know he hit me, and I fell to the ground and hurt my ankle, it was like he was in some sort of a trance, he just walked off leaving me on the floor."

I look around "Julia we need to get you out of here, the fire is spreading, and we don't have much time, can you walk?"

"I'm not sure."

"I'll get her out mate you go and find your brother" Curtis says.

I nod in agreement then make my way further towards the back of the building.

I fumble with my phone; my hands are shaking as I dial 999. I'm standing alone outside the burning building while the man I love, and his best friend are searching for Julia and Sebastian.

After getting through I explain the situation and they tell me they are on the way and will be here soon.

'Oh god please hurry.'

I wait and wait for signs of someone coming through the front door as I stare at it hoping and praying that everyone is alright, but no one appears. I feel sick and shaky. 'Where are they?'

"Evan, Curtis, where are you?" I shout pacing up and down, frantic. I hear a voice and turn to look where it came from and Curtis is walking towards me carrying Julia in his arms.

"Curtis" I call running over to them as he lowers Julia onto the ground.

"Are you okay? Where's Evan?"

Julia is sobbing. "I'm fine Evan's still inside looking for Sebastian" he coughs the smoke having affected his throat. "Julia's hurt her ankle, where's the fire brigade, the ambulance?" Curtis asks sounding panicked.

"They're on their way."

'Oh god Evan's still inside, where the hell is he, and where is Sebastian and why aren't they coming out?'

"Sebastian I'm so sorry, Sebastian..." Julia cries slumped on the ground.

"I need to find them; I need to find Evan" I say distraught. I make my way to the side of the building.

"Kara... no... stop" Curtis shouts running after me and stopping me by grabbing my arm.

"The fire it's too strong and you don't know the building like Evan does, he would never forgive me if I let you go in there and something happened to you."

"EVAN....," I scream crying. I don't know what to do, I feel helpless. Curtis holds me. "I should have stopped him Curtis, I should have stopped him..." I cry as he tries to console me.

I see Julia sat on the ground looking at us and I feel anger bubbling inside of me. I shrug Curtis off and storm over to her. "It's all your fault, yours and Sebastian's you stupid bitch." I slap her hard across the face.

"Kara no she's not worth it" Curtis grabs hold of me and drags me away stopping me from doing anything more.

Julia doesn't say anything she just looks at me and holds her cheek feeling the sting and sobs.

"I hate her Curtis, I hate her," I yell. "Why couldn't they just leave us alone?" I sob.

The noise of sirens fills the air getting louder and louder, we look to see the emergency services driving down the lane towards the Manor at speed.

"It's about bloody time" Curtis says as we watch them come to a halt.

Curtis runs over to one of the firemen as he exits one of the fire engines and explains what has happened and that there are still two people inside. He tells him where he thinks the fire started and that the fire is spreading quickly. There are firemen and ambulance crews, and everyone has their own job to do as they set about trying to put out the fire and secure the area.

Julia and Curtis are taken into the ambulances to be checked over while all I can do is stand and watch and wait for any signs of life.

I watch the front door as the orange flames of the fire continues to light up the windows of the Manor. Water from the fire hoses are being sprayed onto and inside the building and I feel like I'm in a nightmare and I desperately want to wake up. The beautiful building that Evan is lovingly restoring to turn into his new hotel is now ruined and it will take a lot of time and money to get it back to its original state.

"Are you okay madam?" a fireman asks seeing me standing alone disturbing me from my thoughts.

"My boyfriend's in there," I half smile referring to the building "he's looking for his brother." I feel numb, I don't want to think of the possibility of what if Evan doesn't make it out alive, it's too painful.

"We are doing everything we can love to find them I can assure you" he smiles giving my back a comforting rub before walking off to speak to one of his colleagues.

I continue to watch from a safe distance when something catches my eye, a blackened figure is walking towards me from the side of the building. His clothes are black, his face is dirtied from the smuts and he is coughing repeatedly holding his hand over his mouth. He is retching and gasping for breath.

'Oh, thank god Evan.' I rush over to him and he slumps down onto the ground in front of me.

"Evan baby are you hurt, are you okay?" I crouch down at the side of him relieved to see him alive.

"Where's Julia?" he coughs "Did she make it out?"

"She's safe Curtis got her out, she's hurt her ankle but apart from that I think she's going to be fine."

"I'm so sorry" he mumbles repeatedly.

"Evan it's okay it's not your fault don't talk just concentrate on your breathing okay." I look into his sad brown eyes and cup his face. "I'll go and get help, you need help." I go to get up to get a paramedic, but he stops me.

"No wait…" he cries holding my arm.

"Evan you need to see someone."

"I need to see Julia, I love her."

"What?" I stand up and back away from him. The fire must have brought out his true feelings because he's afraid he's lost her.

I feel like I am having an out of body experience as I let his words sink in. The noises and people around me are all fuzzy, my legs feel weak, his words have knocked me for six and I stagger backwards.

"I love her so much we argued, she said she hated me and then I just wanted it to end, if I can't have her then no-one can, I hit her, she fell, I'm so sorry I never meant to…where is she, where's Julia?" he rambles coughing in between his words.

"Evan no, you don't mean that" I frown with tears rolling down my cheeks.

"I'm Sebastian, why do you keep calling me Evan, where is he?"

Wait it's Sebastian who loves Julia, not Evan. Oh my god but then the realisation dawns on me that Sebastian is sat here, and Evan isn't.

"He ran into the building to save you, to save Julia and now he's missing and it's all your fault," I cry shouting in his face shaking. "The firemen are busy looking for him, he hasn't been seen for ages" I sob.

"What no he can't be, he wouldn't do that, why would he do that? Why would he save me after everything I've done to him?" Sebastian coughs sounding shocked.

"Because he's a good man and you're his brother." I snap angrily. We both look at each other and then turn to look at the Manor engulfed in flames.

'No please god no, please let him be alive.'

"EVVVVAAAAAAANNNNNN.........."

Author's Note

Hi, thank you for reading 'Two Much Trouble,' the second book in the 'Two Series', I hope you enjoyed it.

I have loved every minute of writing Kara and Evan's love story. If you have any friends or family members that you think would enjoy reading it please feel free to spread the word. Also if you could take a few minutes to write a review that would be great.

Thank you for choosing my book to read and keep an eye out for the final part of the 'Two Series' continuing Kara and Evan's love story.

Lisa Jane Lordan

x

www.lisajanelordan.com

Acknowledgements

To my wonderful husband and our two beautiful daughters as always thank you for everything, you are my world.

To my lovely family and friends thank you for your continued support.

I would like to say a huge thank you to the team at Partnership Publishing I love working with you and I look forward to producing more books together in the future.

And finally thank you to you, my readers, for buying my books and for continuing to support me, you're the best.

Two Much Trouble

Also available as an eBook

NEXT IN THE 'TWO SERIES'

'Two Much to Lose.'

The Final Part of Kara and Evan's Love Story…

Printed in Great Britain
by Amazon